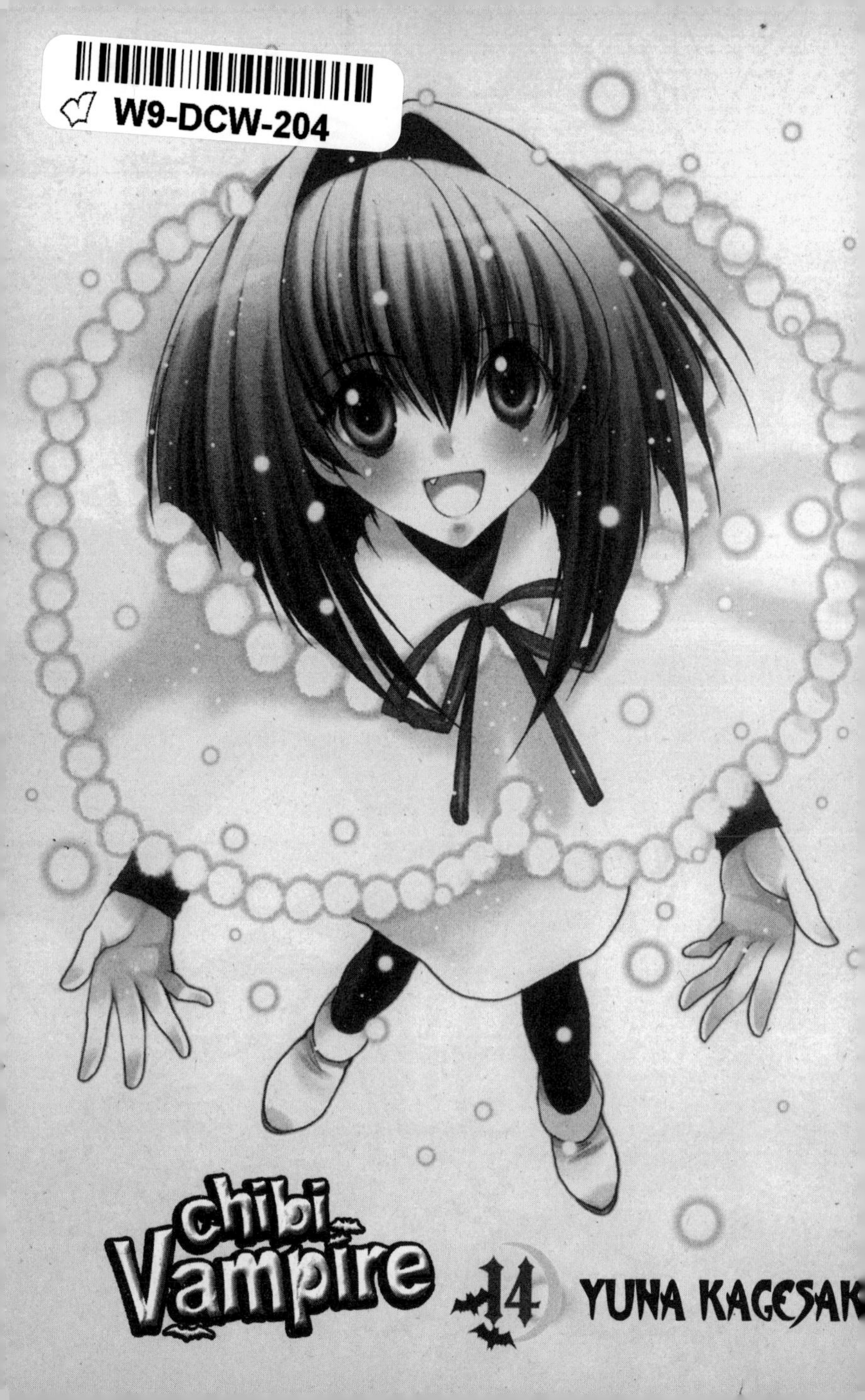
chibi
Vampire
14
YUNA KAGESAK

Chibi Vampire Volume 14
Created by Yuna Kagesaki

Translation - Alexis Kirsch
English Adaptation - Christine Boylan
Retouch and Lettering - Star Print Brokers
Production Artist - Rui Kyo
Graphic Designer - Louis Csontos

Editor - Bryce P. Coleman
Print Production Manager - Lucas Rivera
Managing Editor - Vy Nguyen
Senior Designer - Louis Csontos
Director of Sales and Manufacturing - Allyson De Simone
Associate Publisher - Marco F. Pavia
President and C.O.O. - John Parker
C.E.O. and Chief Creative Officer - Stu Levy

A  Manga

TOKYOPOP and 🐢 are trademarks or registered trademarks of TOKYOPOP Inc.

TOKYOPOP Inc.
5900 Wilshire Blvd. Suite 2000
Los Angeles, CA 90036

E-mail: info@TOKYOPOP.com
Come visit us online at www.TOKYOPOP.com

KARIN Volume 14 © 2008 YUNA KAGESAKI
First published in Japan in 2008 by FUJIMISHOBO CO., LTD.,
Tokyo. English translation rights arranged with KADOKAWA
SHOTEN PUBLISHING CO., LTD., Tokyo through TUTTLE-MORI
AGENCY, INC., Tokyo.
English text copyright © 2009 TOKYOPOP Inc.

ISBN: 978-1-4278-1625-2

First TOKYOPOP printing: September 2009
10 9 8 7 6 5 4 3 2
Printed in the USA

Chibi Vampire

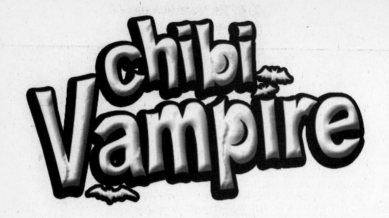

Volume 14

Created by
Yuna Kagesaki

TOKYOPOP®

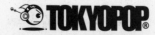

HAMBURG // LONDON // LOS ANGELES // TOKYO

OUR STORY SO FAR...

KARIN MAAKA ISN'T LIKE OTHER GIRLS. ONCE A MONTH, SHE EXPERIENCES PAIN, FATIGUE, HUNGER, IRRITABILITY—AND THEN SHE BLEEDS. FROM HER NOSE. KARIN IS A VAMPIRE, FROM A FAMILY OF VAMPIRES, BUT INSTEAD OF NEEDING TO DRINK BLOOD, SHE HAS AN EXCESS OF BLOOD THAT SHE MUST GIVE TO HER VICTIMS. IF DONE RIGHT, GIVING THIS BLOOD TO HER VICTIM CAN BE AN EXTREMELY POSITIVE THING. THE PROBLEM WITH THIS IS THAT KARIN NEVER SEEMS TO DO THINGS RIGHT...

KARIN IS HAVING A BIT OF BOY TROUBLE. KENTA USUI—THE HANDSOME NEW STUDENT AT HER SCHOOL AND WORK—IS A NICE ENOUGH GUY, BUT HE EXACERBATES KARIN'S PROBLEM. KARIN'S BLOOD PROBLEM, YOU SEE, BECOMES WORSE WHEN SHE'S AROUND PEOPLE WHO HAVE SUFFERED MISFORTUNE, AND KENTA HAS SUFFERED PLENTY OF IT. MAKING THINGS EVEN MORE COMPLICATED, IT'S BECOME CLEAR TO KARIN THAT SHE'S IN LOVE WITH KENTA... AND THIS BECOMES PAINFUL TO KARIN AS SHE SOON DISCOVERS THAT LOVE BETWEEN HUMANS AND VAMPIRES IS FROWNED UPON BECAUSE CHILDREN BETWEEN THE TWO SPECIES LACK REPRODUCTIVE ABILITIES. BUT KENTA'S LOVE FOR KARIN SURPASSES ALL BOUNDARIES AND THE TWO FINALLY HAVE THEIR FIRST KISS. THE MOMENT OF BLISS IS SHORT LIVED, HOWEVER, WHEN A GROUP OF RIVAL VAMPIRES COME TO TOWN, AND KARIN BECOMES THE PAWN IN AN ALL-OUT VAMPIRE VENDETTA! WILL KENTA SAVE BE ABLE TO SAVE HIS TRUE LOVE IN TIME...?

THE MAAKA FAMILY

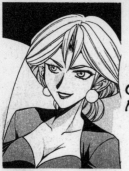

CALERA MARKER

Karin's overbearing mother. While Calera resents that Karin wasn't born a normal vampire, she does love her daughter in her own obnoxious way. Calera has chosen to keep her European last name.

KARIN MAAKA

Our little heroine. Karin is a vampire living in Japan, but instead of sucking blood from her victims, she actually GIVES them some of her blood. She's a vampire in reverse!

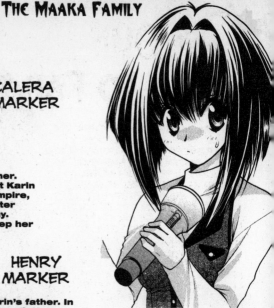

HENRY MARKER

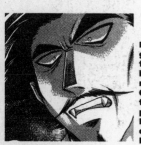

Karin's father. In general, Henry treats Karin a lot better than her mother does, but Calera wears the pants in this particular family. Henry has also chosen to keep his European last name.

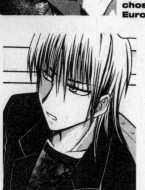

REN MAAKA

Karin's older brother. Ren milks the "sexy creature of the night" thing for all it's worth and spends his nights in the arms (and beds) of attractive young women.

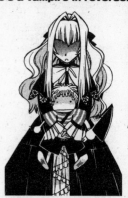

ANJU MAAKA

Karin's little sister. Anju has awoken as a full vampire, and is usually the one who cleans up after Karin's messes. Rarely seen without her "talking" doll, Boogie.

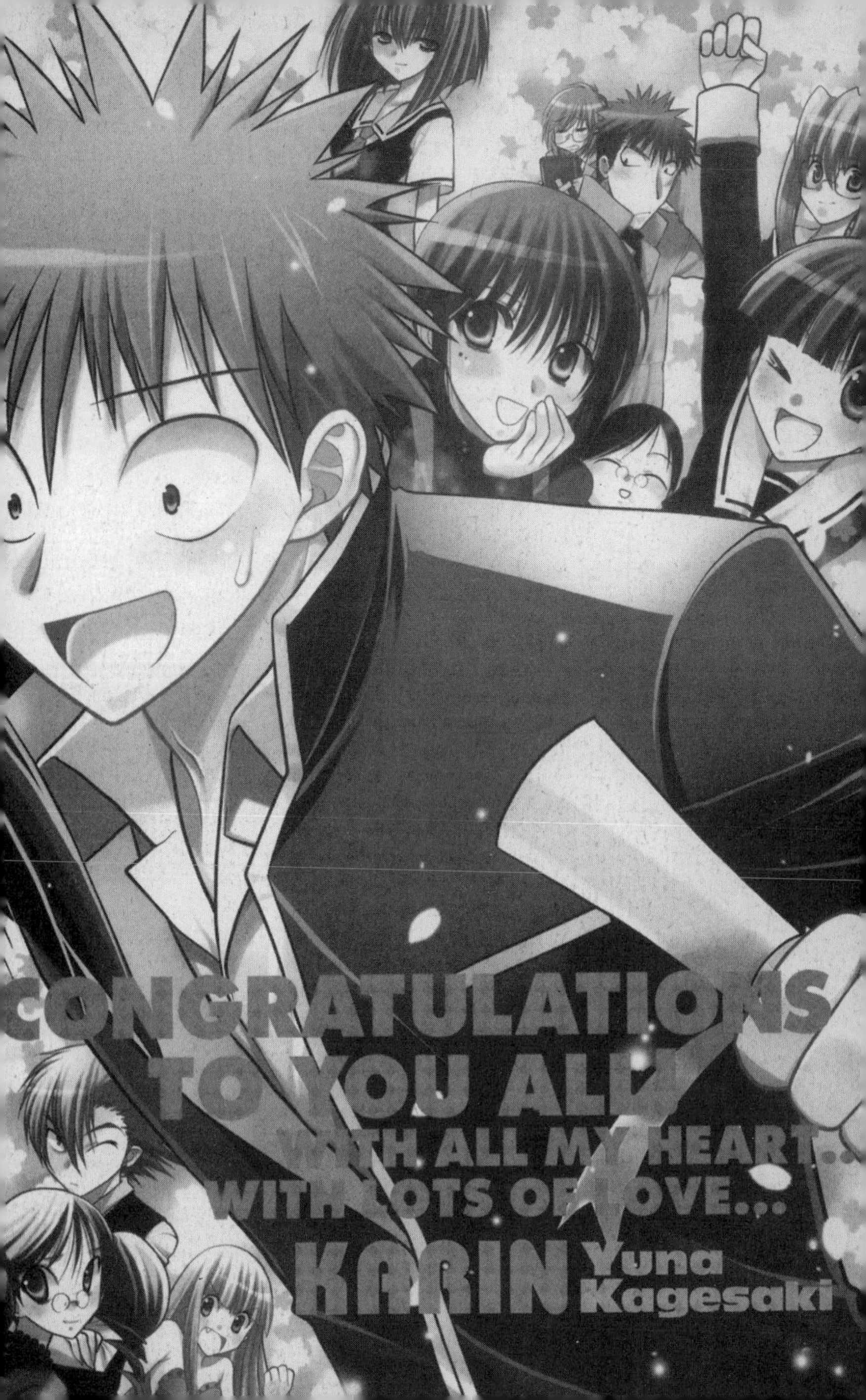
CONGRATULATIONS
TO YOU ALL!
WITH ALL MY HEART...
WITH LOTS OF LOVE...
KARIN
Yuna Kagesaki

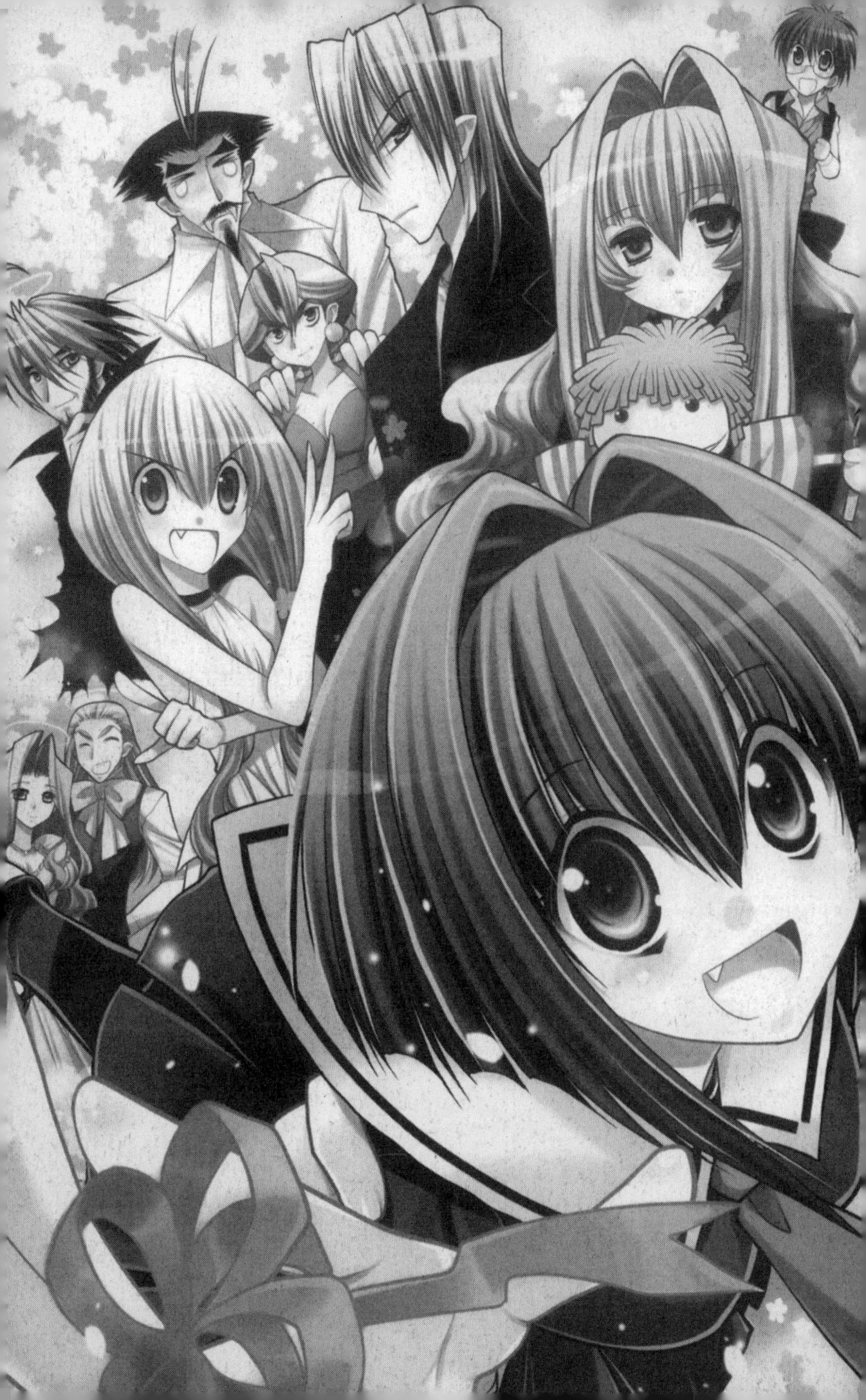

VOL. 14
CONTENTS

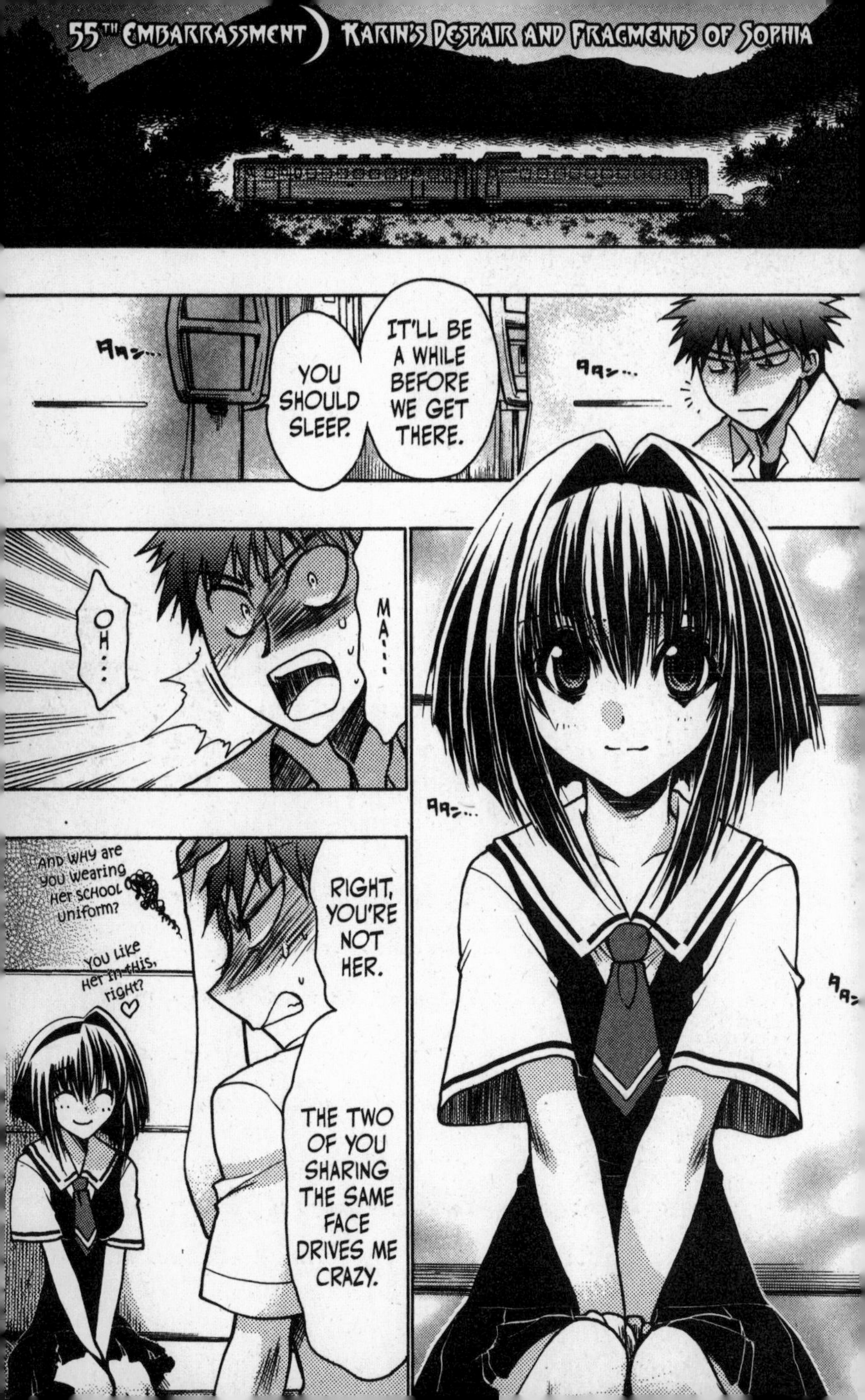
55TH EMBARRASSMENT
KARIN'S DESPAIR AND FRAGMENTS OF SOPHIA
タタン…
タタン…
IT'LL BE A WHILE BEFORE WE GET THERE.
YOU SHOULD SLEEP.
タタン…
タタン…
MA...
OH...
RIGHT, YOU'RE NOT HER.
THE TWO OF YOU SHARING THE SAME FACE DRIVES ME CRAZY.
And WHY are you wearing Her SCHOOL uniform?
You like Her in this, right? ♡

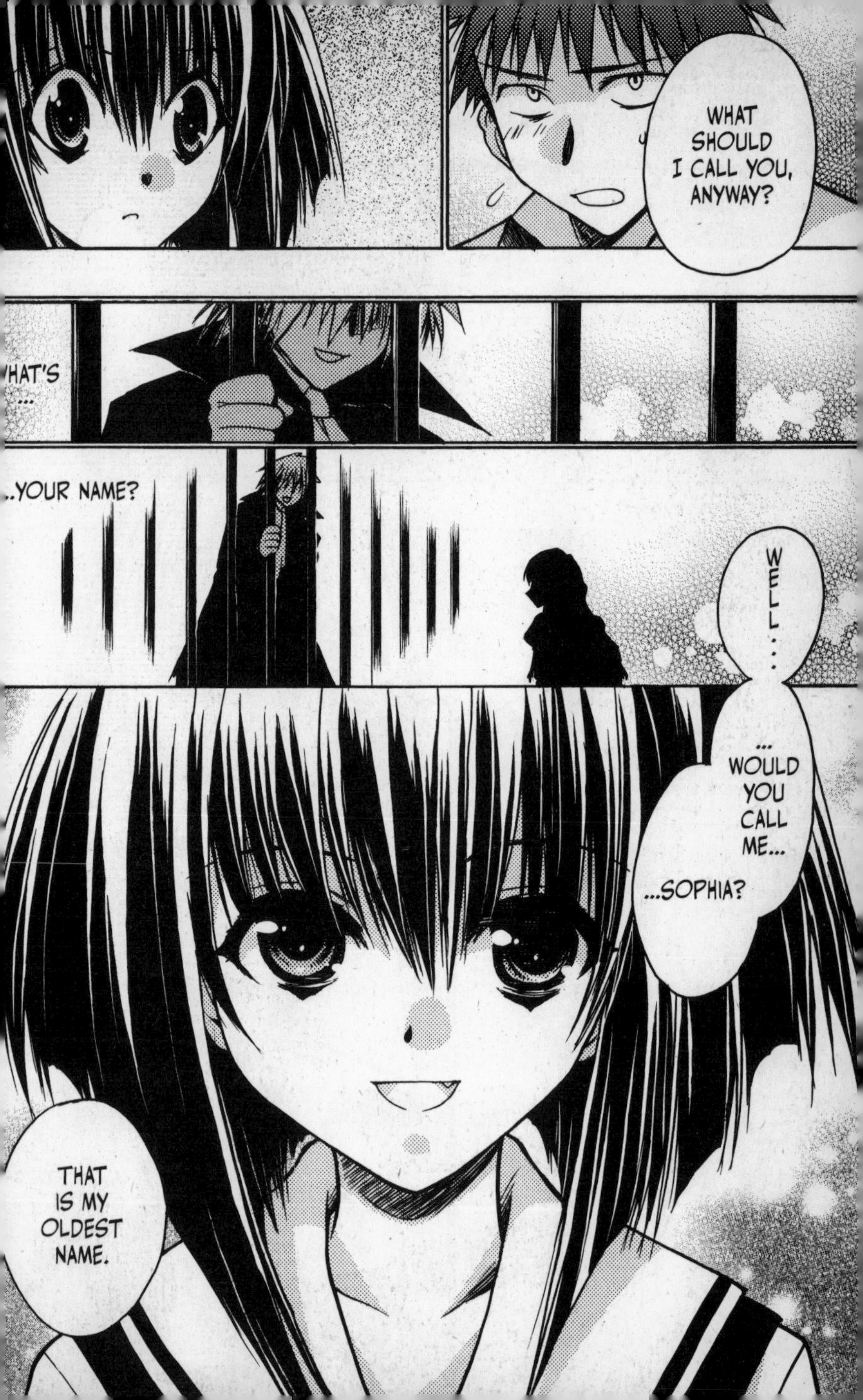
WHAT SHOULD I CALL YOU, ANYWAY?
HAT'S ...
..YOUR NAME?
WELL...
...WOULD YOU CALL ME...
...SOPHIA?
THAT IS MY OLDEST NAME.

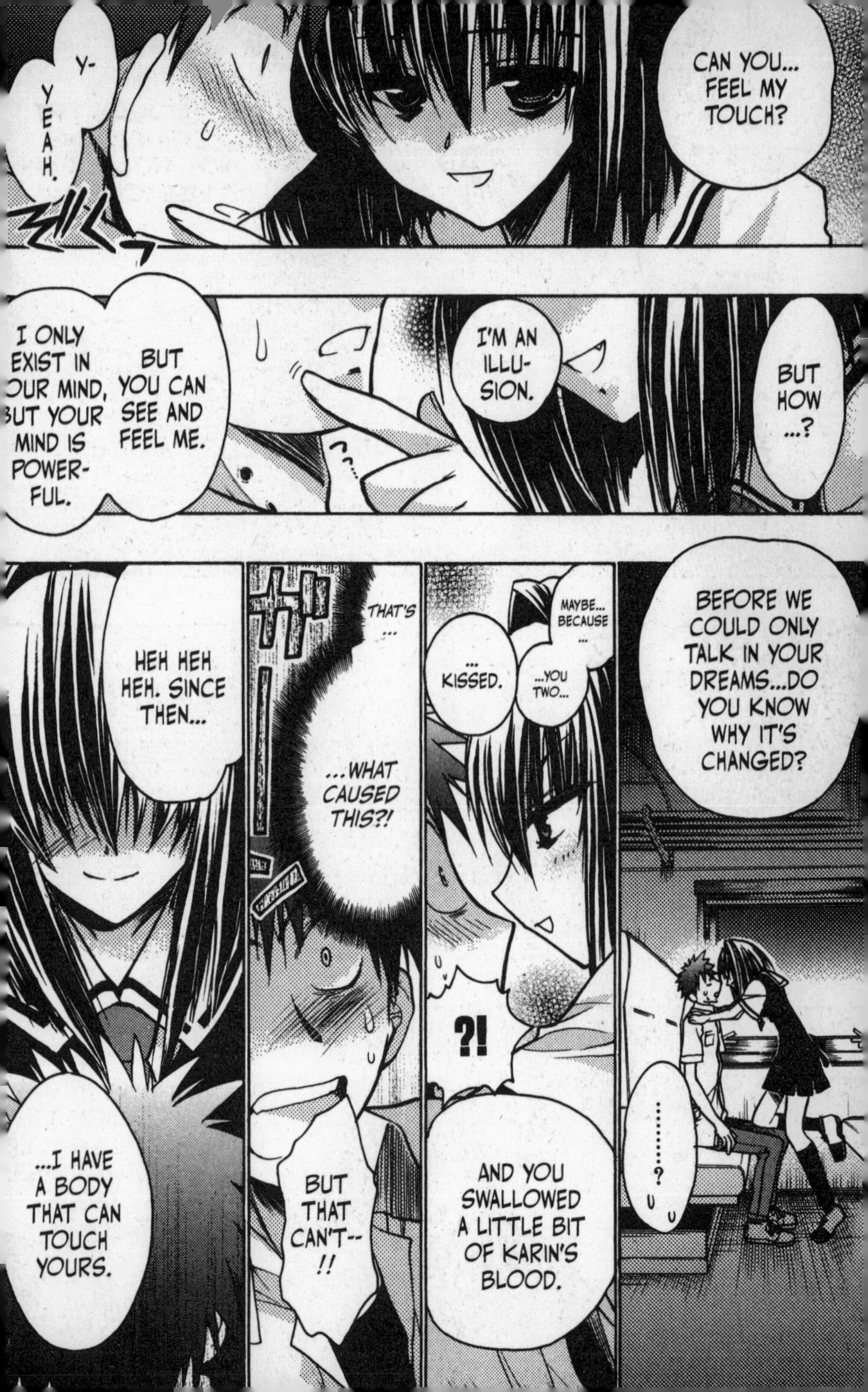
CAN YOU... FEEL MY TOUCH?
Y- YEAH.
BUT HOW ...?
I'M AN ILLUSION.
BUT YOU CAN SEE AND FEEL ME.
I ONLY EXIST IN YOUR MIND, BUT YOUR MIND IS POWERFUL.
BEFORE WE COULD ONLY TALK IN YOUR DREAMS...DO YOU KNOW WHY IT'S CHANGED?
......?
MAYBE... BECAUSE ...
...YOU TWO...
...KISSED.
?!
AND YOU SWALLOWED A LITTLE BIT OF KARIN'S BLOOD.
THAT'S ...
...WHAT CAUSED THIS?!
BUT THAT CAN'T-- !!
HEH HEH HEH. SINCE THEN...
...I HAVE A BODY THAT CAN TOUCH YOURS.

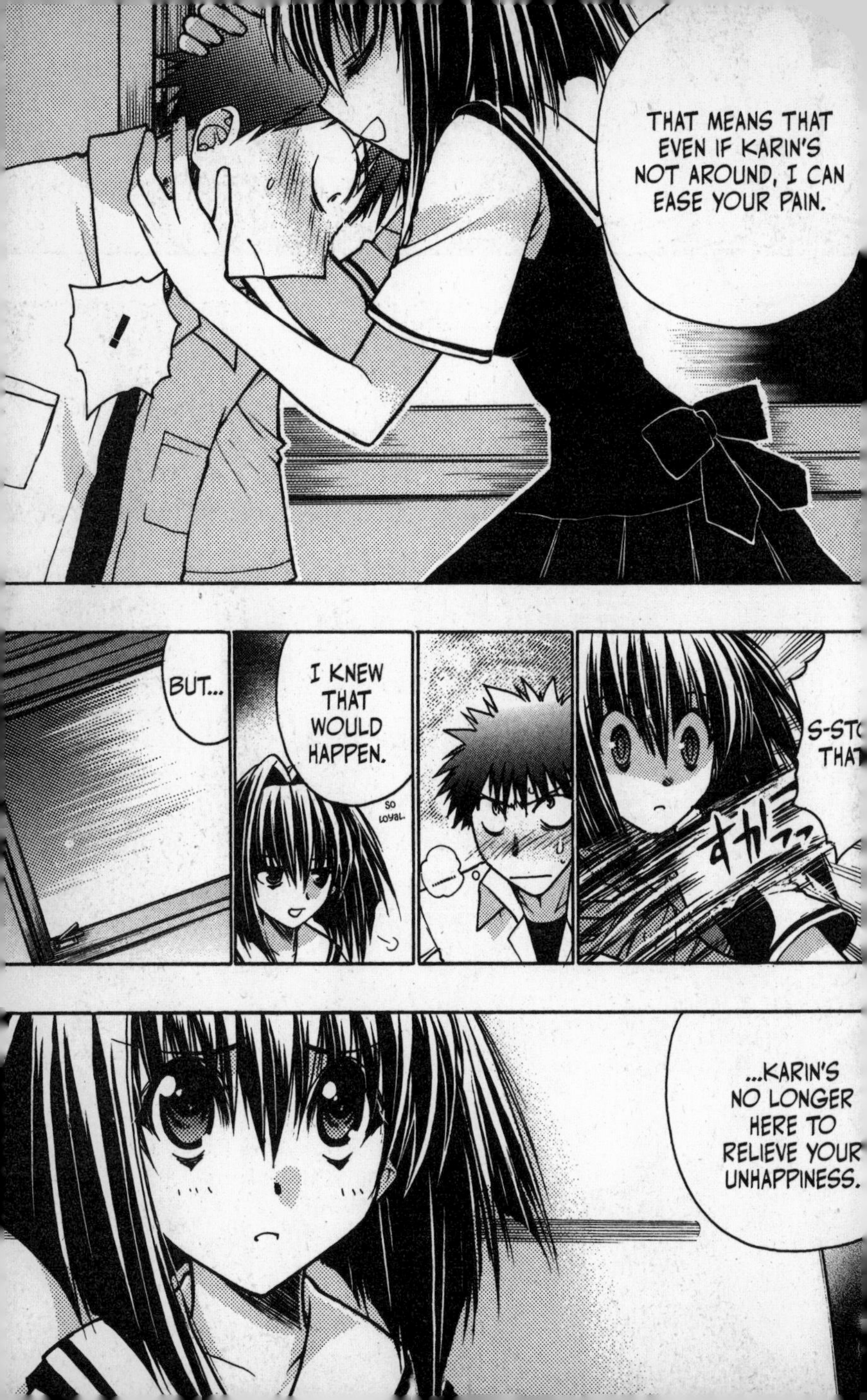
THAT MEANS THAT EVEN IF KARIN'S NOT AROUND, I CAN EASE YOUR PAIN.
!
S-STO THAT
I KNEW THAT WOULD HAPPEN.
SO LOYAL.
BUT...
...KARIN'S NO LONGER HERE TO RELIEVE YOUR UNHAPPINESS.

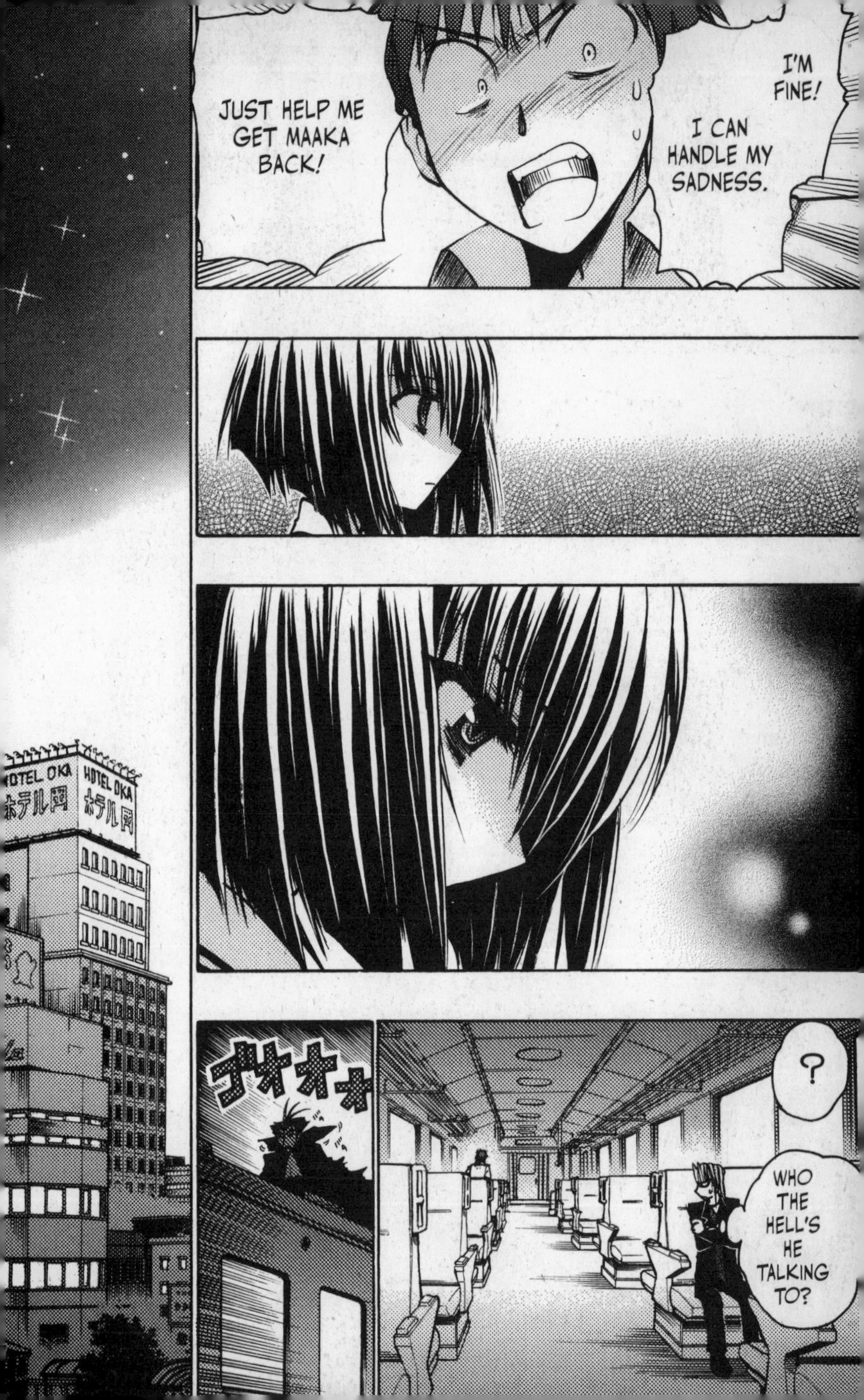
I'M FINE!
I CAN HANDLE MY SADNESS.
JUST HELP ME GET MAAKA BACK!
?
WHO THE HELL'S HE TALKING TO?
HOTEL OKA
ホテル岡
HOTEL OKA
ホテル岡

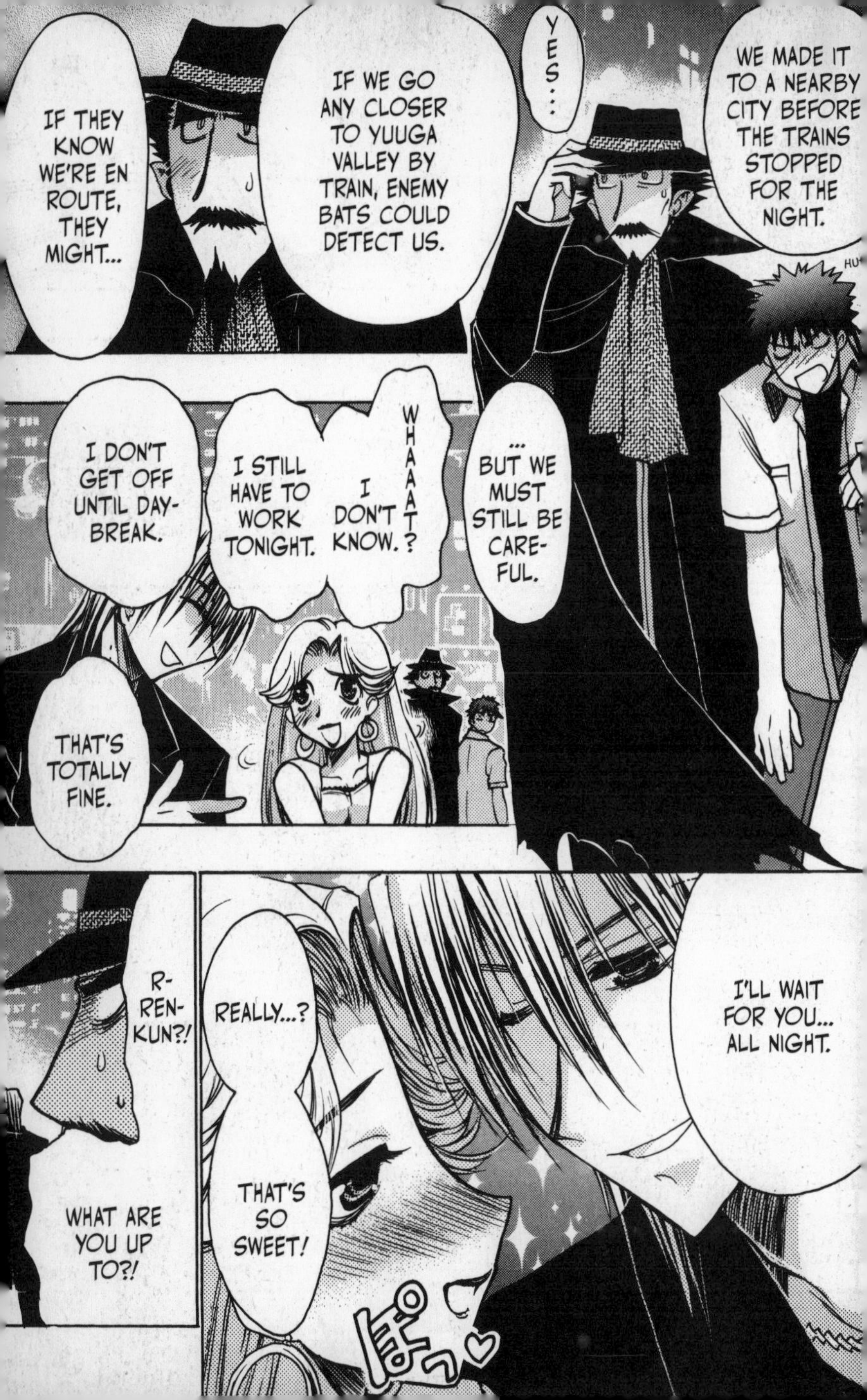
WE MADE IT TO A NEARBY CITY BEFORE THE TRAINS STOPPED FOR THE NIGHT.
YES...
... BUT WE MUST STILL BE CAREFUL.
IF WE GO ANY CLOSER TO YUUGA VALLEY BY TRAIN, ENEMY BATS COULD DETECT US.
IF THEY KNOW WE'RE EN ROUTE, THEY MIGHT...
WHAAAAT?
I DON'T KNOW.
I STILL HAVE TO WORK TONIGHT.
I DON'T GET OFF UNTIL DAY-BREAK.
THAT'S TOTALLY FINE.
I'LL WAIT FOR YOU... ALL NIGHT.
REALLY...?
THAT'S SO SWEET!
ぽっ♡
R-REN-KUN?!
WHAT ARE YOU UP TO?!

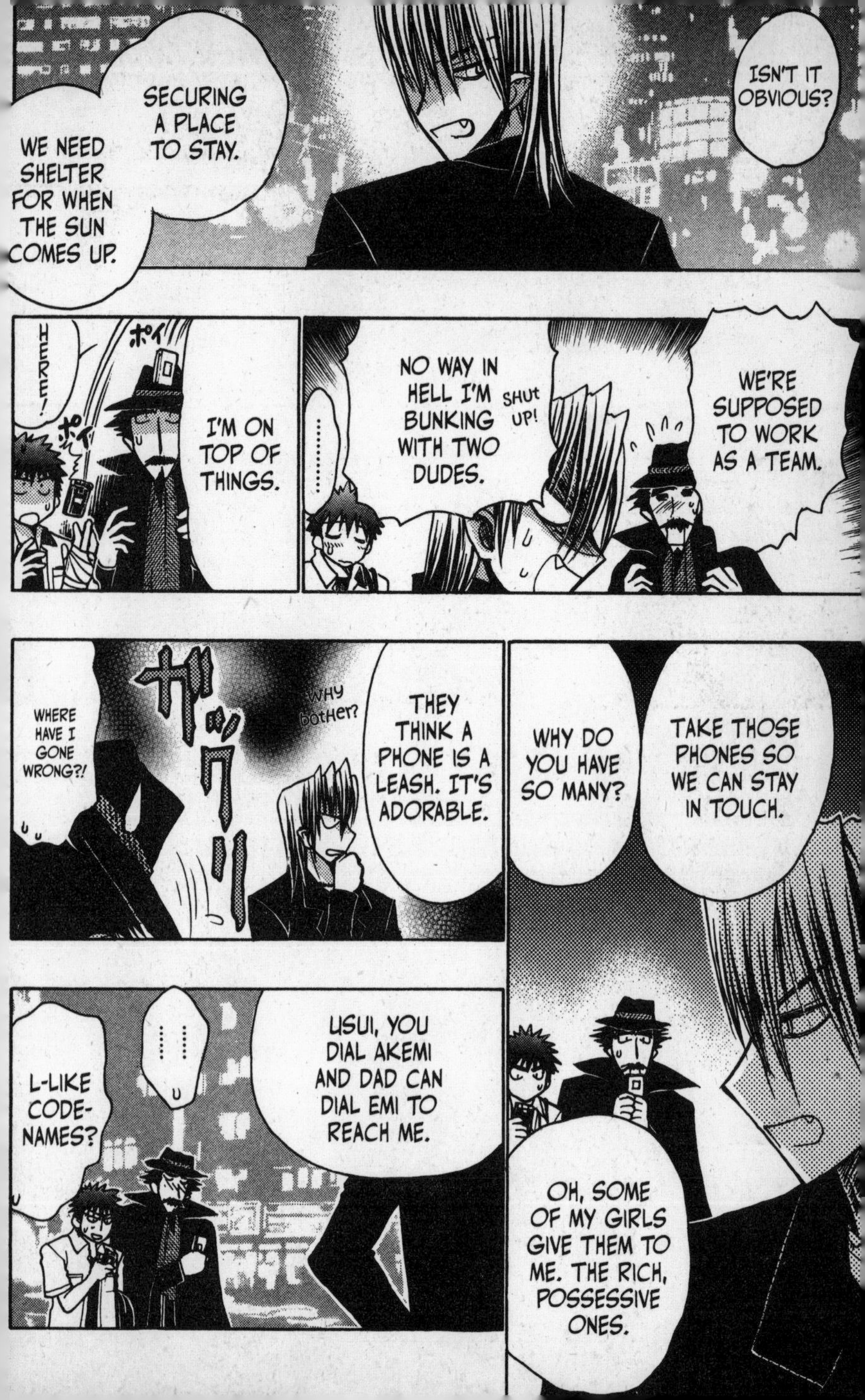
ISN'T IT OBVIOUS?
SECURING A PLACE TO STAY.
WE NEED SHELTER FOR WHEN THE SUN COMES UP.
WE'RE SUPPOSED TO WORK AS A TEAM.
SHUT UP!
NO WAY IN HELL I'M BUNKING WITH TWO DUDES.
......
I'M ON TOP OF THINGS.
ポイ
HERE!
ポイ
TAKE THOSE PHONES SO WE CAN STAY IN TOUCH.
WHY DO YOU HAVE SO MANY?
OH, SOME OF MY GIRLS GIVE THEM TO ME. THE RICH, POSSESSIVE ONES.
THEY THINK A PHONE IS A LEASH. IT'S ADORABLE.
WHY bother?
ガックーリ
WHERE HAVE I GONE WRONG?!
USUI, YOU DIAL AKEMI AND DAD CAN DIAL EMI TO REACH ME.
......
L-LIKE CODE-NAMES?

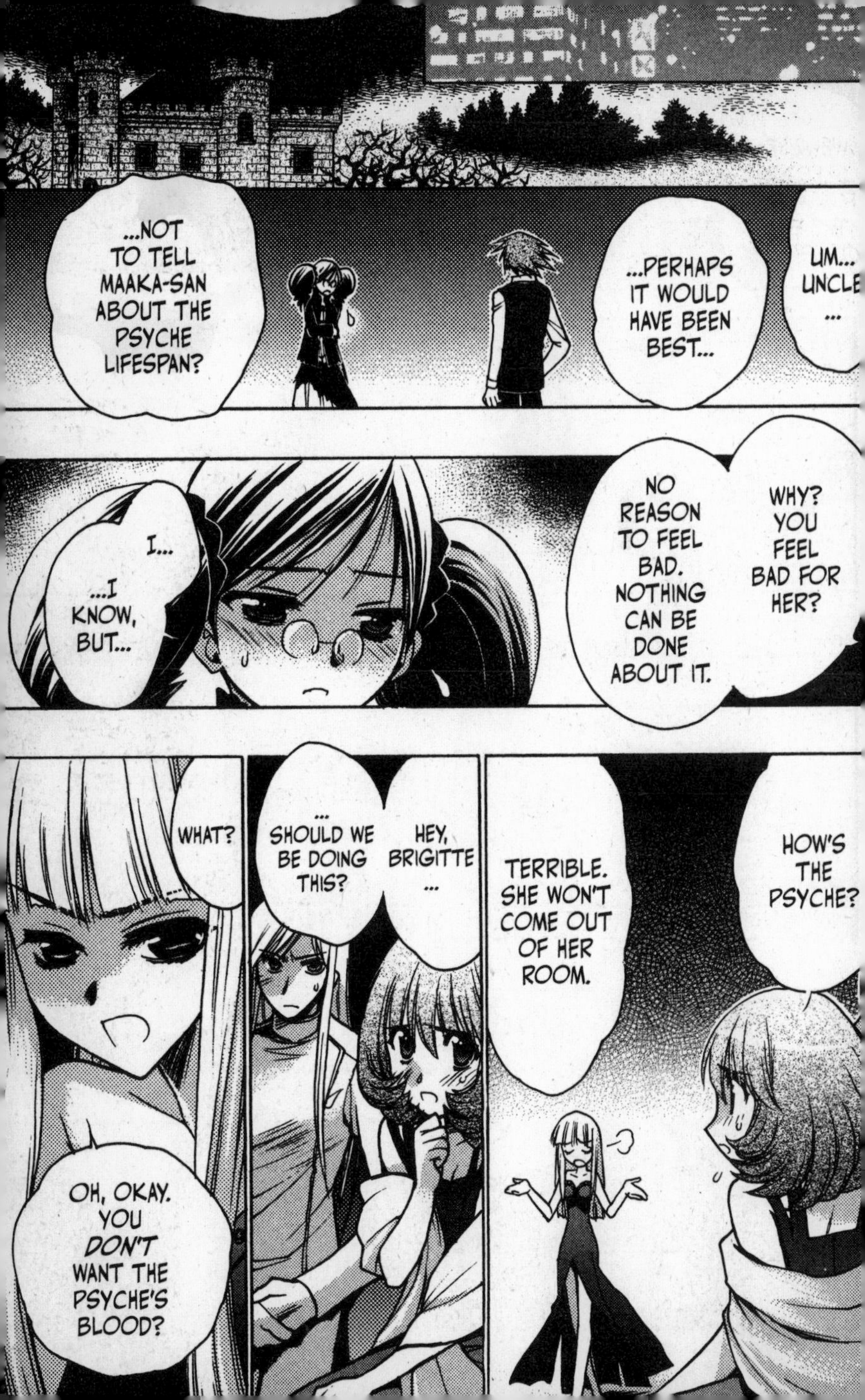
UM... UNCLE ...
...PERHAPS IT WOULD HAVE BEEN BEST...
...NOT TO TELL MAAKA-SAN ABOUT THE PSYCHE LIFESPAN?
WHY? YOU FEEL BAD FOR HER?
NO REASON TO FEEL BAD. NOTHING CAN BE DONE ABOUT IT.
I...
...I KNOW, BUT...
HOW'S THE PSYCHE?
TERRIBLE. SHE WON'T COME OUT OF HER ROOM.
HEY, BRIGITTE ...
... SHOULD WE BE DOING THIS?
WHAT?
OH, OKAY. YOU *DON'T* WANT THE PSYCHE'S BLOOD?

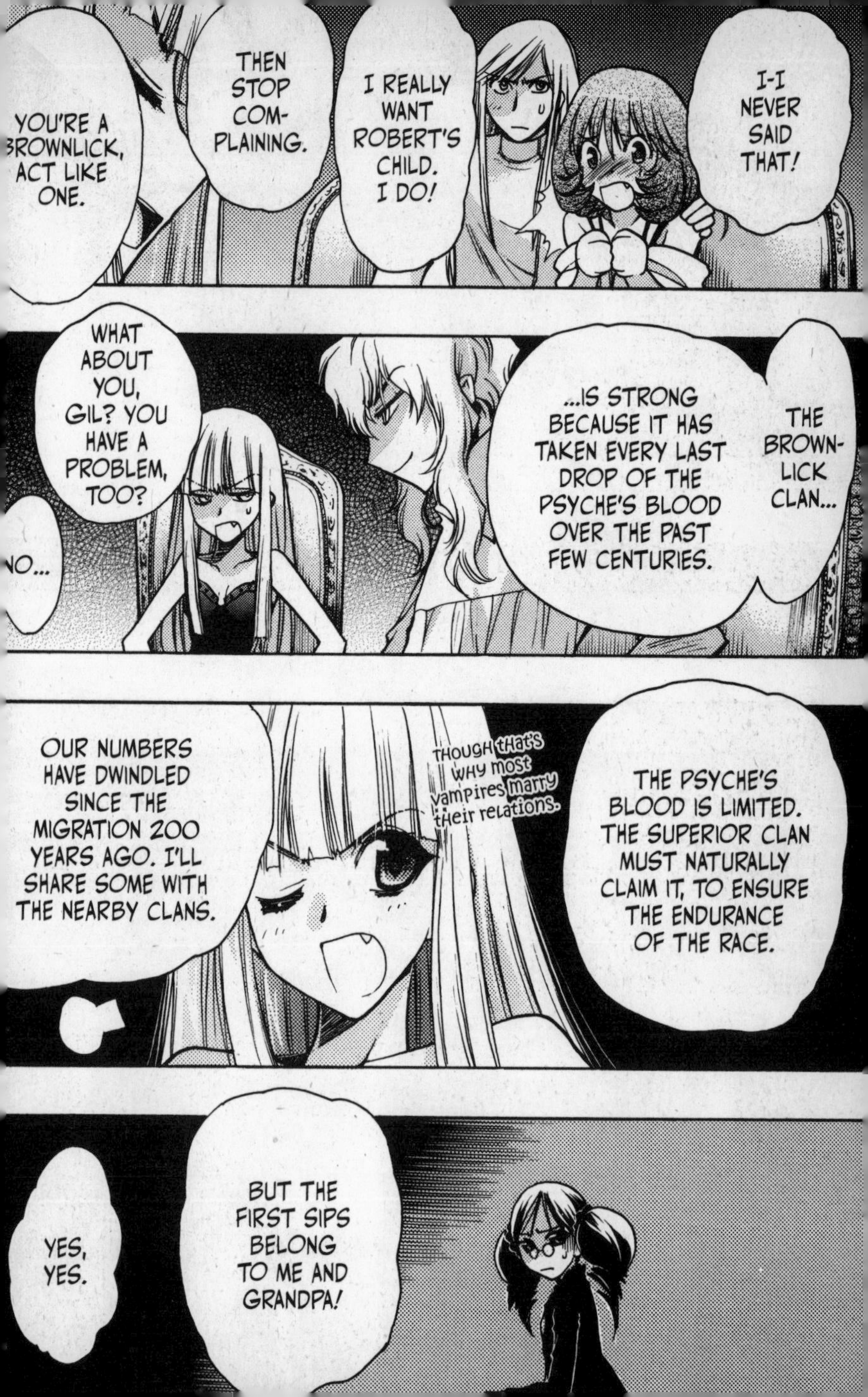
I-I NEVER SAID THAT!
I REALLY WANT ROBERT'S CHILD. I DO!
THEN STOP COM-PLAINING.
YOU'RE A BROWNLICK, ACT LIKE ONE.
THE BROWN-LICK CLAN...
...IS STRONG BECAUSE IT HAS TAKEN EVERY LAST DROP OF THE PSYCHE'S BLOOD OVER THE PAST FEW CENTURIES.
WHAT ABOUT YOU, GIL? YOU HAVE A PROBLEM, TOO?
NO...
THE PSYCHE'S BLOOD IS LIMITED. THE SUPERIOR CLAN MUST NATURALLY CLAIM IT, TO ENSURE THE ENDURANCE OF THE RACE.
THOUGH that's why most vampires marry their relations.
OUR NUMBERS HAVE DWINDLED SINCE THE MIGRATION 200 YEARS AGO. I'LL SHARE SOME WITH THE NEARBY CLANS.
BUT THE FIRST SIPS BELONG TO ME AND GRANDPA!
YES, YES.

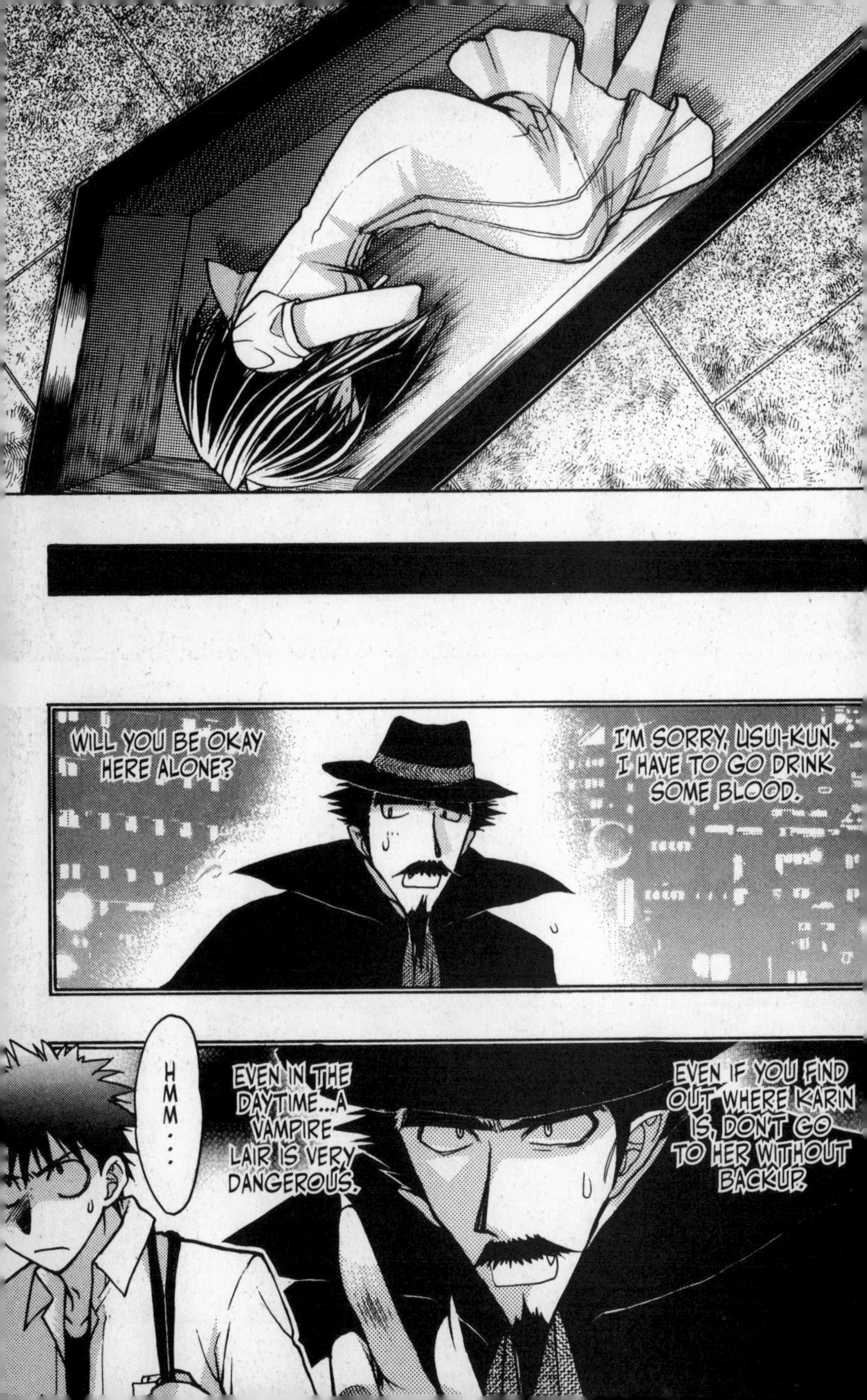
I'M SORRY, USUI-KUN. I HAVE TO GO DRINK SOME BLOOD.
WILL YOU BE OKAY HERE ALONE?
EVEN IF YOU FIND OUT WHERE KARIN IS, DON'T GO TO HER WITHOUT BACKUP.
EVEN IN THE DAYTIME...A VAMPIRE LAIR IS VERY DANGEROUS.
HMM...

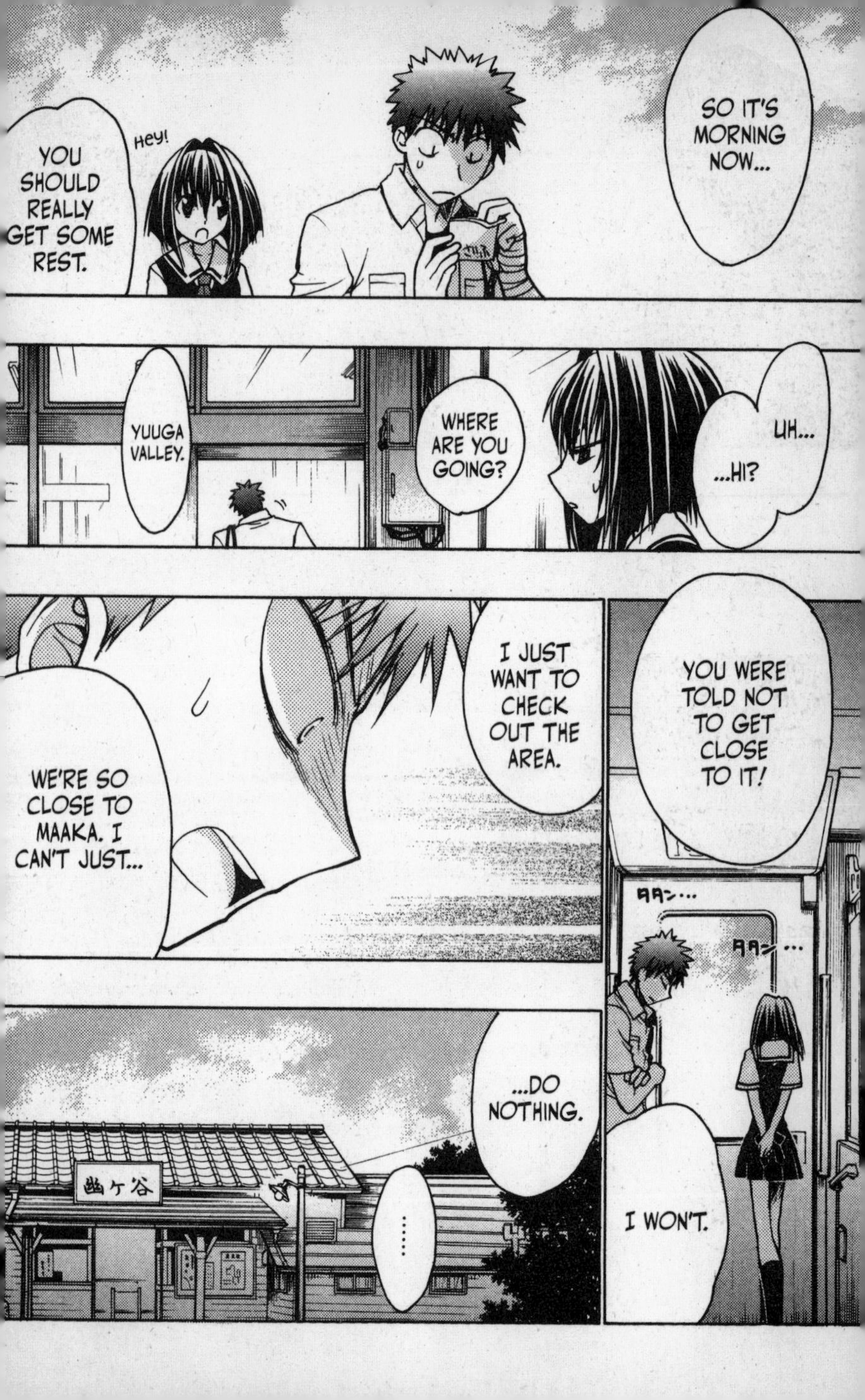
SO IT'S MORNING NOW...
Hey!
YOU SHOULD REALLY GET SOME REST.
UH... ...HI?
WHERE ARE YOU GOING?
YUUGA VALLEY.
YOU WERE TOLD NOT TO GET CLOSE TO IT!
タタン…
タタン…
I WON'T.
I JUST WANT TO CHECK OUT THE AREA.
WE'RE SO CLOSE TO MAAKA. I CAN'T JUST...
...DO NOTHING.
......
幽ケ谷

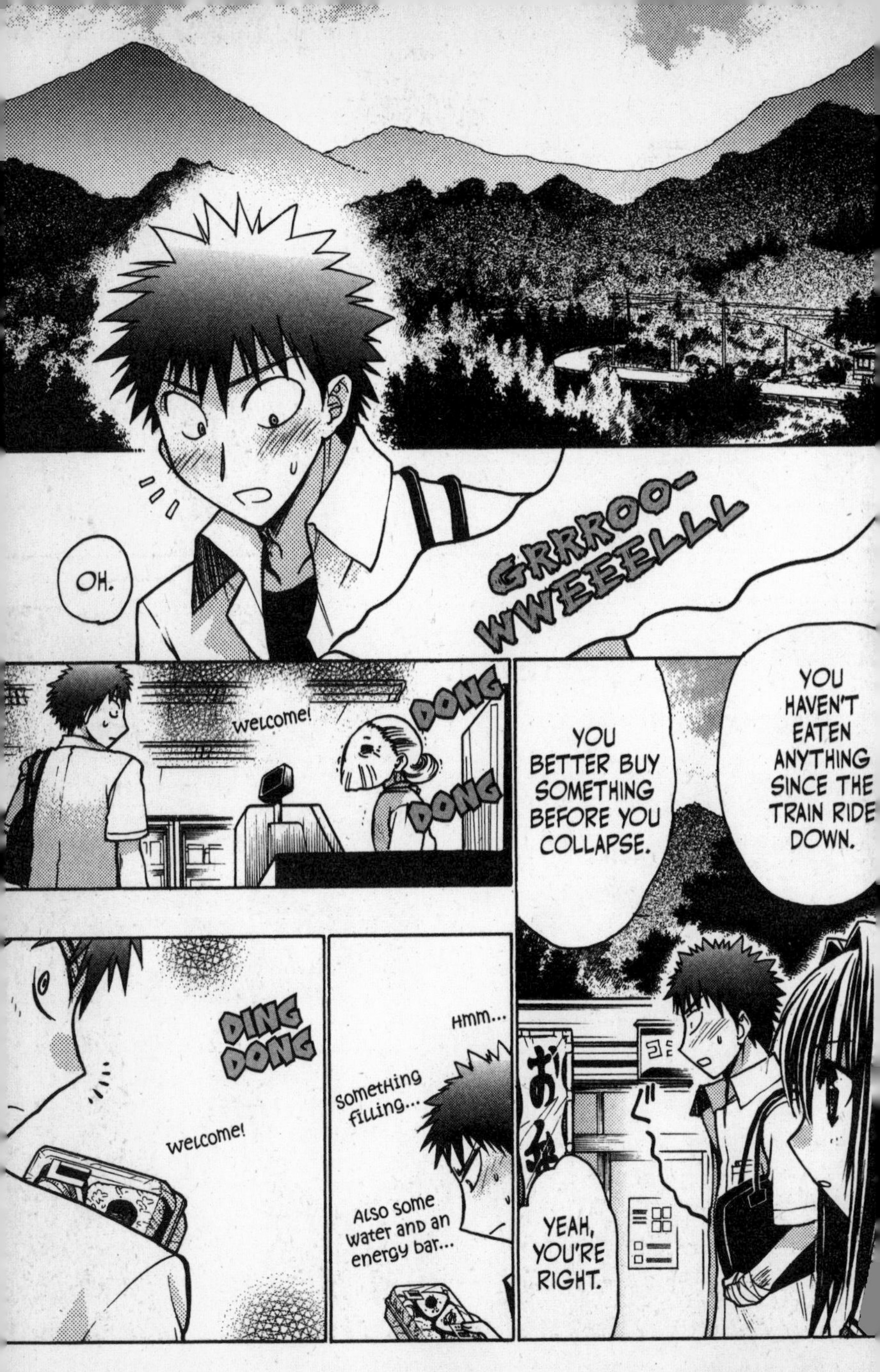
GRRROO-WWEEELLL
OH.
YOU HAVEN'T EATEN ANYTHING SINCE THE TRAIN RIDE DOWN.
YOU BETTER BUY SOMETHING BEFORE YOU COLLAPSE.
YEAH, YOU'RE RIGHT.
DONG DONG
Welcome!
Hmm...
Something filling...
Also some water and an energy bar...
DING DONG
Welcome!

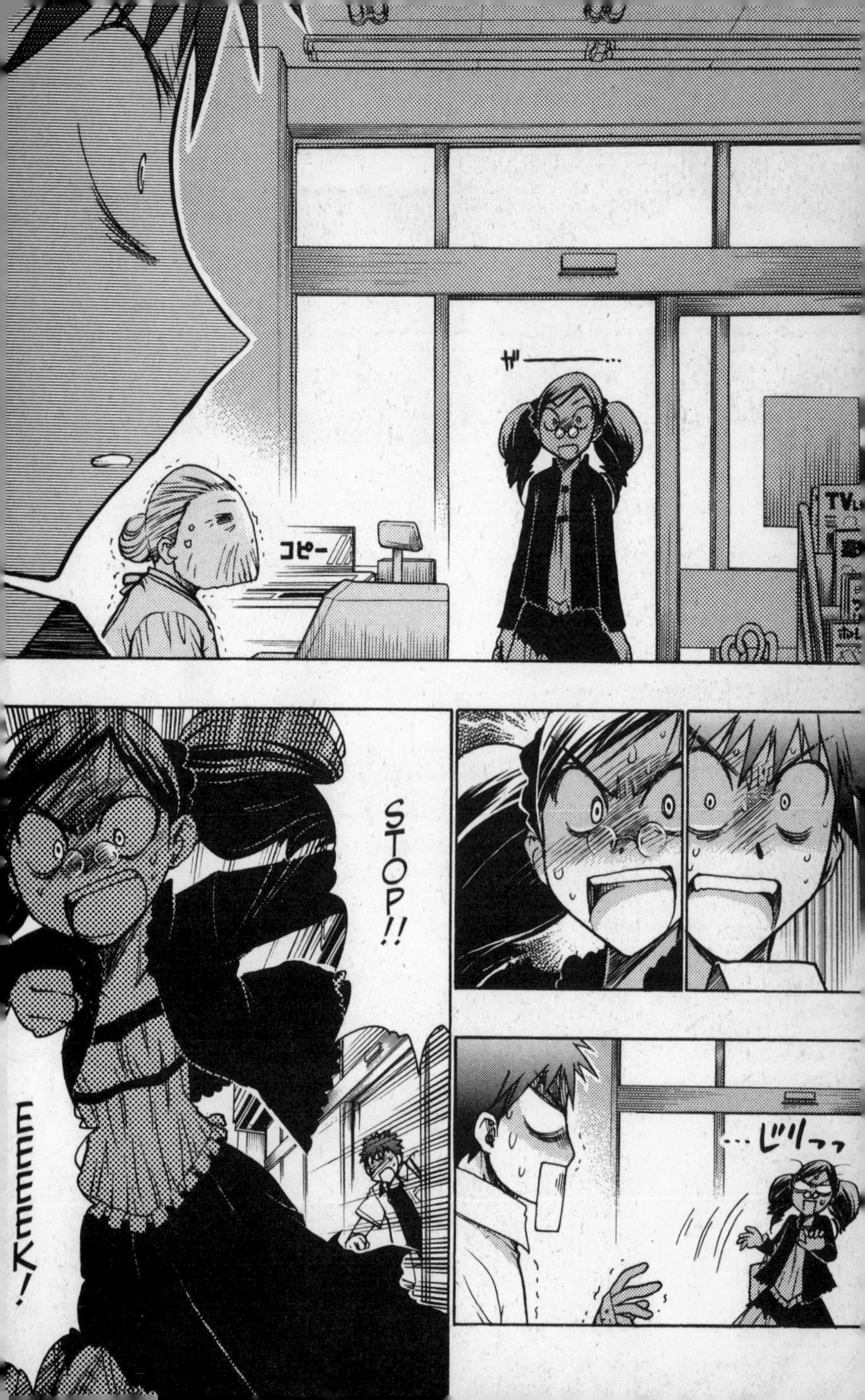
ザ——…
コピー
…ジリッッ
STOP!!
EEEEEEK!

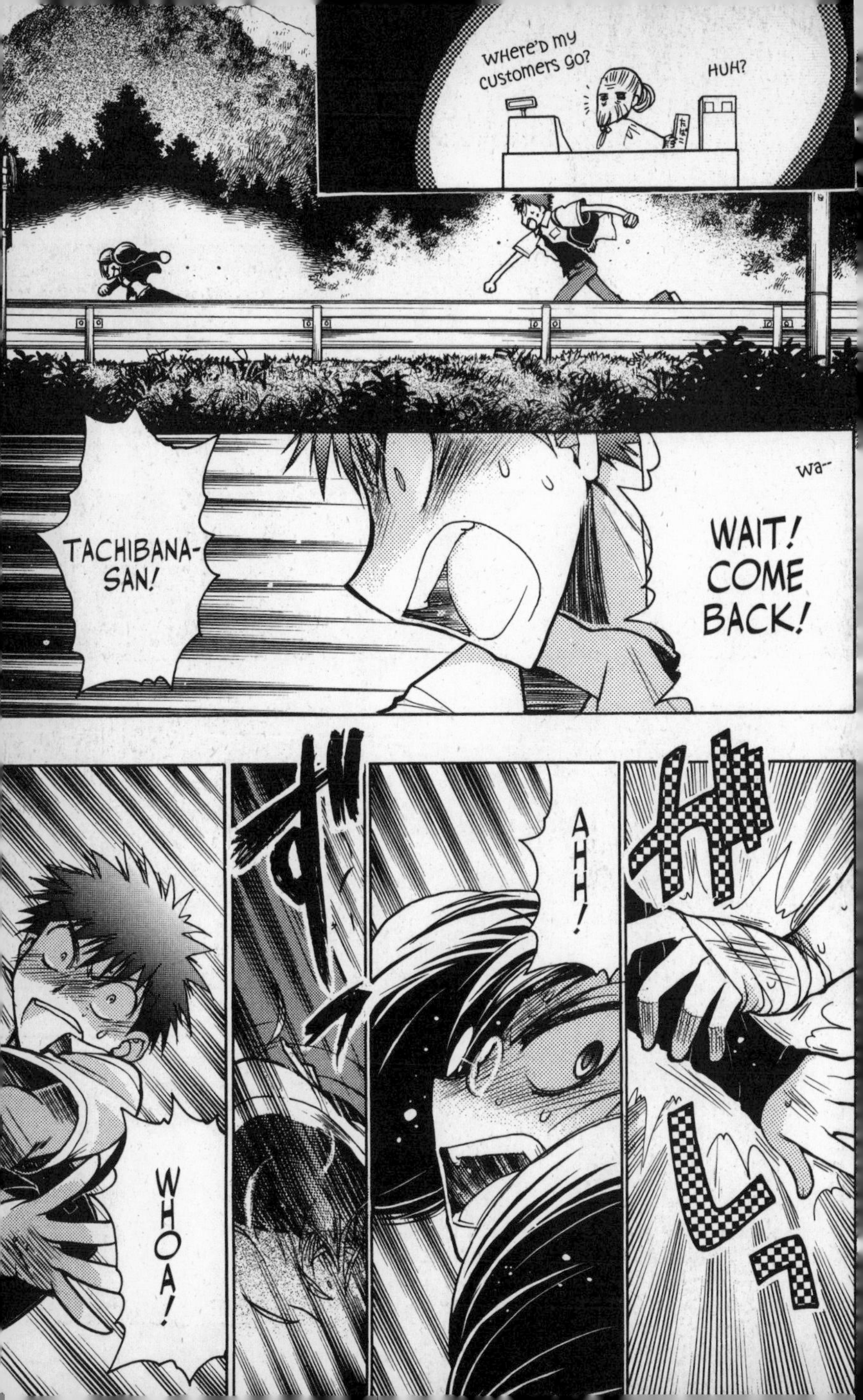
HUH?
Where'd my customers go?
wa-
WAIT! COME BACK!
TACHIBANA-SAN!
AHH!
WHOA!

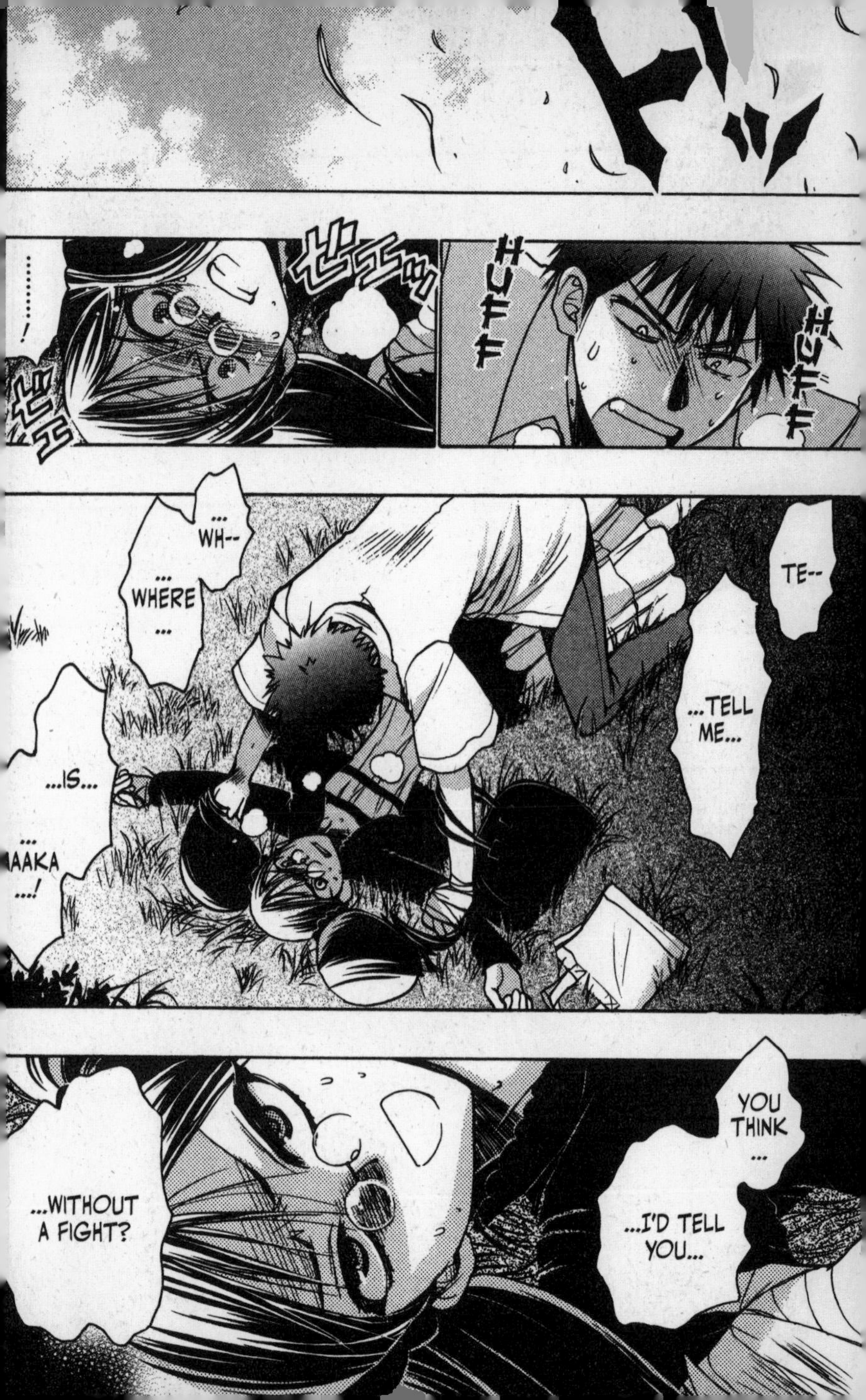

HUFF
HUFF
......!
TE--
...TELL ME...
... WH--
... WHERE ...
...IS...
... AAKA ...!
YOU THINK ...
...I'D TELL YOU...
...WITHOUT A FIGHT?

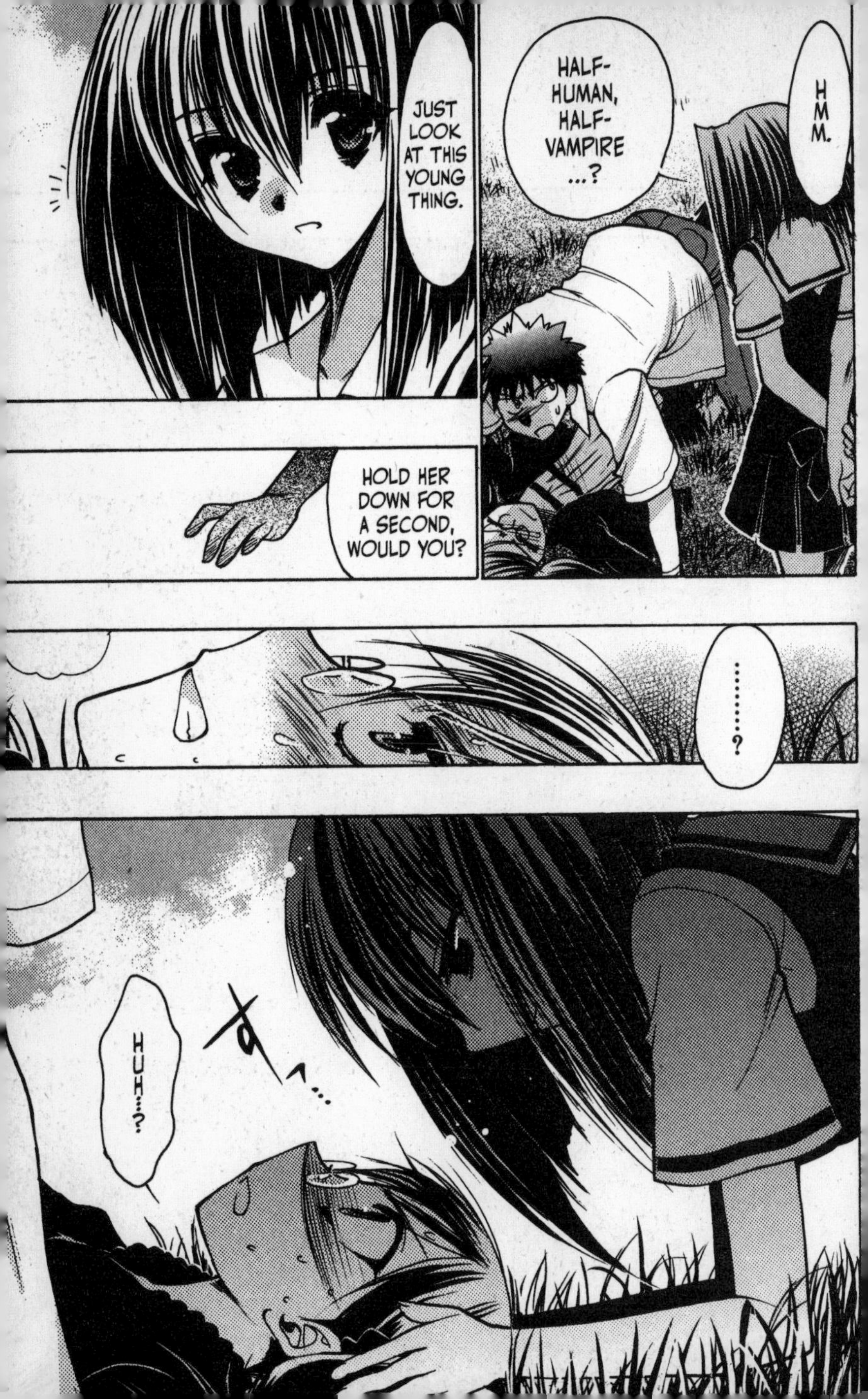
HMM.
HALF-HUMAN, HALF-VAMPIRE ...?
JUST LOOK AT THIS YOUNG THING.
HOLD HER DOWN FOR A SECOND, WOULD YOU?
......?
HUH...?

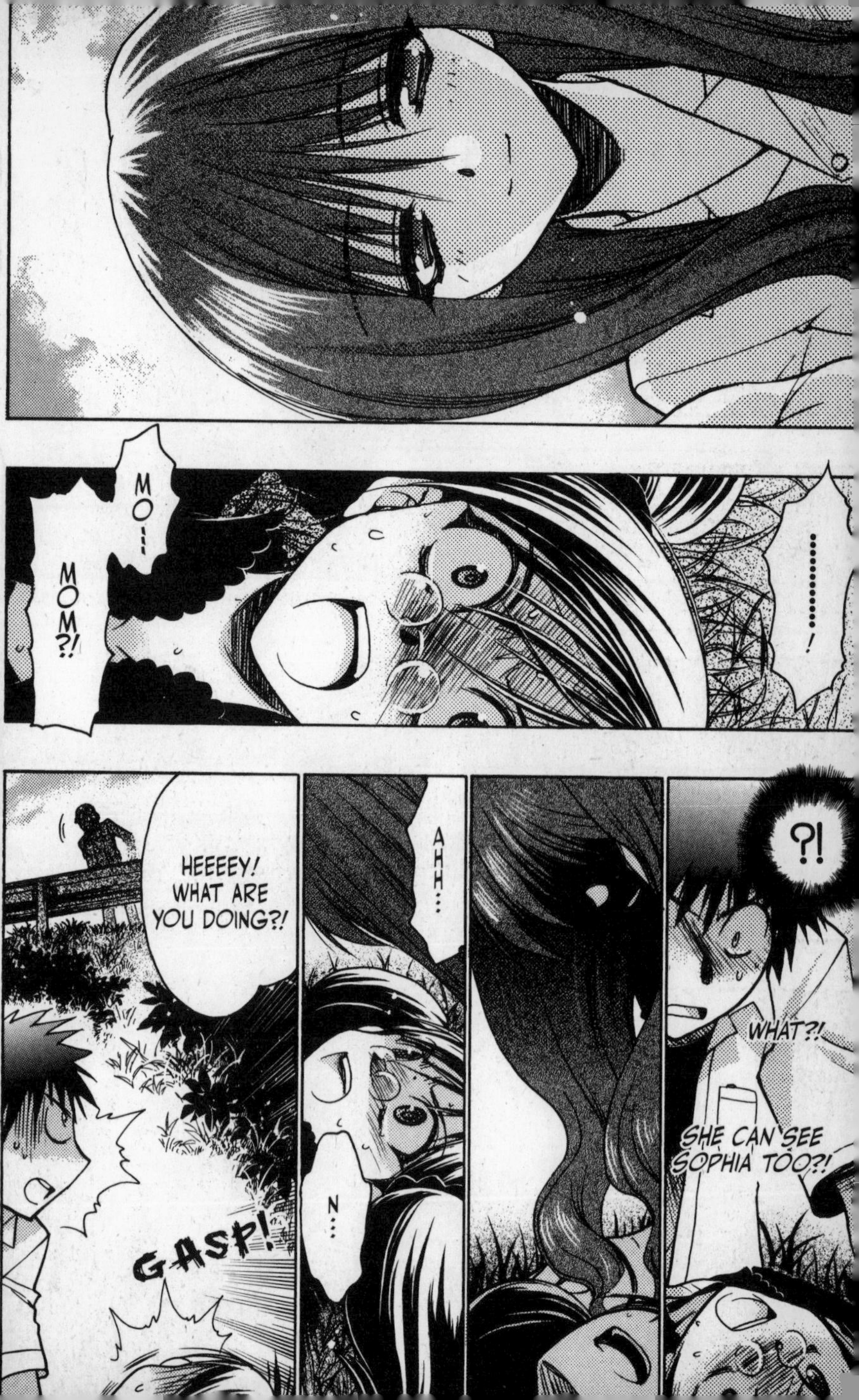
......!
MO... MOM?!
?!
WHAT?!
SHE CAN SEE SOPHIA TOO?!
AHH...
N...
HEEEEY! WHAT ARE YOU DOING?!
GASP!

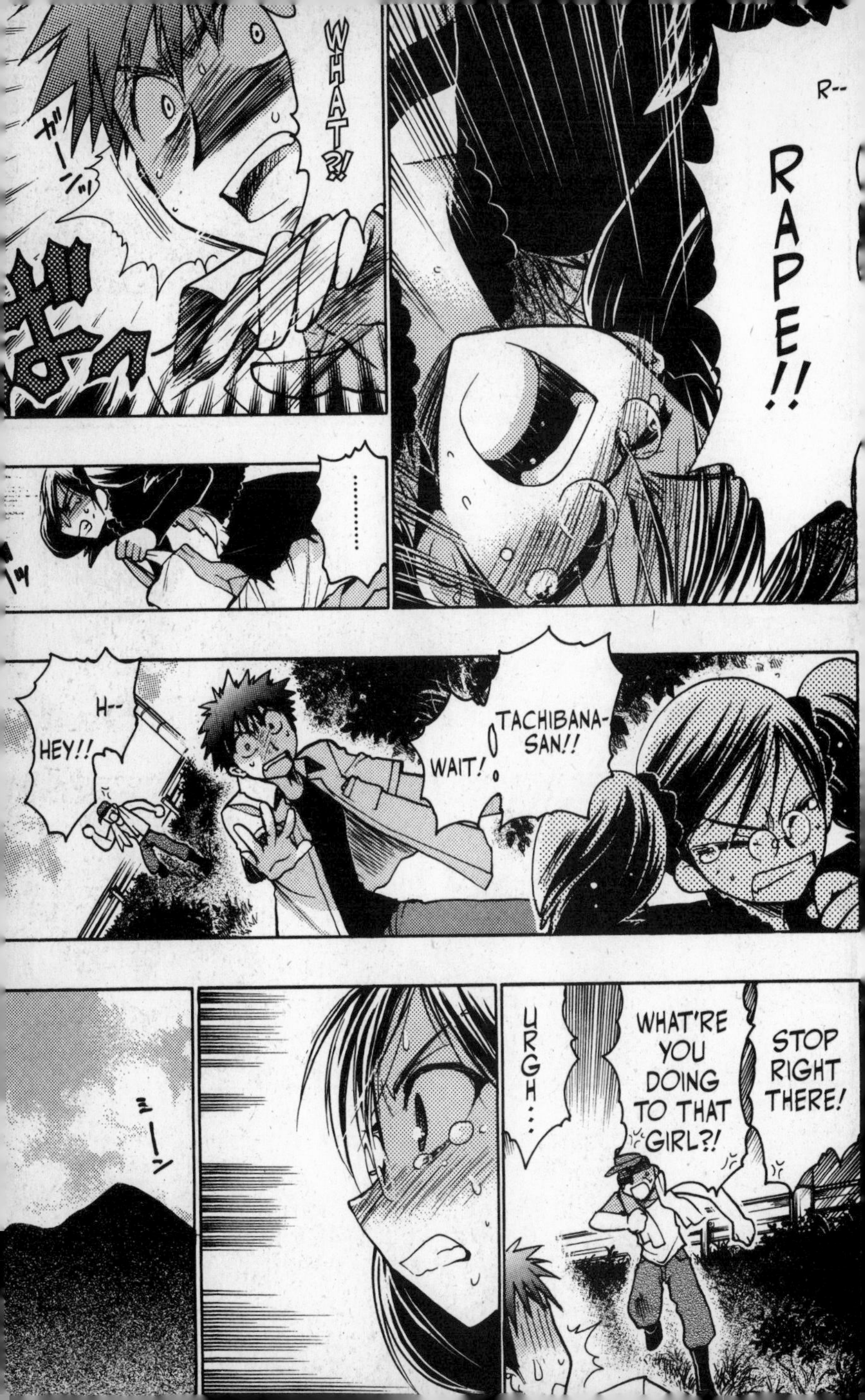
R--
RAPE!!
WHAT?!
ばっ
....
TACHIBANA-SAN!!
WAIT!
H--
HEY!!
STOP RIGHT THERE!
WHAT'RE YOU DOING TO THAT GIRL?!
URGH...
ミーン

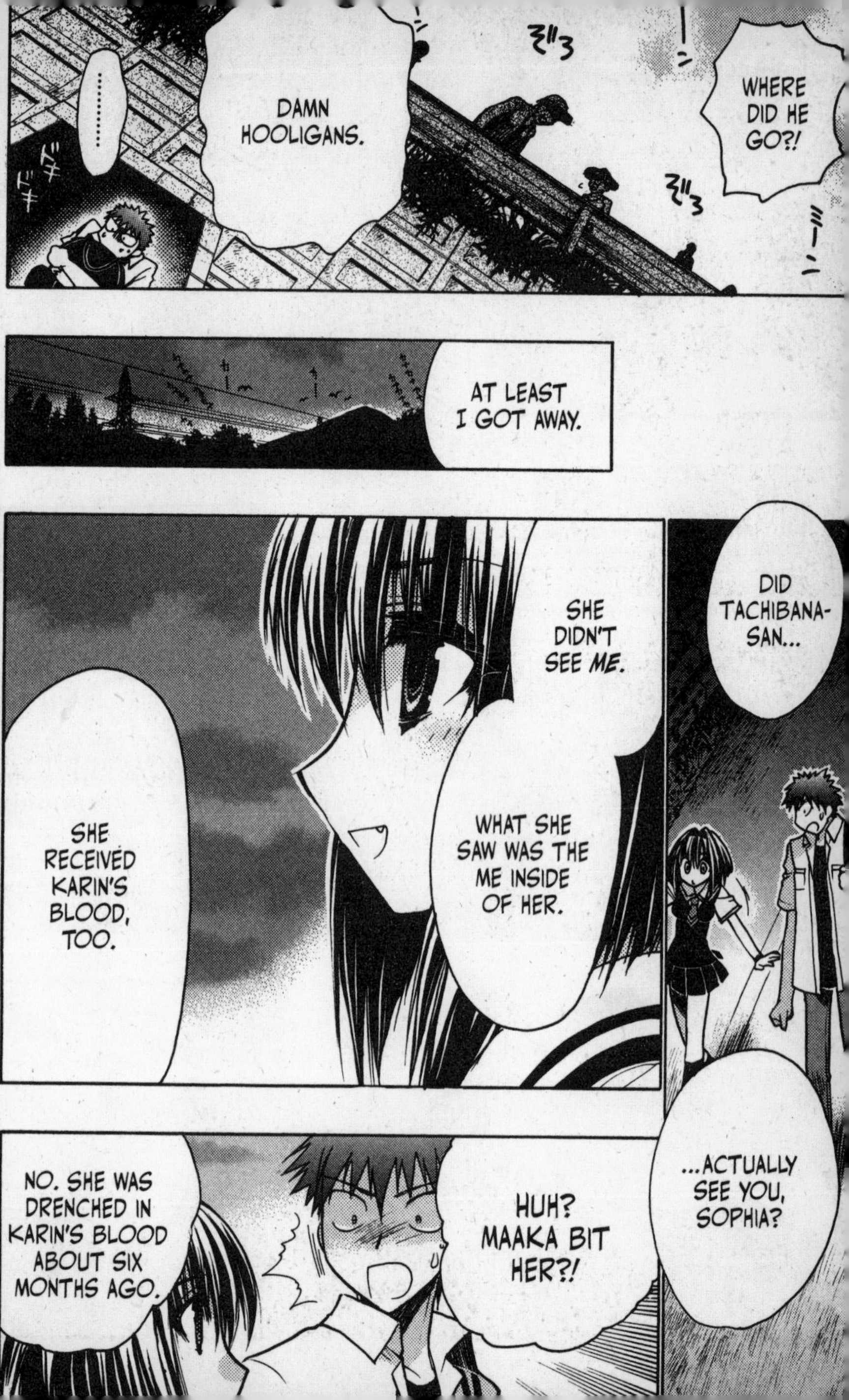
WHERE DID HE GO?!
DAMN HOOLIGANS.
......
AT LEAST I GOT AWAY.
DID TACHIBANA-SAN...
...ACTUALLY SEE YOU, SOPHIA?
SHE DIDN'T SEE *ME*.
WHAT SHE SAW WAS THE ME INSIDE OF HER.
SHE RECEIVED KARIN'S BLOOD, TOO.
HUH? MAAKA BIT HER?!
NO. SHE WAS DRENCHED IN KARIN'S BLOOD ABOUT SIX MONTHS AGO.

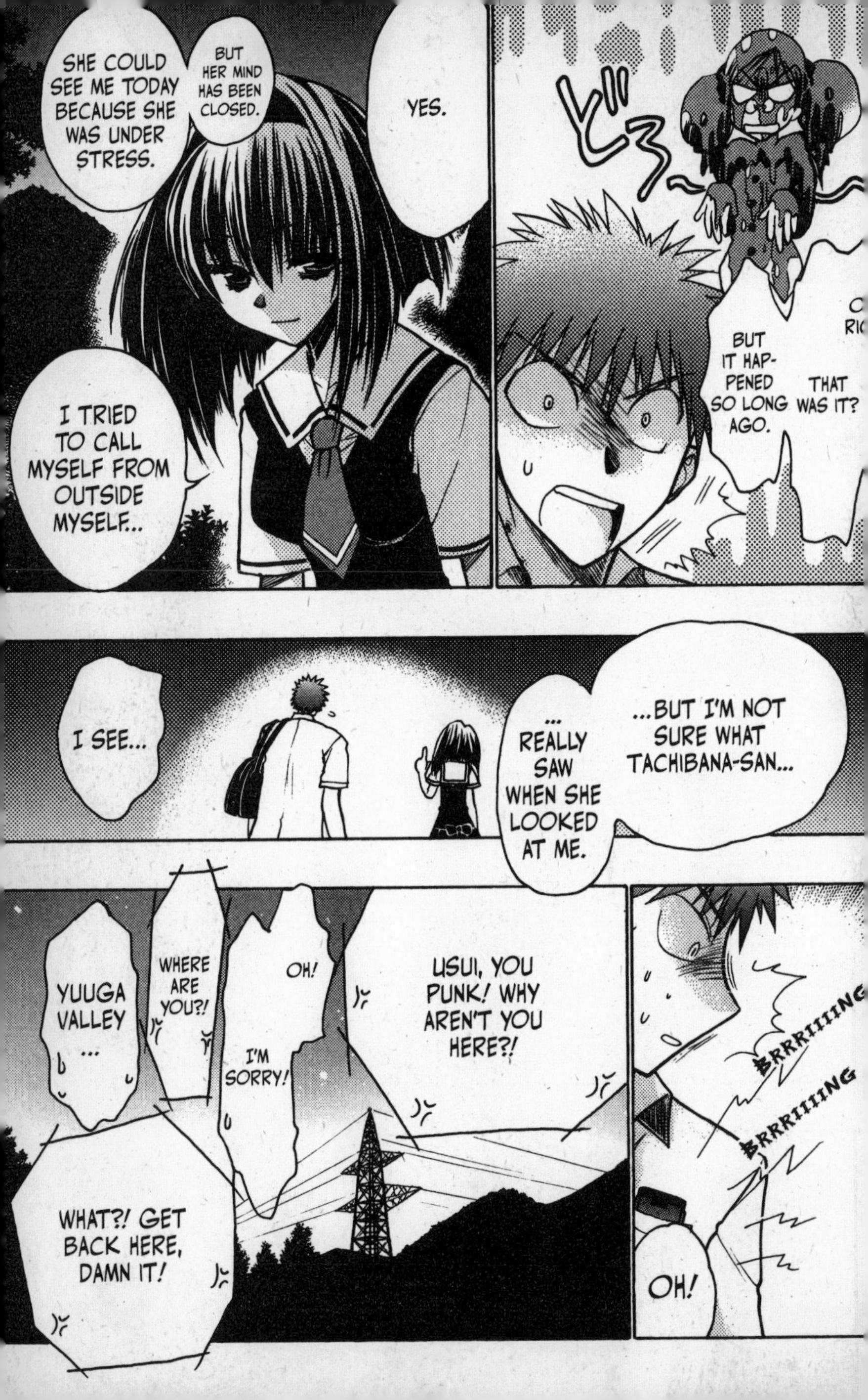
どろ~
THAT WAS IT?
BUT IT HAPPENED SO LONG AGO.
YES.
BUT HER MIND HAS BEEN CLOSED.
SHE COULD SEE ME TODAY BECAUSE SHE WAS UNDER STRESS.
I TRIED TO CALL MYSELF FROM OUTSIDE MYSELF...
...BUT I'M NOT SURE WHAT TACHIBANA-SAN...
...REALLY SAW WHEN SHE LOOKED AT ME.
I SEE...
BRRRIIIING
BRRRIIIING
OH!
USUI, YOU PUNK! WHY AREN'T YOU HERE?!
OH!
I'M SORRY!
WHERE ARE YOU?!
YUUGA VALLEY...
WHAT?! GET BACK HERE, DAMN IT!

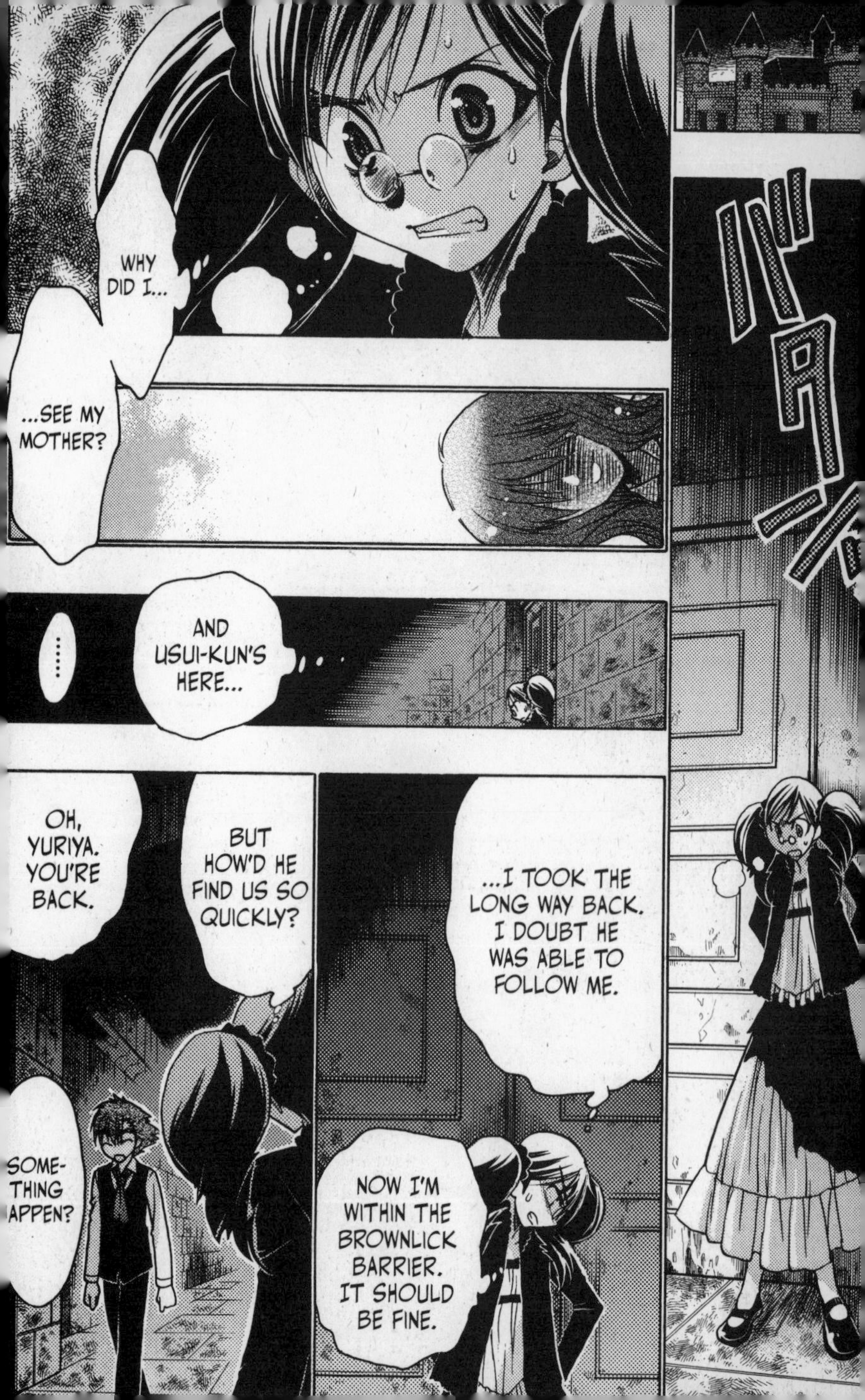

バタン
WHY DID I...
...SEE MY MOTHER?
AND USUI-KUN'S HERE...
......
...I TOOK THE LONG WAY BACK. I DOUBT HE WAS ABLE TO FOLLOW ME.
NOW I'M WITHIN THE BROWNLICK BARRIER. IT SHOULD BE FINE.
BUT HOW'D HE FIND US SO QUICKLY?
OH, YURIYA. YOU'RE BACK.
SOME-THING APPEN?

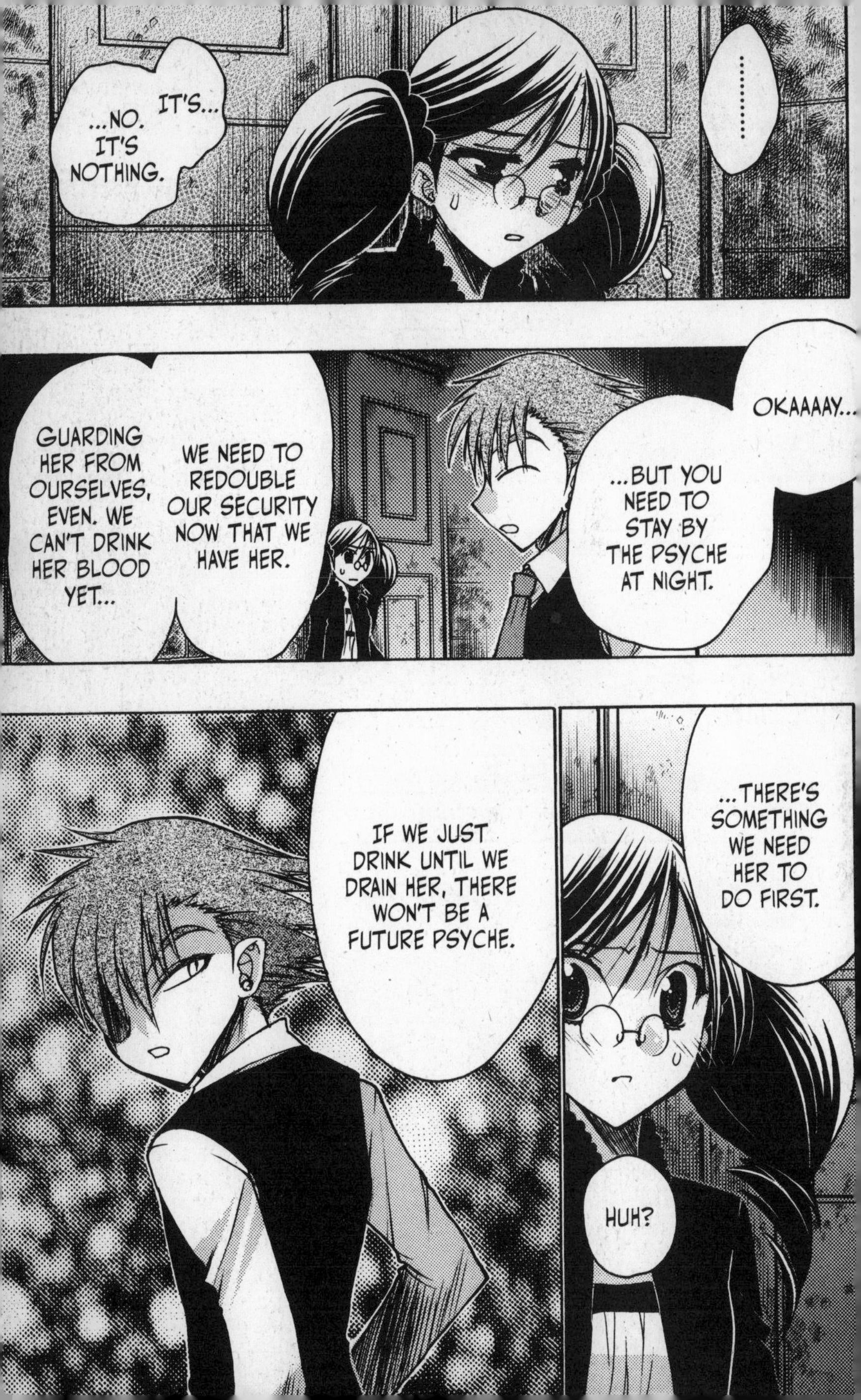
....
IT'S...
...NO. IT'S NOTHING.
OKAAAAY...
...BUT YOU NEED TO STAY BY THE PSYCHE AT NIGHT.
WE NEED TO REDOUBLE OUR SECURITY NOW THAT WE HAVE HER.
GUARDING HER FROM OURSELVES, EVEN. WE CAN'T DRINK HER BLOOD YET...
...THERE'S SOMETHING WE NEED HER TO DO FIRST.
HUH?
IF WE JUST DRINK UNTIL WE DRAIN HER, THERE WON'T BE A FUTURE PSYCHE.

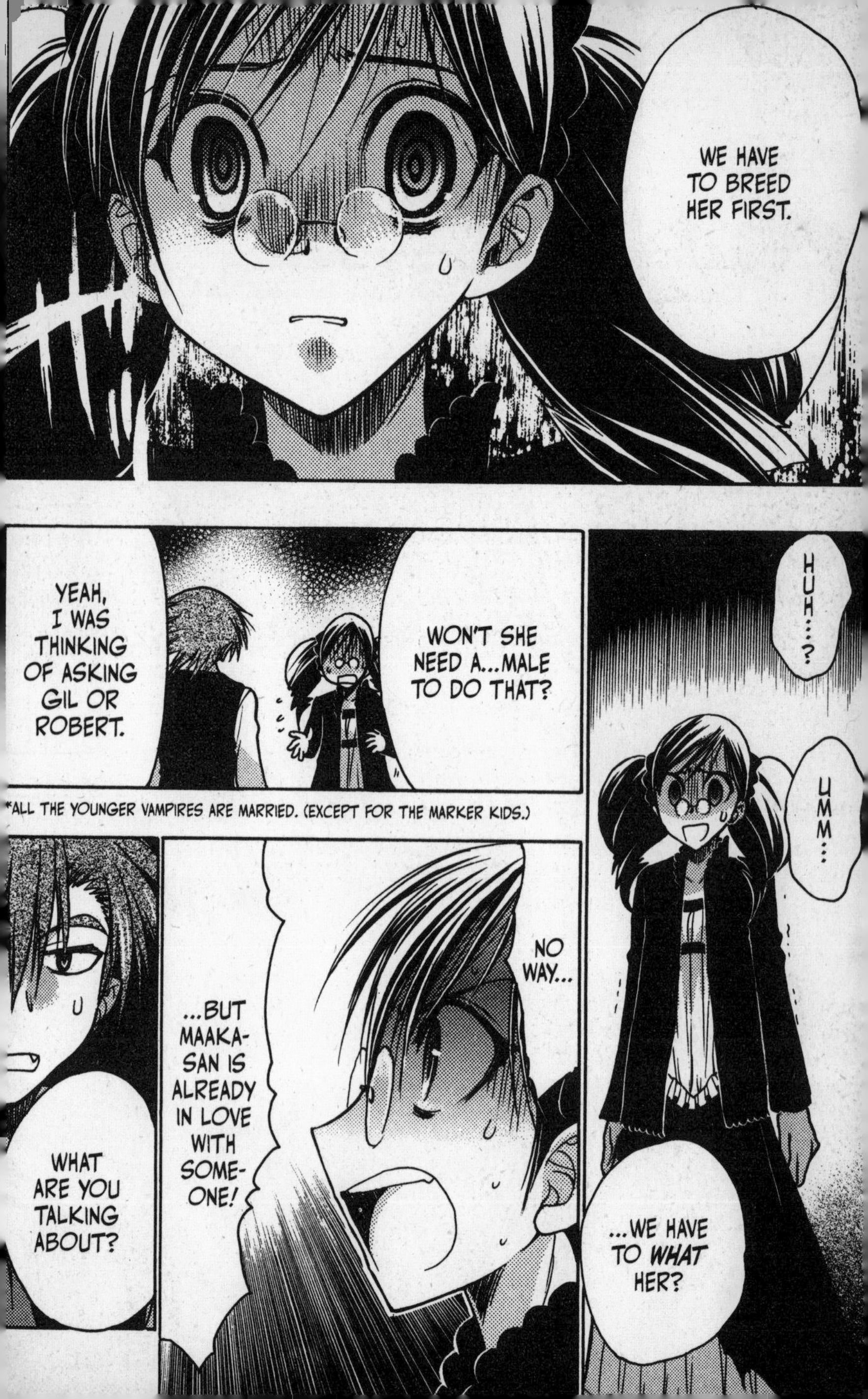
WE HAVE TO BREED HER FIRST.
HUH...?
UMM...
...WE HAVE TO WHAT HER?
WON'T SHE NEED A...MALE TO DO THAT?
YEAH, I WAS THINKING OF ASKING GIL OR ROBERT.
*ALL THE YOUNGER VAMPIRES ARE MARRIED. (EXCEPT FOR THE MARKER KIDS.)
NO WAY...
...BUT MAAKA-SAN IS ALREADY IN LOVE WITH SOME-ONE!
WHAT ARE YOU TALKING ABOUT?

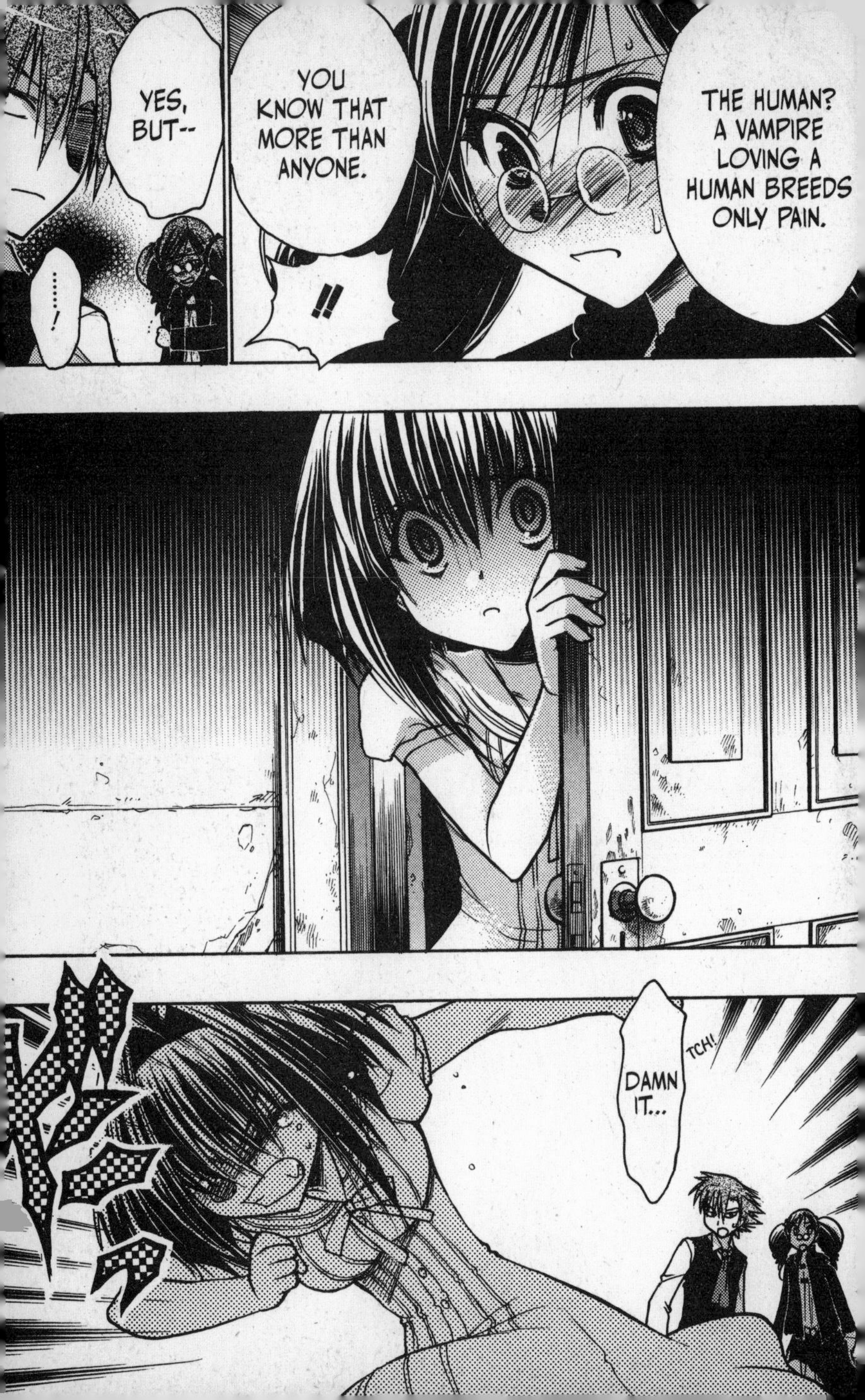
THE HUMAN? A VAMPIRE LOVING A HUMAN BREEDS ONLY PAIN.
YOU KNOW THAT MORE THAN ANYONE.
!!
YES, BUT--
......!
TCH!
DAMN IT...

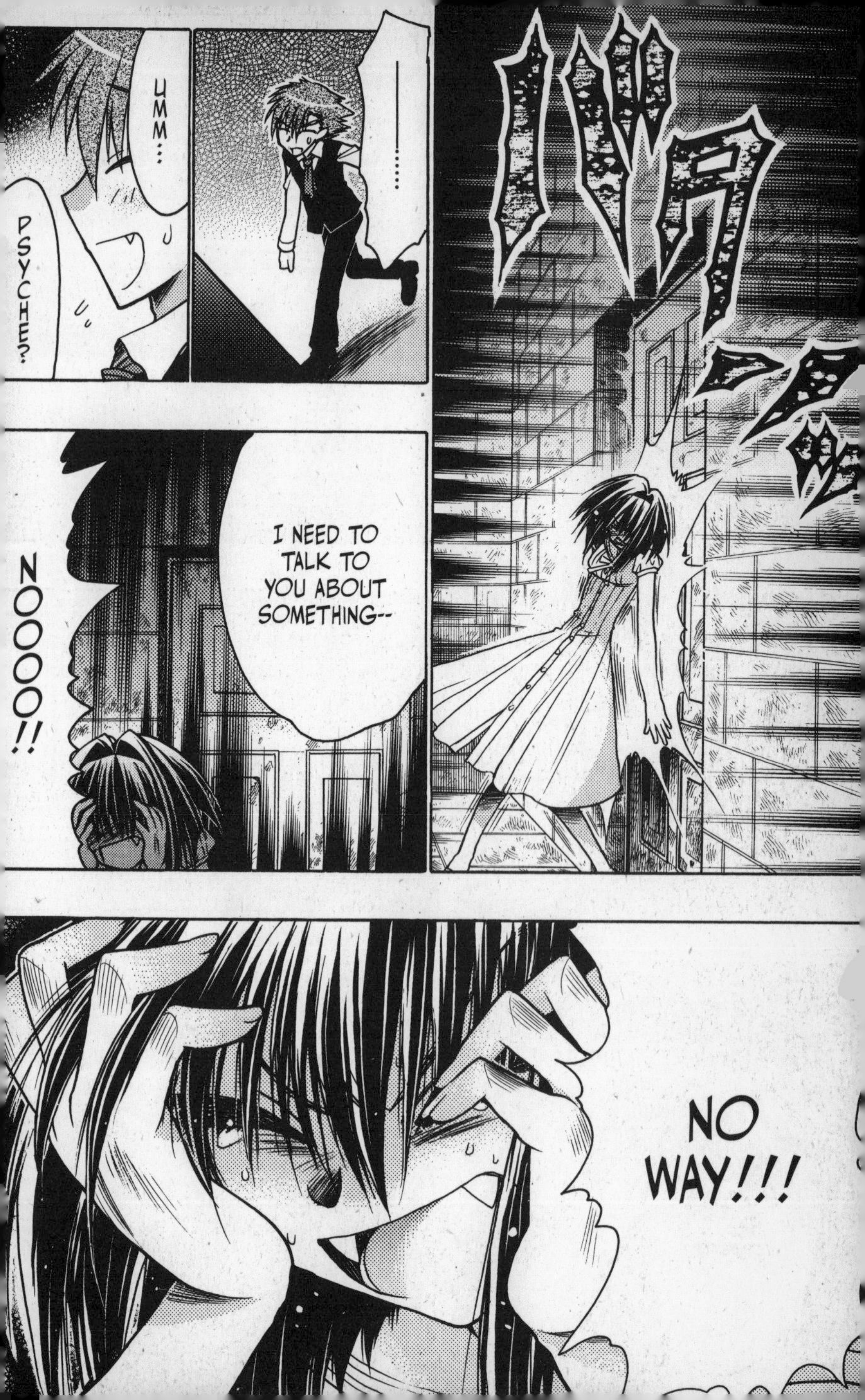
......
UMM... PSYCHE?
I NEED TO TALK TO YOU ABOUT SOMETHING--
NOOOOO!!
NO WAY!!!

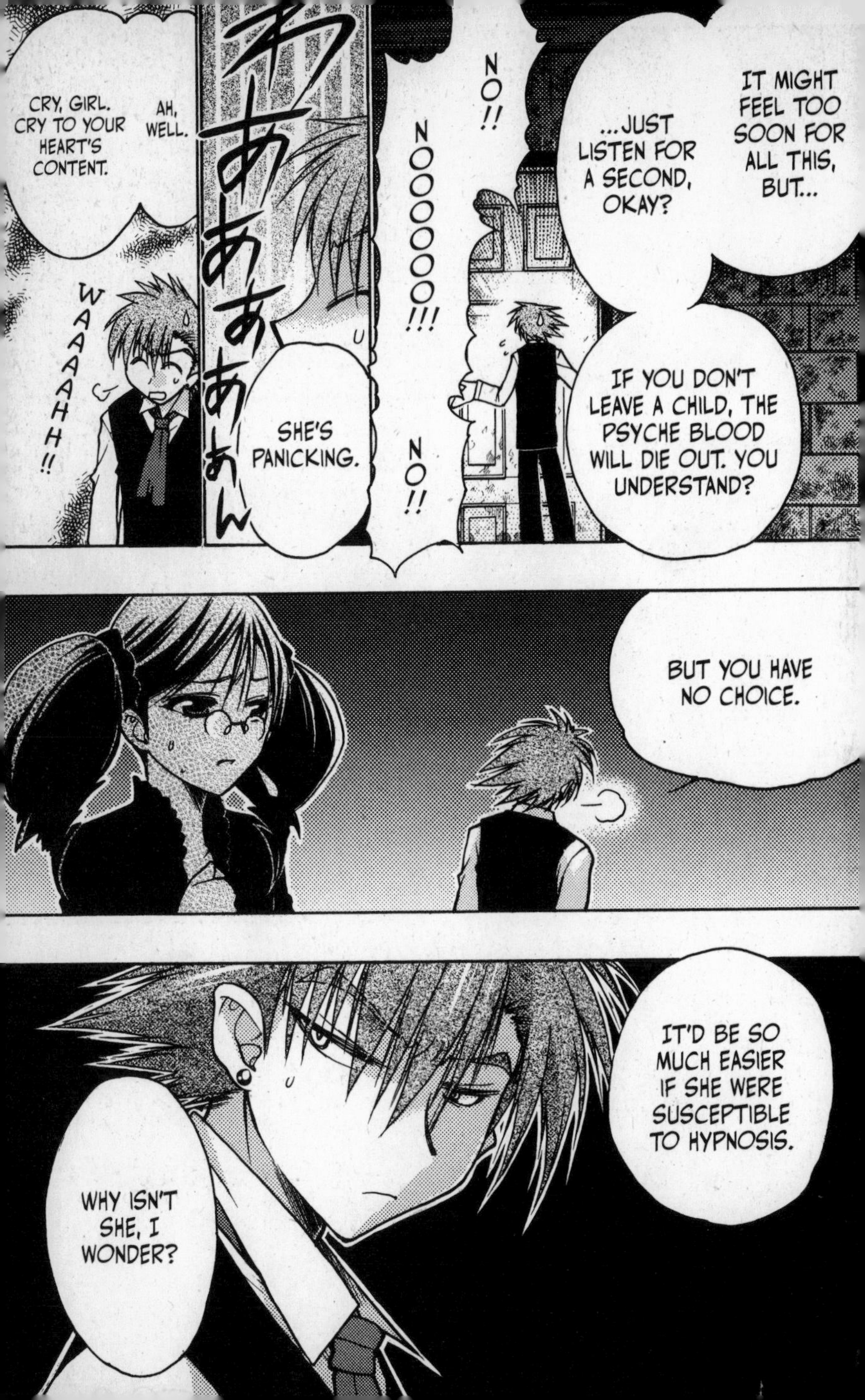
IT MIGHT FEEL TOO SOON FOR ALL THIS, BUT...
...JUST LISTEN FOR A SECOND, OKAY?
IF YOU DON'T LEAVE A CHILD, THE PSYCHE BLOOD WILL DIE OUT. YOU UNDERSTAND?
NO!!
NOOOOOOO!!!
NO!!
SHE'S PANICKING.
AH, WELL.
CRY, GIRL. CRY TO YOUR HEART'S CONTENT.
WAAAAAHH!!
BUT YOU HAVE NO CHOICE.
IT'D BE SO MUCH EASIER IF SHE WERE SUSCEPTIBLE TO HYPNOSIS.
WHY ISN'T SHE, I WONDER?

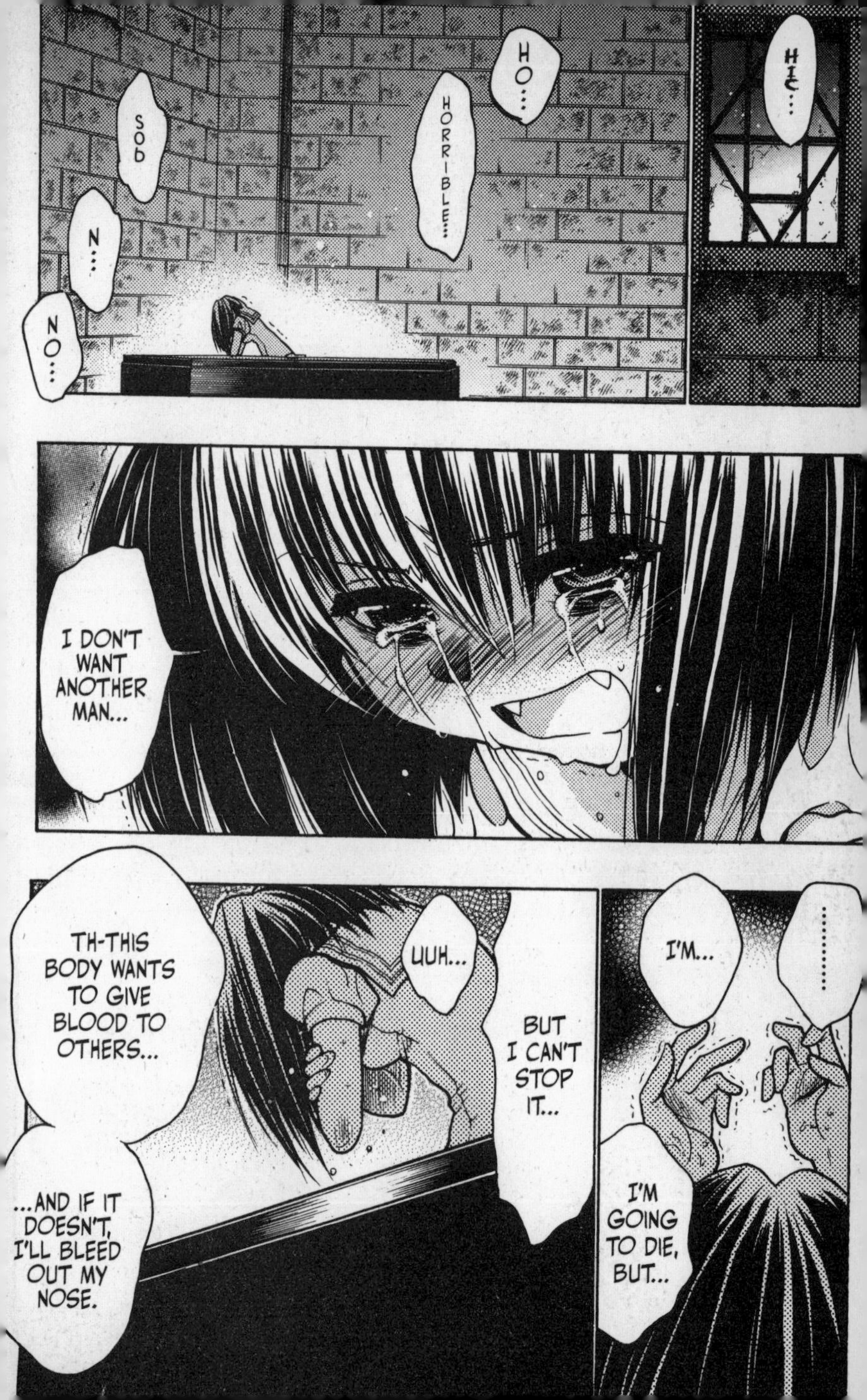
HIC...
HO...
HORRIBLE...
SOB
N...
NO...
I DON'T WANT ANOTHER MAN...
......
I'M...
I'M GOING TO DIE, BUT...
UUH...
BUT I CAN'T STOP IT...
TH-THIS BODY WANTS TO GIVE BLOOD TO OTHERS...
...AND IF IT DOESN'T, I'LL BLEED OUT MY NOSE.

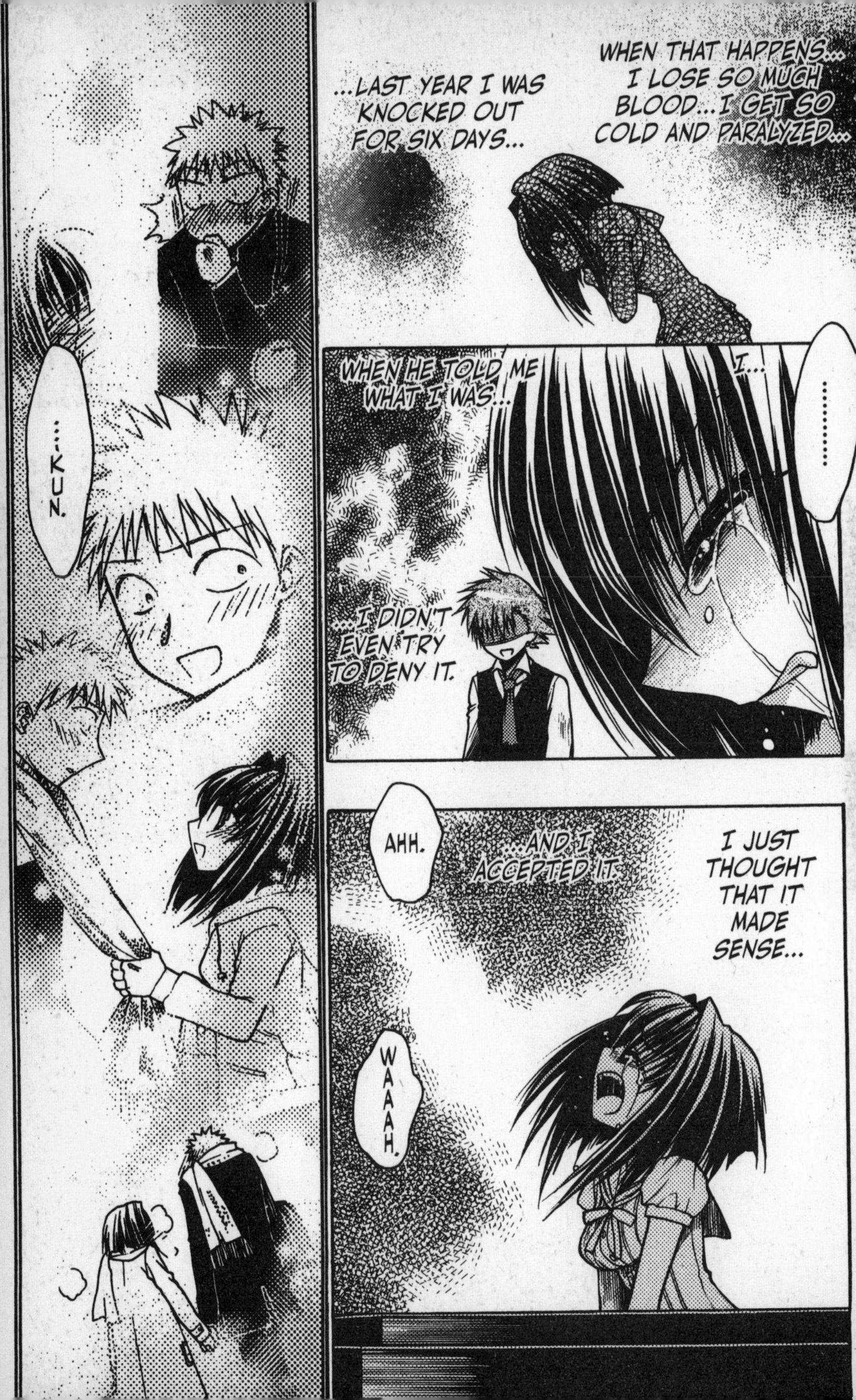
WHEN THAT HAPPENS... I LOSE SO MUCH BLOOD... I GET SO COLD AND PARALYZED...
...LAST YEAR I WAS KNOCKED OUT FOR SIX DAYS...
......
I...
WHEN HE TOLD ME WHAT I WAS...
...I DIDN'T EVEN TRY TO DENY IT.
I JUST THOUGHT THAT IT MADE SENSE...
...AND I ACCEPTED IT.
AHH.
WAAAAH.
...KUN.

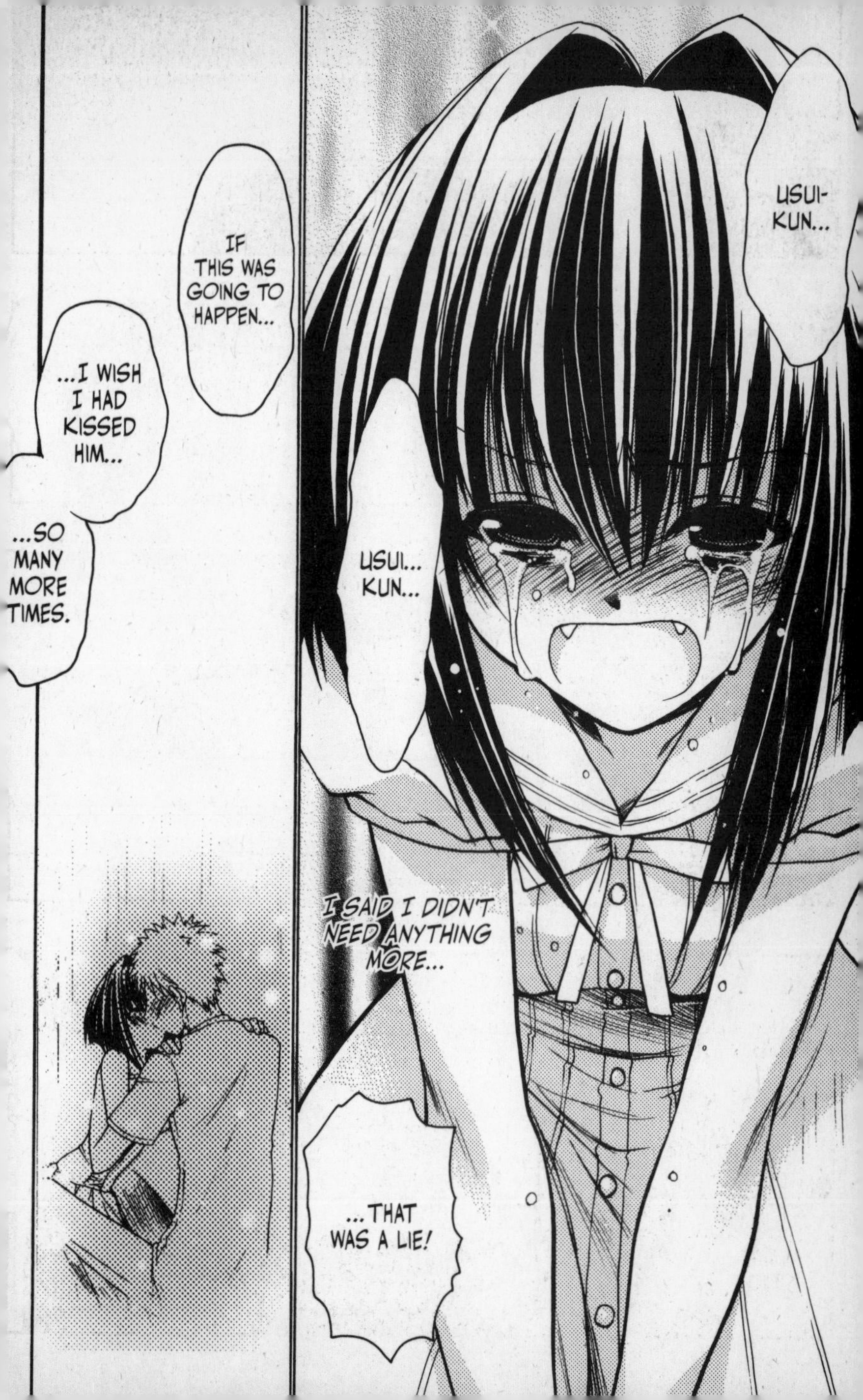
USUI-KUN...
USUI... KUN...
I SAID I DIDN'T NEED ANYTHING MORE...
...THAT WAS A LIE!
IF THIS WAS GOING TO HAPPEN...
...I WISH I HAD KISSED HIM...
...SO MANY MORE TIMES.

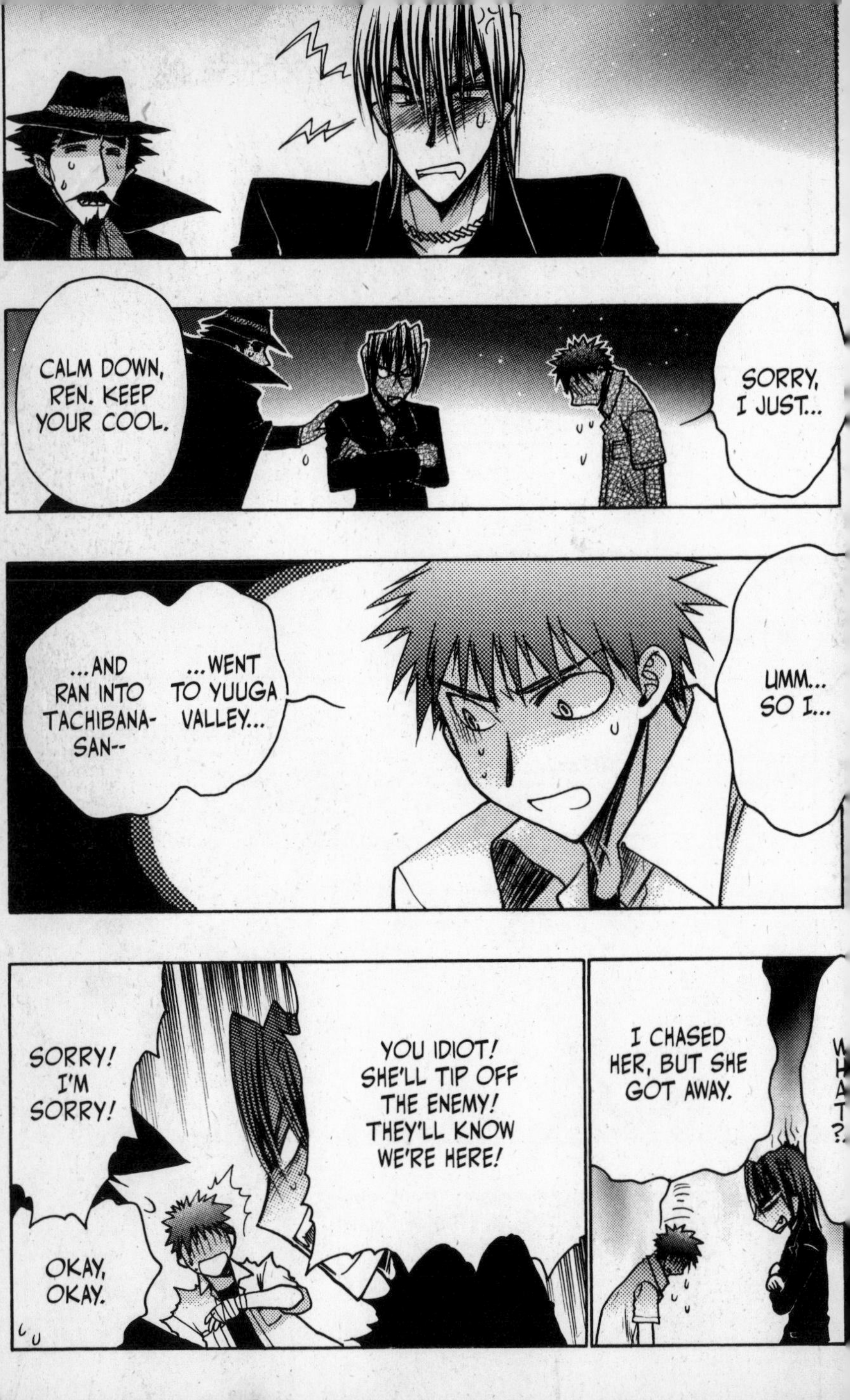
SORRY, I JUST...
CALM DOWN, REN. KEEP YOUR COOL.
UMM... SO I...
...WENT TO YUUGA VALLEY...
...AND RAN INTO TACHIBANA-SAN--
WHAT?!
I CHASED HER, BUT SHE GOT AWAY.
YOU IDIOT! SHE'LL TIP OFF THE ENEMY! THEY'LL KNOW WE'RE HERE!
SORRY! I'M SORRY!
OKAY, OKAY.

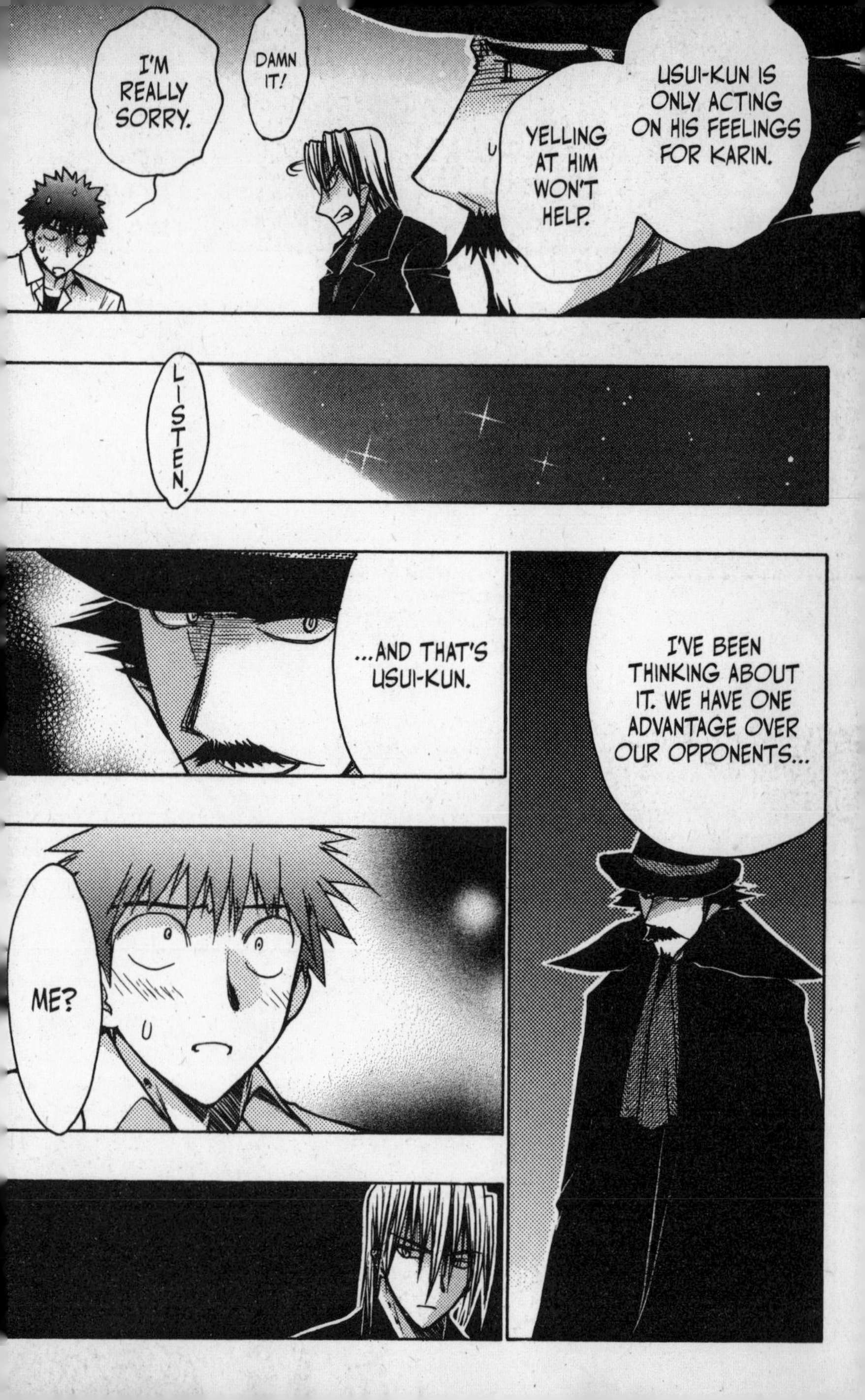
USUI-KUN IS ONLY ACTING ON HIS FEELINGS FOR KARIN.
YELLING AT HIM WON'T HELP.
DAMN IT!
I'M REALLY SORRY.
LISTEN.
I'VE BEEN THINKING ABOUT IT. WE HAVE ONE ADVANTAGE OVER OUR OPPONENTS...
...AND THAT'S USUI-KUN.
ME?

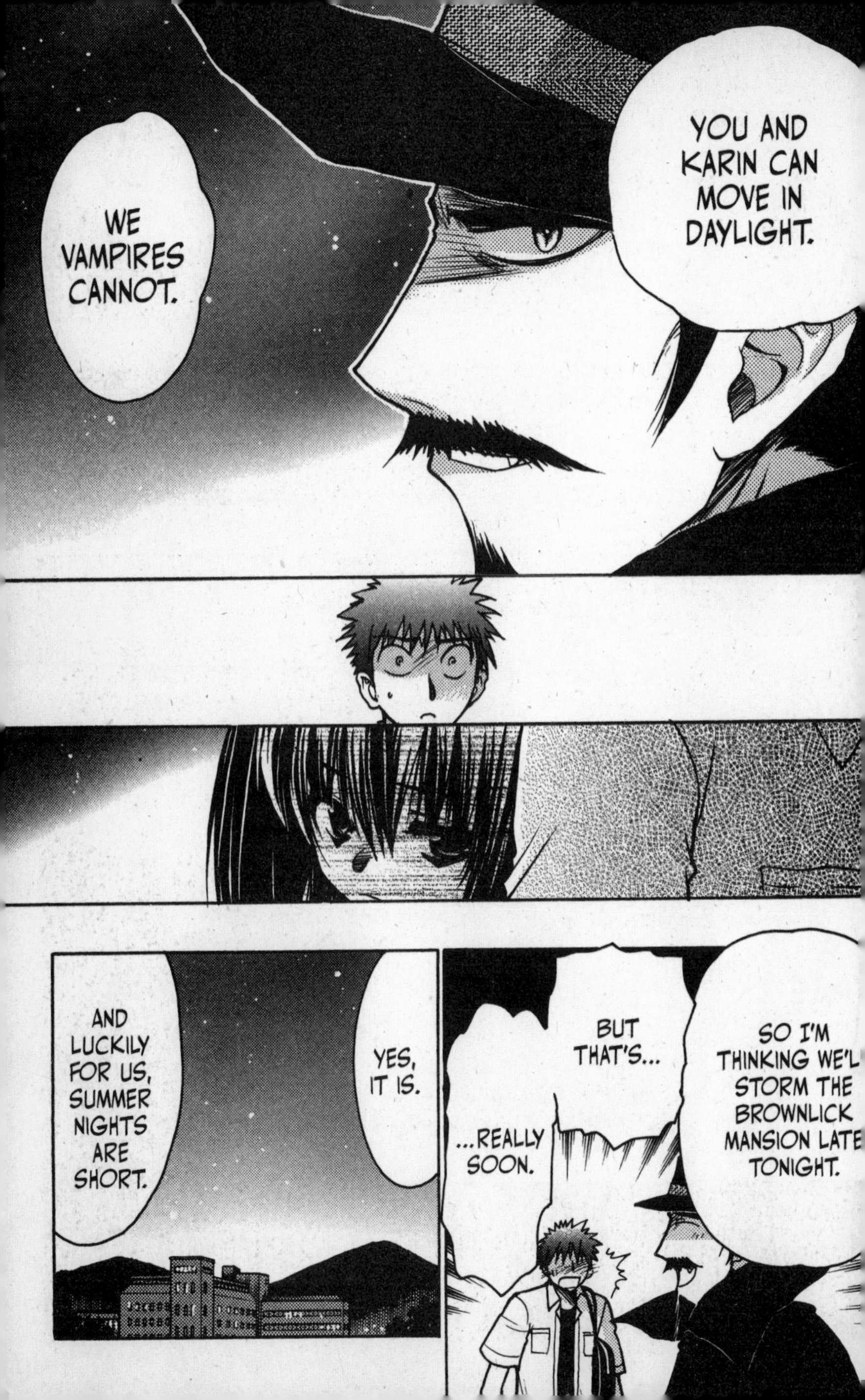
YOU AND KARIN CAN MOVE IN DAYLIGHT.
WE VAMPIRES CANNOT.
SO I'M THINKING WE'L STORM THE BROWNLICK MANSION LATE TONIGHT.
BUT THAT'S...
...REALLY SOON.
YES, IT IS.
AND LUCKILY FOR US, SUMMER NIGHTS ARE SHORT.

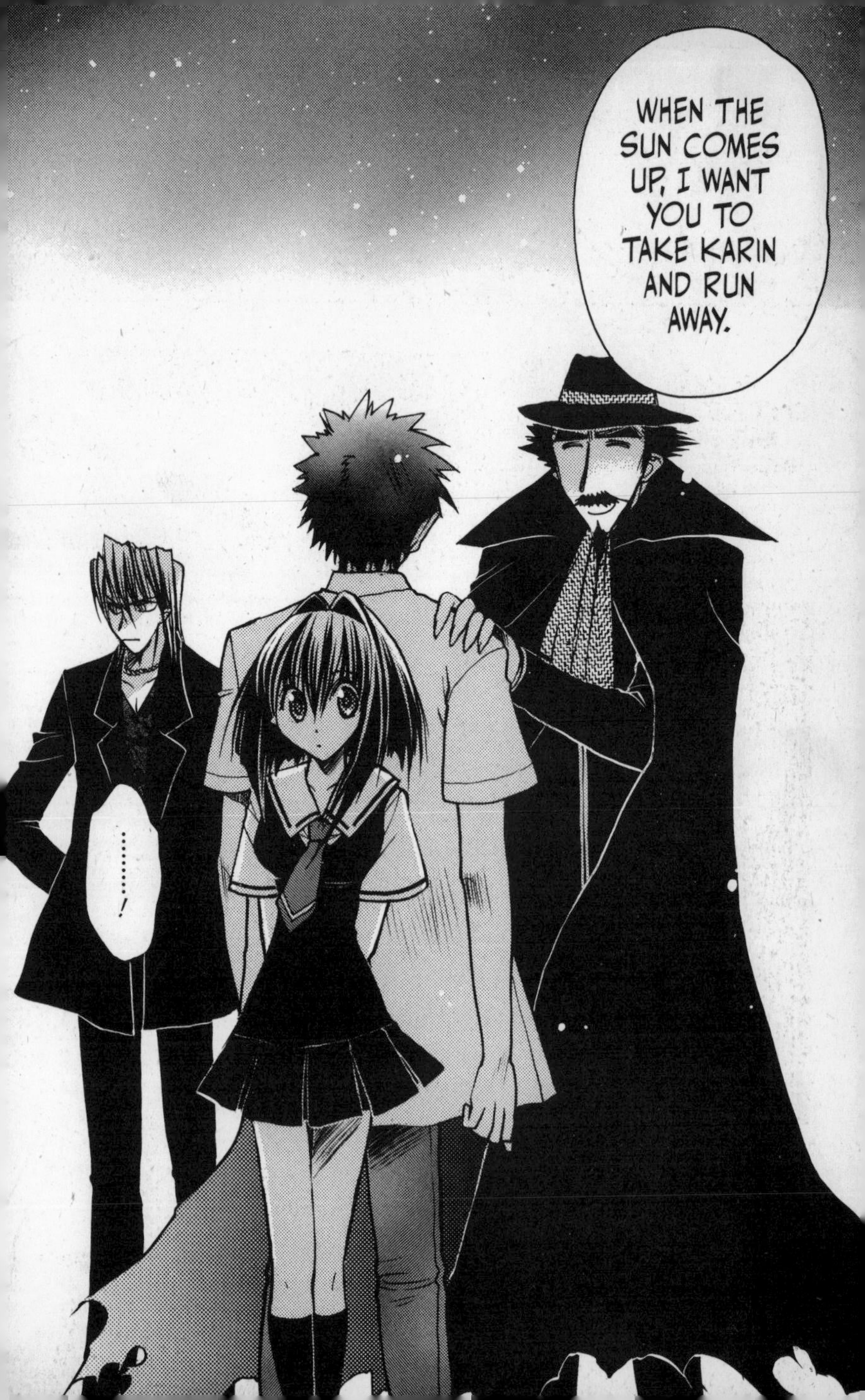
WHEN THE SUN COMES UP, I WANT YOU TO TAKE KARIN AND RUN AWAY.
.......!

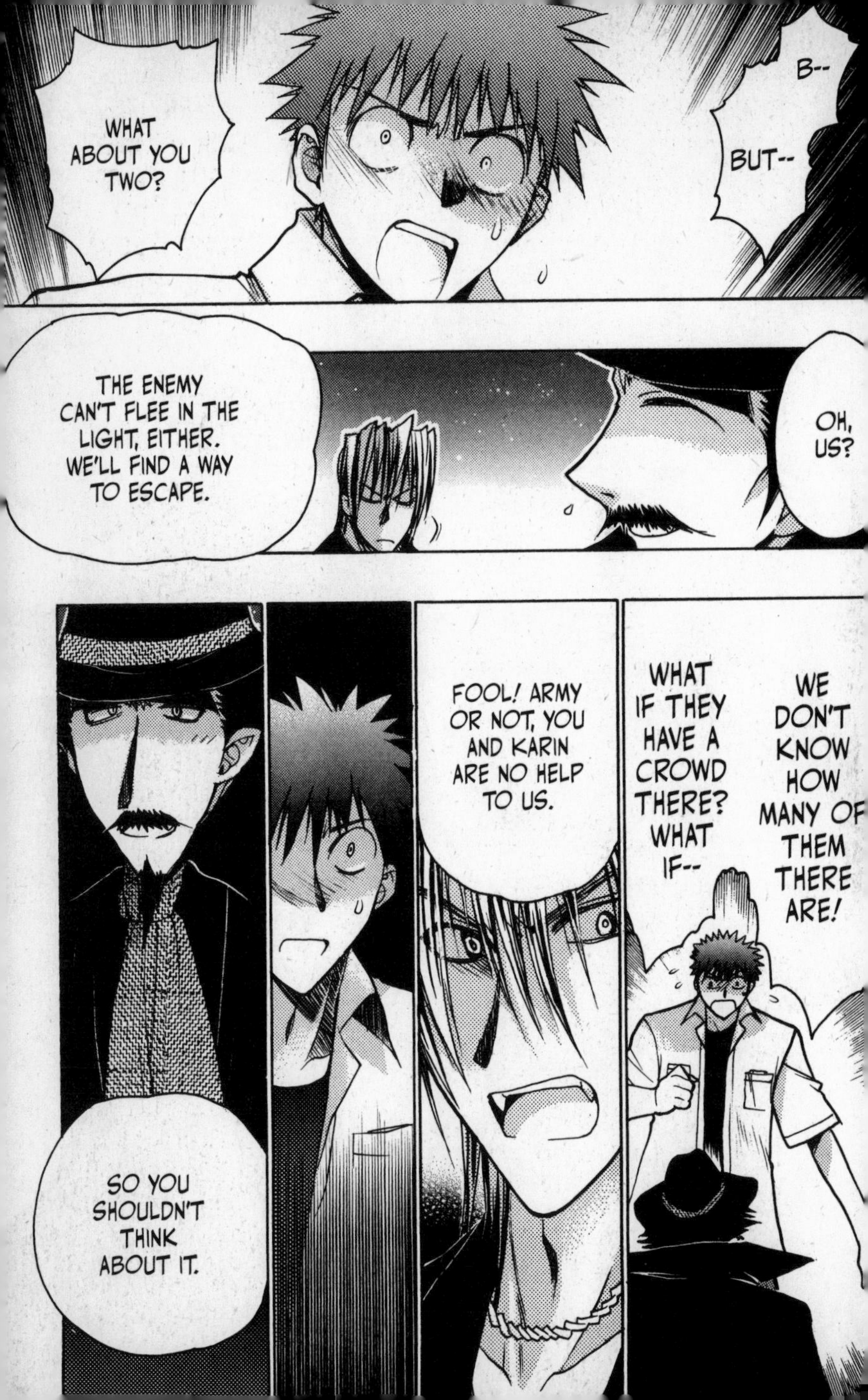
B-- BUT--
WHAT ABOUT YOU TWO?
OH, US?
THE ENEMY CAN'T FLEE IN THE LIGHT, EITHER. WE'LL FIND A WAY TO ESCAPE.
WE DON'T KNOW HOW MANY OF THEM THERE ARE!
WHAT IF THEY HAVE A CROWD THERE? WHAT IF--
FOOL! ARMY OR NOT, YOU AND KARIN ARE NO HELP TO US.
SO YOU SHOULDN'T THINK ABOUT IT.

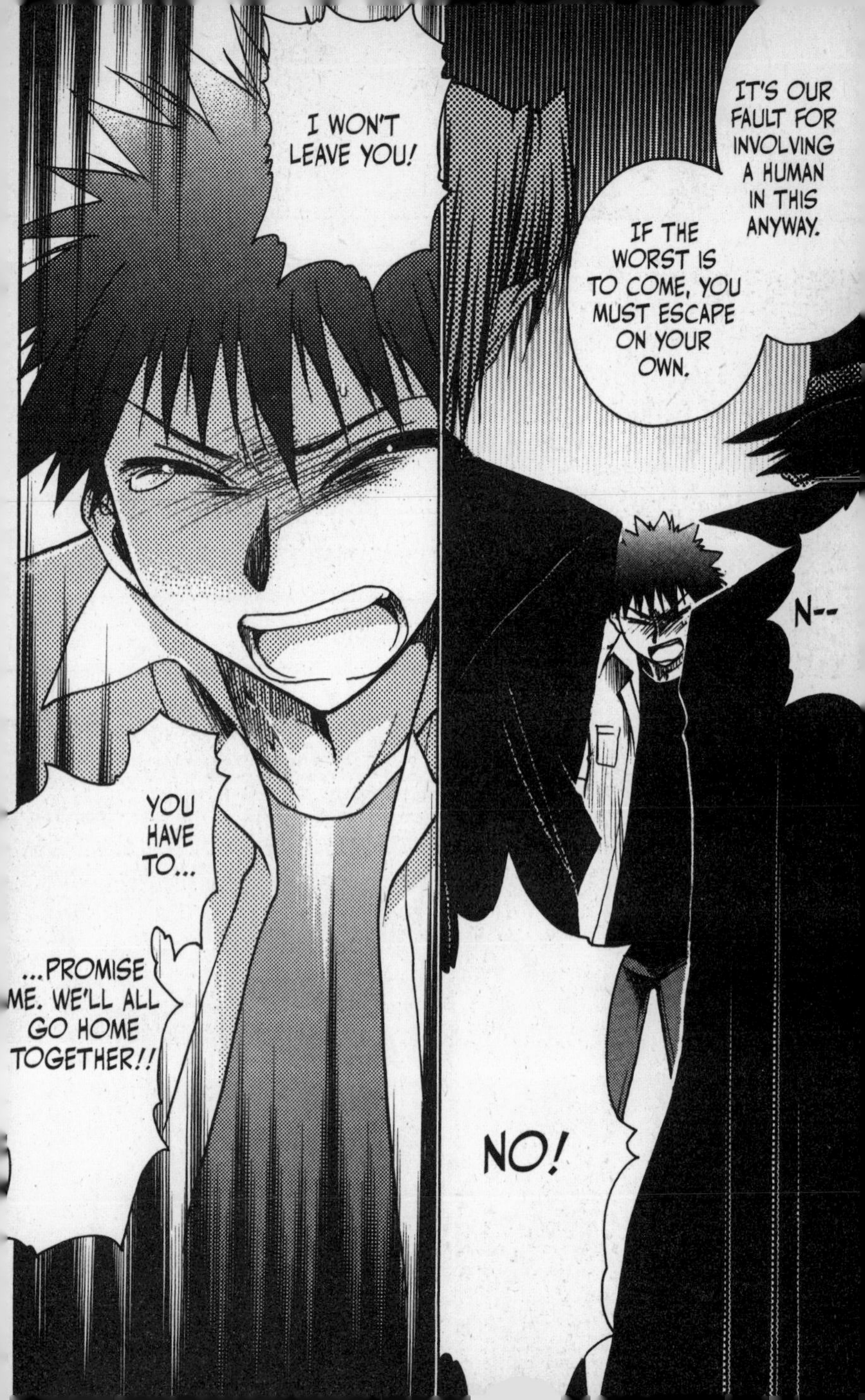
IT'S OUR FAULT FOR INVOLVING A HUMAN IN THIS ANYWAY.
IF THE WORST IS TO COME, YOU MUST ESCAPE ON YOUR OWN.
N--
NO!
I WON'T LEAVE YOU!
YOU HAVE TO...
...PROMISE ME. WE'LL ALL GO HOME TOGETHER!!

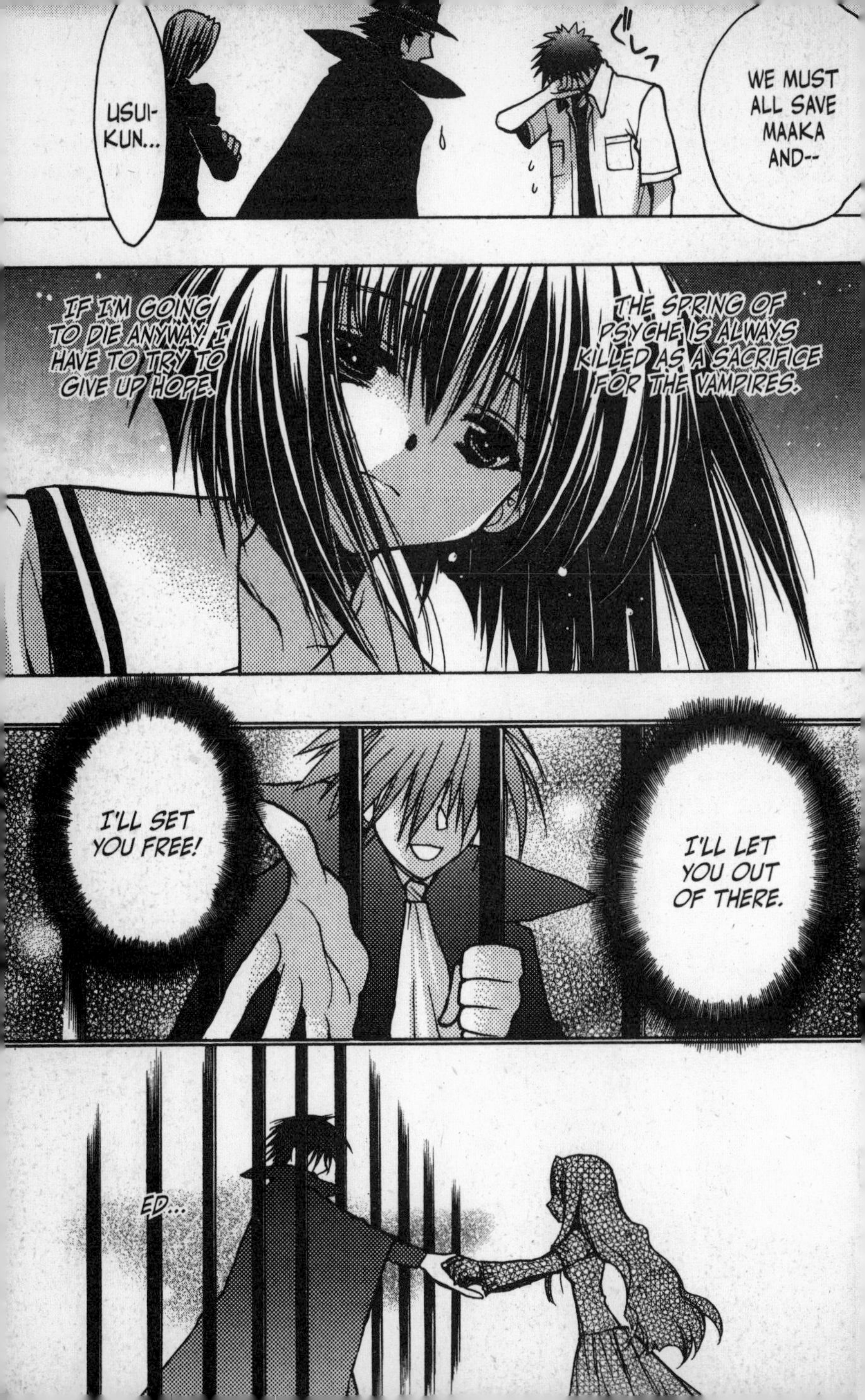
WE MUST ALL SAVE MAAKA AND--
USUI-KUN...
THE SPRING OF PSYCHE IS ALWAYS KILLED AS A SACRIFICE FOR THE VAMPIRES.
IF I'M GOING TO DIE ANYWAY I HAVE TO TRY TO GIVE UP HOPE.
I'LL LET YOU OUT OF THERE.
I'LL SET YOU FREE!
ED...

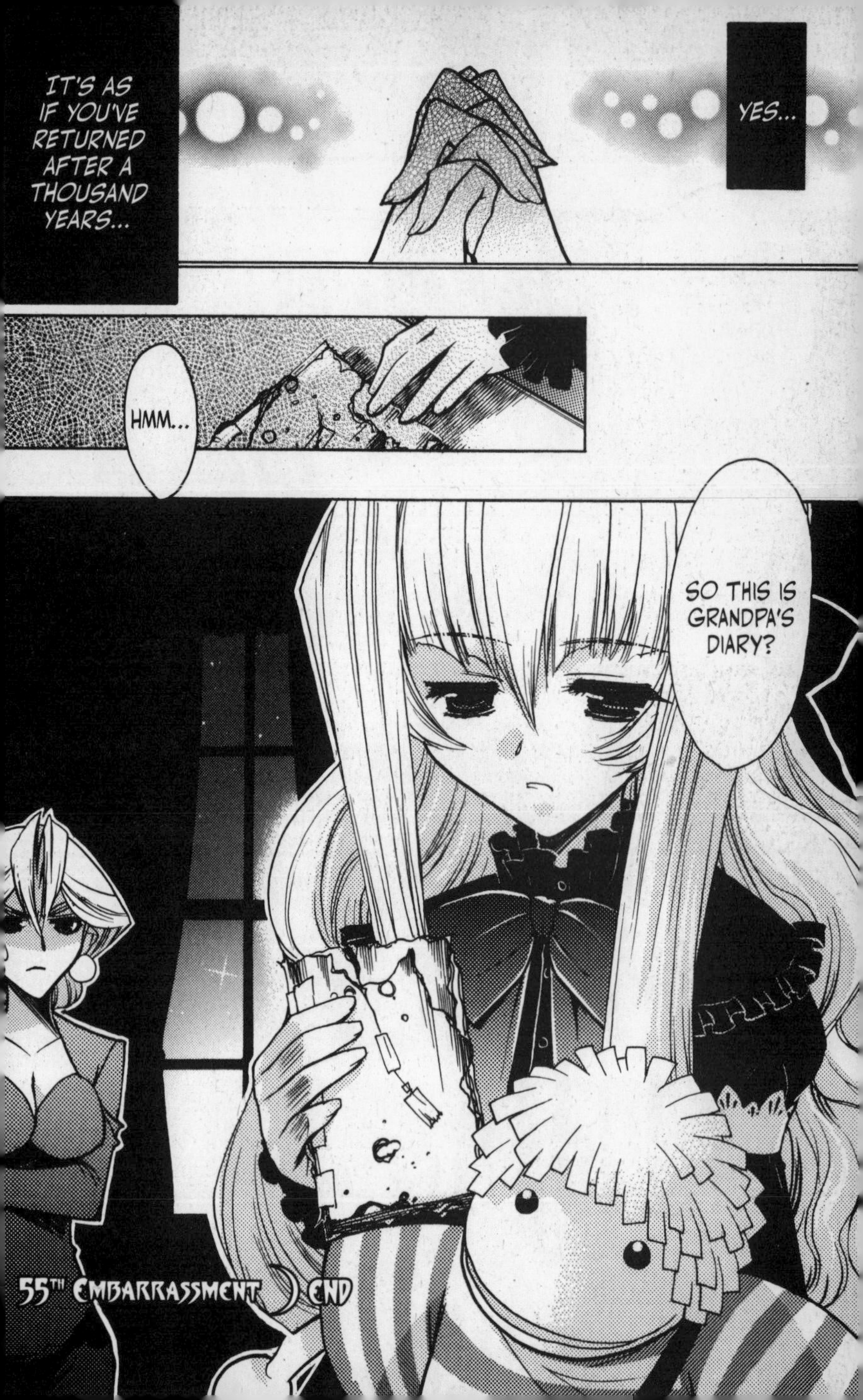
YES...
IT'S AS IF YOU'VE RETURNED AFTER A THOUSAND YEARS...
HMM...
SO THIS IS GRANDPA'S DIARY?
55TH EMBARRASSMENT END

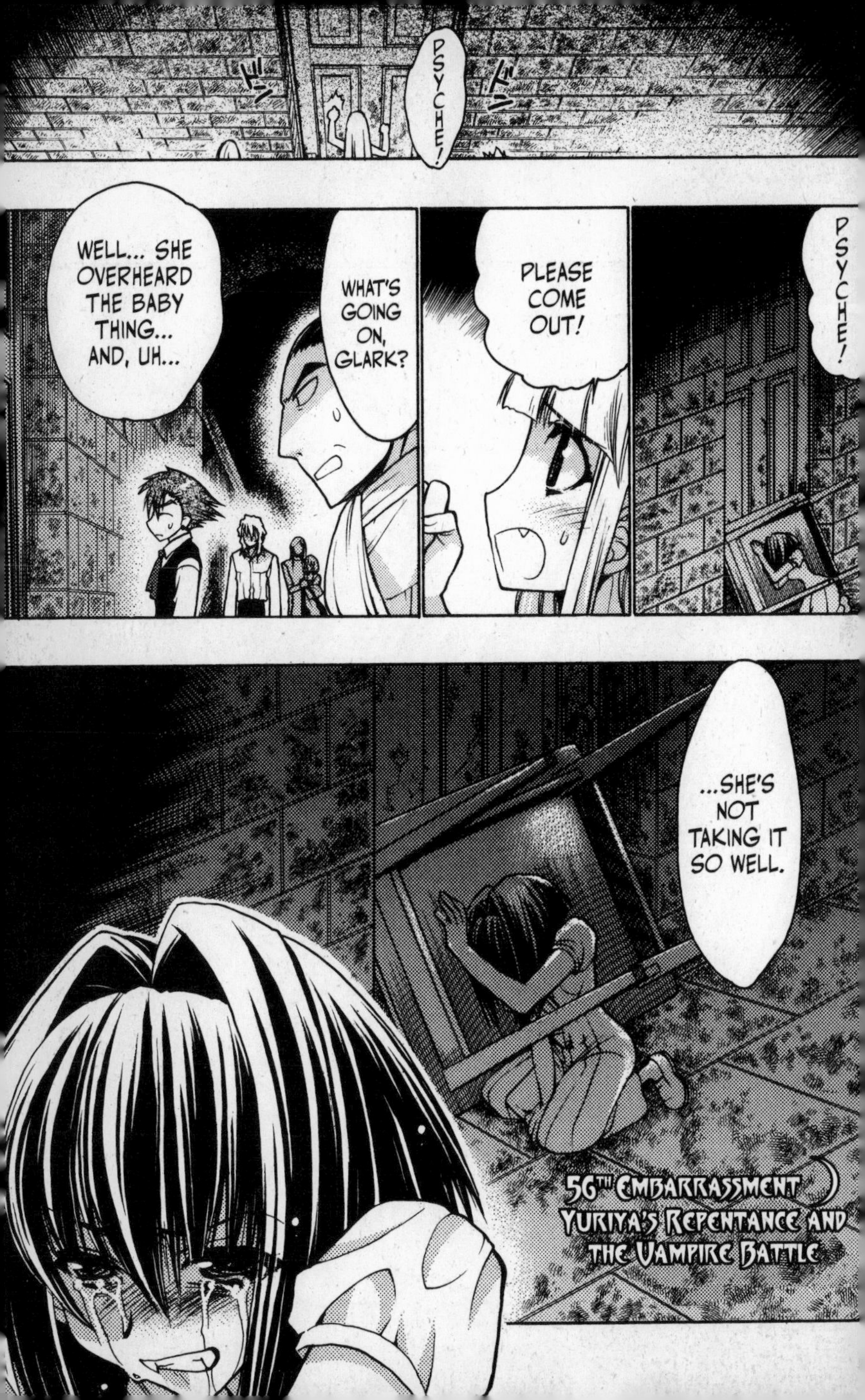
PSYCHE!
PSYCHE!
PLEASE COME OUT!
WHAT'S GOING ON, GLARK?
WELL... SHE OVERHEARD THE BABY THING... AND, UH...
...SHE'S NOT TAKING IT SO WELL.
56TH EMBARRASSMENT
YURIYA'S REPENTANCE AND THE VAMPIRE BATTLE

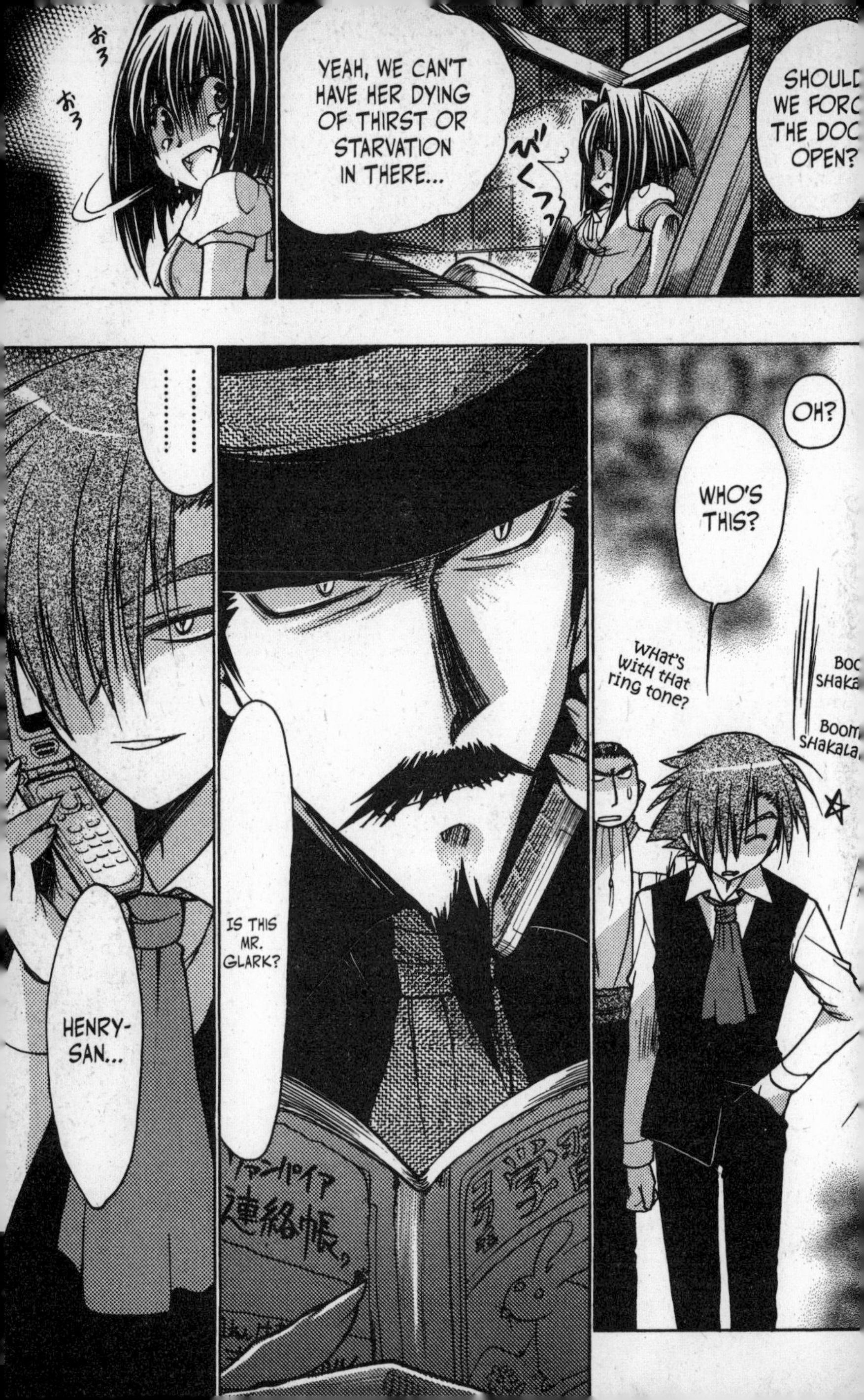

SHOULD WE FORC THE DOC OPEN?
ぷくっ
YEAH, WE CAN'T HAVE HER DYING OF THIRST OR STARVATION IN THERE...
おろ
おろ
OH?
WHO'S THIS?
BOO SHAKA
BOOM SHAKALA
WHAT'S WITH THAT RING TONE?
IS THIS MR. GLARK?
ヴァンパイア連絡帳
......
HENRY-SAN...

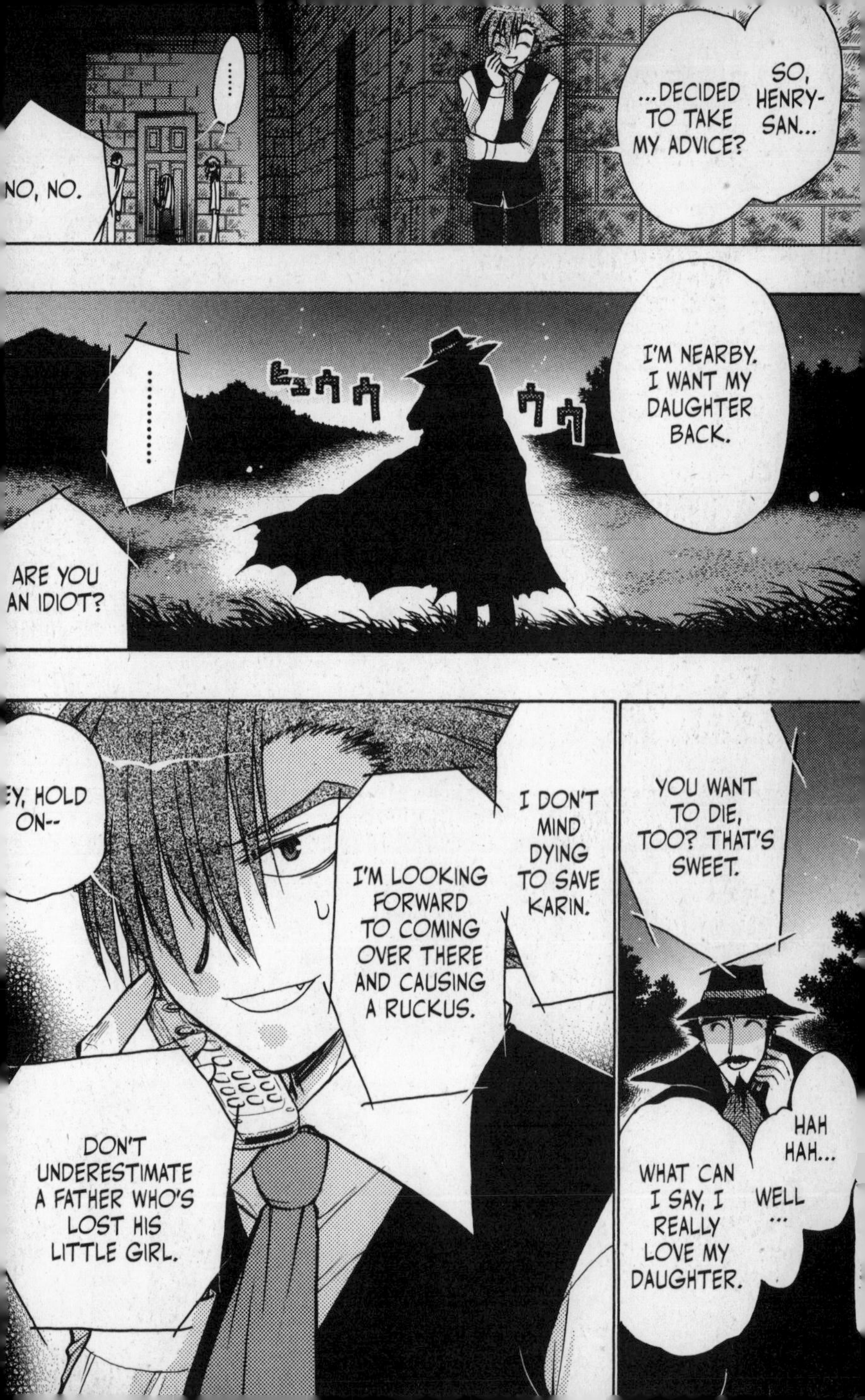
SO, HENRY-SAN...
...DECIDED TO TAKE MY ADVICE?
...
NO, NO.
I'M NEARBY. I WANT MY DAUGHTER BACK.
ヒュウウ
ウウ
......
ARE YOU AN IDIOT?
YOU WANT TO DIE, TOO? THAT'S SWEET.
HAH HAH...
WELL ...
WHAT CAN I SAY, I REALLY LOVE MY DAUGHTER.
I DON'T MIND DYING TO SAVE KARIN.
I'M LOOKING FORWARD TO COMING OVER THERE AND CAUSING A RUCKUS.
EY, HOLD ON--
DON'T UNDERESTIMATE A FATHER WHO'S LOST HIS LITTLE GIRL.

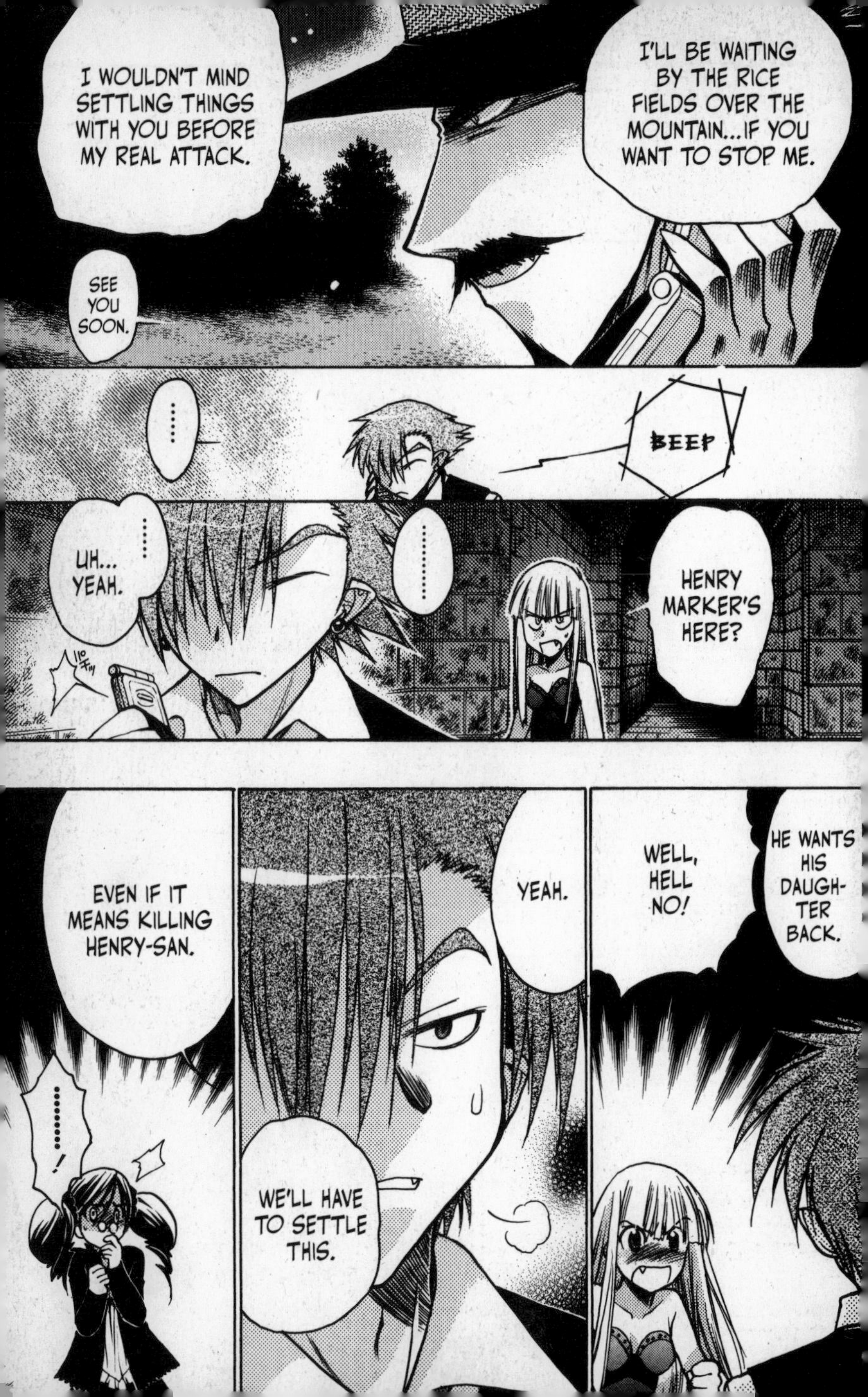
I'LL BE WAITING BY THE RICE FIELDS OVER THE MOUNTAIN...IF YOU WANT TO STOP ME.
I WOULDN'T MIND SETTLING THINGS WITH YOU BEFORE MY REAL ATTACK.
SEE YOU SOON.
BEEP
......
HENRY MARKER'S HERE?
....
......
UH... YEAH.
HE WANTS HIS DAUGH-TER BACK.
WELL, HELL NO!
YEAH.
WE'LL HAVE TO SETTLE THIS.
EVEN IF IT MEANS KILLING HENRY-SAN.
........!

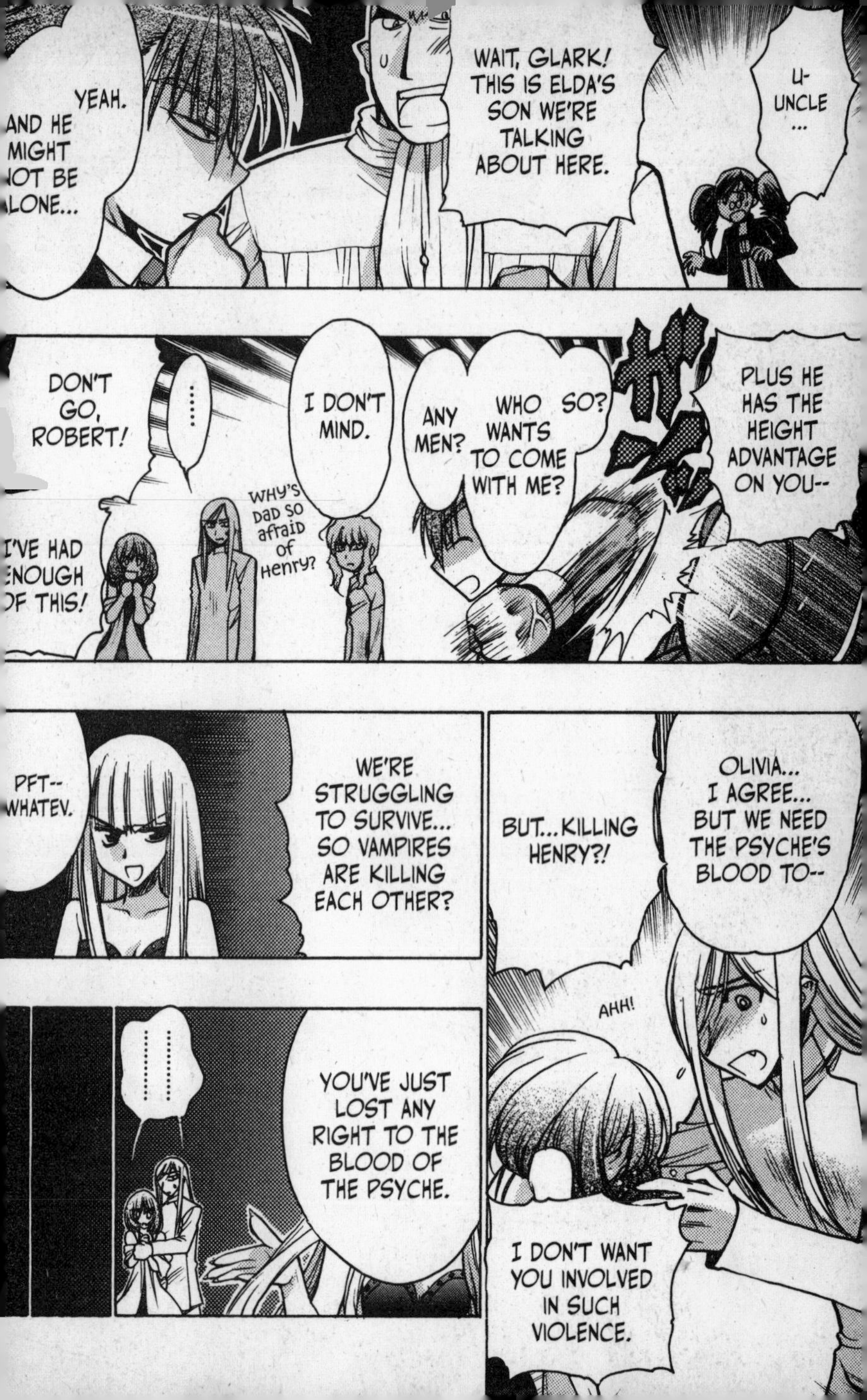
U-UNCLE...
WAIT, GLARK! THIS IS ELDA'S SON WE'RE TALKING ABOUT HERE.
YEAH.
AND HE MIGHT IOT BE LONE...
PLUS HE HAS THE HEIGHT ADVANTAGE ON YOU--
SO? WHO WANTS TO COME WITH ME?
ANY MEN?
I DON'T MIND.
WHY'S DAD SO afraid of Henry?
......
DON'T GO, ROBERT!
I'VE HAD ENOUGH OF THIS!
OLIVIA... I AGREE... BUT WE NEED THE PSYCHE'S BLOOD TO--
BUT...KILLING HENRY?!
AHH!
I DON'T WANT YOU INVOLVED IN SUCH VIOLENCE.
WE'RE STRUGGLING TO SURVIVE... SO VAMPIRES ARE KILLING EACH OTHER?
PFT-- WHATEV.
YOU'VE JUST LOST ANY RIGHT TO THE BLOOD OF THE PSYCHE.
......

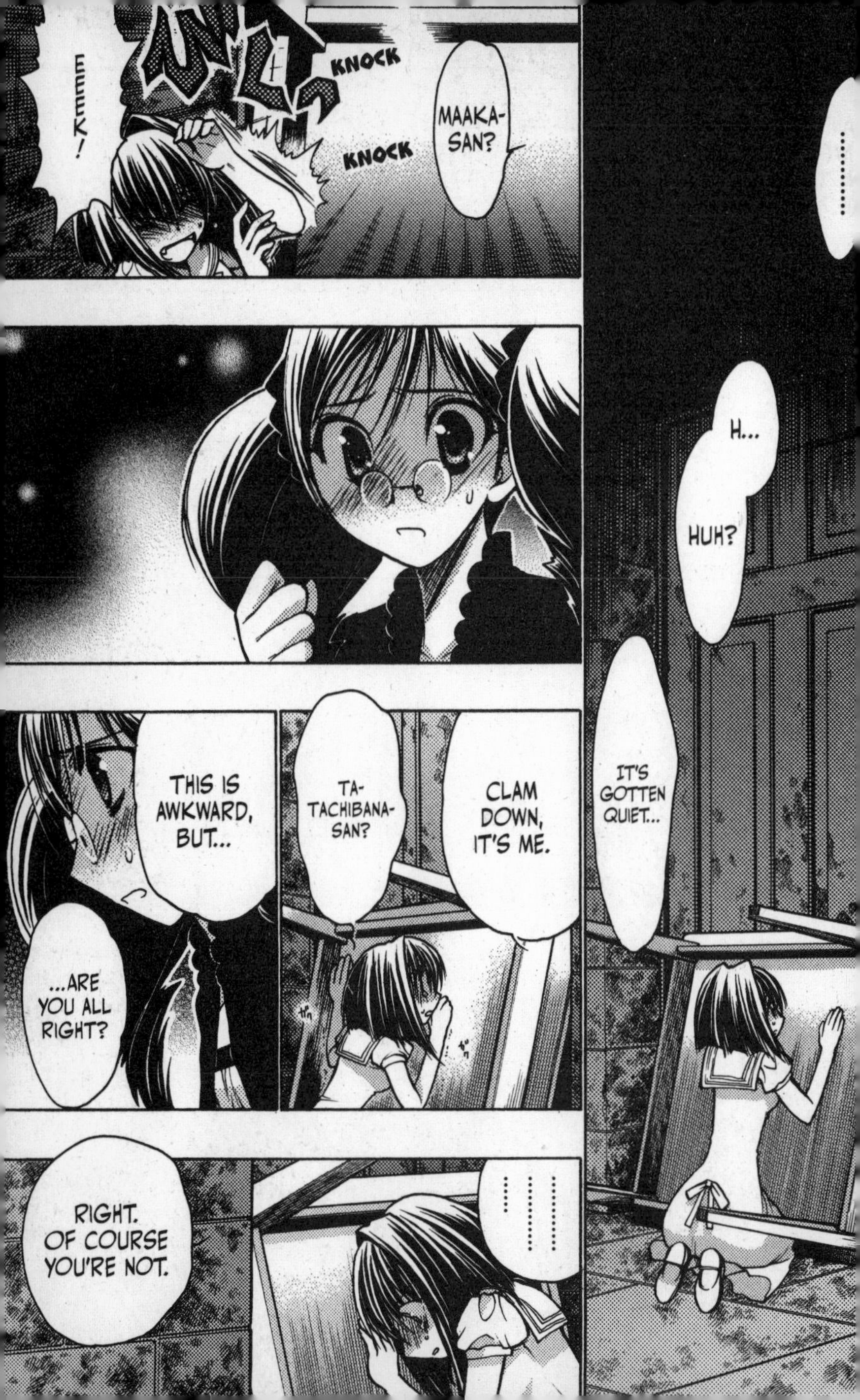
......
H...
HUH?
IT'S GOTTEN QUIET...
MAAKA-SAN?
KNOCK
KNOCK
EEEEK!
CLAM DOWN, IT'S ME.
TA-TACHIBANA-SAN?
THIS IS AWKWARD, BUT...
...ARE YOU ALL RIGHT?
......
RIGHT. OF COURSE YOU'RE NOT.

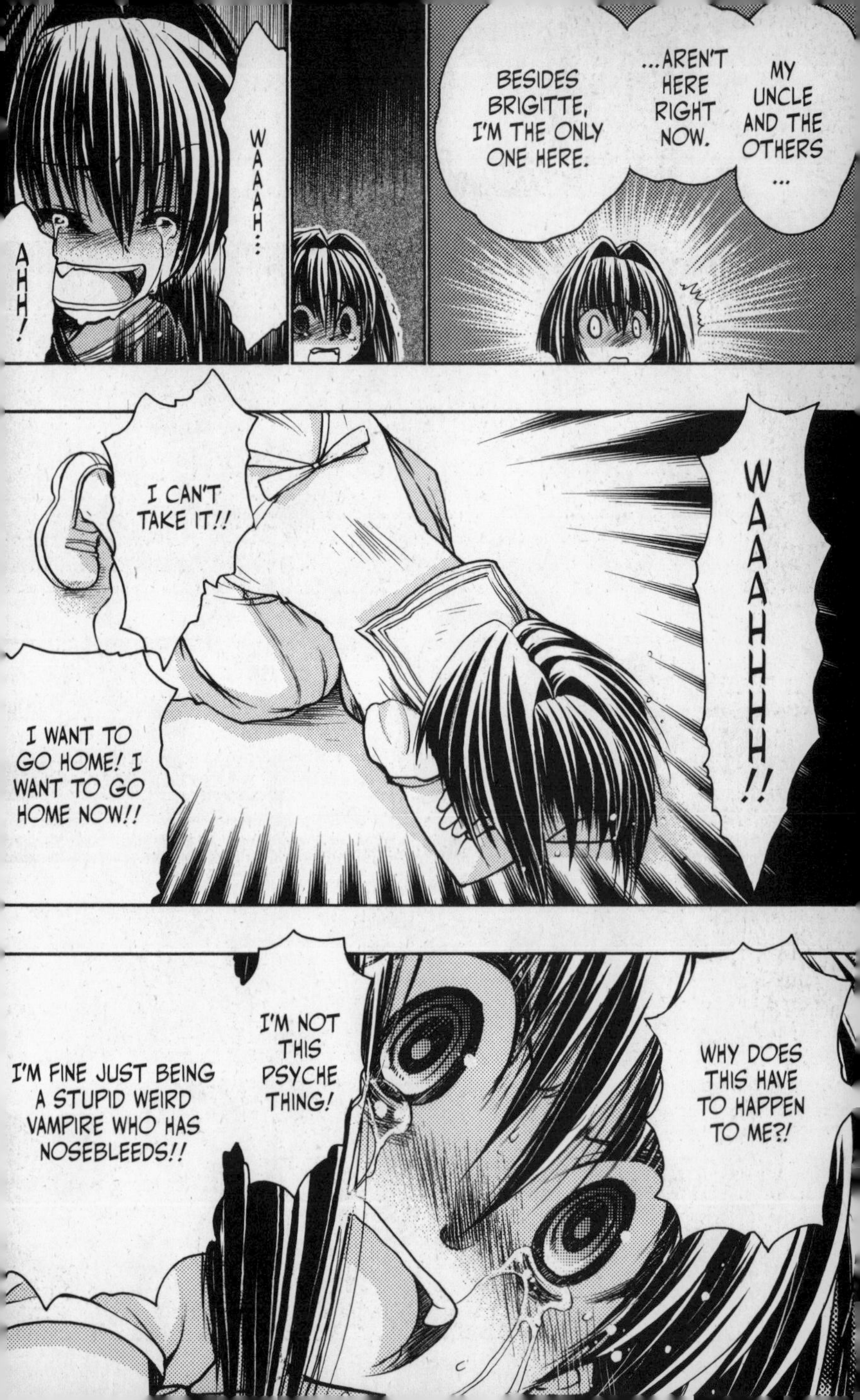
MY UNCLE AND THE OTHERS...
...AREN'T HERE RIGHT NOW.
BESIDES BRIGITTE, I'M THE ONLY ONE HERE.
WAAAAH...
AHH!
WAAAAHHHH!!
I CAN'T TAKE IT!!
I WANT TO GO HOME! I WANT TO GO HOME NOW!!
WHY DOES THIS HAVE TO HAPPEN TO ME?!
I'M NOT THIS PSYCHE THING!
I'M FINE JUST BEING A STUPID WEIRD VAMPIRE WHO HAS NOSEBLEEDS!!

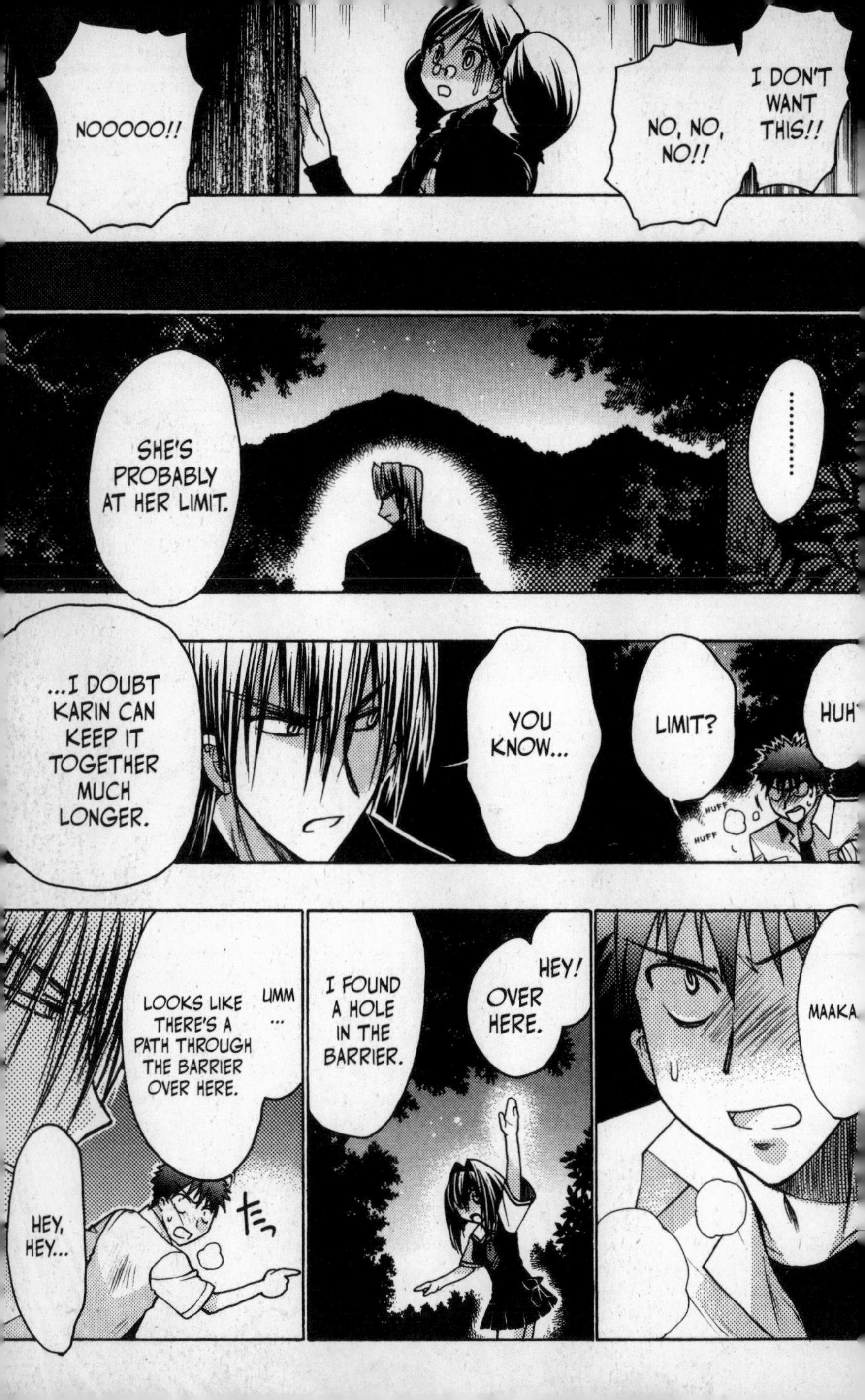
I DON'T WANT THIS!!
NO, NO, NO!!
NOOOOO!!
......
SHE'S PROBABLY AT HER LIMIT.
HUH
LIMIT?
HUFF HUFF
YOU KNOW...
...I DOUBT KARIN CAN KEEP IT TOGETHER MUCH LONGER.
MAAKA.
HEY! OVER HERE.
I FOUND A HOLE IN THE BARRIER.
UMM ...
LOOKS LIKE THERE'S A PATH THROUGH THE BARRIER OVER HERE.
HEY, HEY...

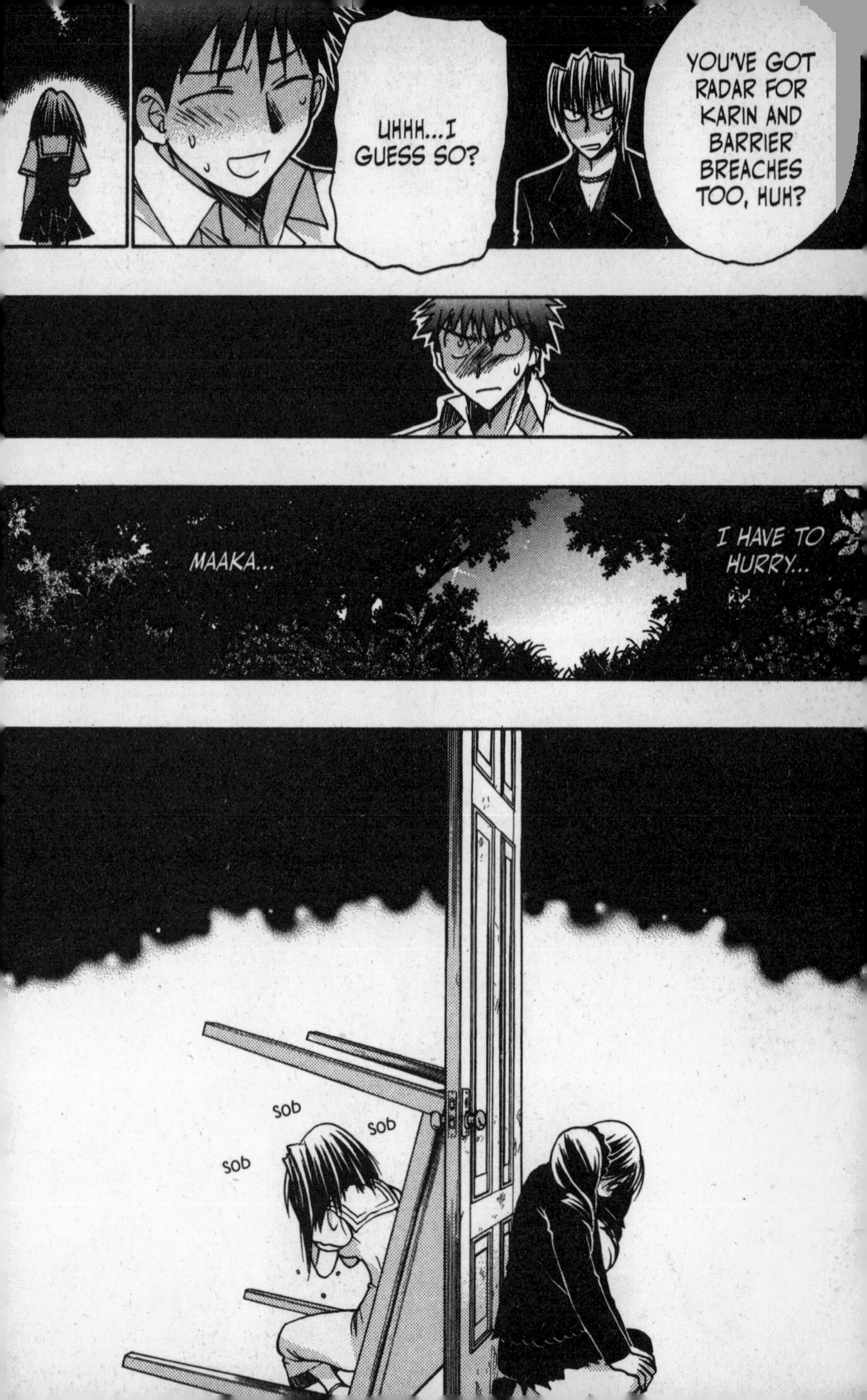
YOU'VE GOT RADAR FOR KARIN AND BARRIER BREACHES TOO, HUH?
UHHH...I GUESS SO?
I HAVE TO HURRY...
MAAKA...
sob
sob
sob

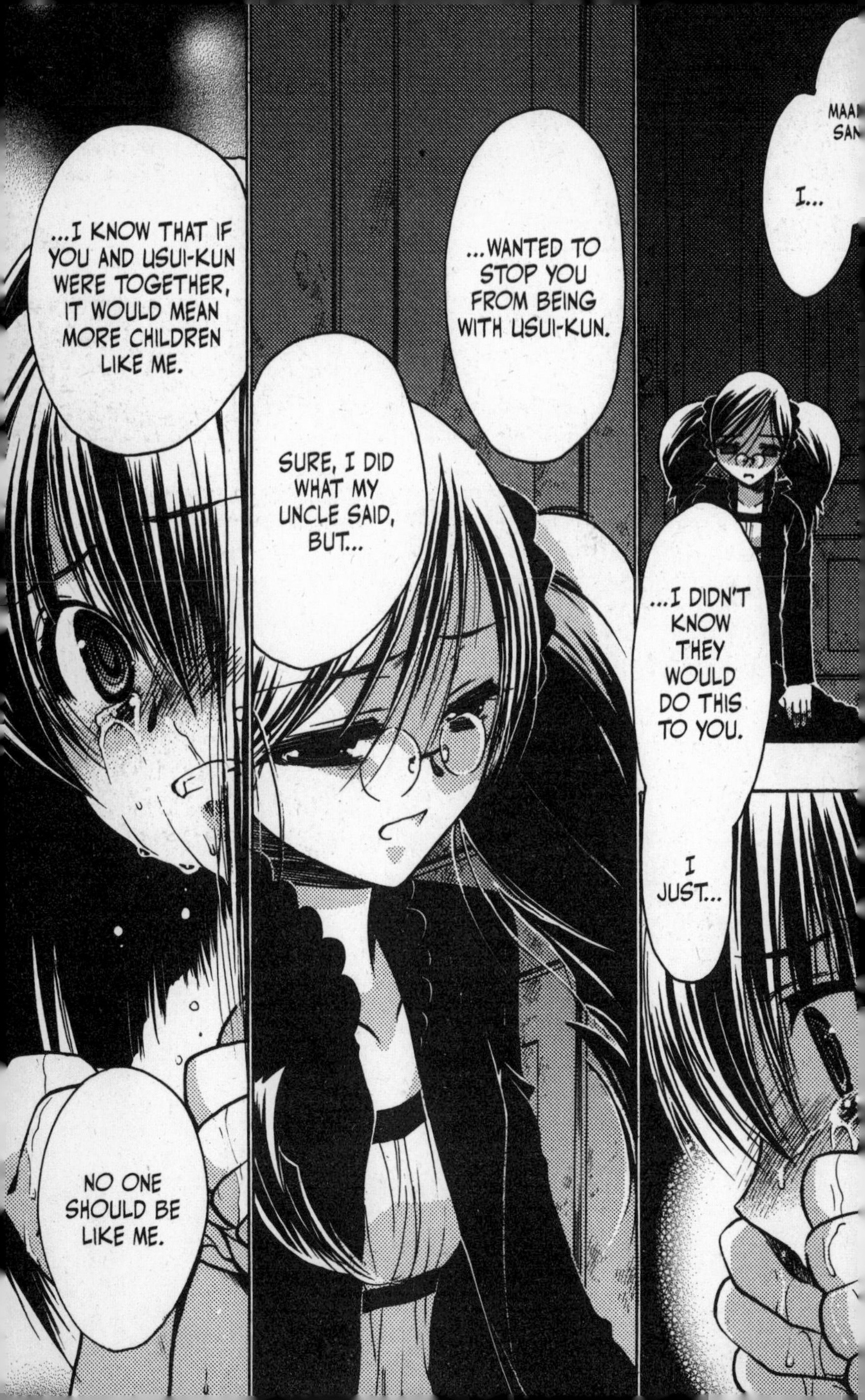

MAA SAN
I...
...I DIDN'T KNOW THEY WOULD DO THIS TO YOU.
I JUST...
...WANTED TO STOP YOU FROM BEING WITH USUI-KUN.
SURE, I DID WHAT MY UNCLE SAID, BUT...
...I KNOW THAT IF YOU AND USUI-KUN WERE TOGETHER, IT WOULD MEAN MORE CHILDREN LIKE ME.
NO ONE SHOULD BE LIKE ME.

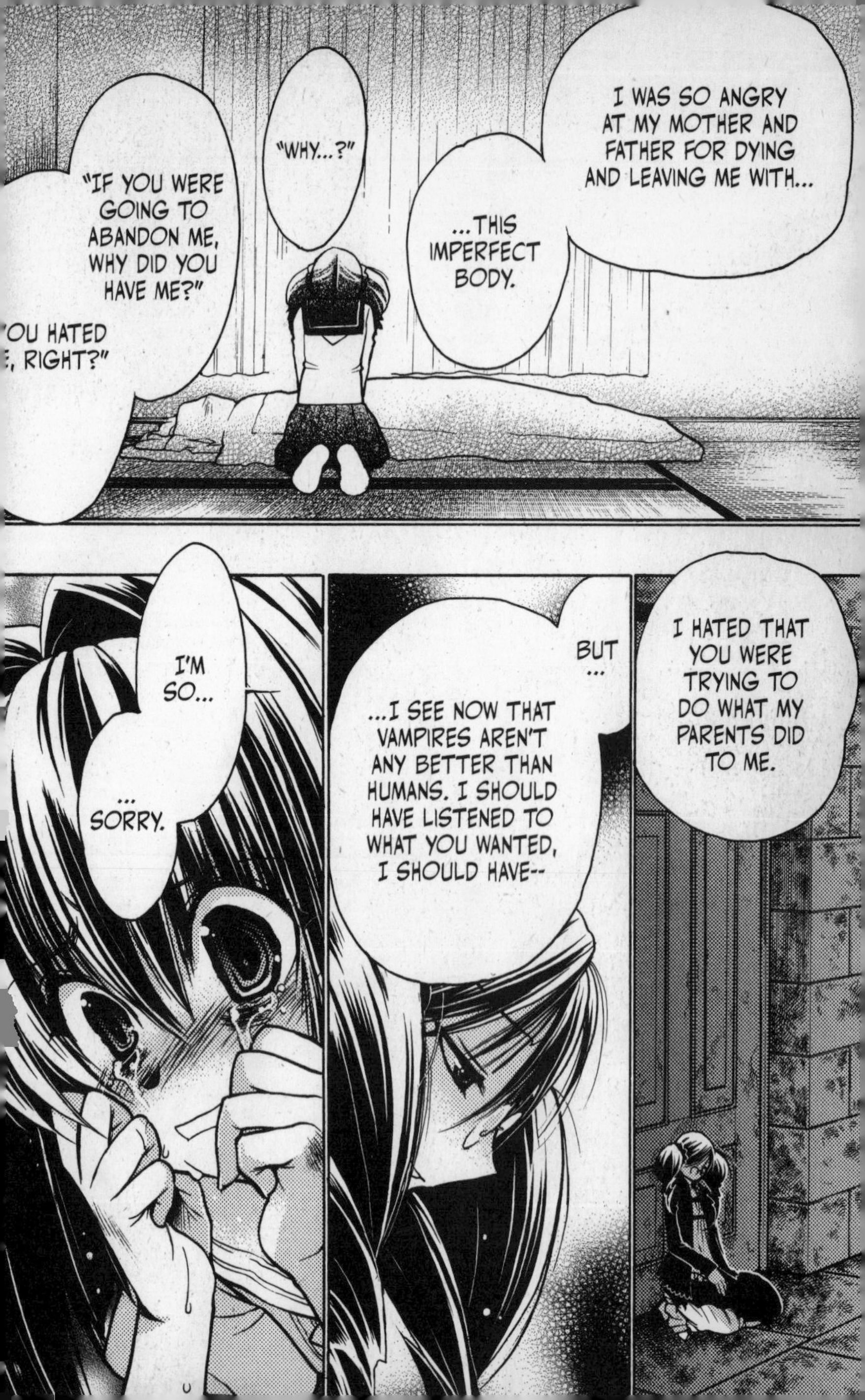
I WAS SO ANGRY AT MY MOTHER AND FATHER FOR DYING AND LEAVING ME WITH...
...THIS IMPERFECT BODY.
"WHY...?"
"IF YOU WERE GOING TO ABANDON ME, WHY DID YOU HAVE ME?"
OU HATED , RIGHT?"
I HATED THAT YOU WERE TRYING TO DO WHAT MY PARENTS DID TO ME.
BUT...
...I SEE NOW THAT VAMPIRES AREN'T ANY BETTER THAN HUMANS. I SHOULD HAVE LISTENED TO WHAT YOU WANTED, I SHOULD HAVE--
I'M SO...
...SORRY.

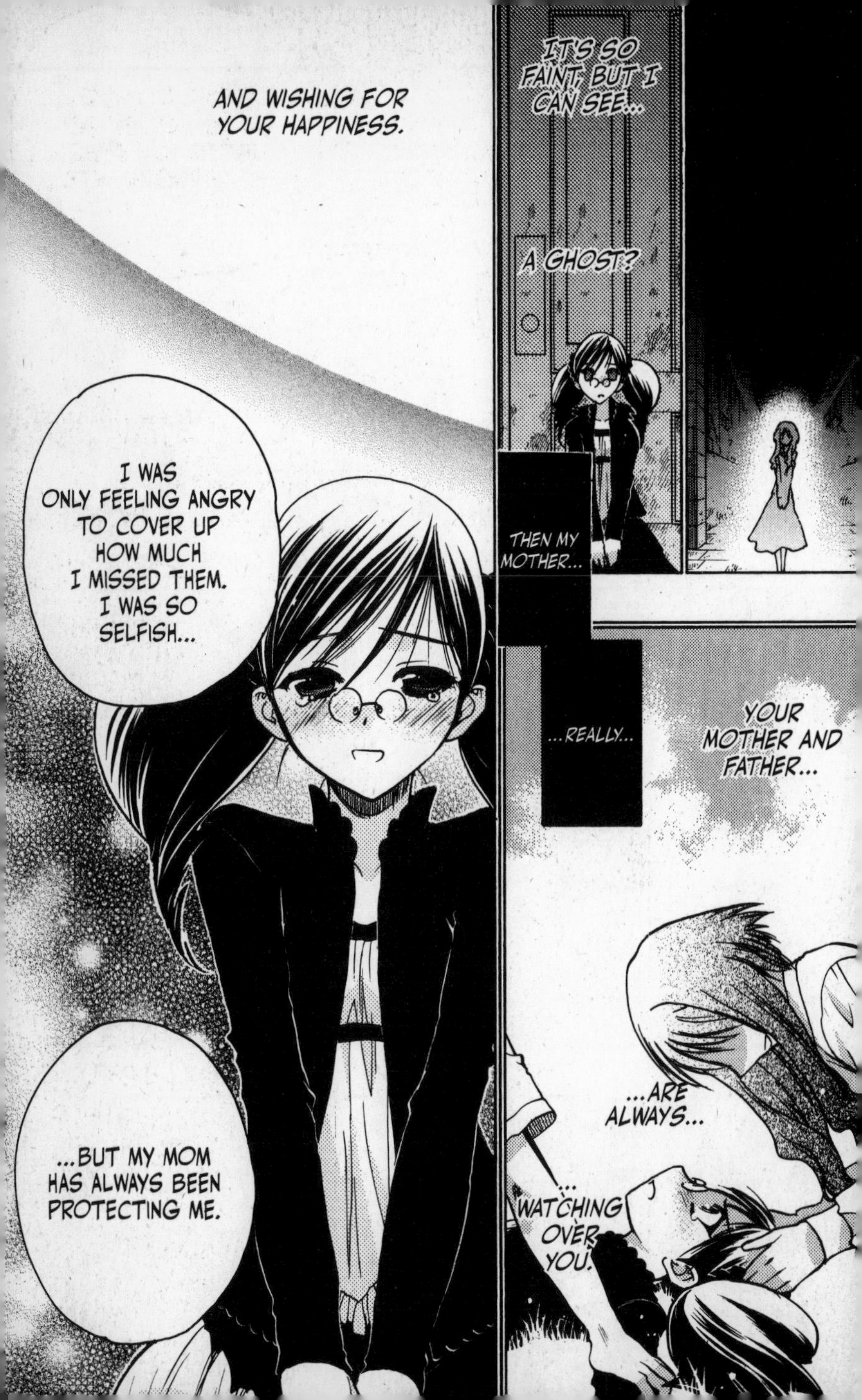
IT'S SO FAINT, BUT I CAN SEE...
A GHOST?
THEN MY MOTHER...
...REALLY...
YOUR MOTHER AND FATHER...
...ARE ALWAYS...
...WATCHING OVER YOU.
AND WISHING FOR YOUR HAPPINESS.
I WAS ONLY FEELING ANGRY TO COVER UP HOW MUCH I MISSED THEM. I WAS SO SELFISH...
...BUT MY MOM HAS ALWAYS BEEN PROTECTING ME.

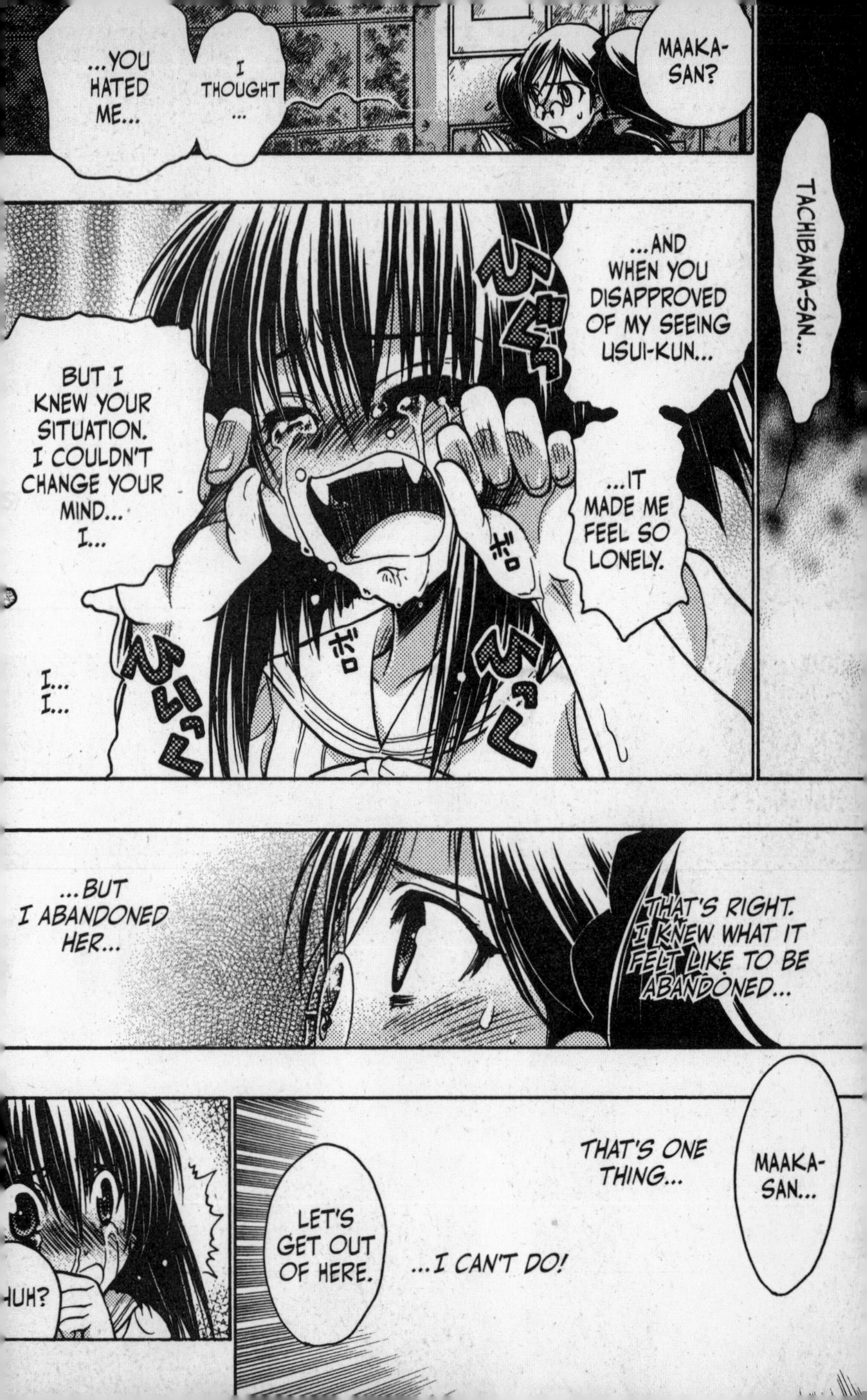
TACHIBANA-SAN...
MAAKA-SAN?
I THOUGHT ...
...YOU HATED ME...
...AND WHEN YOU DISAPPROVED OF MY SEEING USUI-KUN...
...IT MADE ME FEEL SO LONELY.
ボロ
ボロ
BUT I KNEW YOUR SITUATION. I COULDN'T CHANGE YOUR MIND... I...
I... I...
ひっく
THAT'S RIGHT. I KNEW WHAT IT FELT LIKE TO BE ABANDONED...
...BUT I ABANDONED HER...
MAAKA-SAN...
THAT'S ONE THING...
...I CAN'T DO!
LET'S GET OUT OF HERE.
HUH?

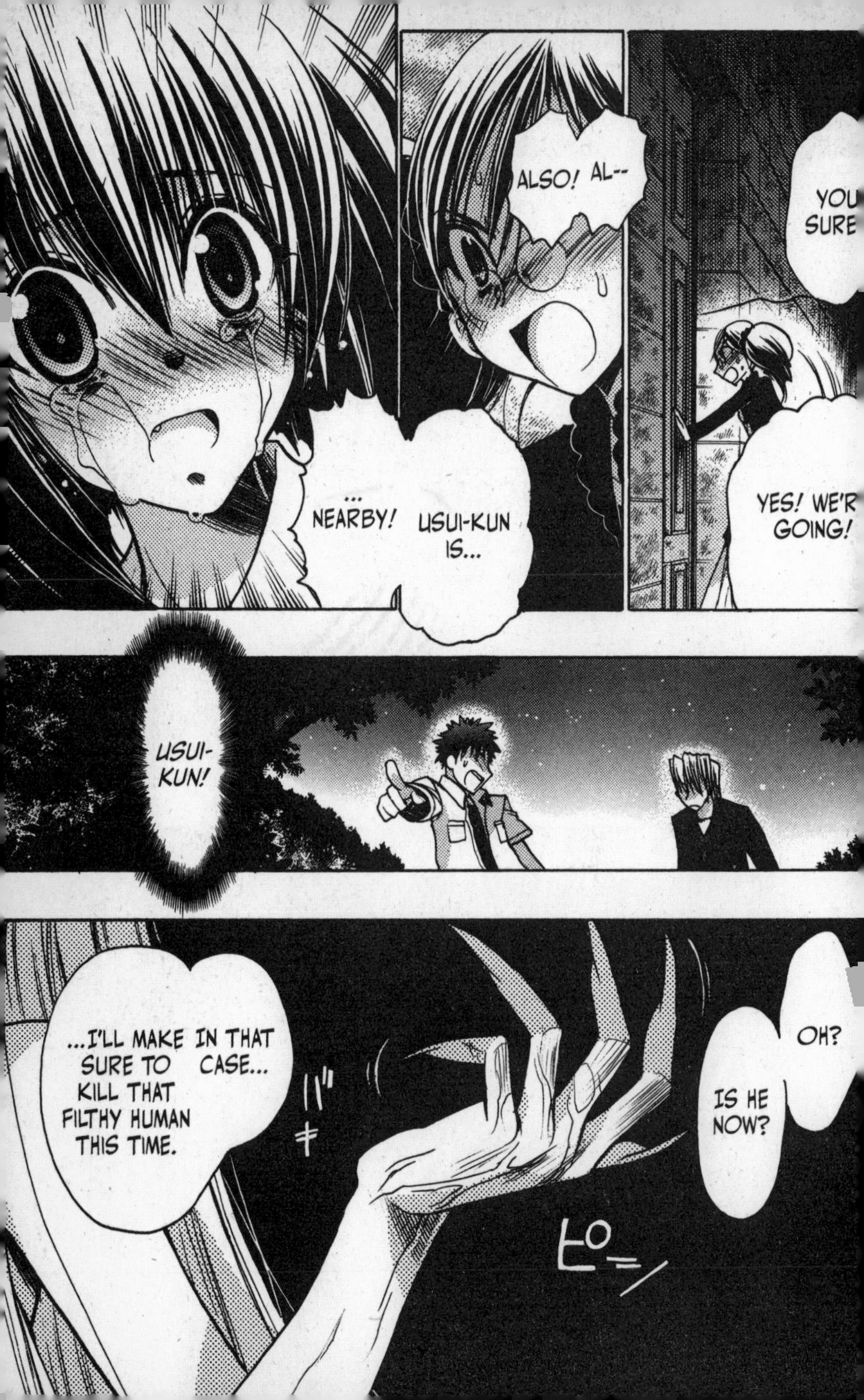
YOU SURE
YES! WE'R GOING!
ALSO! AL--
USUI-KUN IS...
...NEARBY!
USUI-KUN!
OH?
IS HE NOW?
IN THAT CASE...
...I'LL MAKE SURE TO KILL THAT FILTHY HUMAN THIS TIME.

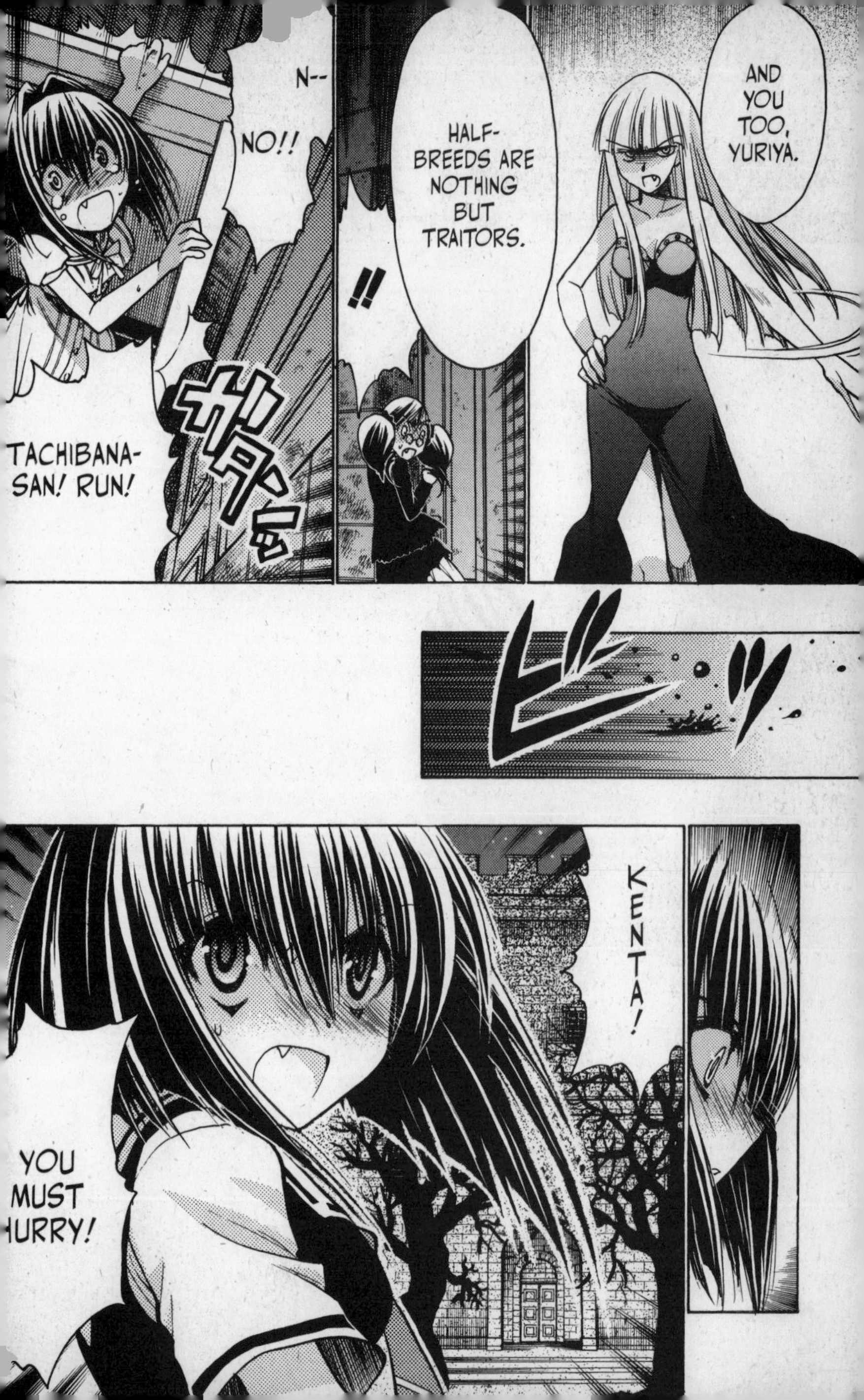
AND YOU TOO, YURIYA.
HALF-BREEDS ARE NOTHING BUT TRAITORS.
!!
N--
NO!!
TACHIBANA-SAN! RUN!
KENTA!
YOU MUST HURRY!

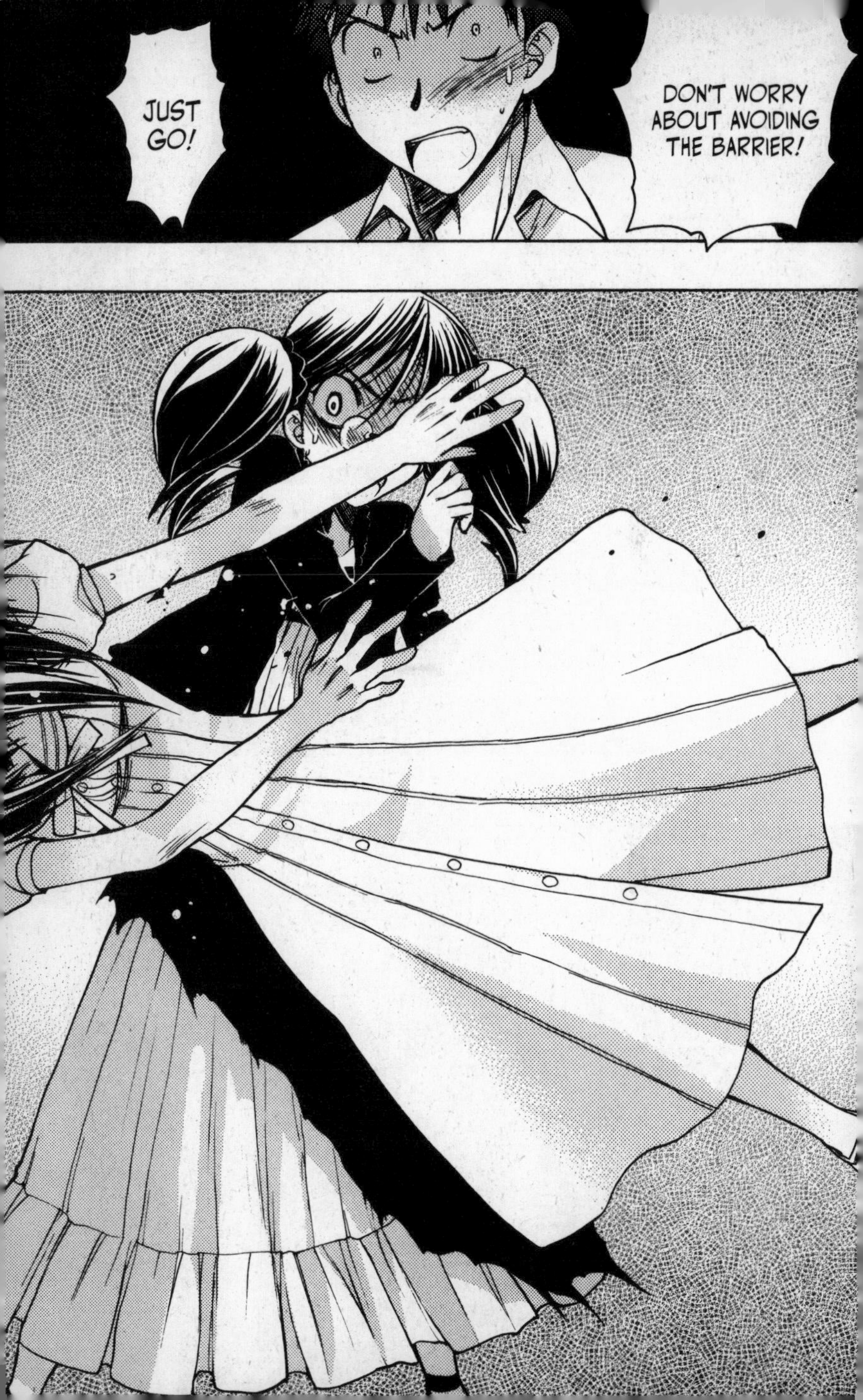
DON'T WORRY ABOUT AVOIDING THE BARRIER!
JUST GO!

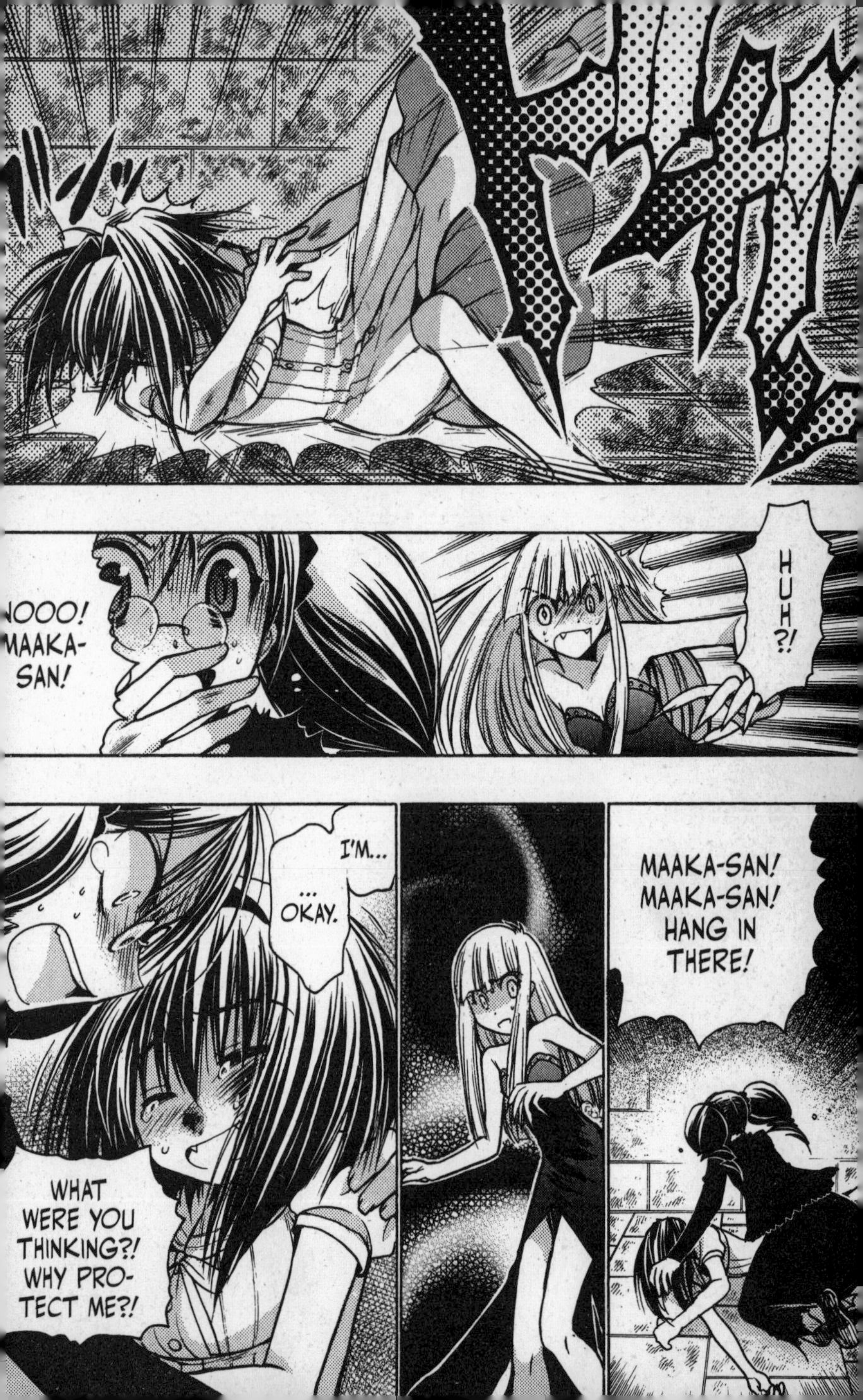
HUH?!
NOOO! MAAKA-SAN!
MAAKA-SAN! MAAKA-SAN! HANG IN THERE!
I'M...
...OKAY.
WHAT WERE YOU THINKING?! WHY PRO-TECT ME?!

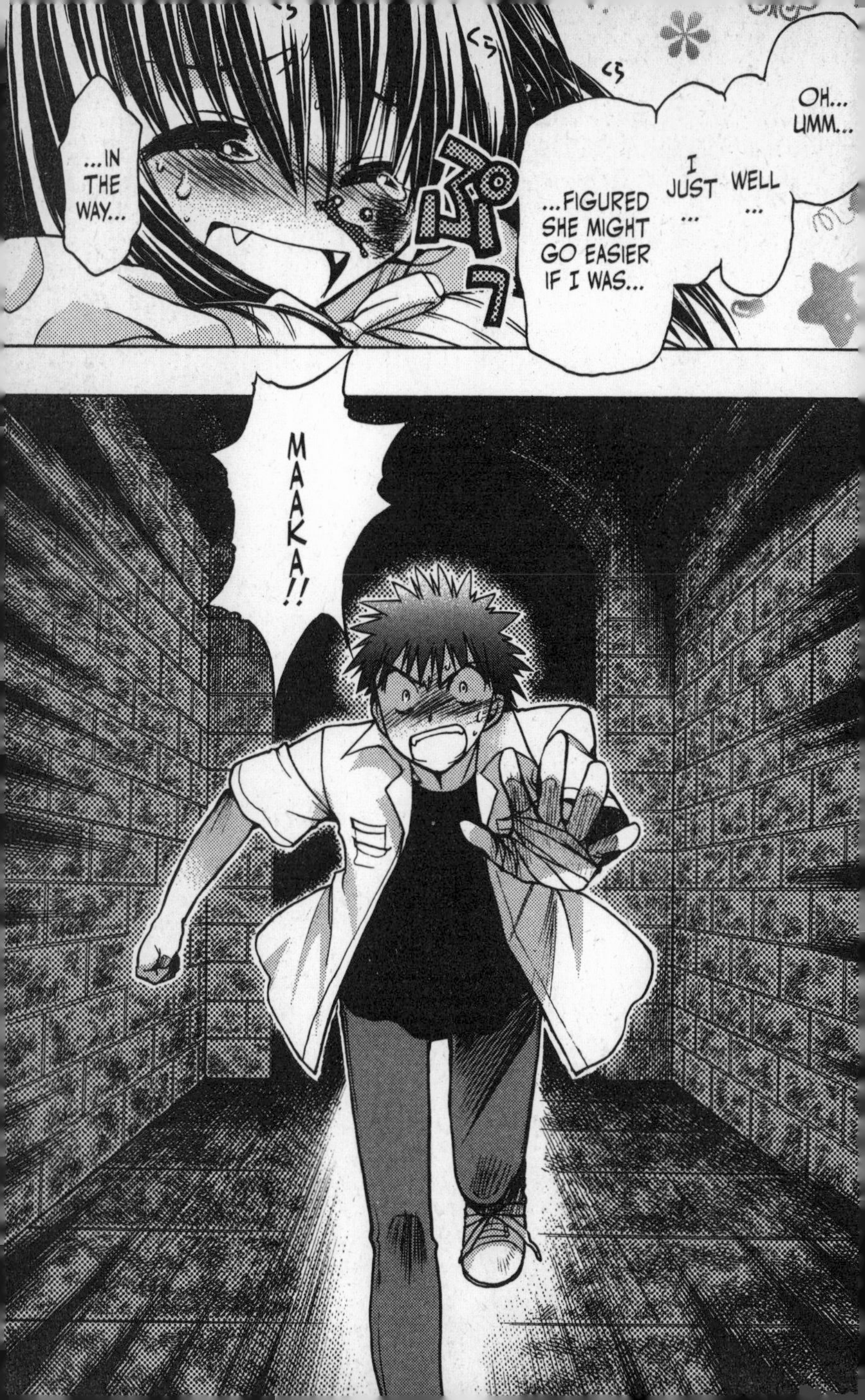

OH... UMM...
WELL ...
I JUST ...
...FIGURED SHE MIGHT GO EASIER IF I WAS...
...IN THE WAY...
MAAKA!!

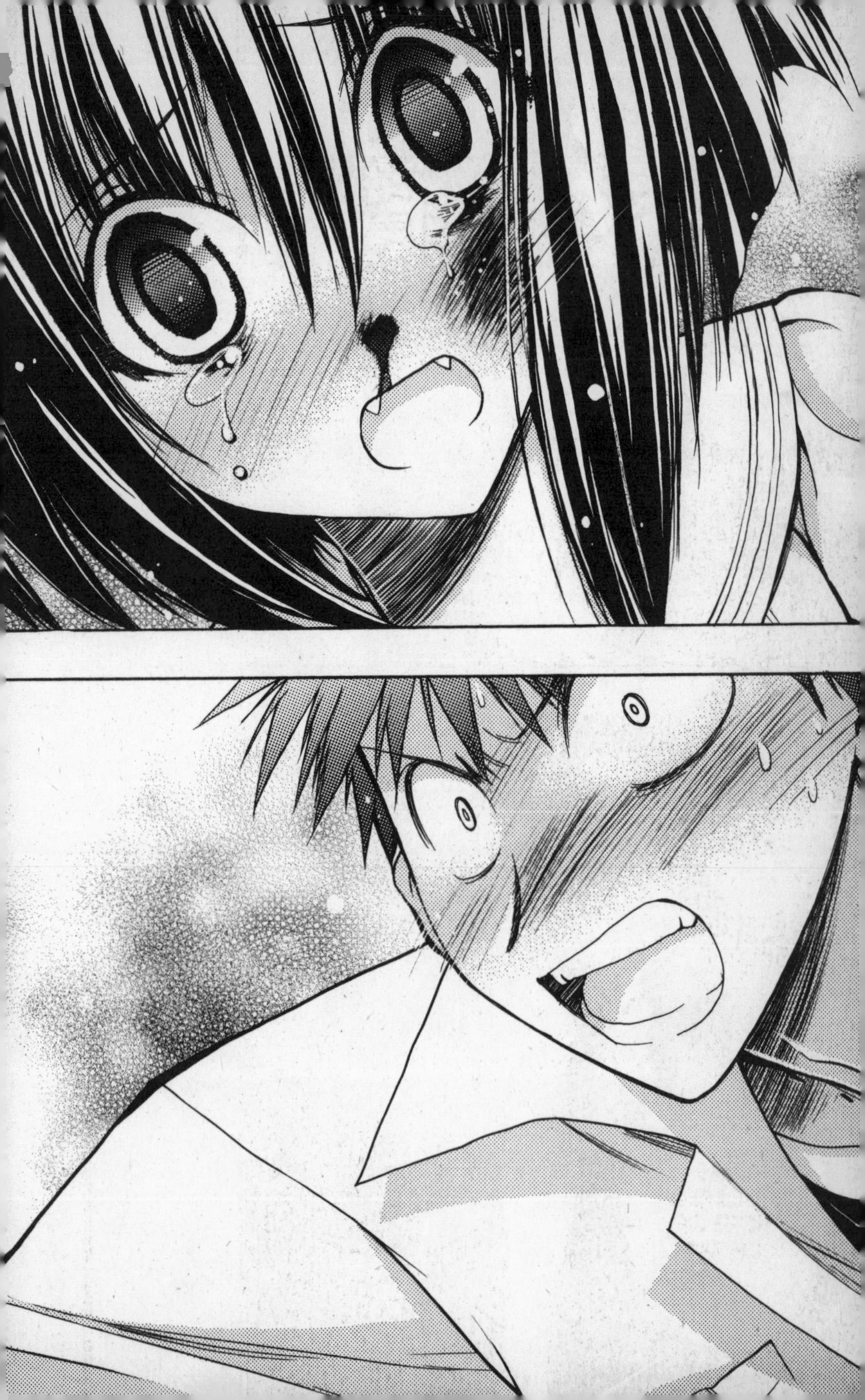

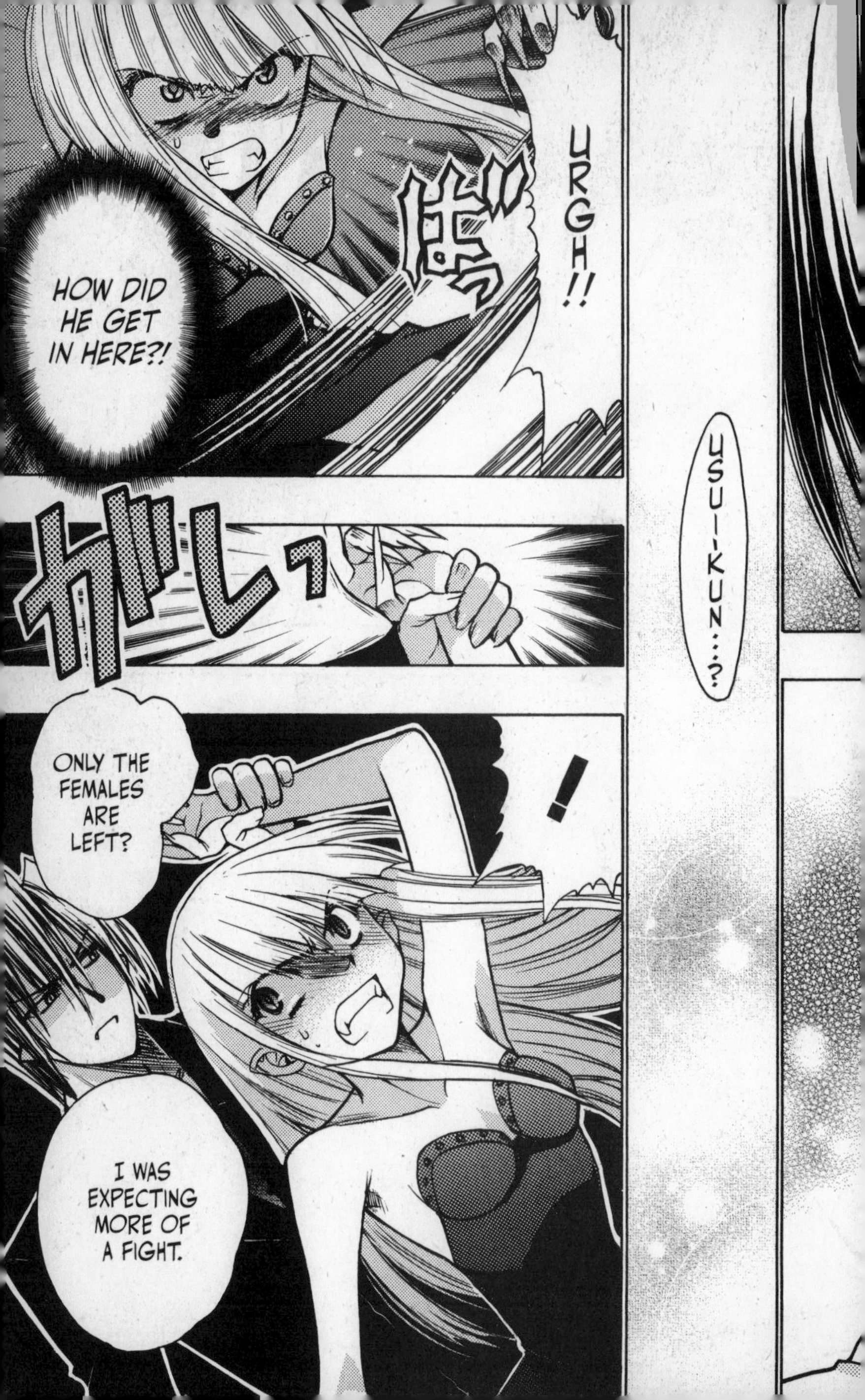
USUI-KUN...?
URGH!!
はっ
HOW DID HE GET IN HERE?!
ガしっ
!
ONLY THE FEMALES ARE LEFT?
I WAS EXPECTING MORE OF A FIGHT.

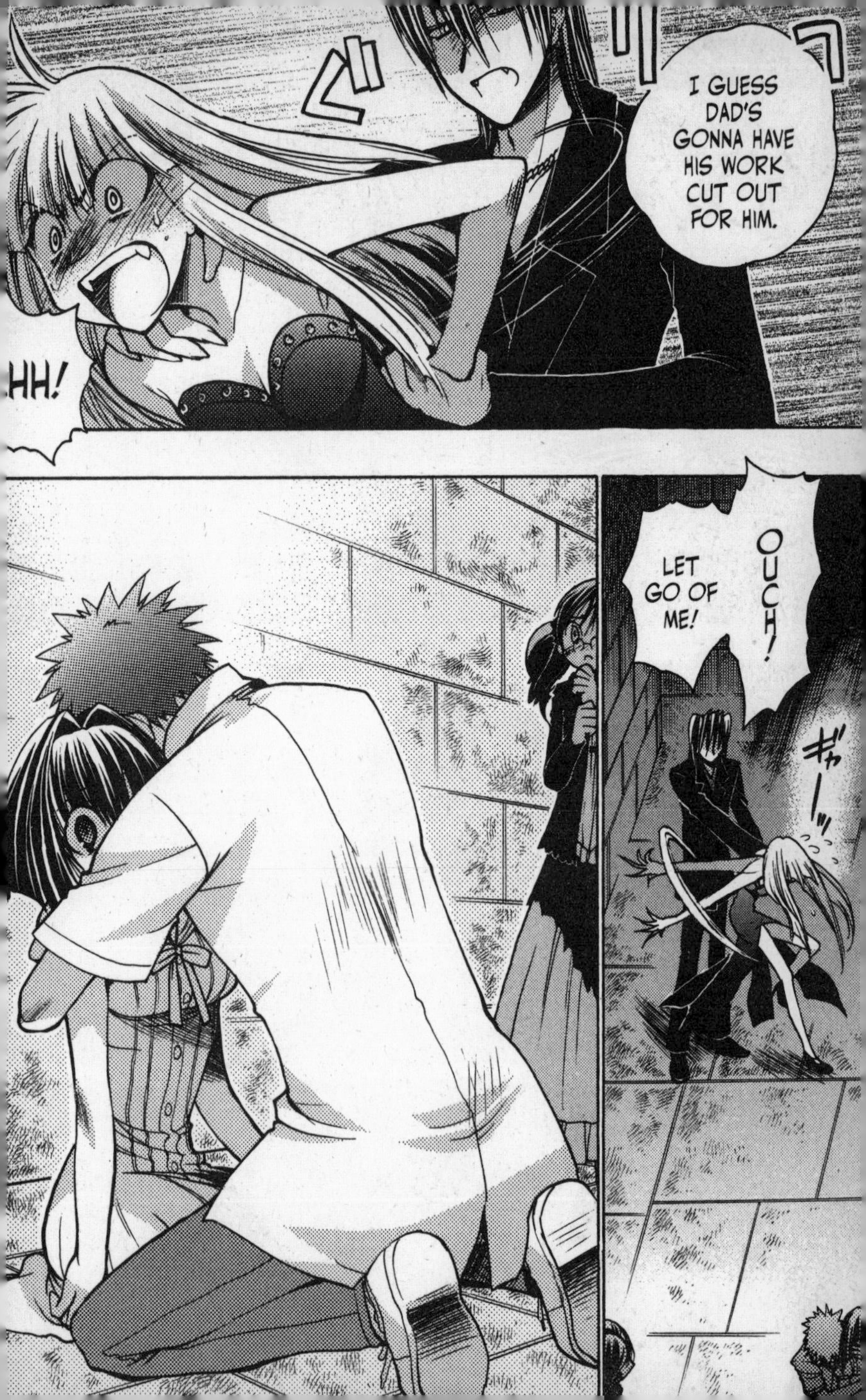
I GUESS DAD'S GONNA HAVE HIS WORK CUT OUT FOR HIM.
HH!
OUCH!
LET GO OF ME!
ギャー!!!

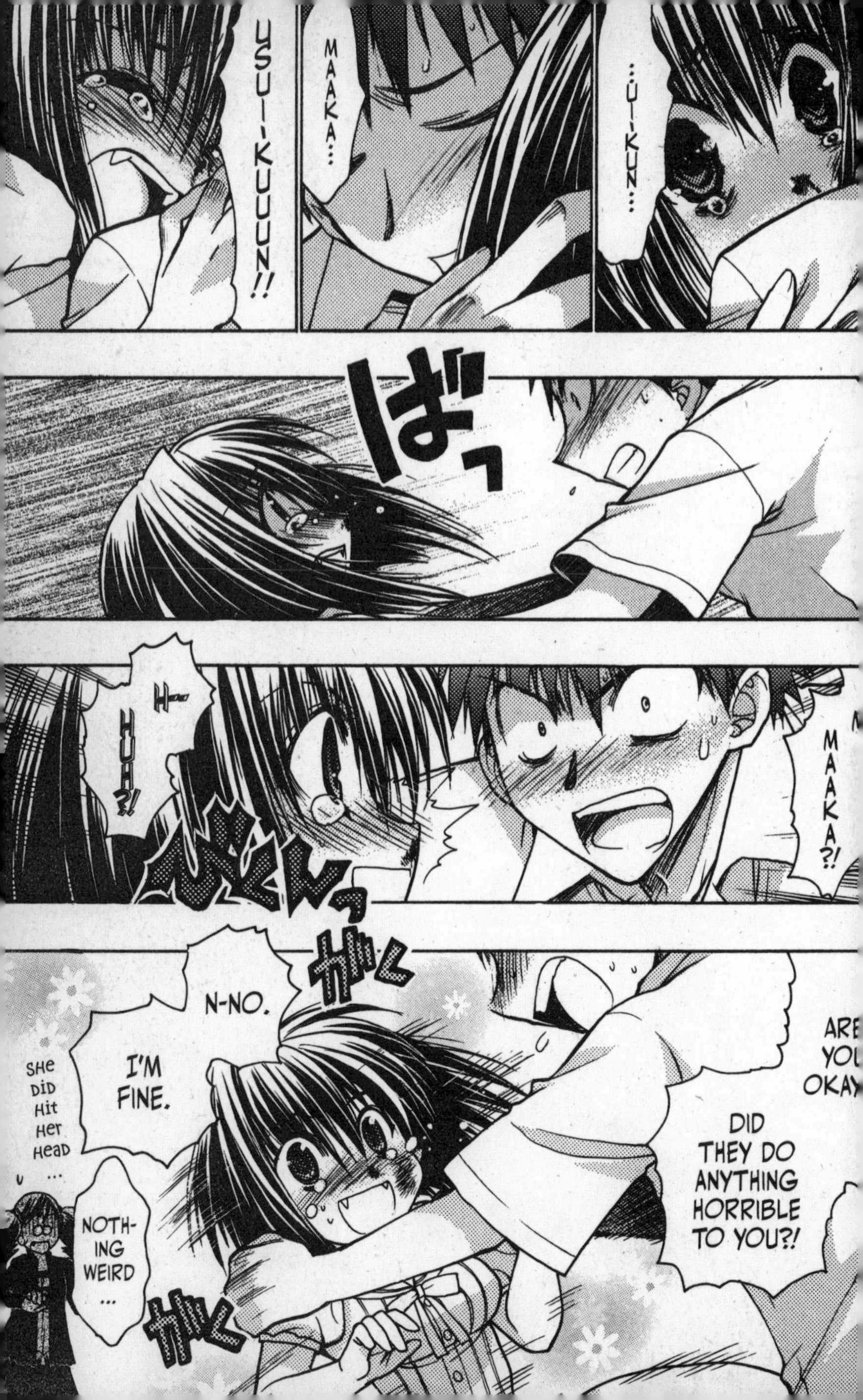
...UI-KUN...
MAAKA...
USUI-KUUUUN!!
ばっ
MAAKA?!
H-HUH?!
ARE YOU OKAY
DID THEY DO ANYTHING HORRIBLE TO YOU?!
N-NO.
I'M FINE.
NOTH-ING WEIRD...
SHE DID HIT HER HEAD...

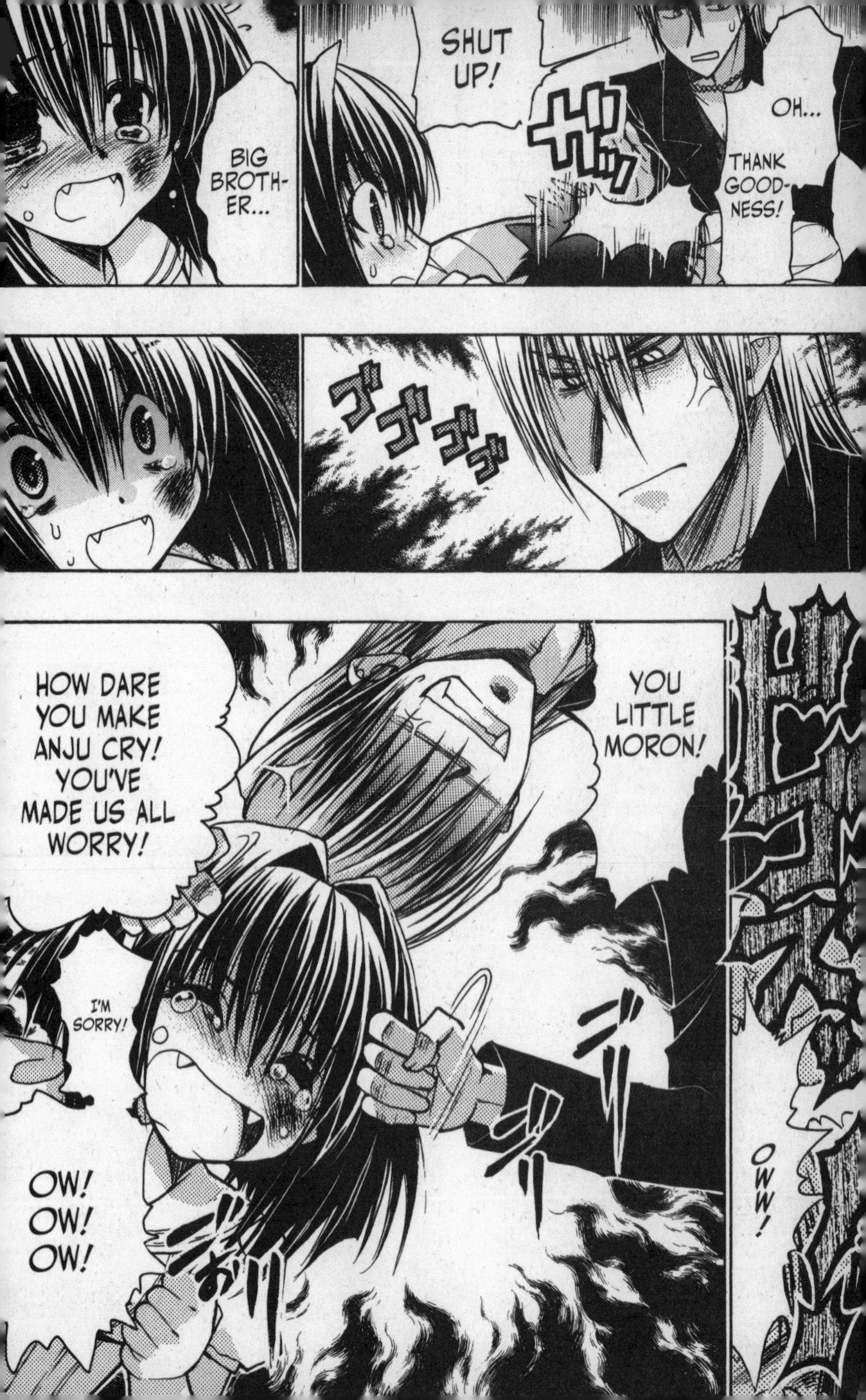
OH...
THANK GOODNESS!
SHUT UP!
BIG BROTHER...
OWW!
YOU LITTLE MORON!
HOW DARE YOU MAKE ANJU CRY! YOU'VE MADE US ALL WORRY!
I'M SORRY!
OW! OW! OW!

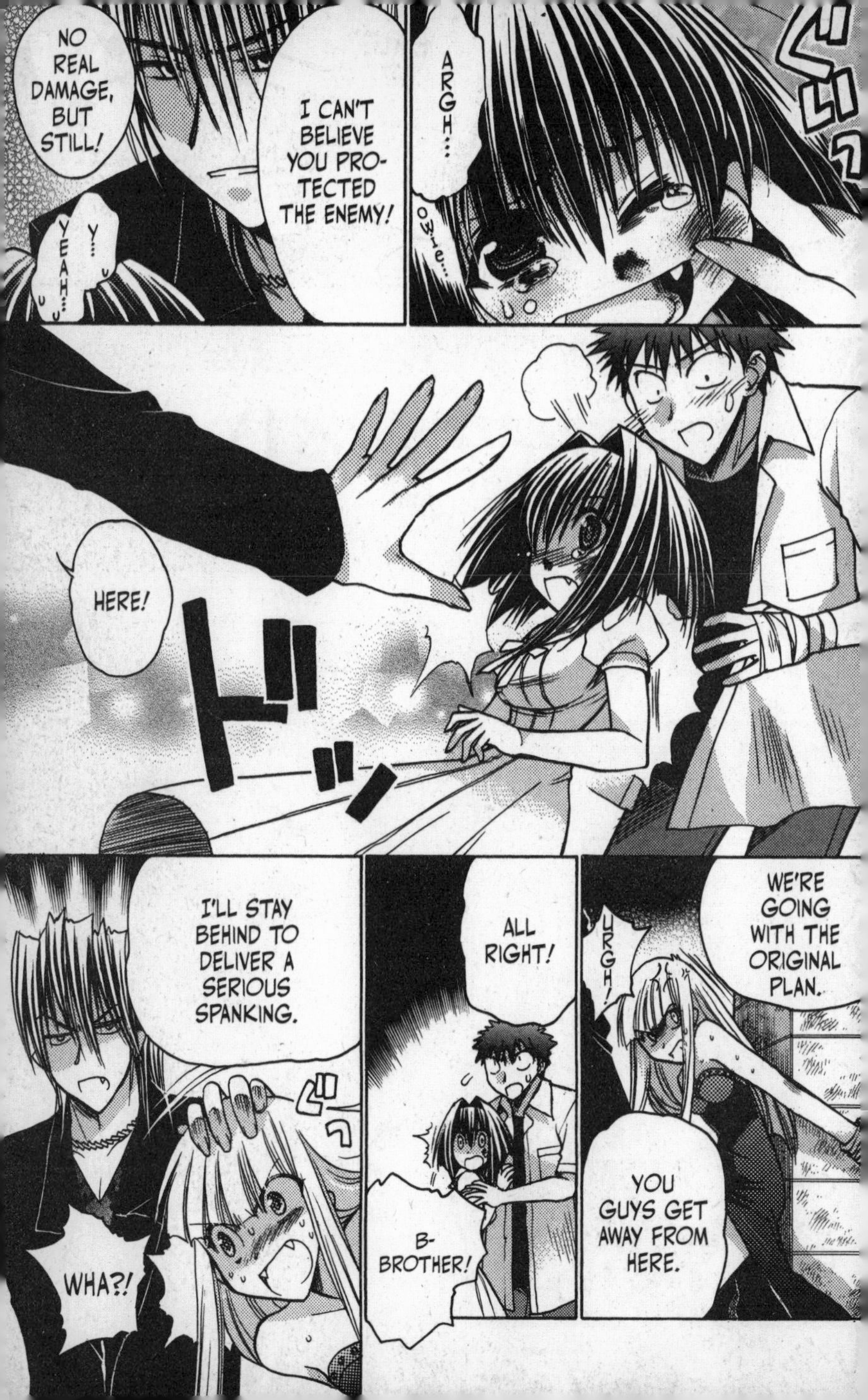
ARGH...
OWIE...
I CAN'T BELIEVE YOU PROTECTED THE ENEMY!
NO REAL DAMAGE, BUT STILL!
Y... YEAH...
HERE!
WE'RE GOING WITH THE ORIGINAL PLAN.
URGH!
YOU GUYS GET AWAY FROM HERE.
ALL RIGHT!
B-BROTHER!
I'LL STAY BEHIND TO DELIVER A SERIOUS SPANKING.
WHA?!

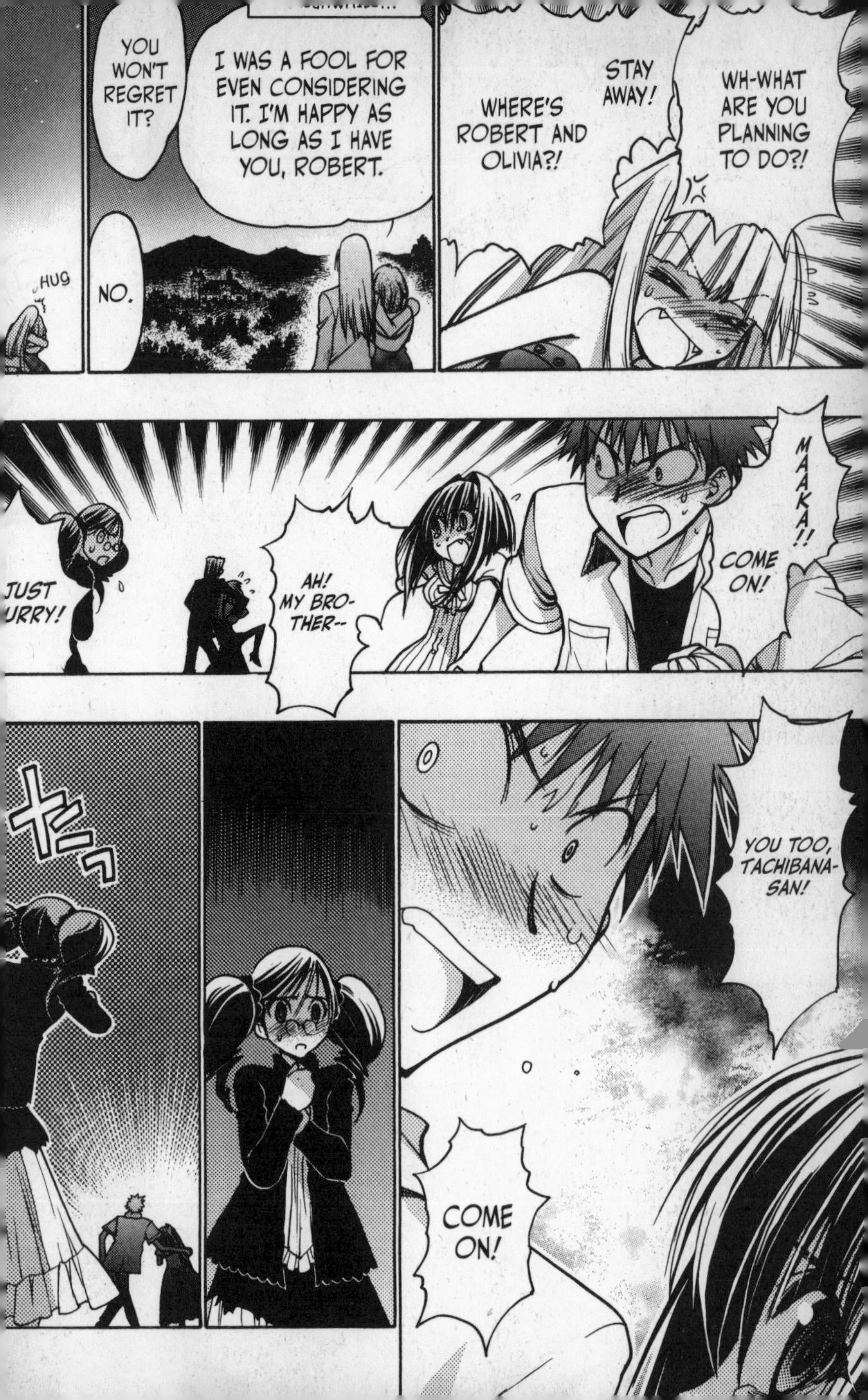
WH-WHAT ARE YOU PLANNING TO DO?!
STAY AWAY!
WHERE'S ROBERT AND OLIVIA?!
I WAS A FOOL FOR EVEN CONSIDERING IT. I'M HAPPY AS LONG AS I HAVE YOU, ROBERT.
YOU WON'T REGRET IT?
NO.
HUG
MAAKA!!
COME ON!
AH! MY BRO-THER--
JUST
URRY!
YOU TOO, TACHIBANA-SAN!
COME ON!

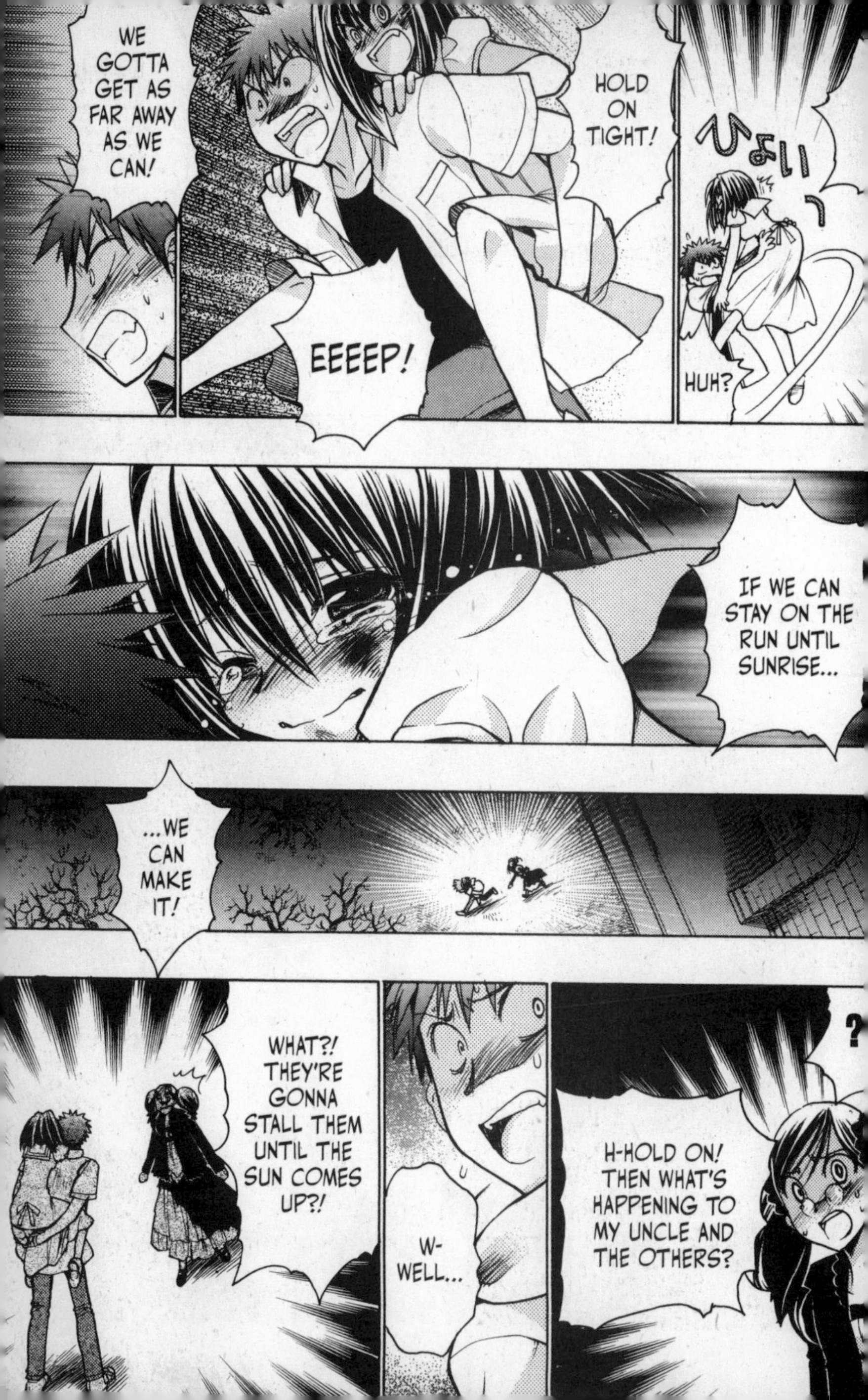
ひょいっ
HUH?
HOLD ON TIGHT!
EEEEP!
WE GOTTA GET AS FAR AWAY AS WE CAN!
IF WE CAN STAY ON THE RUN UNTIL SUNRISE...
...WE CAN MAKE IT!
?
H-HOLD ON! THEN WHAT'S HAPPENING TO MY UNCLE AND THE OTHERS?
W-WELL...
WHAT?! THEY'RE GONNA STALL THEM UNTIL THE SUN COMES UP?!

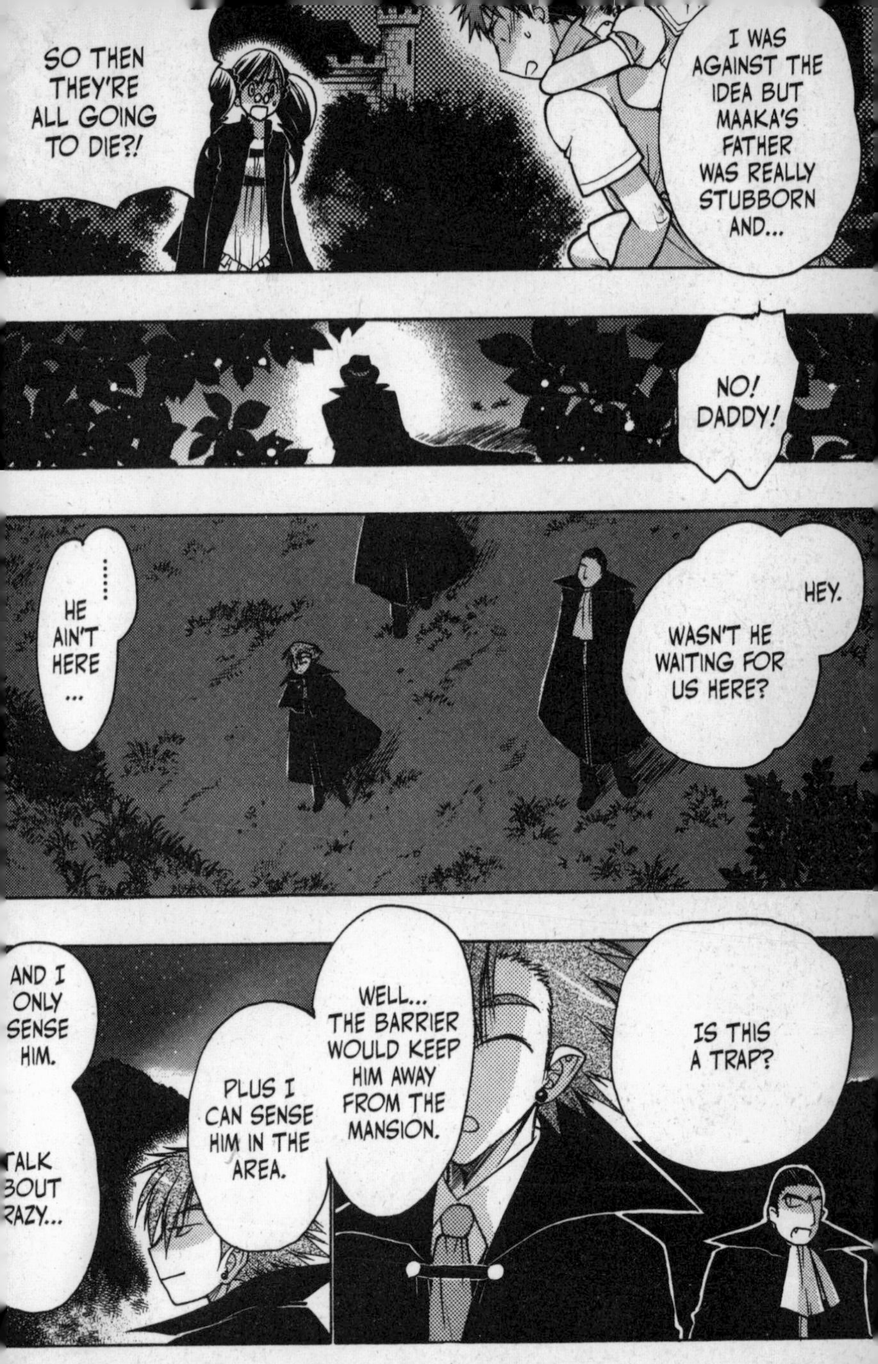
I WAS AGAINST THE IDEA BUT MAAKA'S FATHER WAS REALLY STUBBORN AND...
SO THEN THEY'RE ALL GOING TO DIE?!
NO! DADDY!
HEY.
WASN'T HE WAITING FOR US HERE?
......
HE AIN'T HERE ...
IS THIS A TRAP?
WELL... THE BARRIER WOULD KEEP HIM AWAY FROM THE MANSION.
PLUS I CAN SENSE HIM IN THE AREA.
AND I ONLY SENSE HIM.
TALK BOUT RAZY...

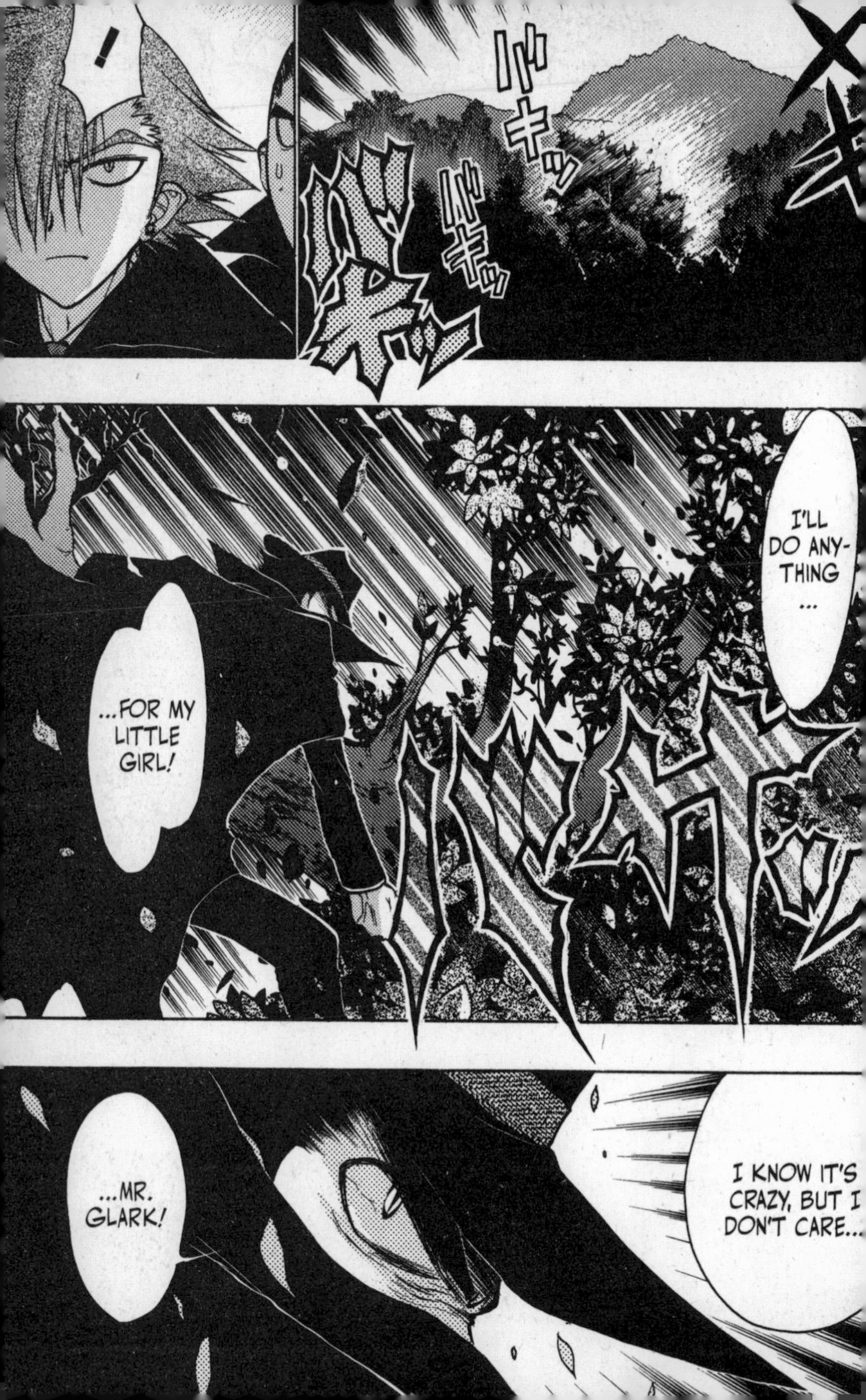
!
I'LL DO ANY-THING ...
...FOR MY LITTLE GIRL!
I KNOW IT'S CRAZY, BUT I DON'T CARE...
...MR. GLARK!

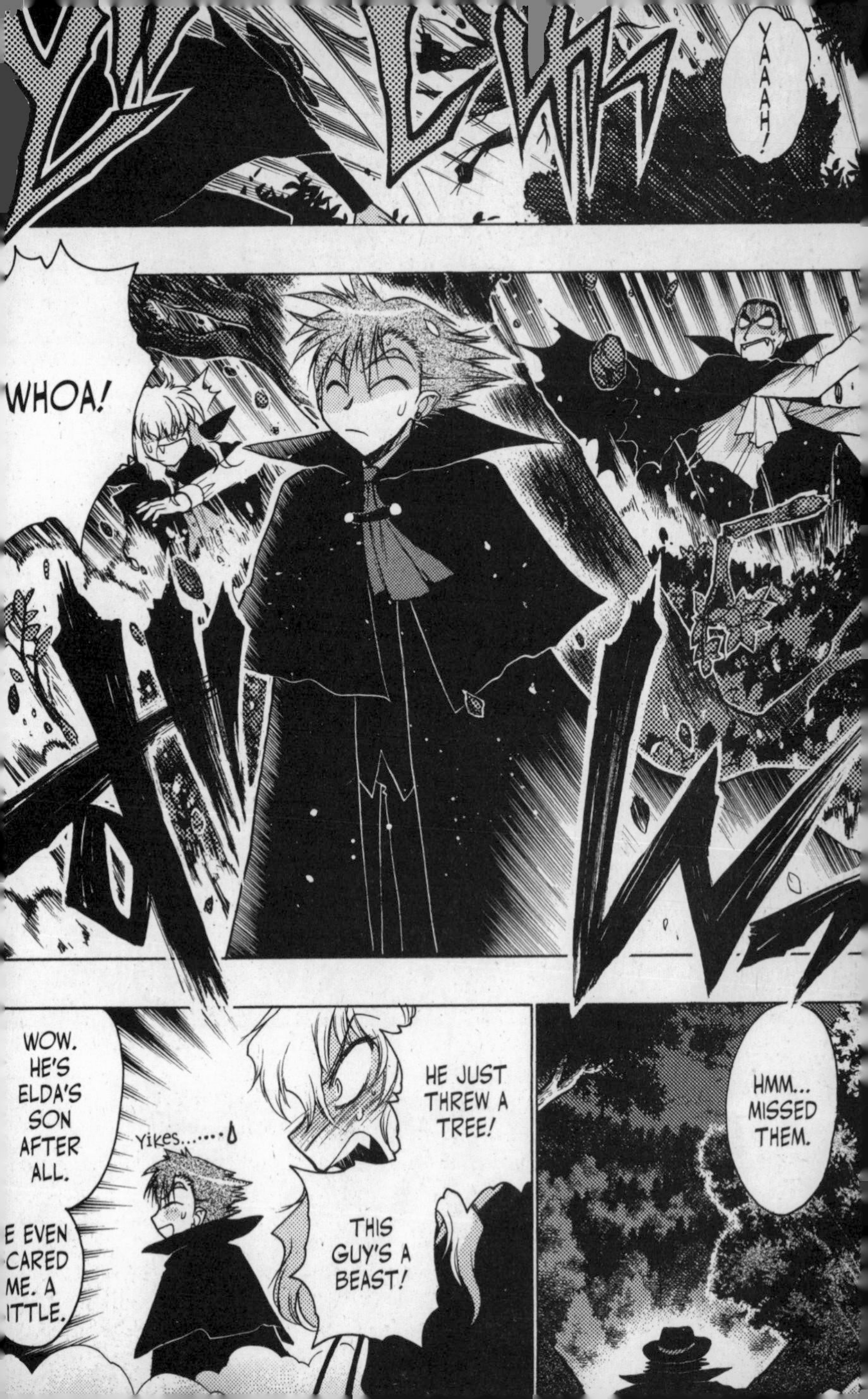
YAAAH!
WHOA!
HMM... MISSED THEM.
HE JUST THREW A TREE!
THIS GUY'S A BEAST!
WOW. HE'S ELDA'S SON AFTER ALL.
Yikes......
E EVEN CARED ME. A ITTLE.

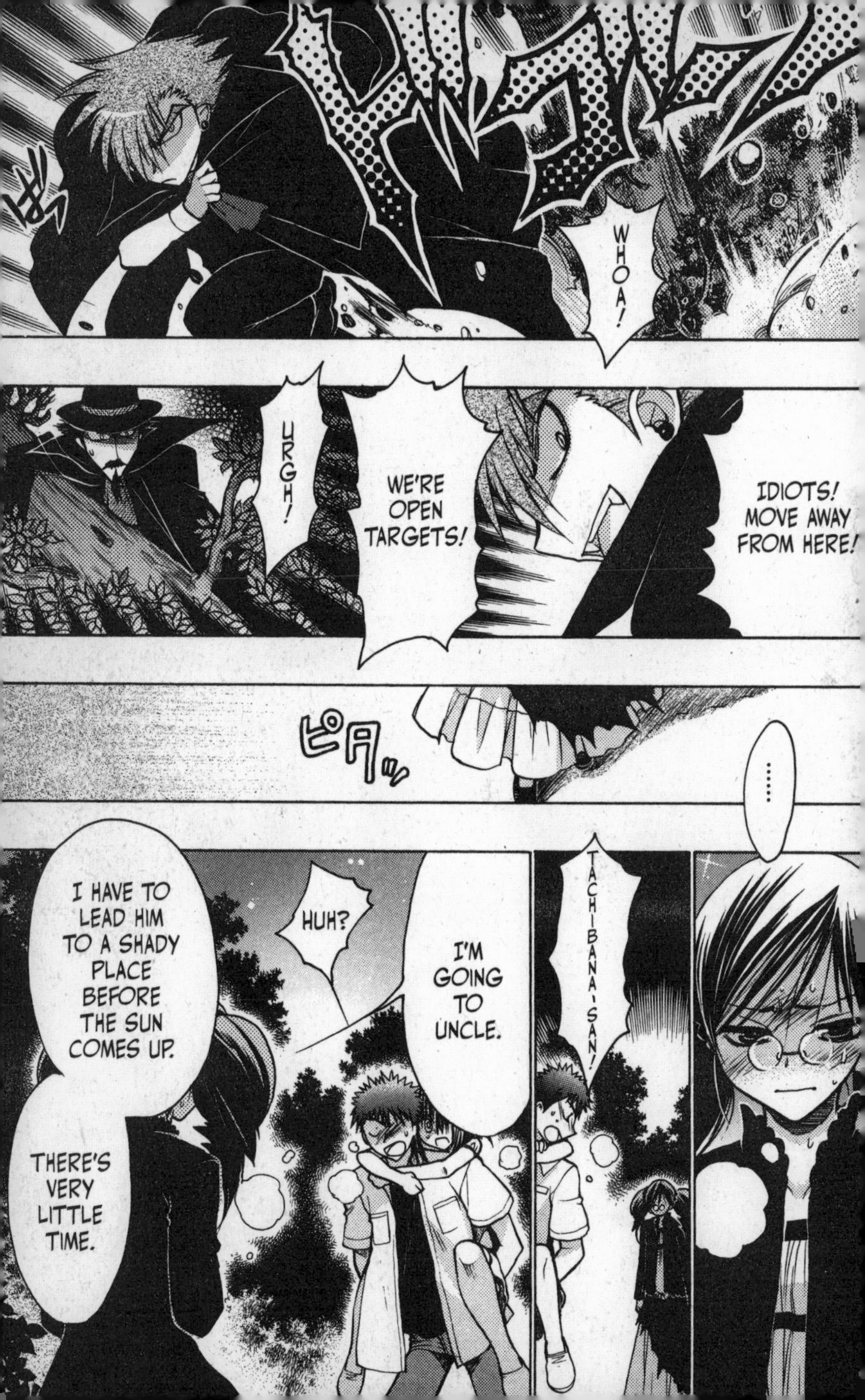
WHOA!
IDIOTS! MOVE AWAY FROM HERE!
WE'RE OPEN TARGETS!
URGH!
......
ピタッ
TACHIBANA-SAN!
I'M GOING TO UNCLE.
HUH?
I HAVE TO LEAD HIM TO A SHADY PLACE BEFORE THE SUN COMES UP.
THERE'S VERY LITTLE TIME.

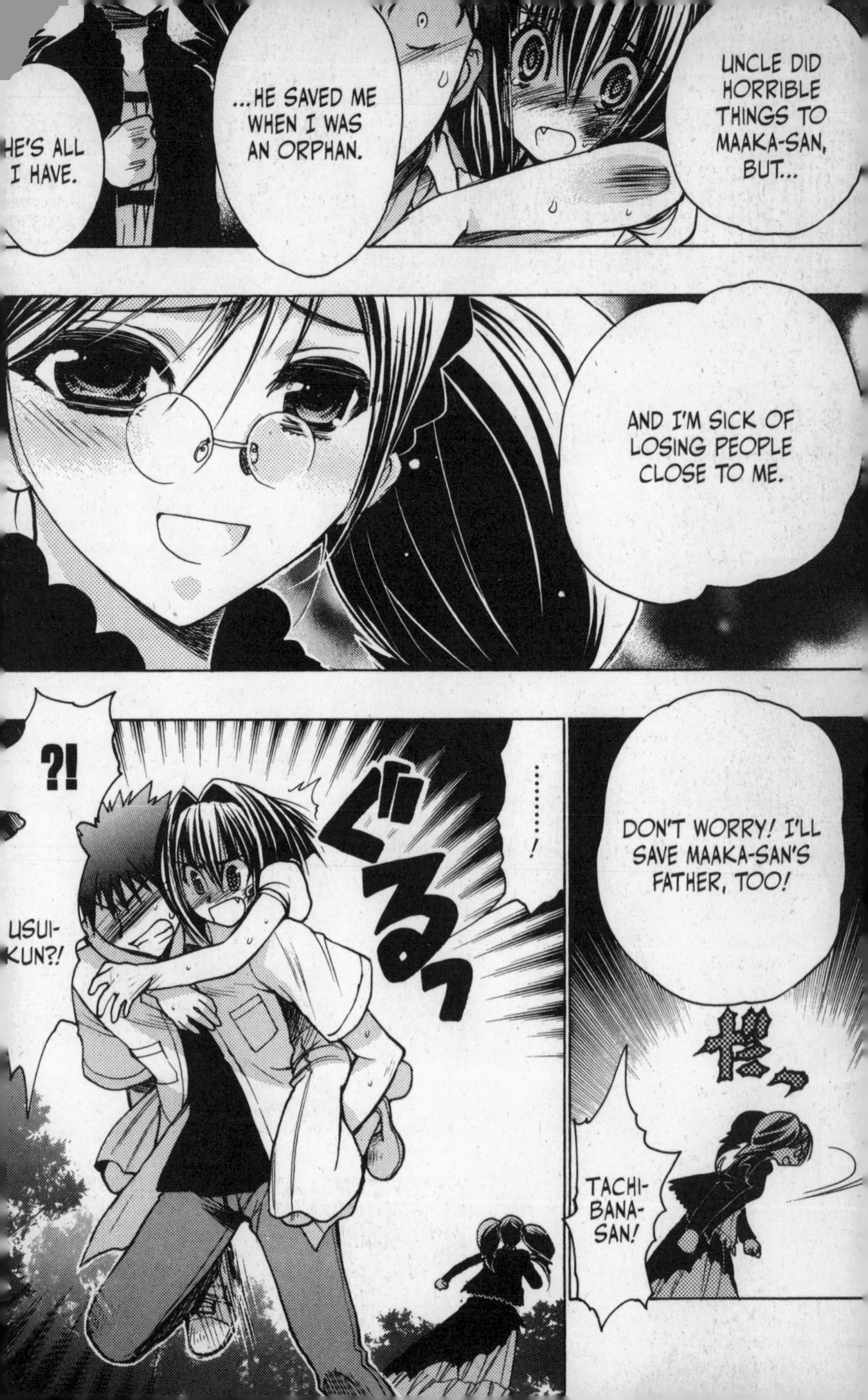

UNCLE DID HORRIBLE THINGS TO MAAKA-SAN, BUT...
...HE SAVED ME WHEN I WAS AN ORPHAN.
HE'S ALL I HAVE.
AND I'M SICK OF LOSING PEOPLE CLOSE TO ME.
DON'T WORRY! I'LL SAVE MAAKA-SAN'S FATHER, TOO!
TACHI-BANA-SAN!
......!
?!
USUI-KUN?!

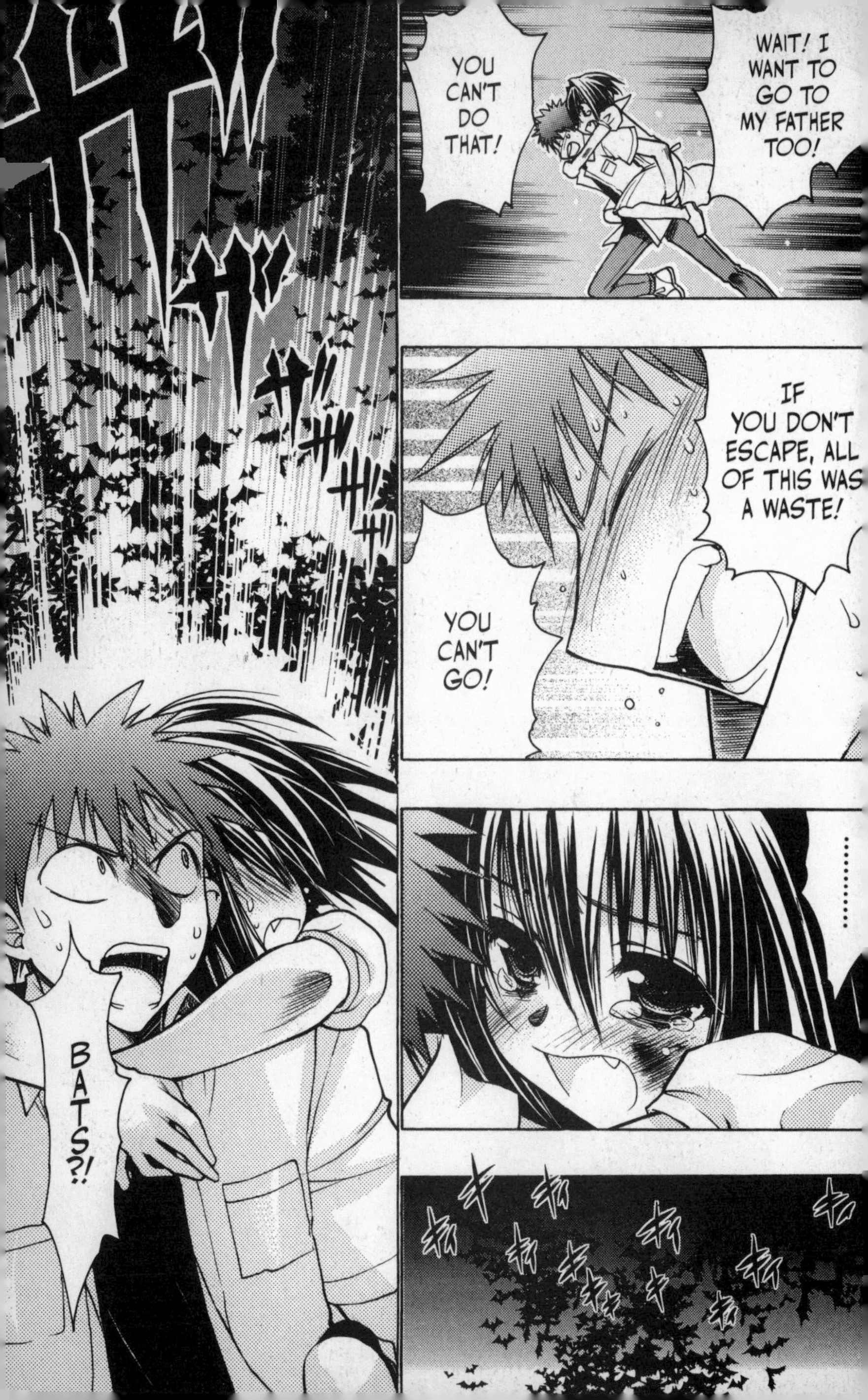
WAIT! I WANT TO GO TO MY FATHER TOO!
YOU CAN'T DO THAT!
IF YOU DON'T ESCAPE, ALL OF THIS WAS A WASTE!
YOU CAN'T GO!
......
BATS?!

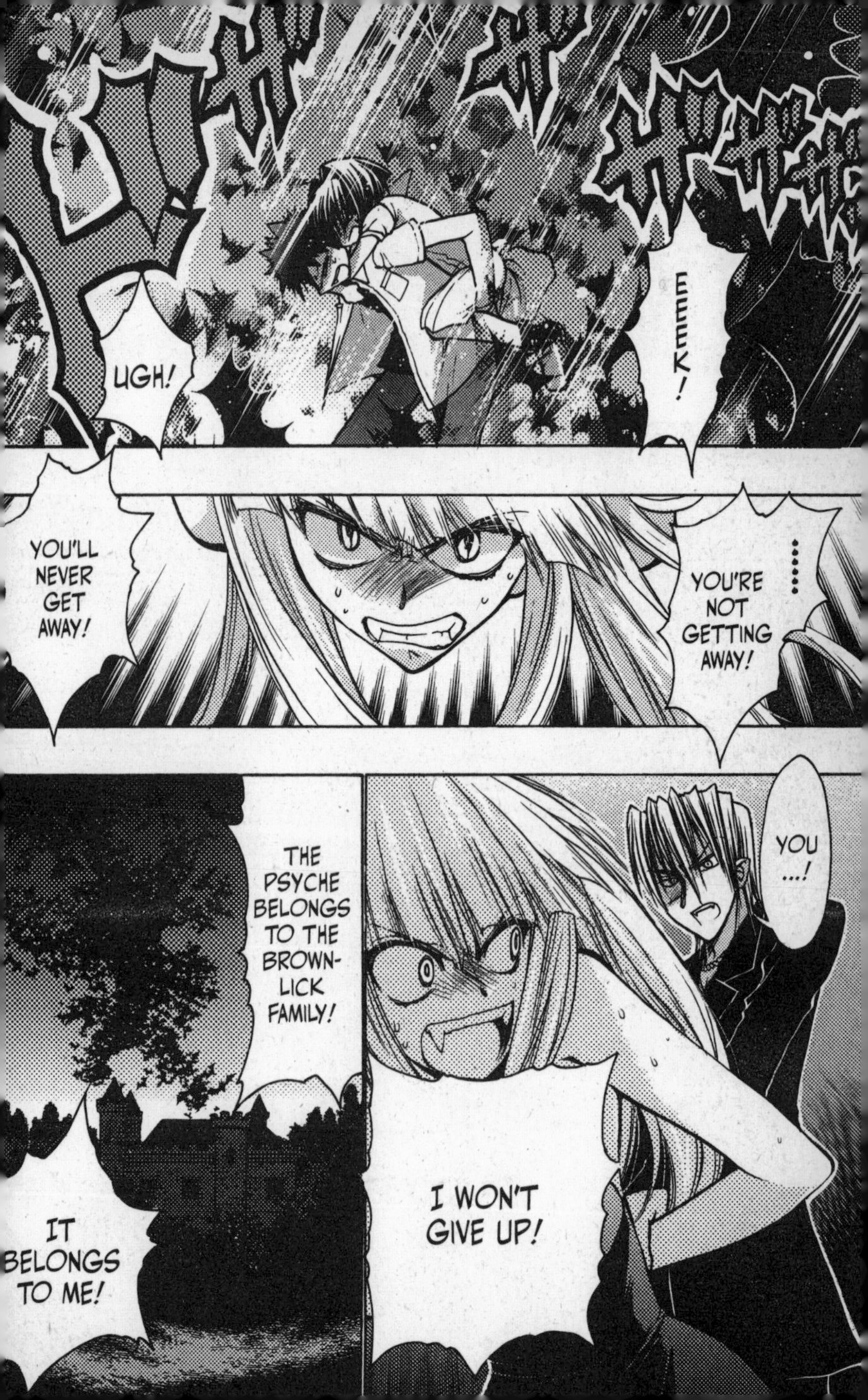
EEEK!
UGH!
......
YOU'RE NOT GETTING AWAY!
YOU'LL NEVER GET AWAY!
YOU ...!
I WON'T GIVE UP!
THE PSYCHE BELONGS TO THE BROWN-LICK FAMILY!
IT BELONGS TO ME!

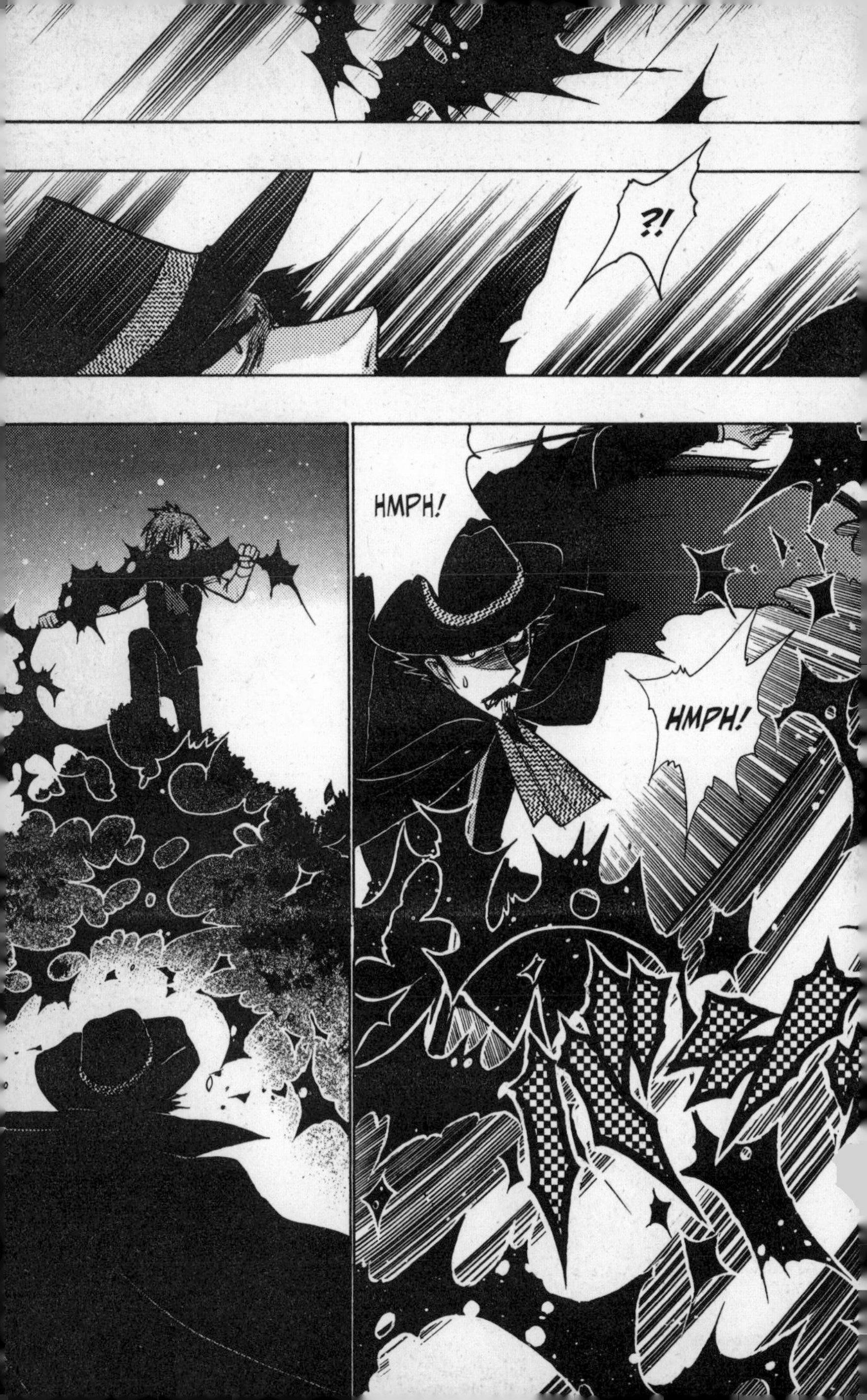
?!
HMPH!
HMPH!

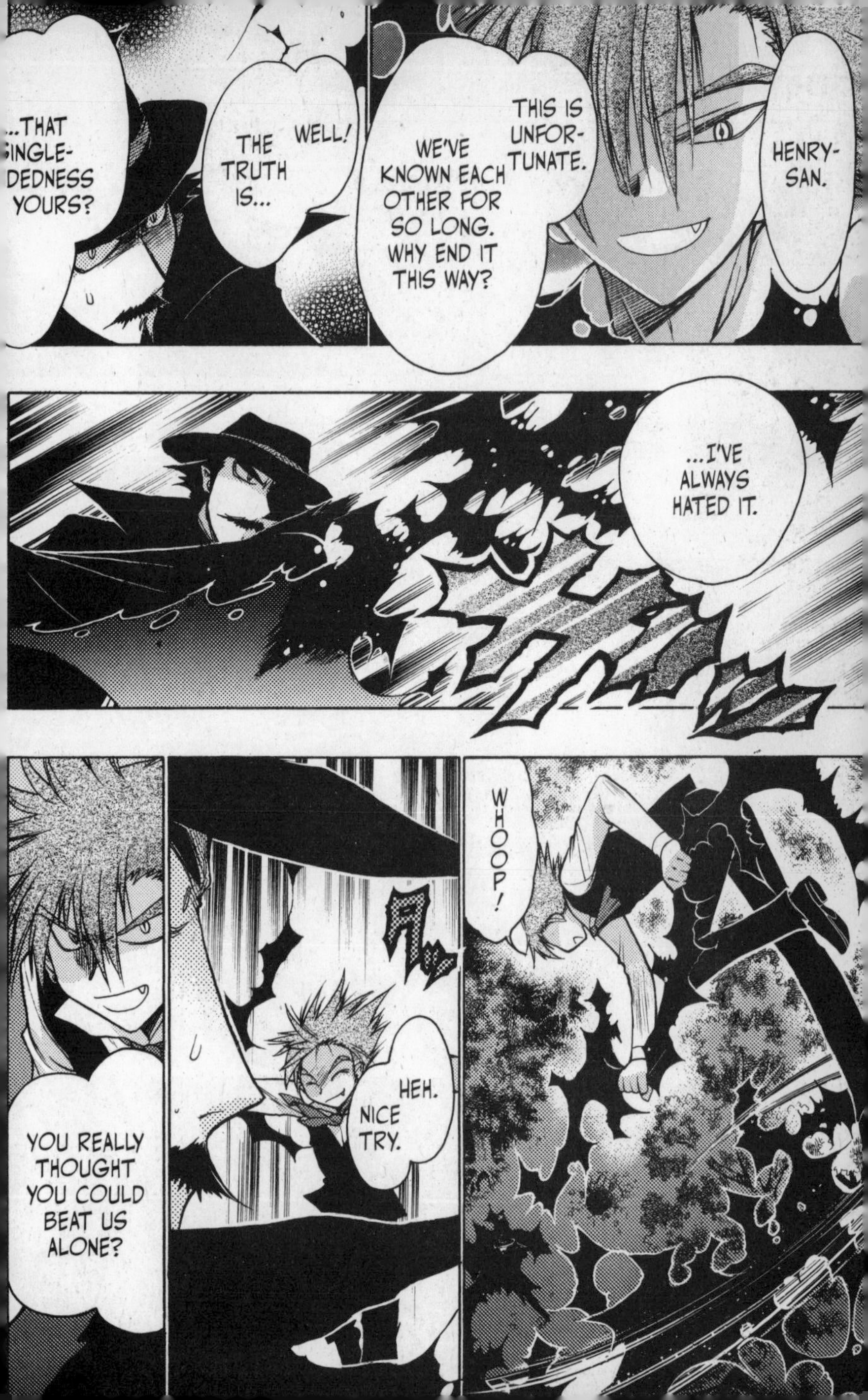
HENRY-SAN.
THIS IS UNFORTUNATE.
WE'VE KNOWN EACH OTHER FOR SO LONG. WHY END IT THIS WAY?
WELL!
THE TRUTH IS...
...THAT SINGLE-DEDNESS YOURS?
...I'VE ALWAYS HATED IT.
WHOOP!
HEH. NICE TRY.
YOU REALLY THOUGHT YOU COULD BEAT US ALONE?

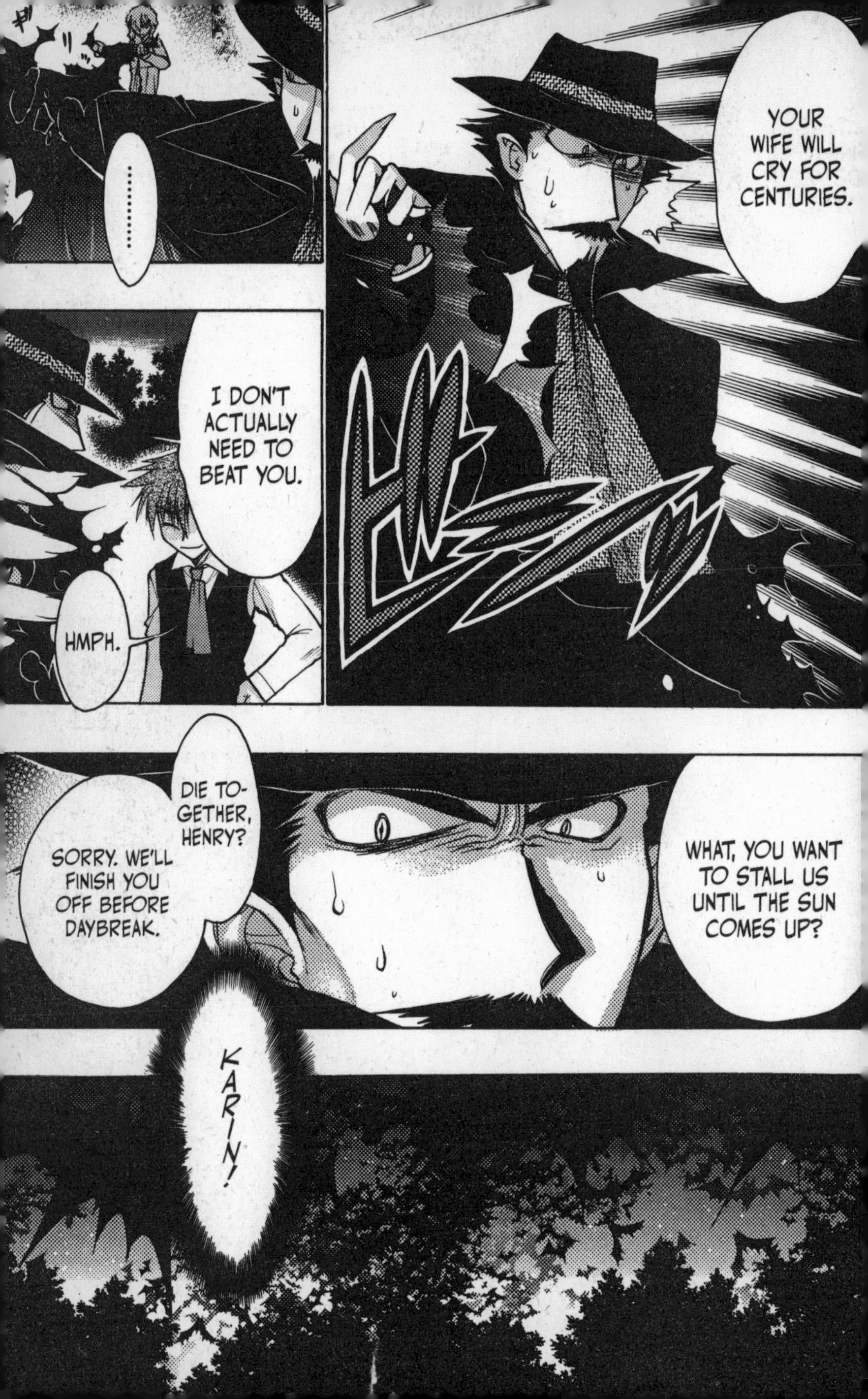
YOUR WIFE WILL CRY FOR CENTURIES.
....
I DON'T ACTUALLY NEED TO BEAT YOU.
HMPH.
WHAT, YOU WANT TO STALL US UNTIL THE SUN COMES UP?
DIE TO-GETHER, HENRY?
SORRY. WE'LL FINISH YOU OFF BEFORE DAYBREAK.
KARIN!

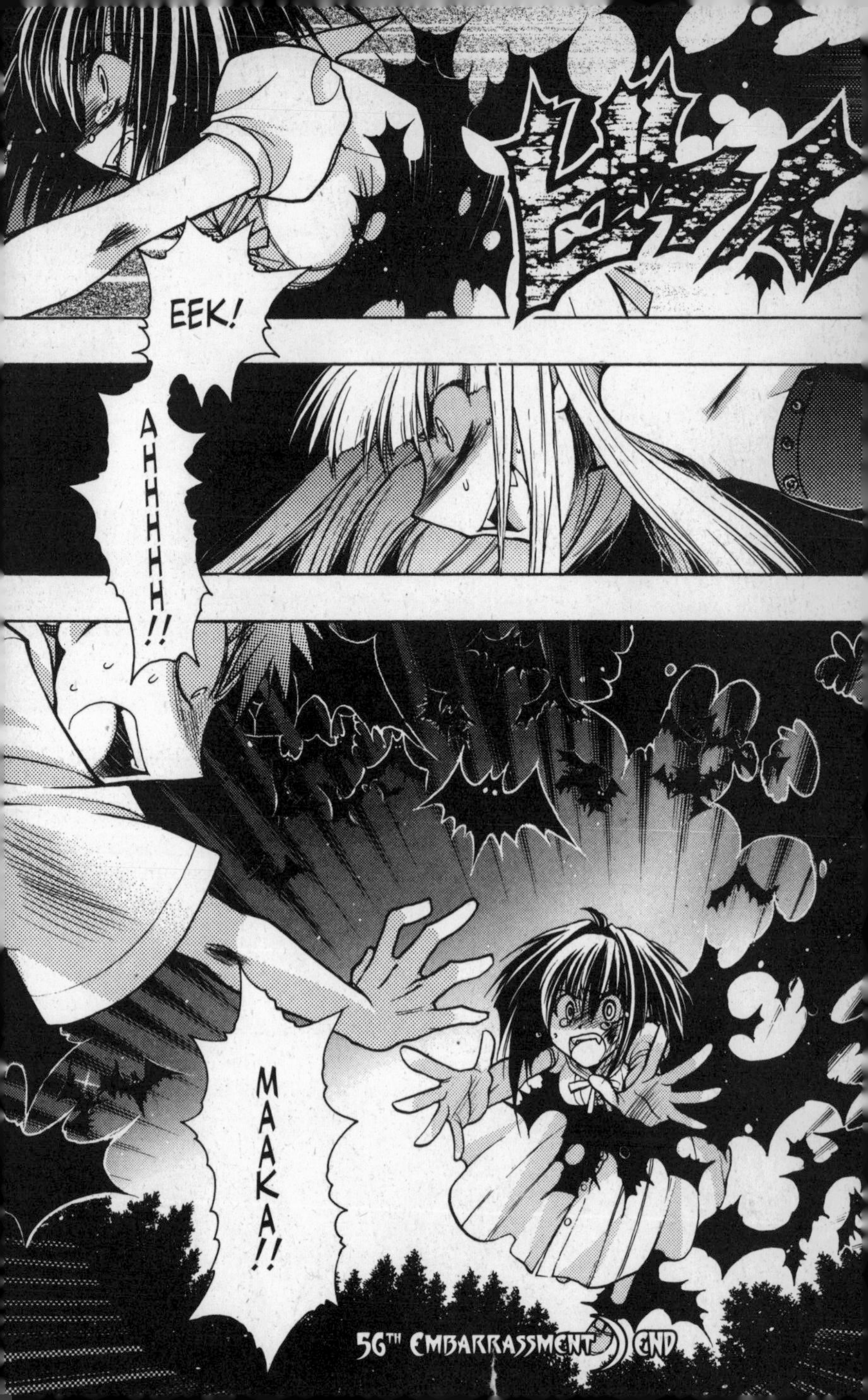
EEK!
AHHHHHH!!
MAAKA!!
56TH EMBARRASSMENT END

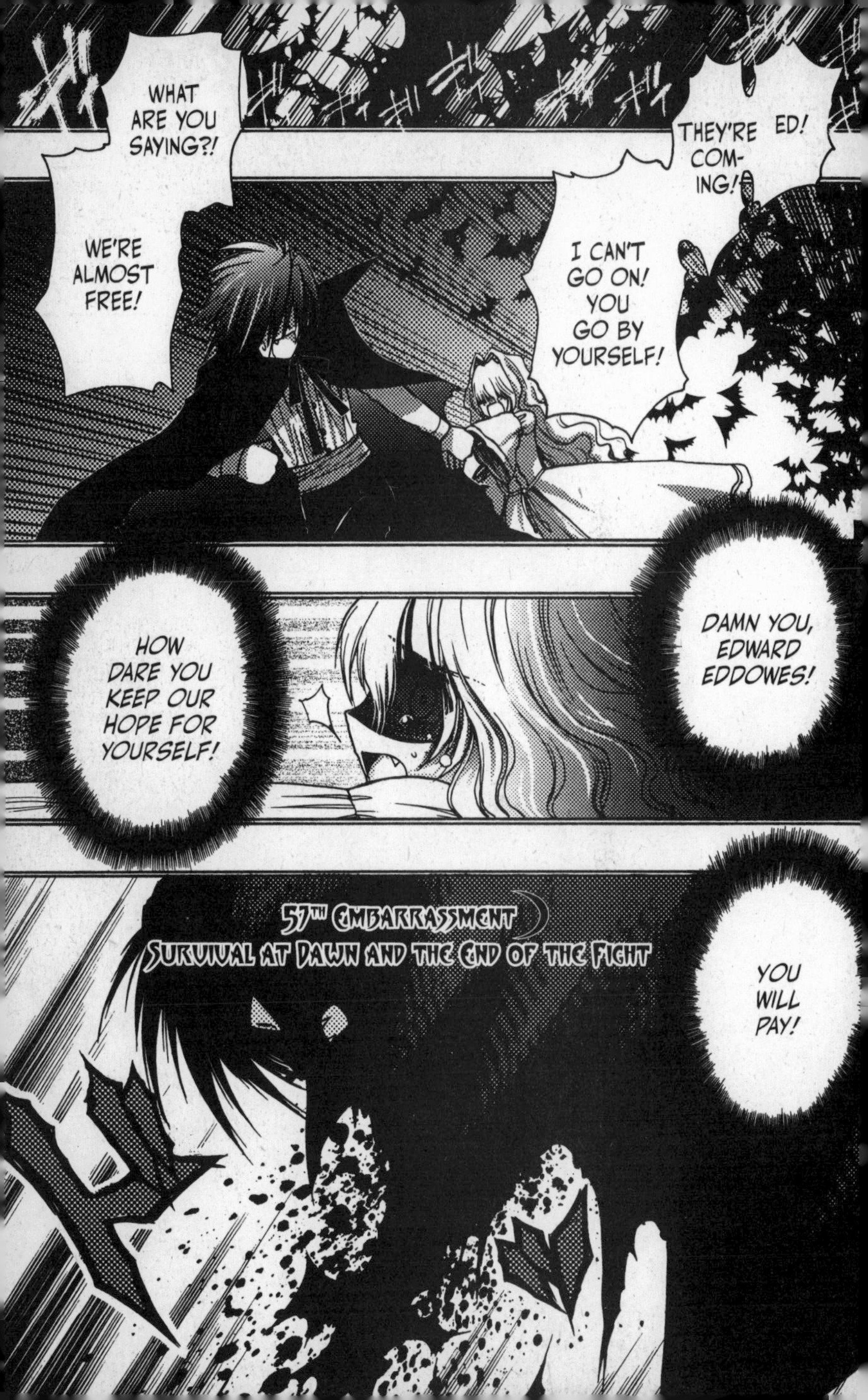
ED!
THEY'RE COMING!
I CAN'T GO ON! YOU GO BY YOURSELF!
WHAT ARE YOU SAYING?!
WE'RE ALMOST FREE!
DAMN YOU, EDWARD EDDOWES!
HOW DARE YOU KEEP OUR HOPE FOR YOURSELF!
YOU WILL PAY!
57TH EMBARRASSMENT
SURVIVAL AT DAWN AND THE END OF THE FIGHT

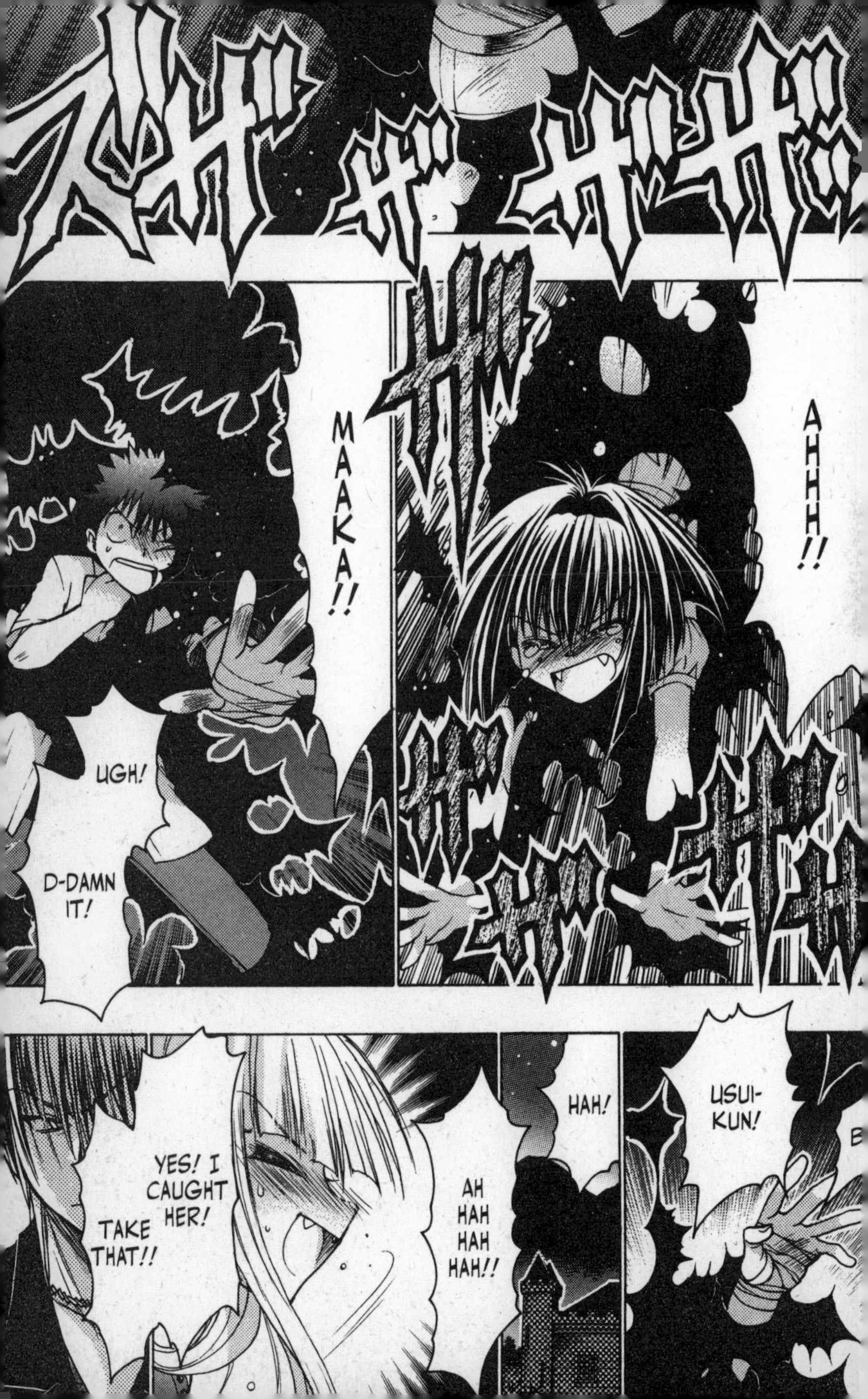
AHHH!!
MAAKA!!
UGH!
D-DAMN IT!
USUI-KUN!
B
HAH!
AH HAH HAH HAH!!
YES! I CAUGHT HER!
TAKE THAT!!

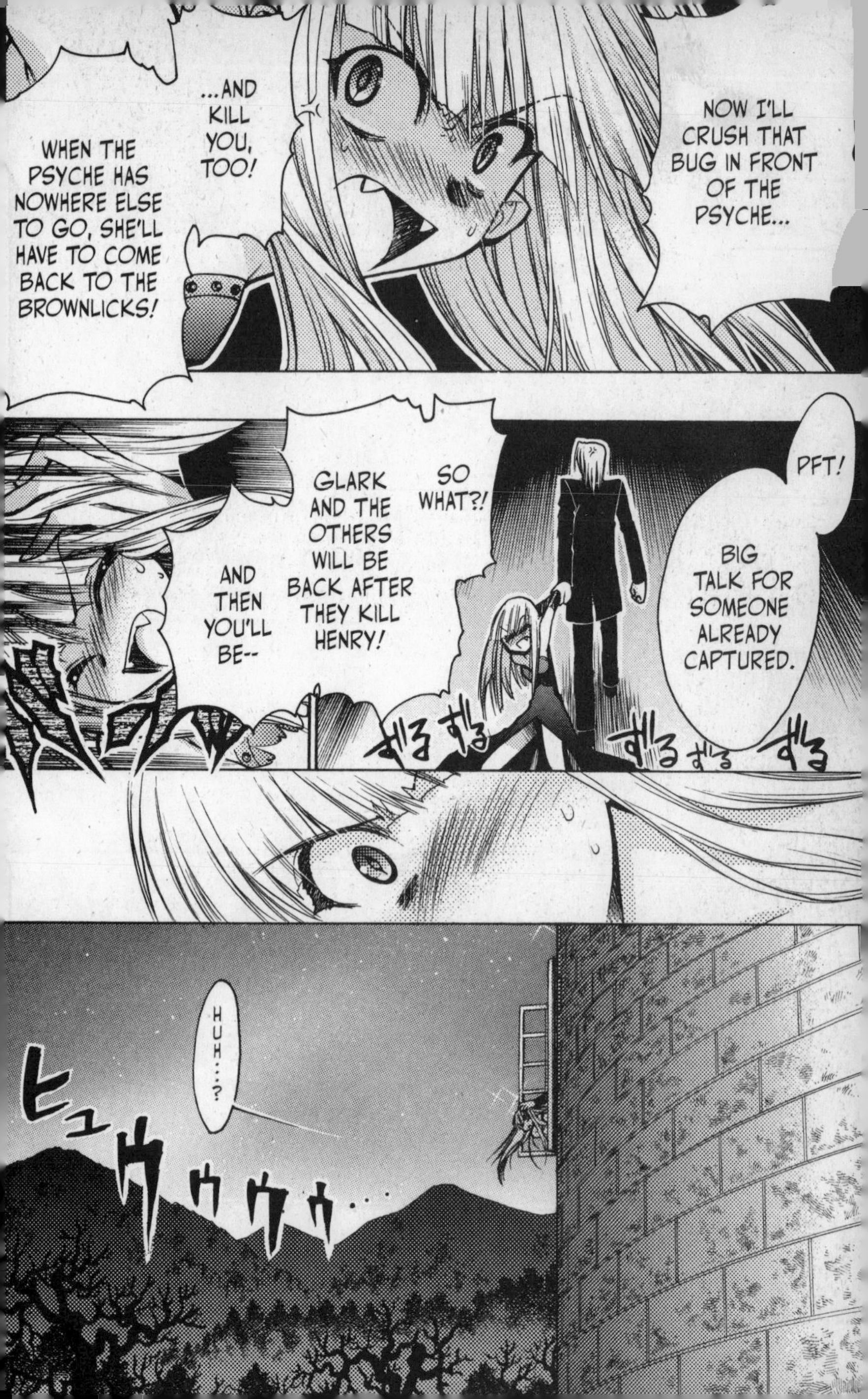
NOW I'LL CRUSH THAT BUG IN FRONT OF THE PSYCHE...
...AND KILL YOU, TOO!
WHEN THE PSYCHE HAS NOWHERE ELSE TO GO, SHE'LL HAVE TO COME BACK TO THE BROWNLICKS!
PFT!
BIG TALK FOR SOMEONE ALREADY CAPTURED.
ずる ずるずる ずるずる
SO WHAT?!
GLARK AND THE OTHERS WILL BE BACK AFTER THEY KILL HENRY!
AND THEN YOU'LL BE--
HUH...?
ヒュウウウウ…

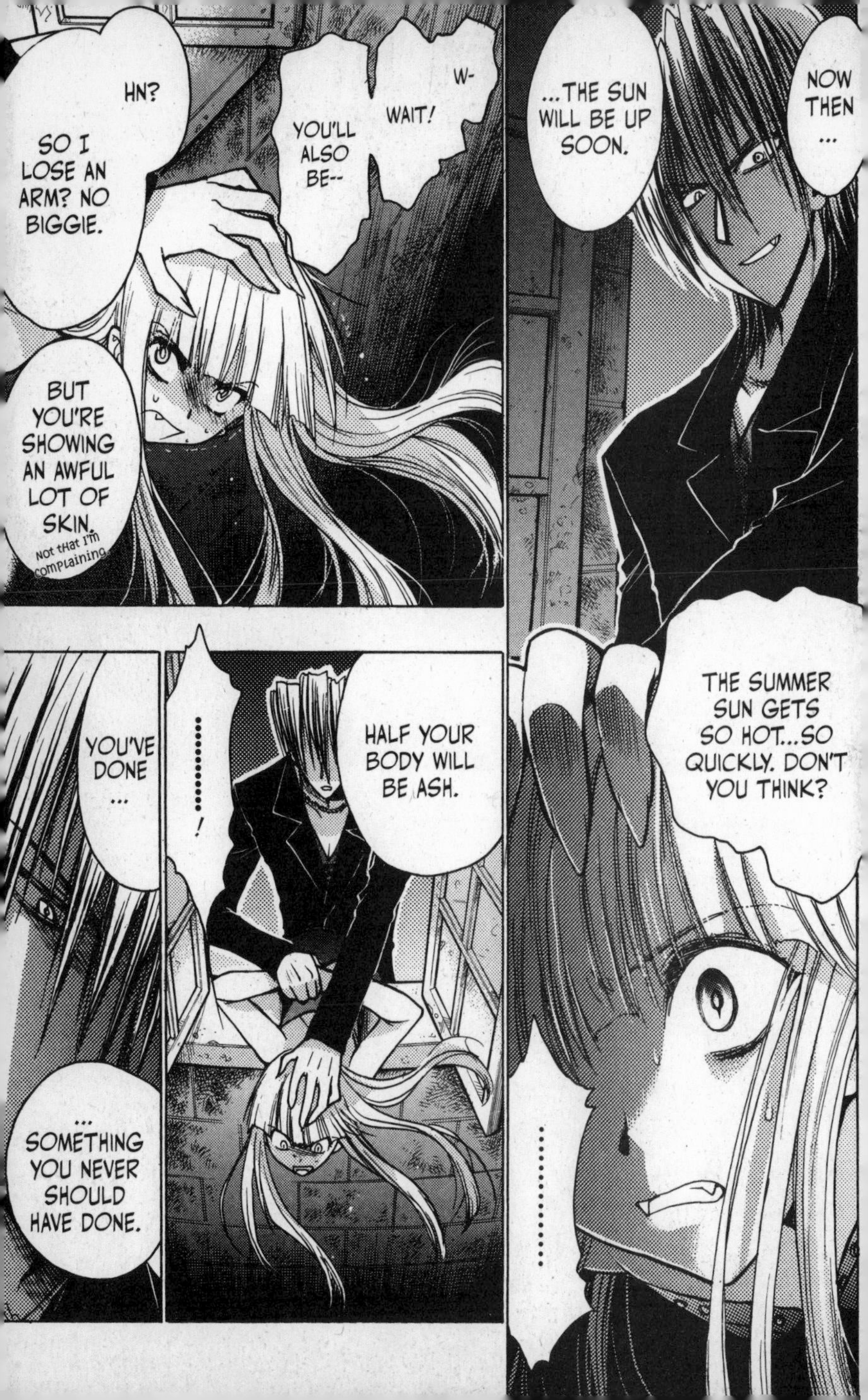
NOW THEN ...
...THE SUN WILL BE UP SOON.
HN?
W-
WAIT!
YOU'LL ALSO BE--
SO I LOSE AN ARM? NO BIGGIE.
BUT YOU'RE SHOWING AN AWFUL LOT OF SKIN.
Not that I'm complaining
THE SUMMER SUN GETS SO HOT...SO QUICKLY. DON'T YOU THINK?
....
HALF YOUR BODY WILL BE ASH.
.........!
YOU'VE DONE ...
... SOMETHING YOU NEVER SHOULD HAVE DONE.

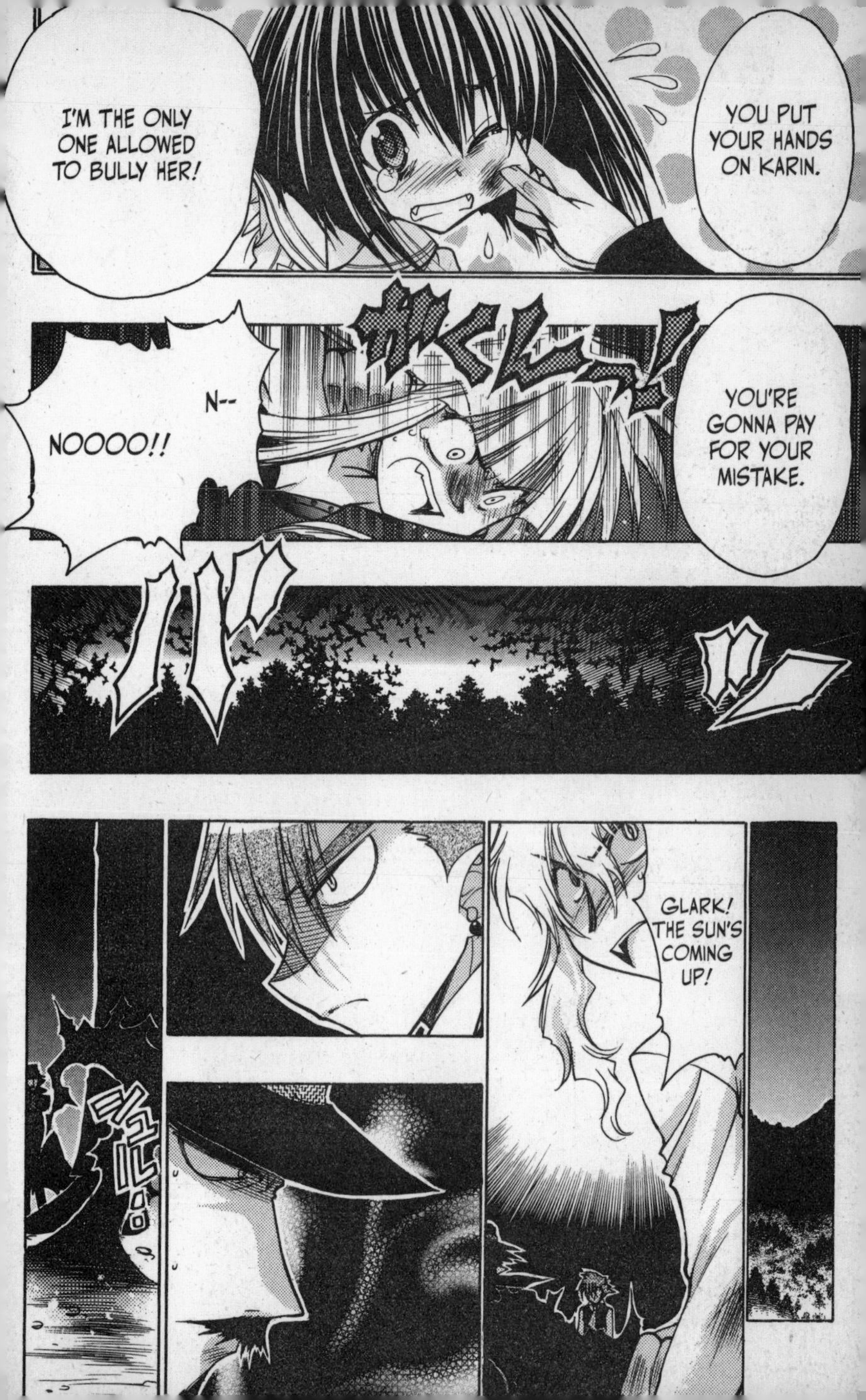
YOU PUT YOUR HANDS ON KARIN.
I'M THE ONLY ONE ALLOWED TO BULLY HER!
YOU'RE GONNA PAY FOR YOUR MISTAKE.
N-- NOOOO!!
GLARK! THE SUN'S COMING UP!
EH!?

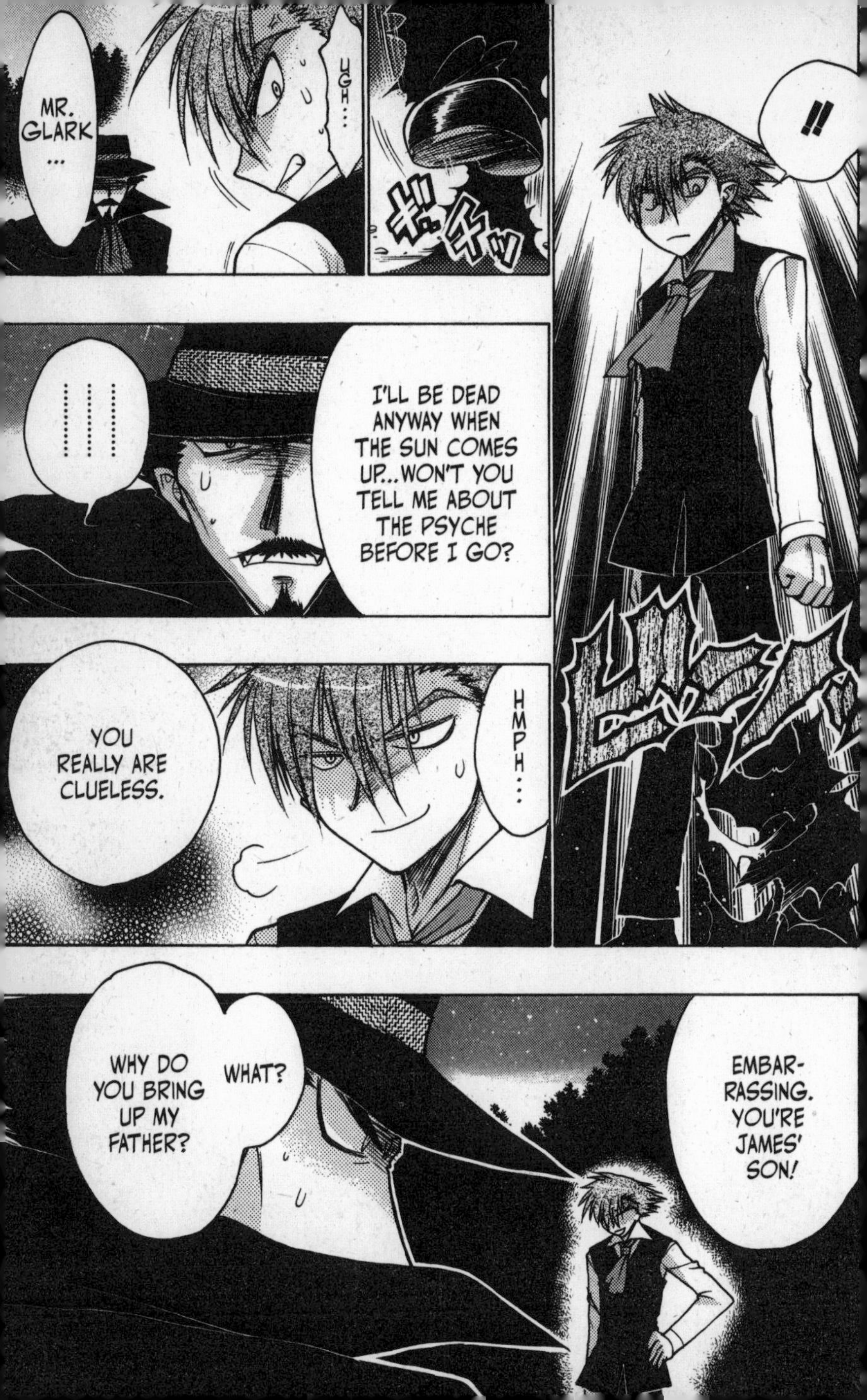
!!
ギュッ
UGH...
MR. GLARK...
I'LL BE DEAD ANYWAY WHEN THE SUN COMES UP...WON'T YOU TELL ME ABOUT THE PSYCHE BEFORE I GO?
......
HMPH...
YOU REALLY ARE CLUELESS.
EMBAR-RASSING. YOU'RE JAMES' SON!
WHAT?
WHY DO YOU BRING UP MY FATHER?

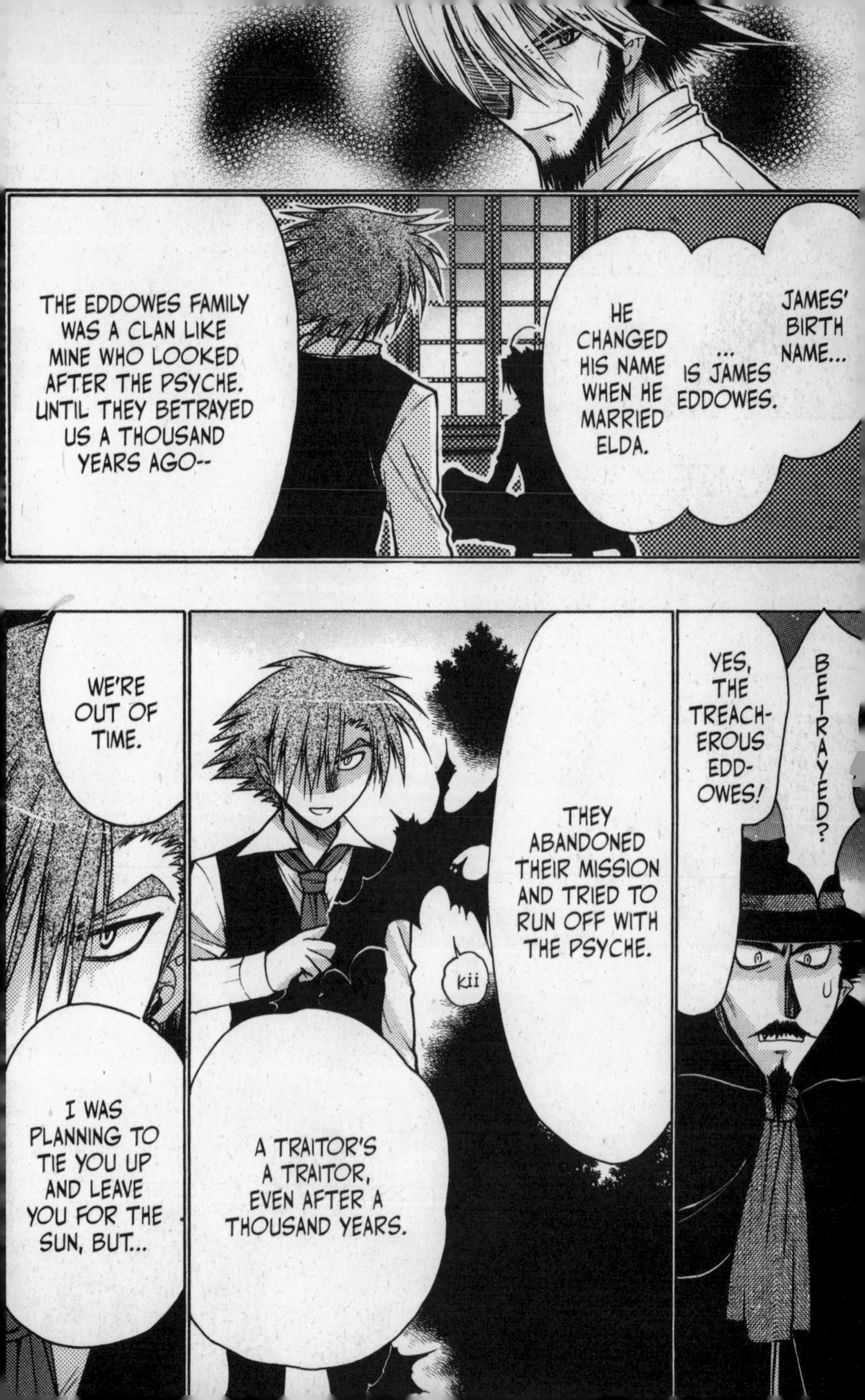
JAMES' BIRTH NAME...
... IS JAMES EDDOWES.
HE CHANGED HIS NAME WHEN HE MARRIED ELDA.
THE EDDOWES FAMILY WAS A CLAN LIKE MINE WHO LOOKED AFTER THE PSYCHE. UNTIL THEY BETRAYED US A THOUSAND YEARS AGO--
BETRAYED?
YES, THE TREACH-EROUS EDD-OWES!
THEY ABANDONED THEIR MISSION AND TRIED TO RUN OFF WITH THE PSYCHE.
kii
A TRAITOR'S A TRAITOR, EVEN AFTER A THOUSAND YEARS.
WE'RE OUT OF TIME.
I WAS PLANNING TO TIE YOU UP AND LEAVE YOU FOR THE SUN, BUT...

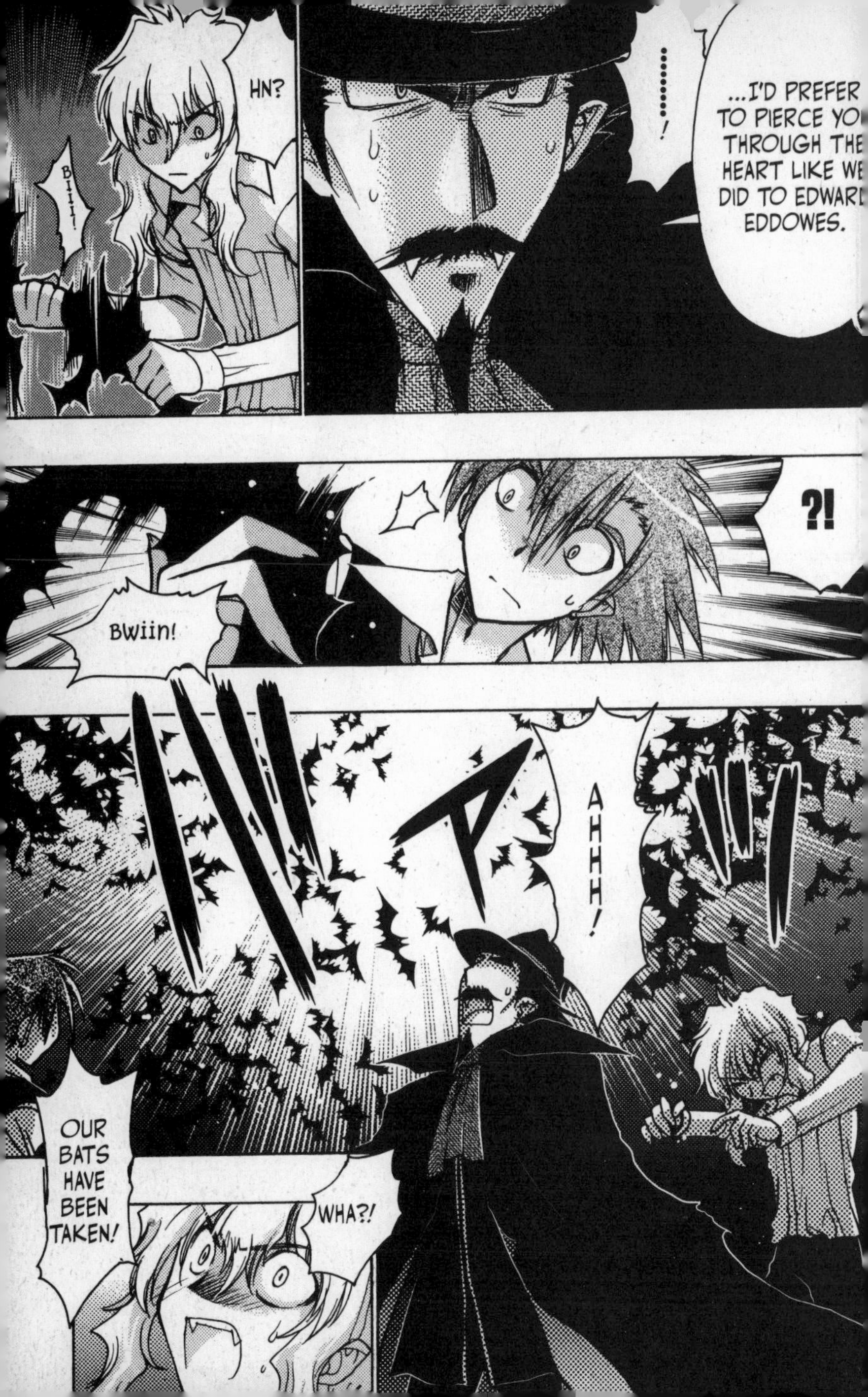
...I'D PREFER TO PIERCE YO THROUGH THE HEART LIKE WE DID TO EDWAR EDDOWES.
........!
HN?
BIIII!
?!
BWiin!
AHHHH!
WHA?!
OUR BATS HAVE BEEN TAKEN!

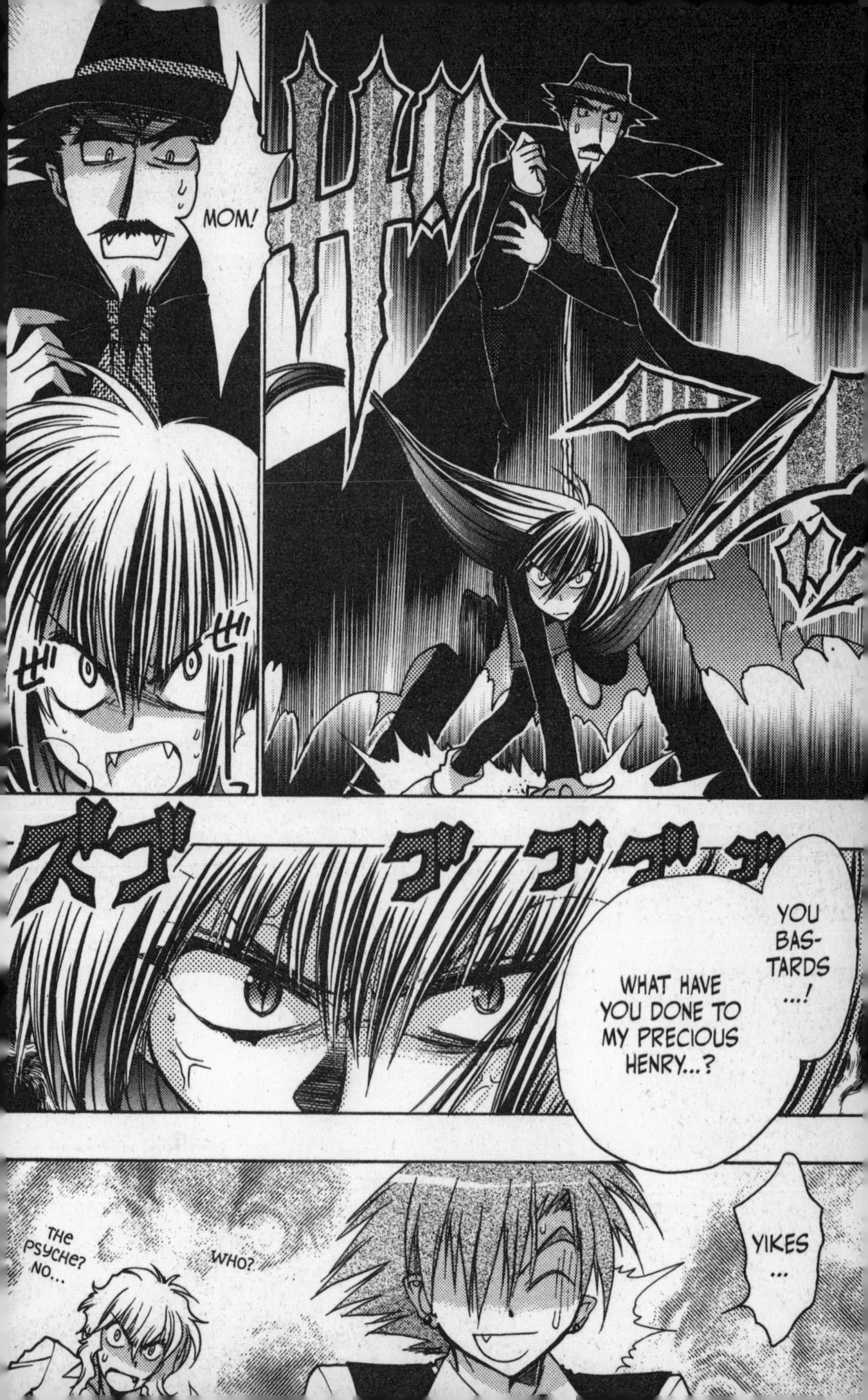
MOM!
ぜ ぜ
YOU BASTARDS...!
WHAT HAVE YOU DONE TO MY PRECIOUS HENRY...?
YIKES...
WHO?
THE PSYCHE? NO...

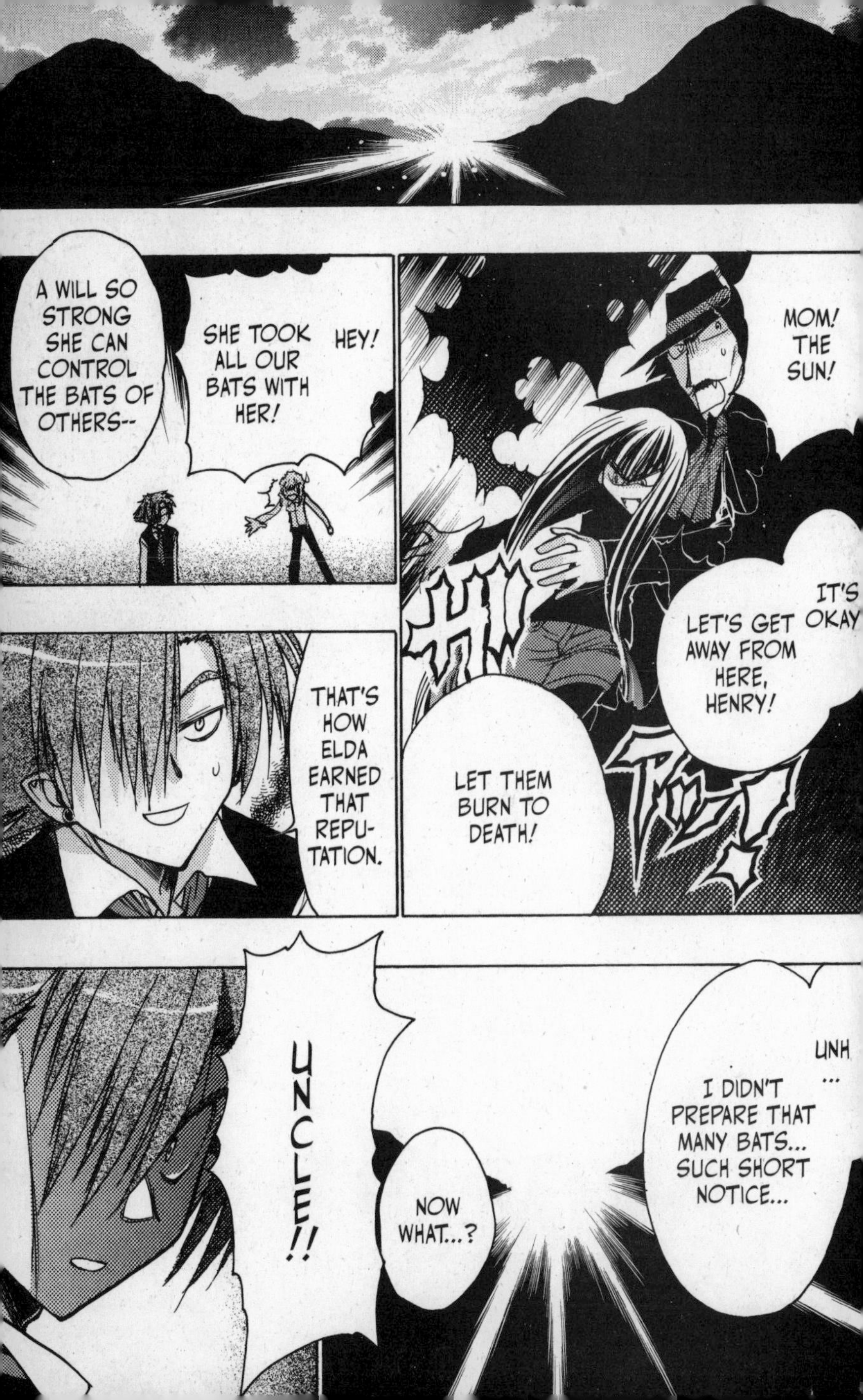
MOM! THE SUN!
IT'S OKAY
LET'S GET AWAY FROM HERE, HENRY!
LET THEM BURN TO DEATH!
HEY!
SHE TOOK ALL OUR BATS WITH HER!
A WILL SO STRONG SHE CAN CONTROL THE BATS OF OTHERS--
THAT'S HOW ELDA EARNED THAT REPUTATION.
UNH ...
I DIDN'T PREPARE THAT MANY BATS... SUCH SHORT NOTICE...
NOW WHAT...?
UNCLE!!

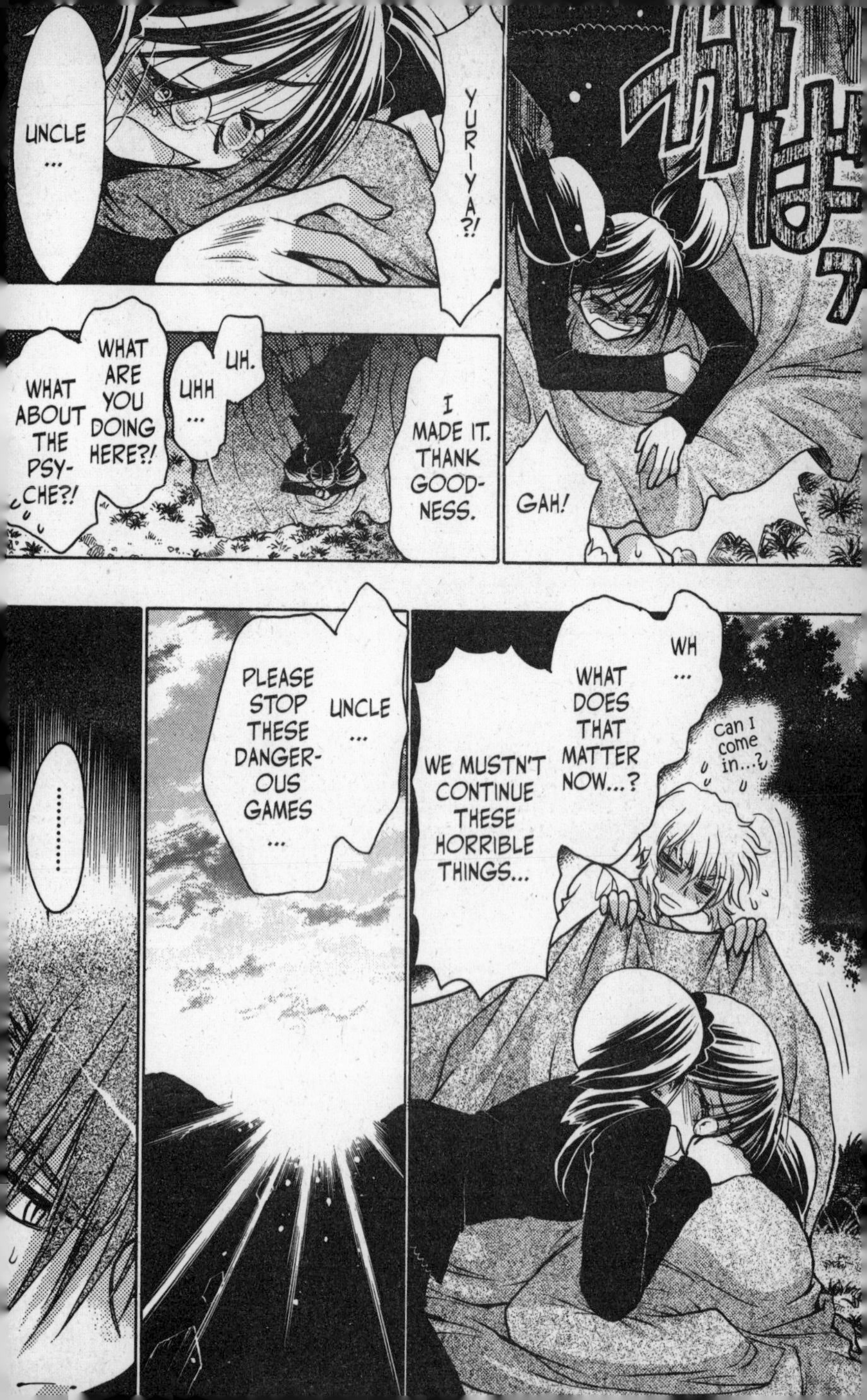
わはっ
GAH!
YURIYA?!
UNCLE ...
I MADE IT. THANK GOODNESS.
UH.
UHH ...
WHAT ARE YOU DOING HERE?!
WHAT ABOUT THE PSYCHE?!
WH ... WHAT DOES THAT MATTER NOW...?
Can I come in...?
WE MUSTN'T CONTINUE THESE HORRIBLE THINGS...
UNCLE ...
PLEASE STOP THESE DANGEROUS GAMES ...
....

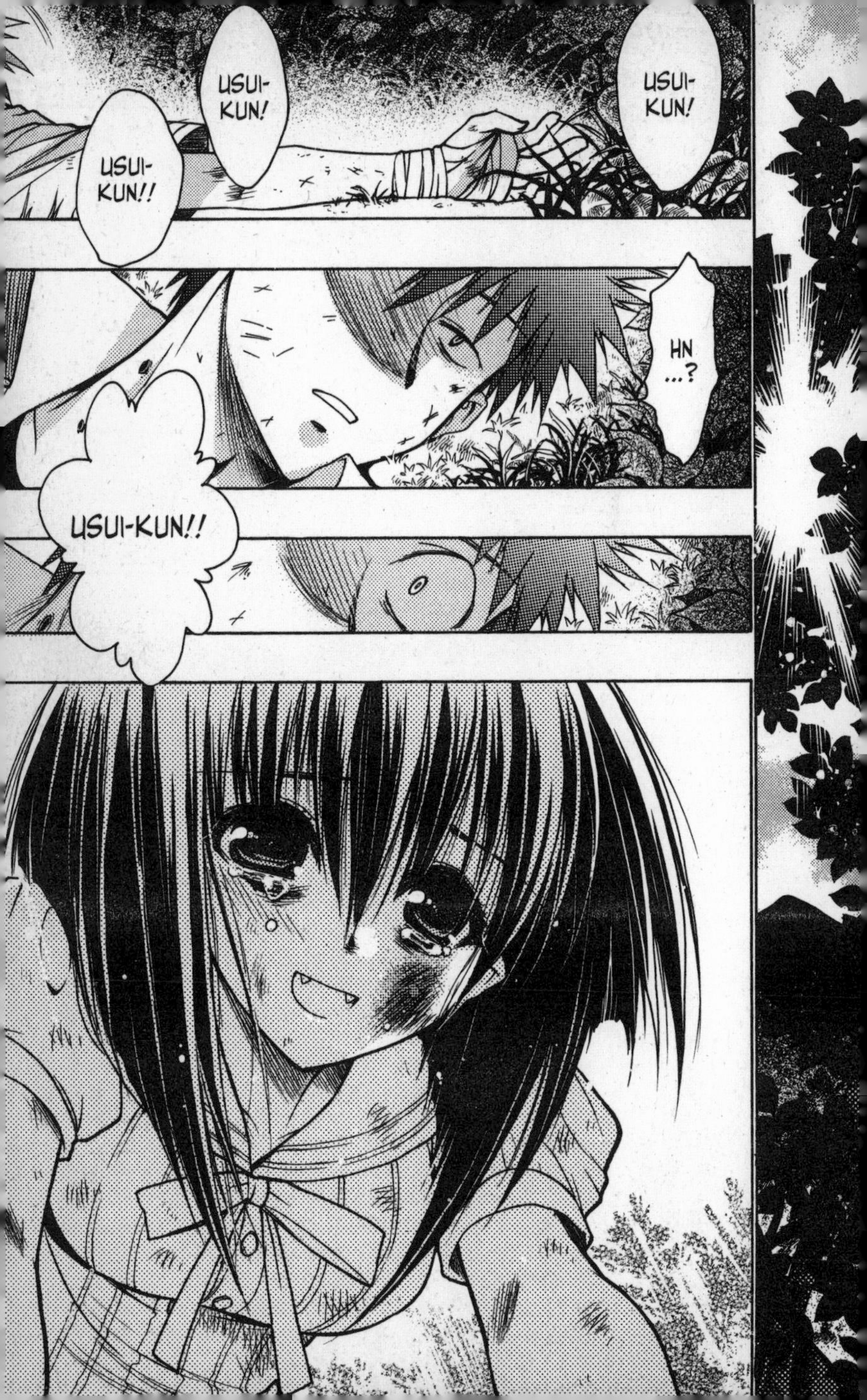
USUI-KUN!
USUI-KUN!
USUI-KUN!!
HN ...?
USUI-KUN!!

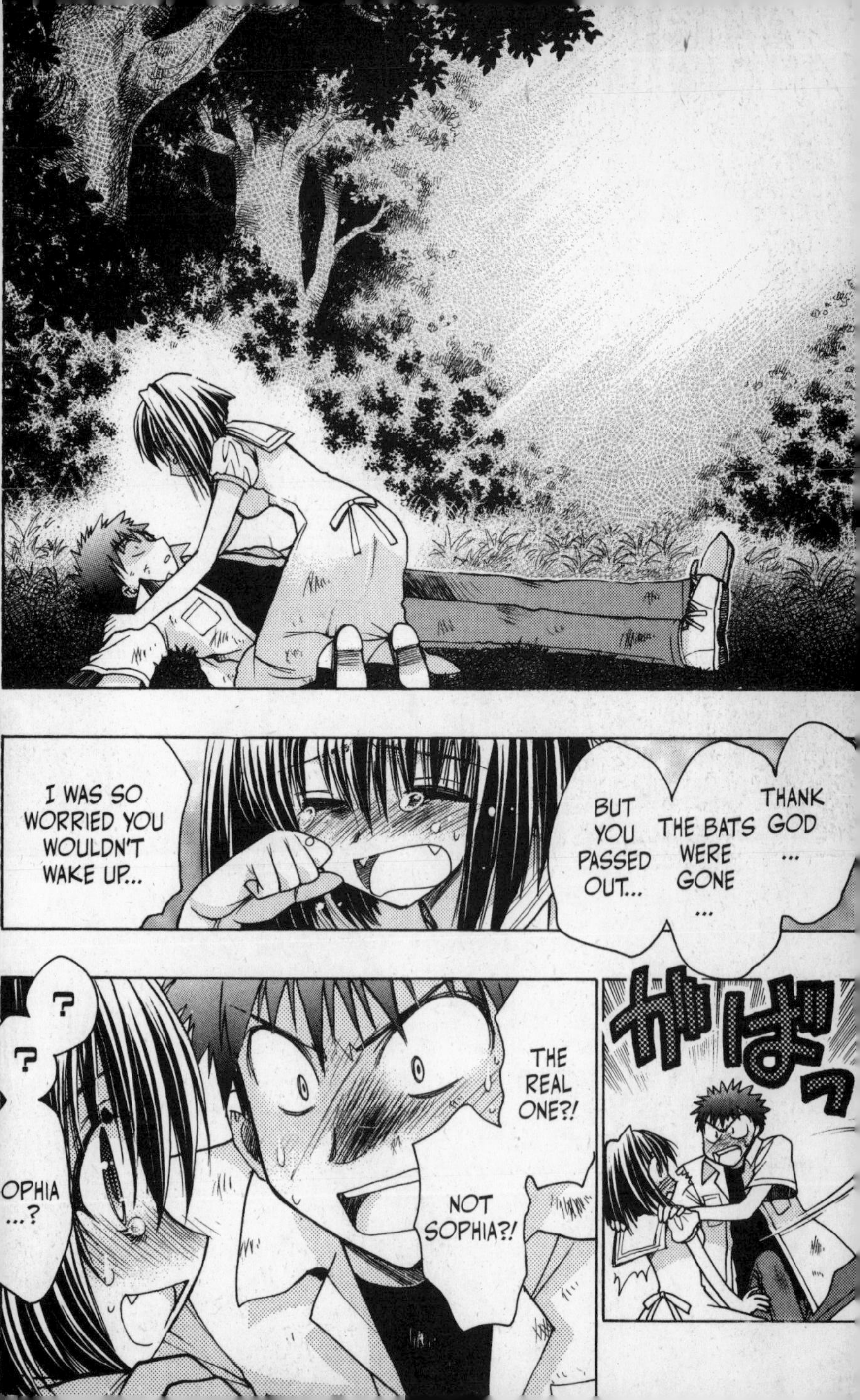
THANK GOD...
THE BATS WERE GONE...
BUT YOU PASSED OUT...
I WAS SO WORRIED YOU WOULDN'T WAKE UP...
がばっ
THE REAL ONE?!
NOT SOPHIA?!
? ?
OPHIA ...?

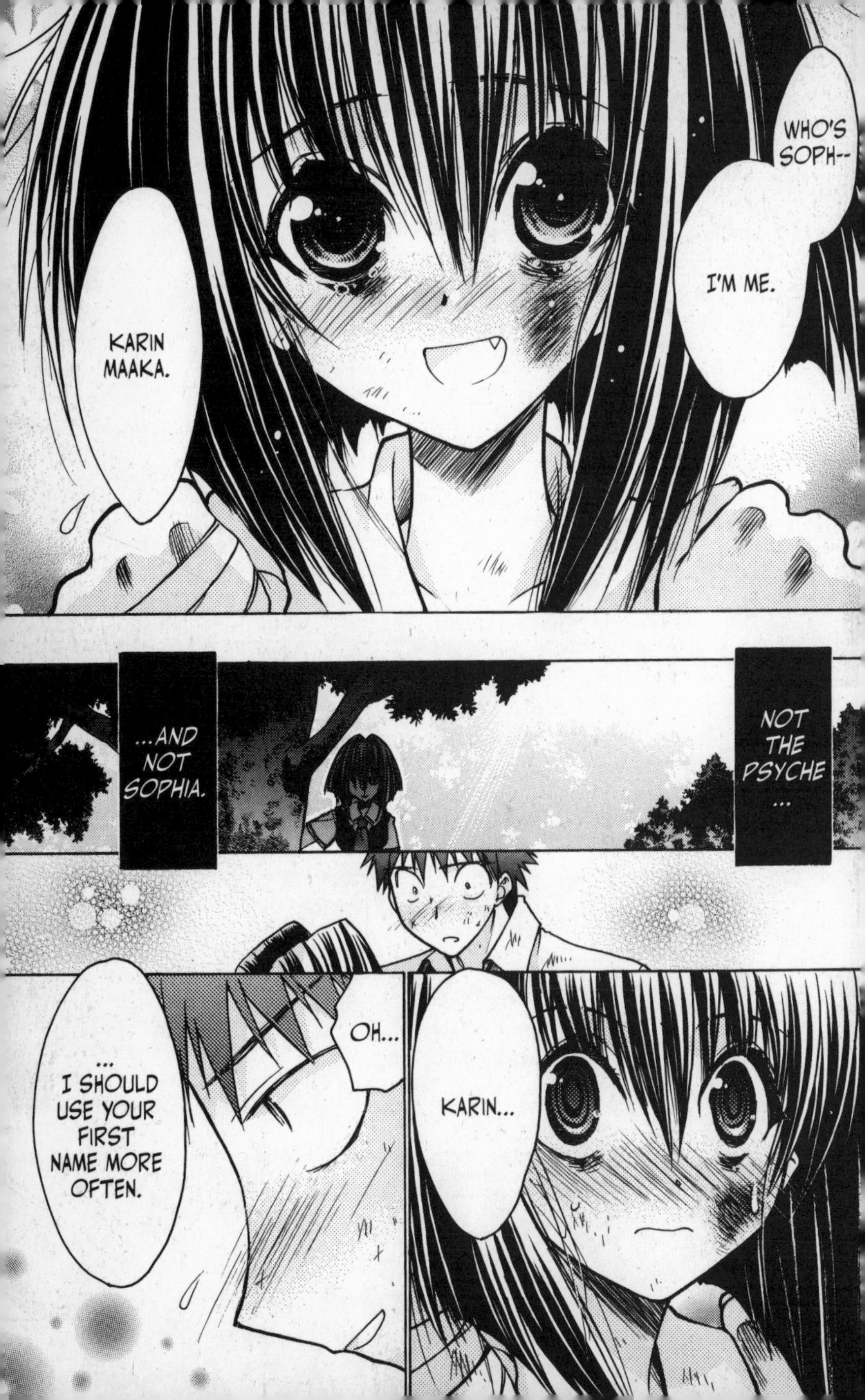
WHO'S SOPH--
I'M ME.
KARIN MAAKA.
NOT THE PSYCHE ...
...AND NOT SOPHIA.
KARIN...
OH...
... I SHOULD USE YOUR FIRST NAME MORE OFTEN.

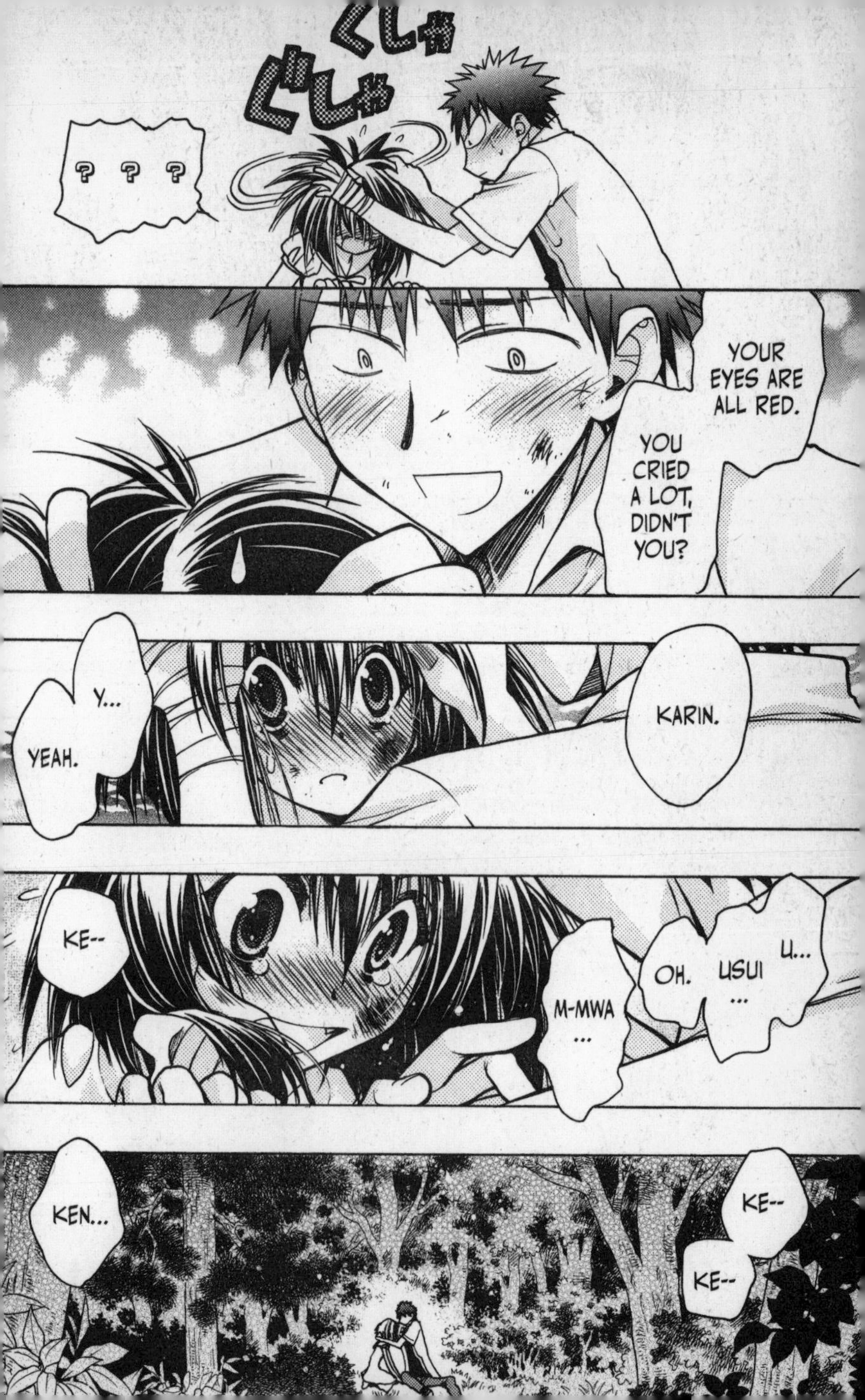
くしゃ
くしゃ
???
YOUR EYES ARE ALL RED.
YOU CRIED A LOT, DIDN'T YOU?
KARIN.
Y...
YEAH.
U...
USUI ...
OH.
M-MWA ...
KE--
KE--
KE--
KEN...

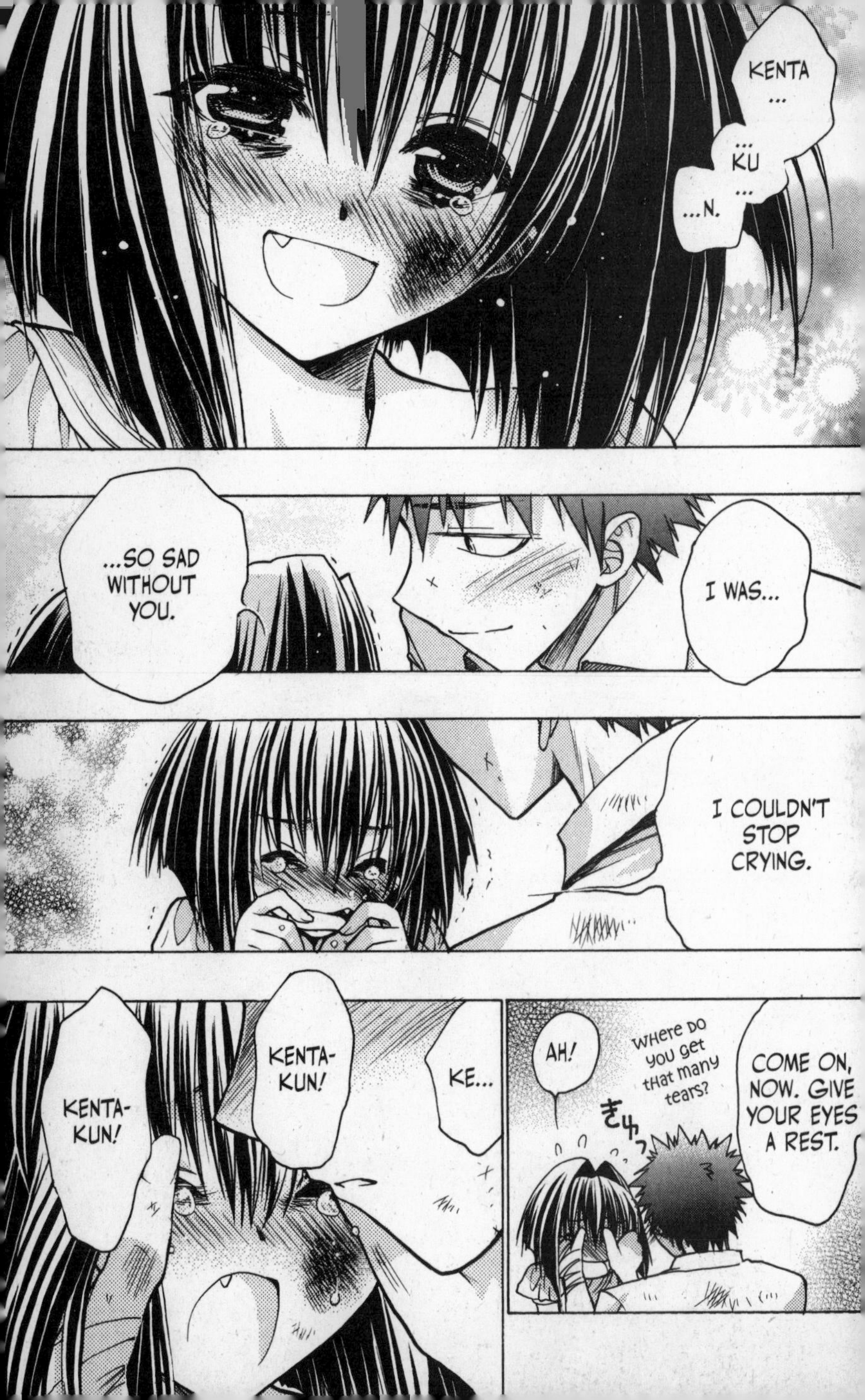
KENTA ...
... KU ... ...N.
I WAS...
...SO SAD WITHOUT YOU.
I COULDN'T STOP CRYING.
COME ON, NOW. GIVE YOUR EYES A REST.
Where do you get that many tears?
きゅっ
AH!
KE...
KENTA-KUN!
KENTA-KUN!

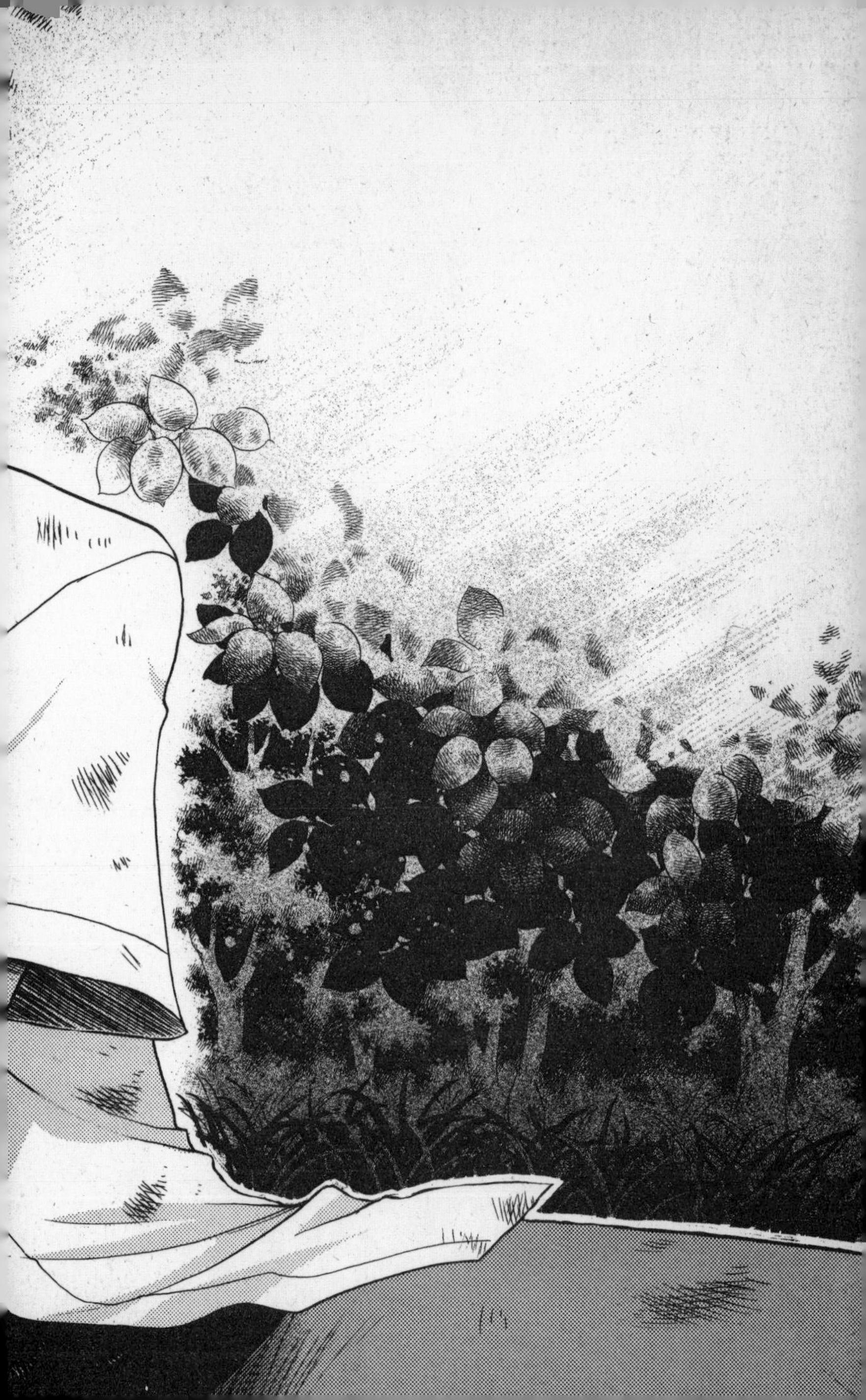

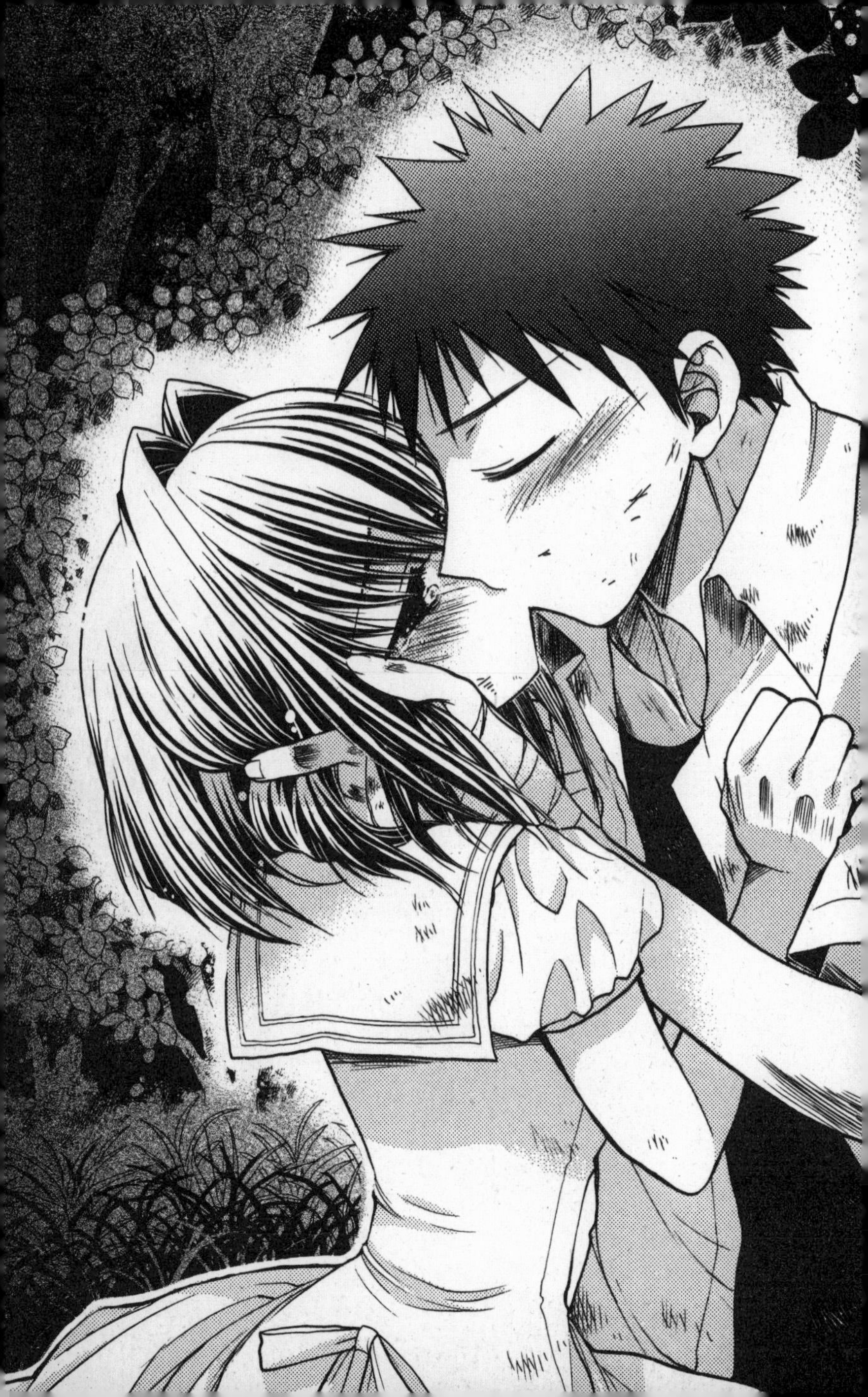

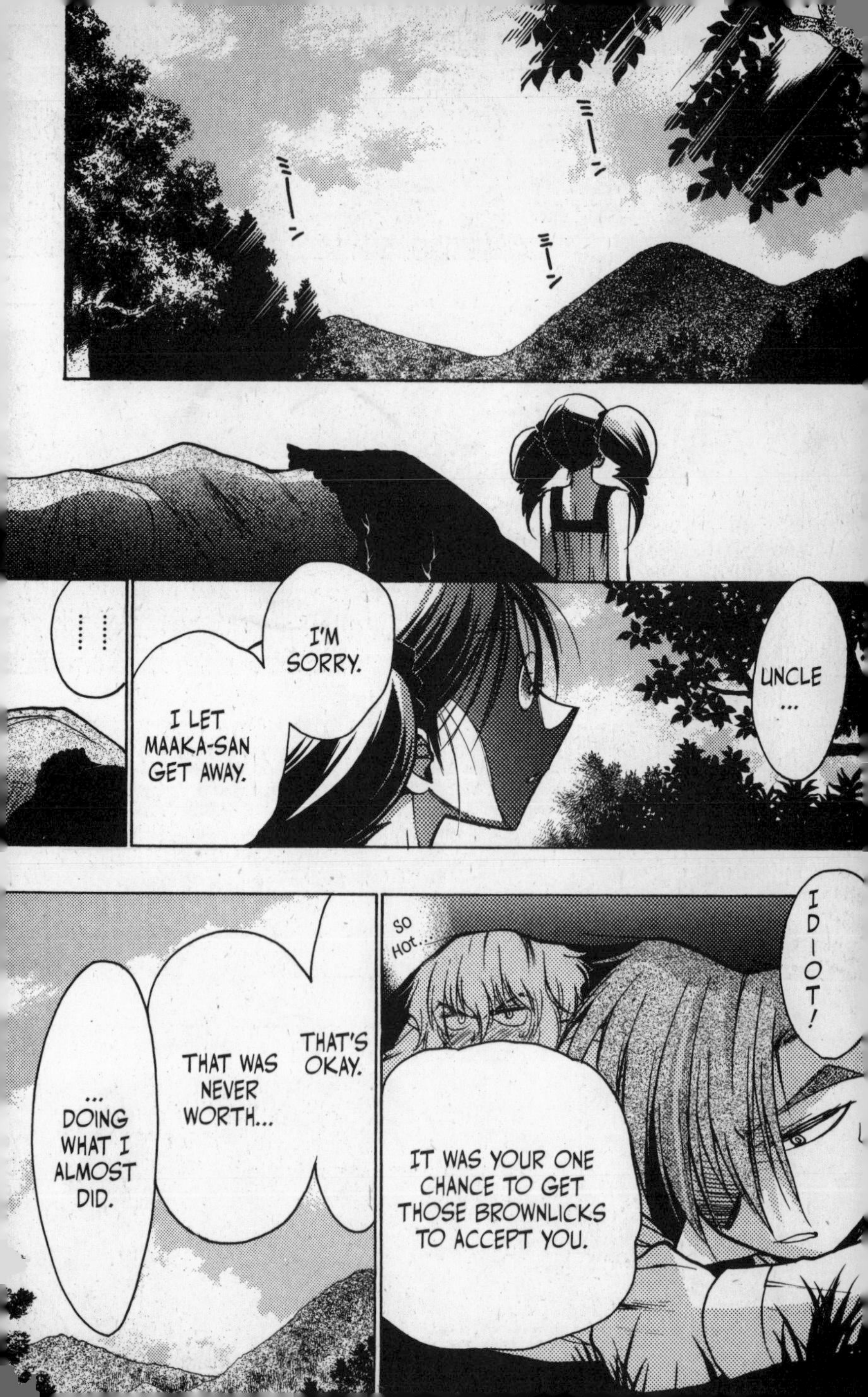
ミーーン
ミーーン
ミーーン
UNCLE ...
I'M SORRY.
I LET MAAKA-SAN GET AWAY.
......
IDIOT!
SO HOT...
IT WAS YOUR ONE CHANCE TO GET THOSE BROWNLICKS TO ACCEPT YOU.
THAT'S OKAY.
THAT WAS NEVER WORTH...
... DOING WHAT I ALMOST DID.

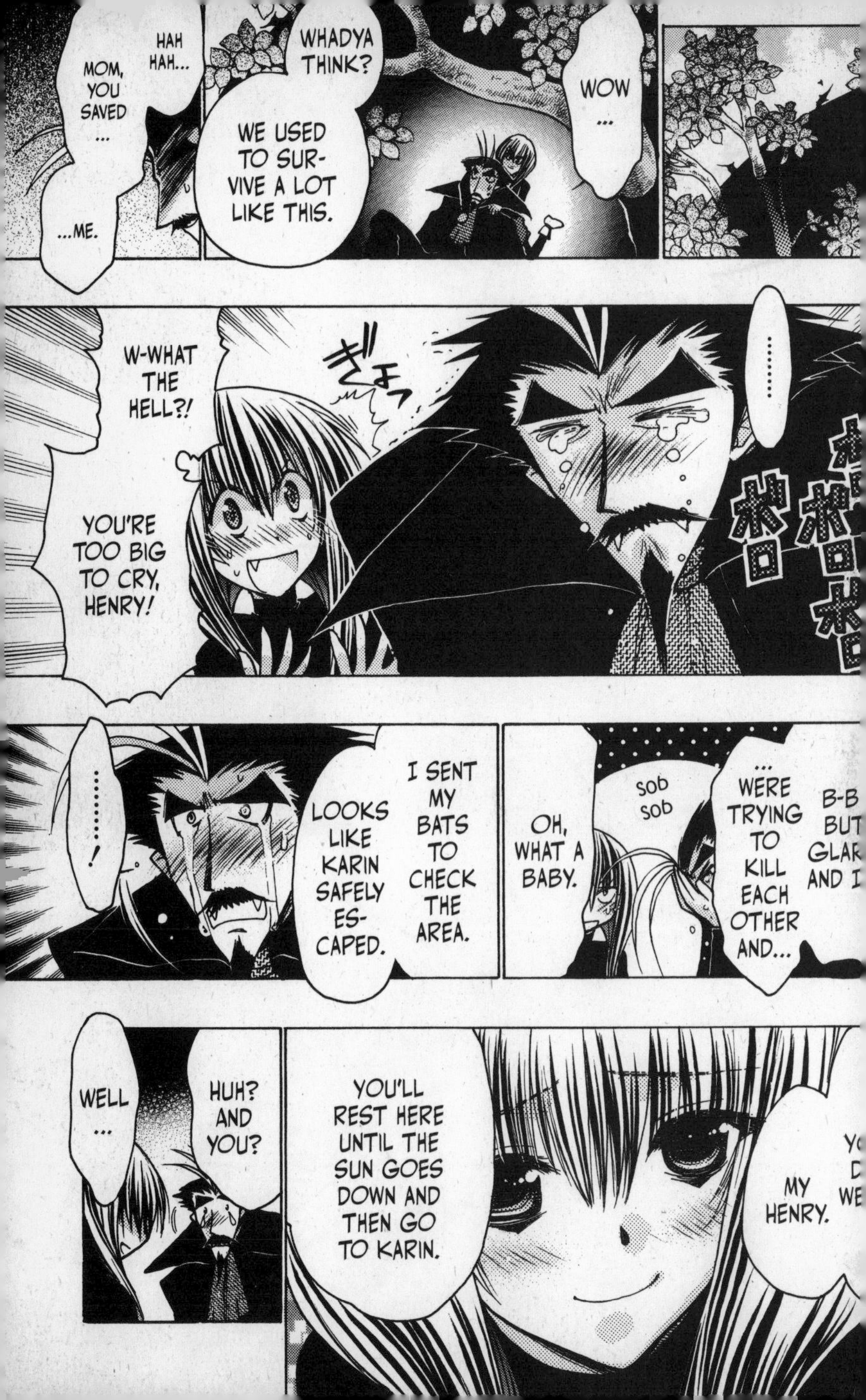
WOW ...
WHADYA THINK?
WE USED TO SUR-VIVE A LOT LIKE THIS.
HAH HAH...
MOM, YOU SAVED ...
...ME.
......
ボロボロ ボロ
ぎょっ
W-WHAT THE HELL?!
YOU'RE TOO BIG TO CRY, HENRY!
B-B BUT GLAR AND I
... WERE TRYING TO KILL EACH OTHER AND...
sob sob
OH, WHAT A BABY.
I SENT MY BATS TO CHECK THE AREA.
LOOKS LIKE KARIN SAFELY ES-CAPED.
......!
MY HENRY.
YOU'LL REST HERE UNTIL THE SUN GOES DOWN AND THEN GO TO KARIN.
HUH? AND YOU?
WELL ...

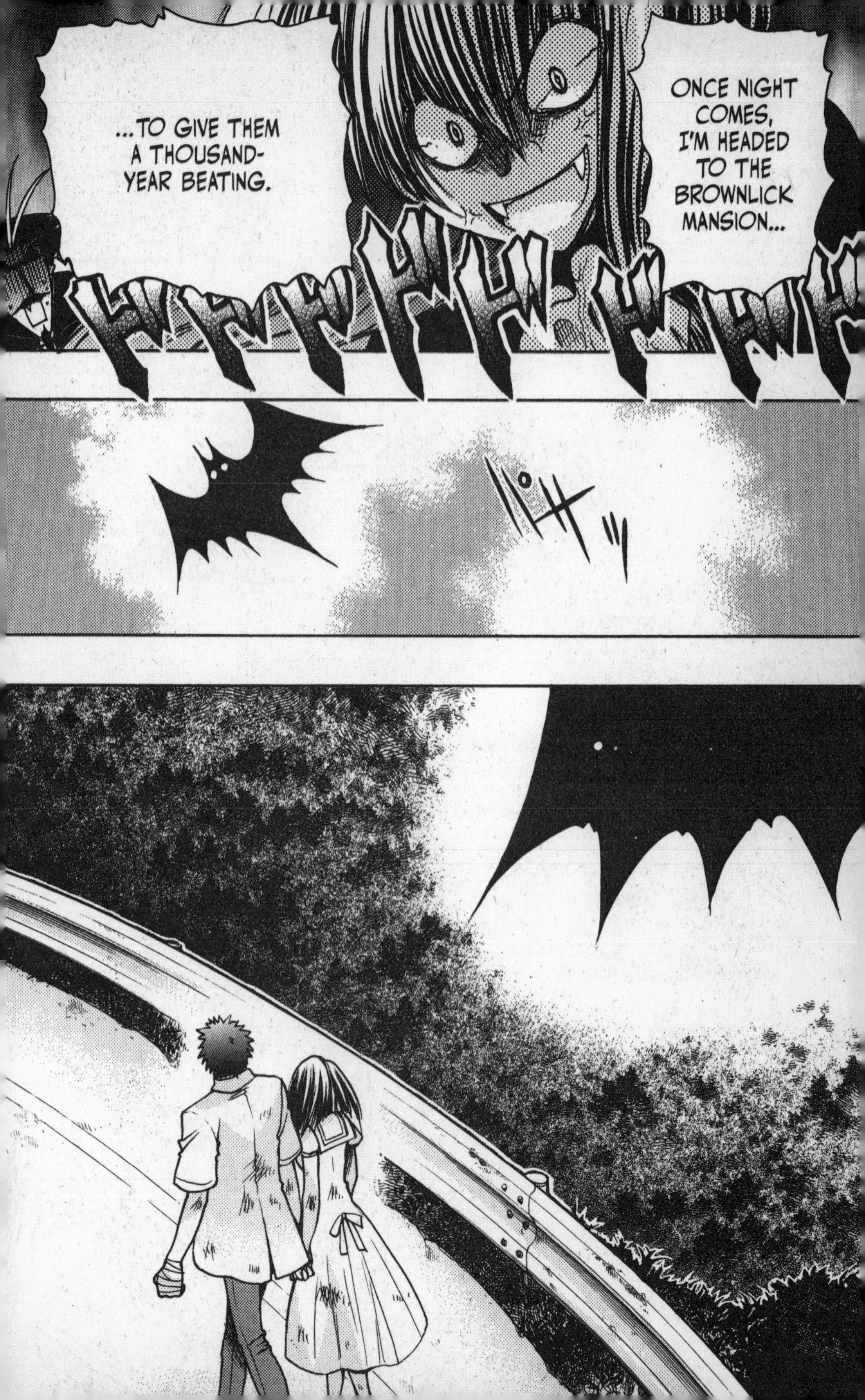
ONCE NIGHT COMES, I'M HEADED TO THE BROWNLICK MANSION...
...TO GIVE THEM A THOUSAND-YEAR BEATING.

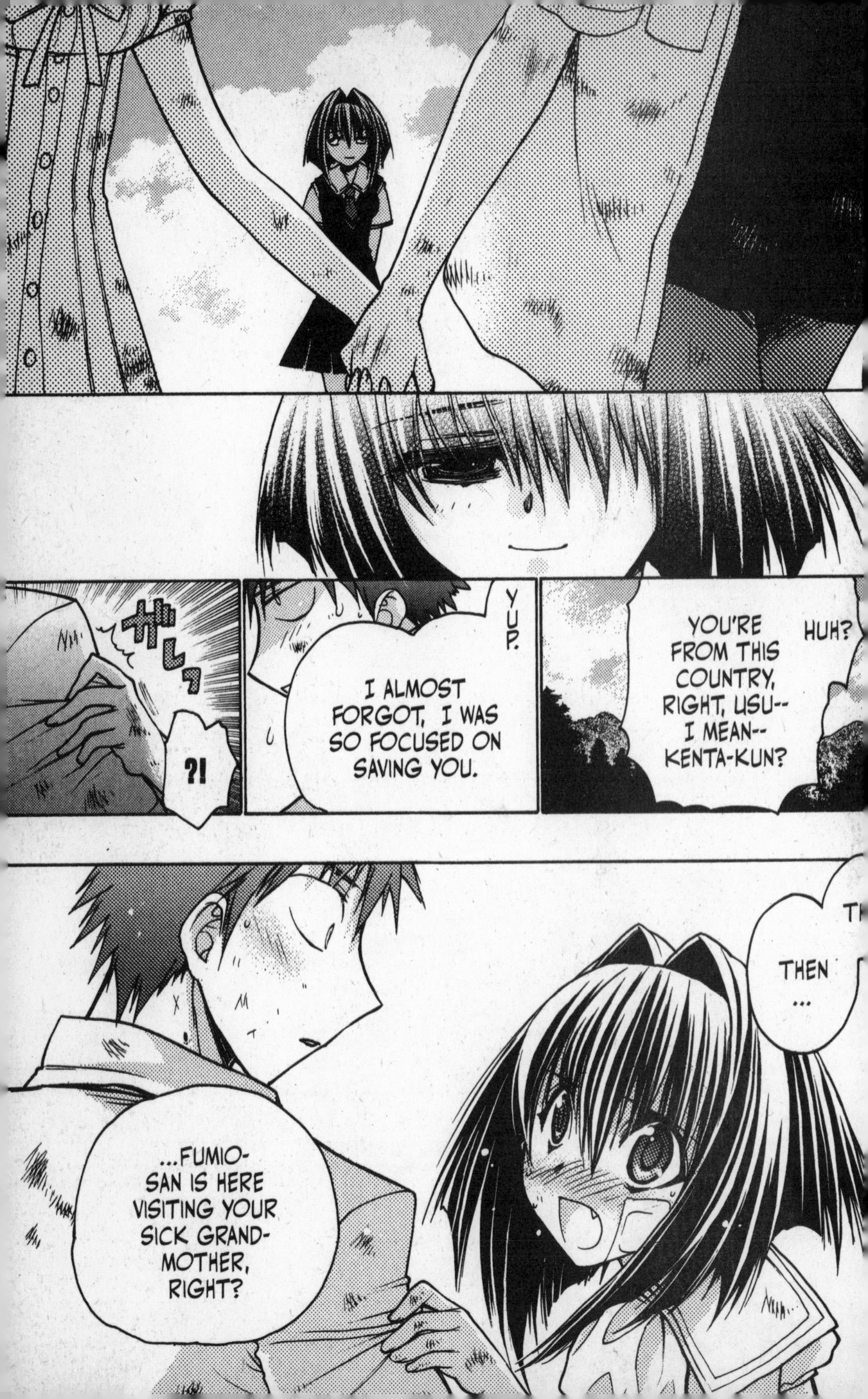
HUH?
YOU'RE FROM THIS COUNTRY, RIGHT, USU-- I MEAN-- KENTA-KUN?
YUP.
I ALMOST FORGOT, I WAS SO FOCUSED ON SAVING YOU.
?!
THEN...
...FUMIO-SAN IS HERE VISITING YOUR SICK GRAND-MOTHER, RIGHT?

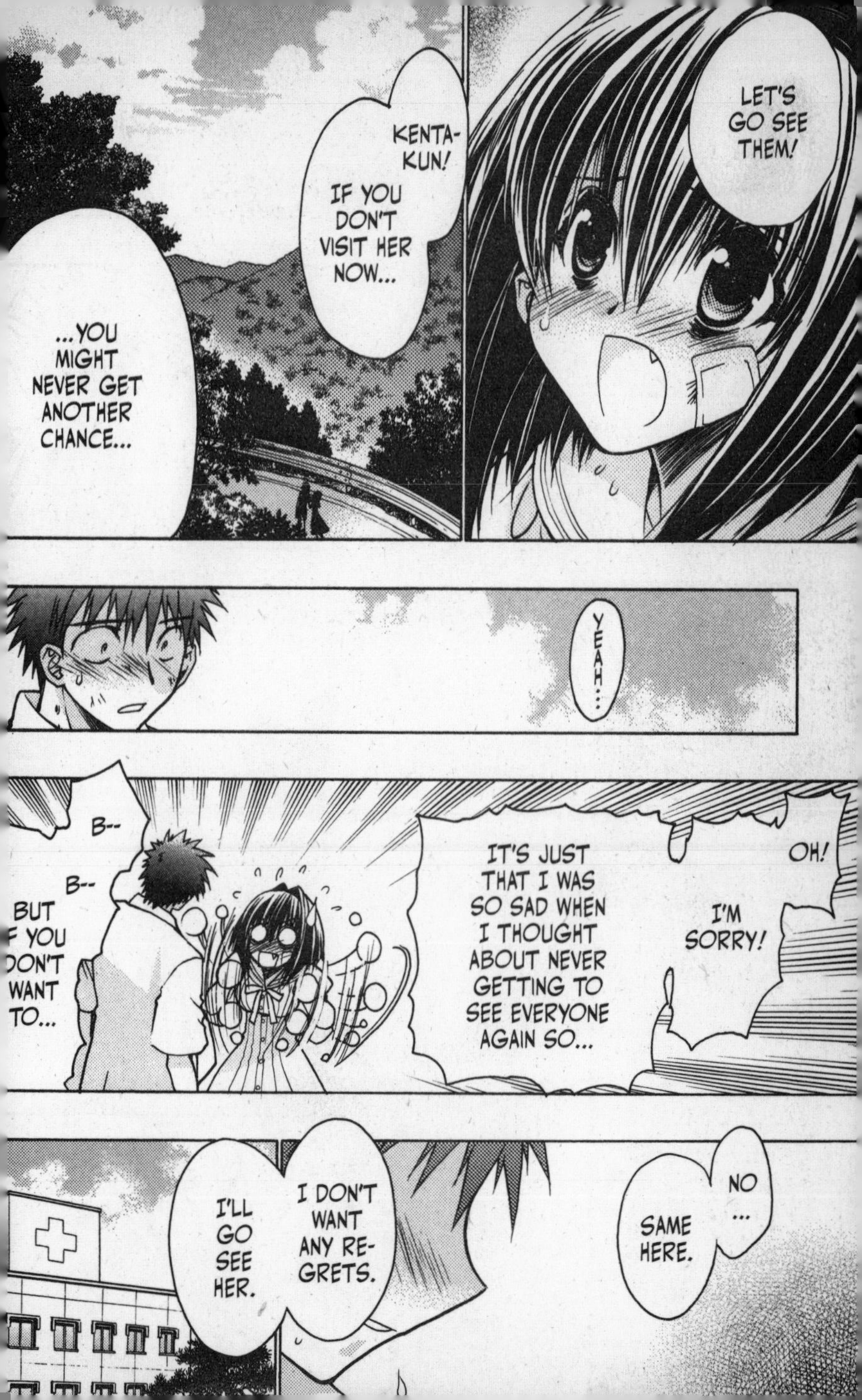

LET'S GO SEE THEM!
KENTA-KUN!
IF YOU DON'T VISIT HER NOW...
...YOU MIGHT NEVER GET ANOTHER CHANCE...
YEAH...
OH!
I'M SORRY!
IT'S JUST THAT I WAS SO SAD WHEN I THOUGHT ABOUT NEVER GETTING TO SEE EVERYONE AGAIN SO...
B--
B--
BUT F YOU DON'T WANT TO...
NO...
SAME HERE.
I DON'T WANT ANY RE-GRETS.
I'LL GO SEE HER.

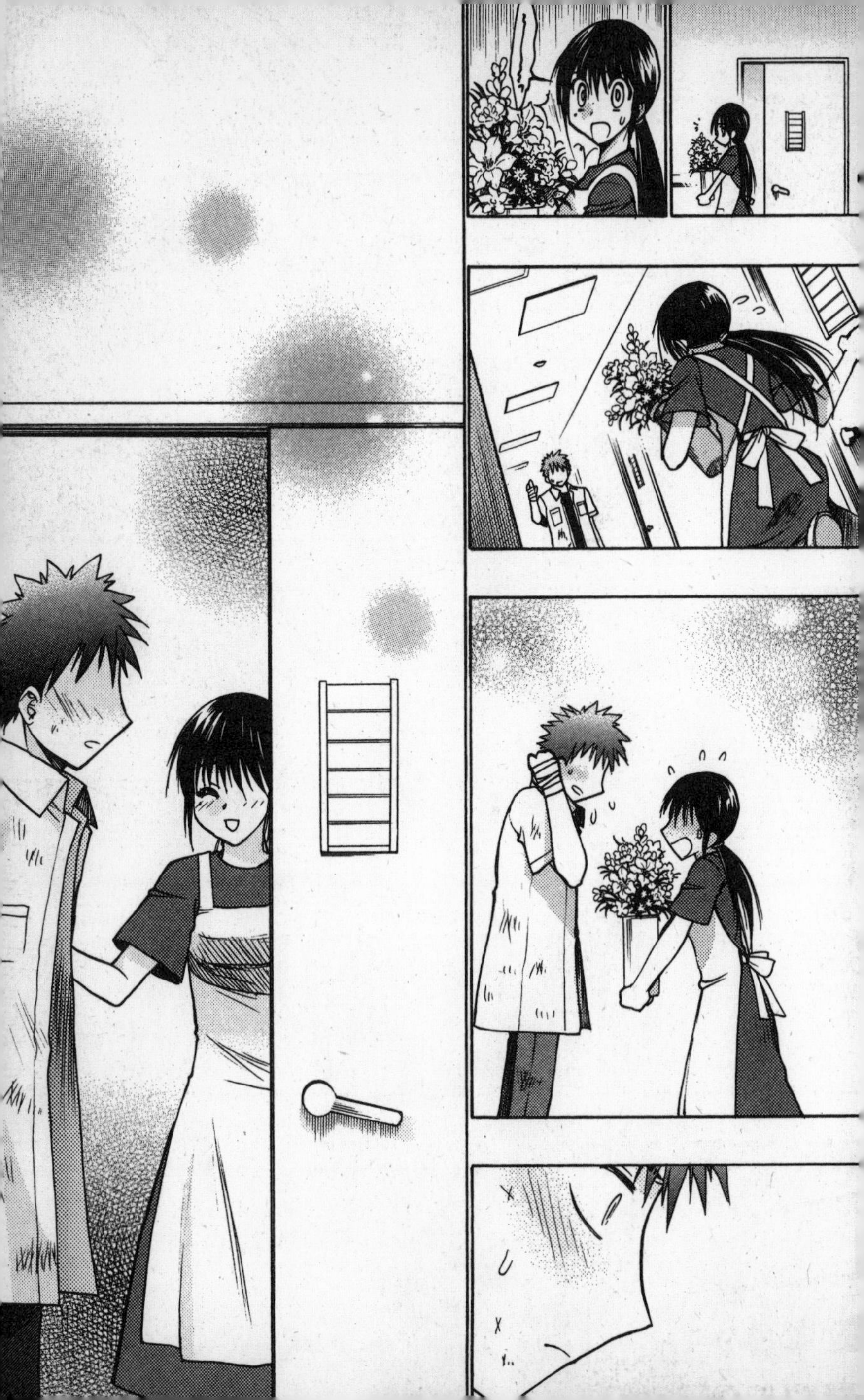

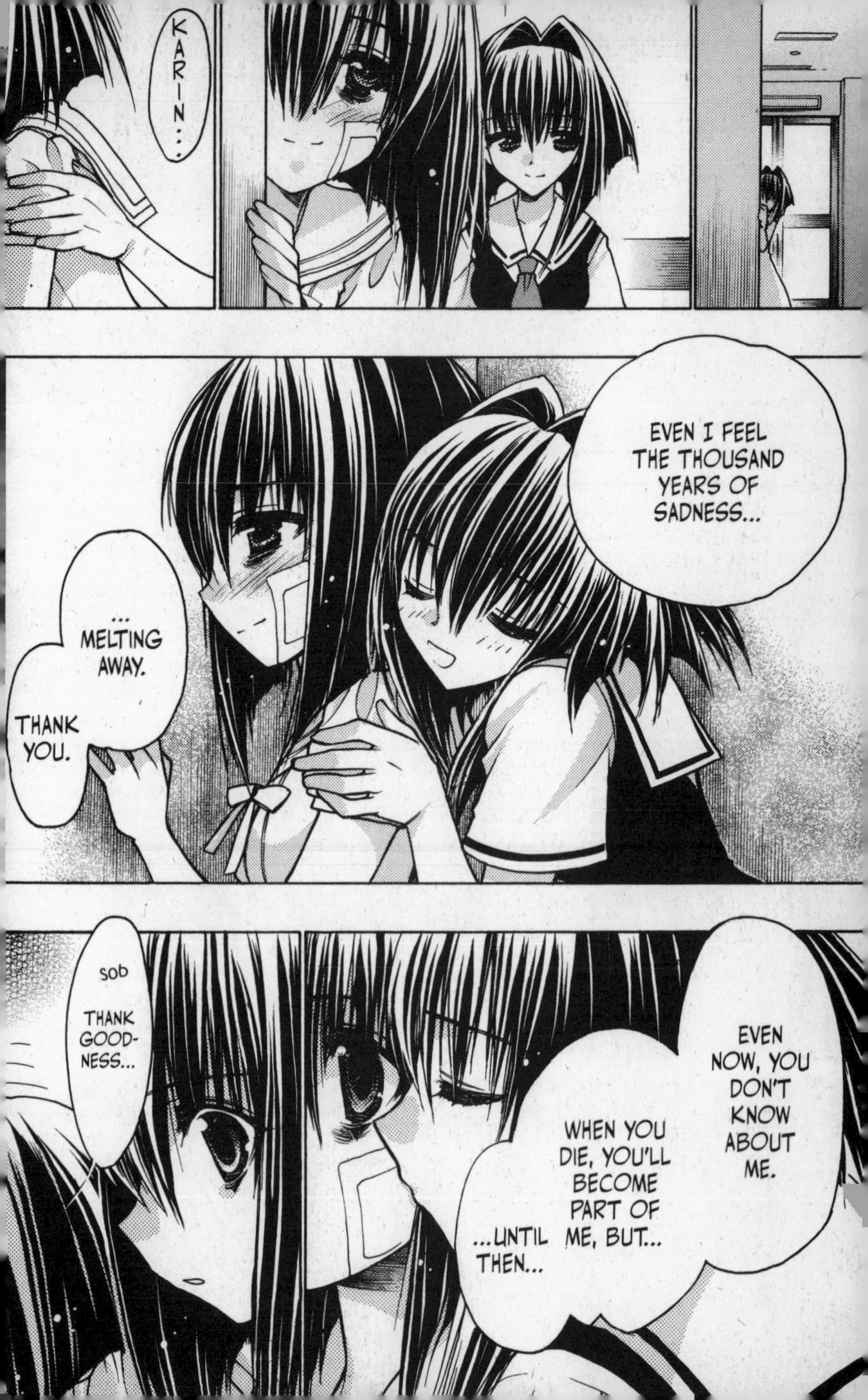
KARIN...
EVEN I FEEL THE THOUSAND YEARS OF SADNESS...
...MELTING AWAY.
THANK YOU.
EVEN NOW, YOU DON'T KNOW ABOUT ME.
WHEN YOU DIE, YOU'LL BECOME PART OF ME, BUT...
...UNTIL THEN...
sob
THANK GOOD-NESS...

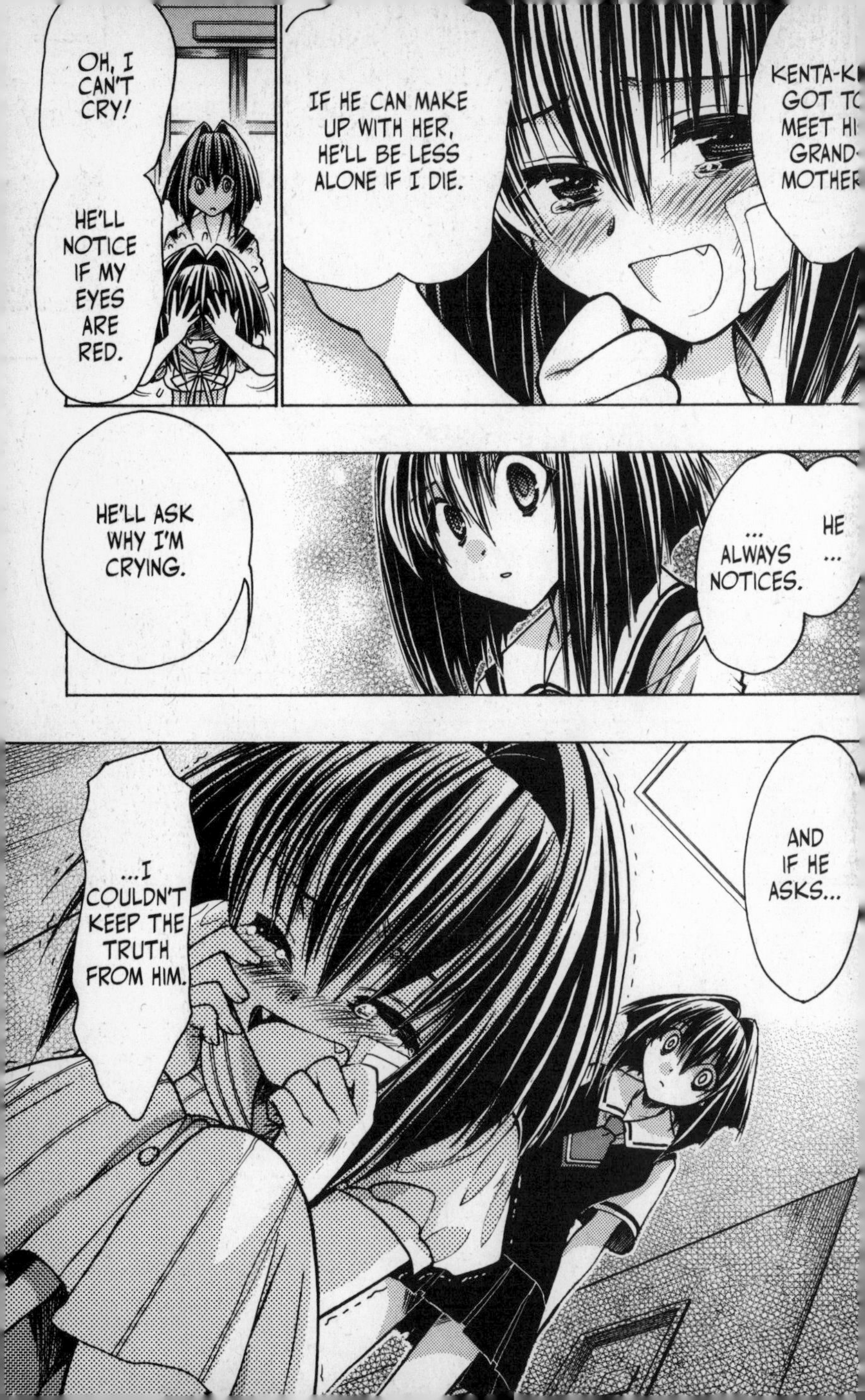
KENTA-K GOT T MEET HI GRAND-MOTHER
IF HE CAN MAKE UP WITH HER, HE'LL BE LESS ALONE IF I DIE.
OH, I CAN'T CRY!
HE'LL NOTICE IF MY EYES ARE RED.
HE ... ALWAYS NOTICES.
HE'LL ASK WHY I'M CRYING.
AND IF HE ASKS...
...I COULDN'T KEEP THE TRUTH FROM HIM.

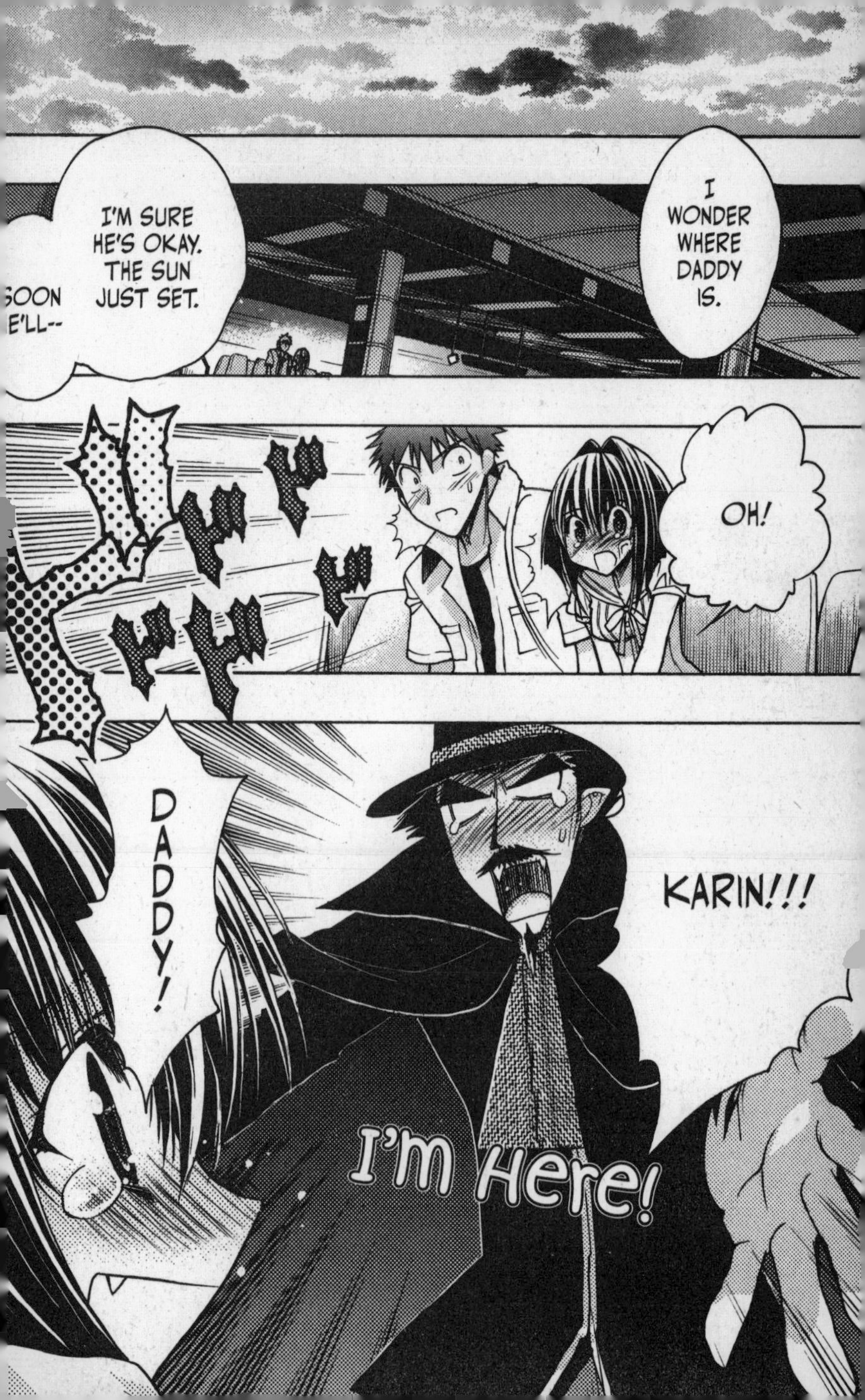
I WONDER WHERE DADDY IS.
I'M SURE HE'S OKAY. THE SUN JUST SET.
SOON E'LL--
OH!
KARIN!!!
DADDY!
I'm Here!

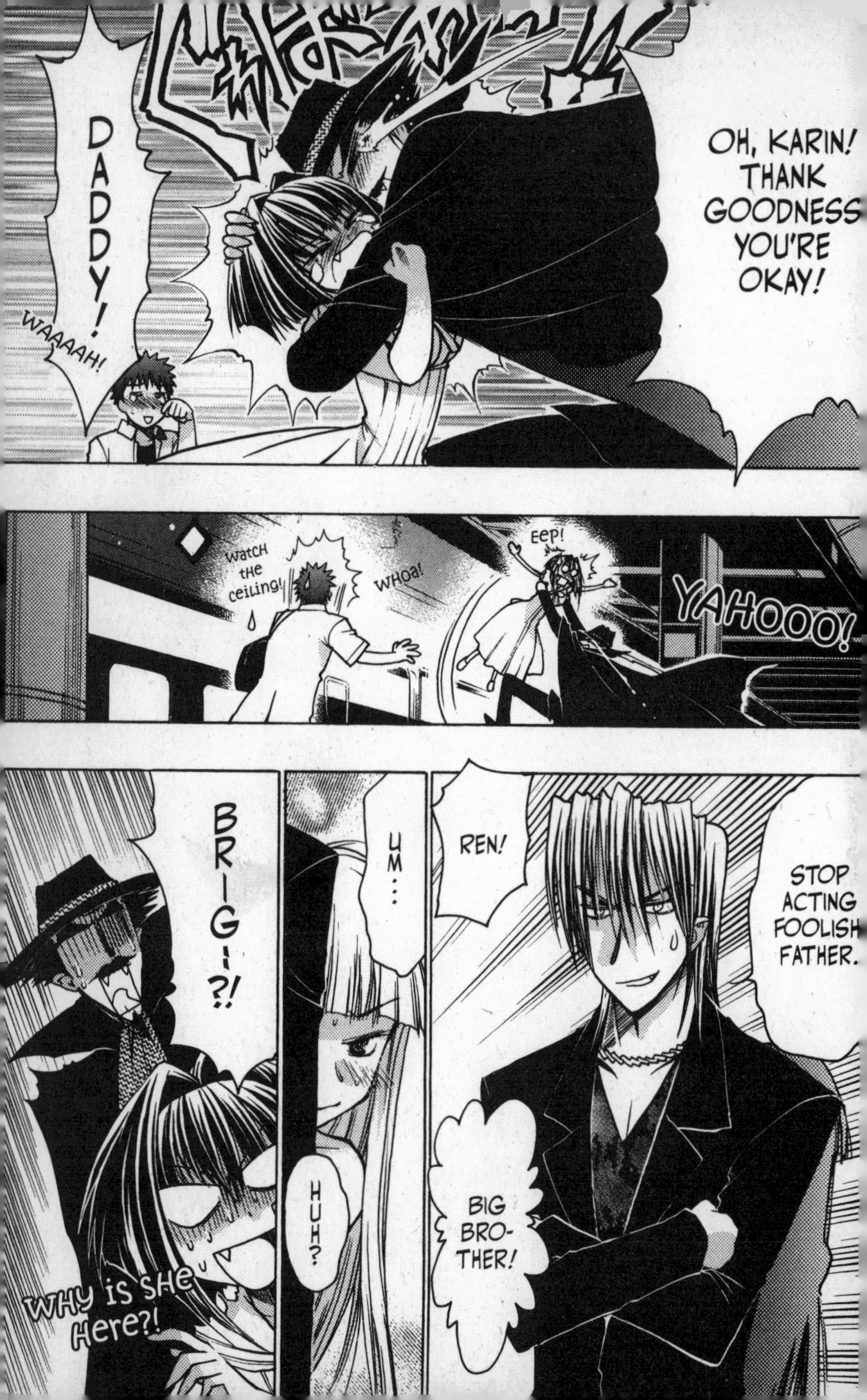
OH, KARIN! THANK GOODNESS YOU'RE OKAY!
DADDY!
WAAAAH!
YAHOOOO!
EEP!
WHOA!
WATCH THE CEILING!
STOP ACTING FOOLISH FATHER.
REN!
BIG BROTHER!
UM...
HUH?
BRIG-?!
WHY IS SHE HERE?!

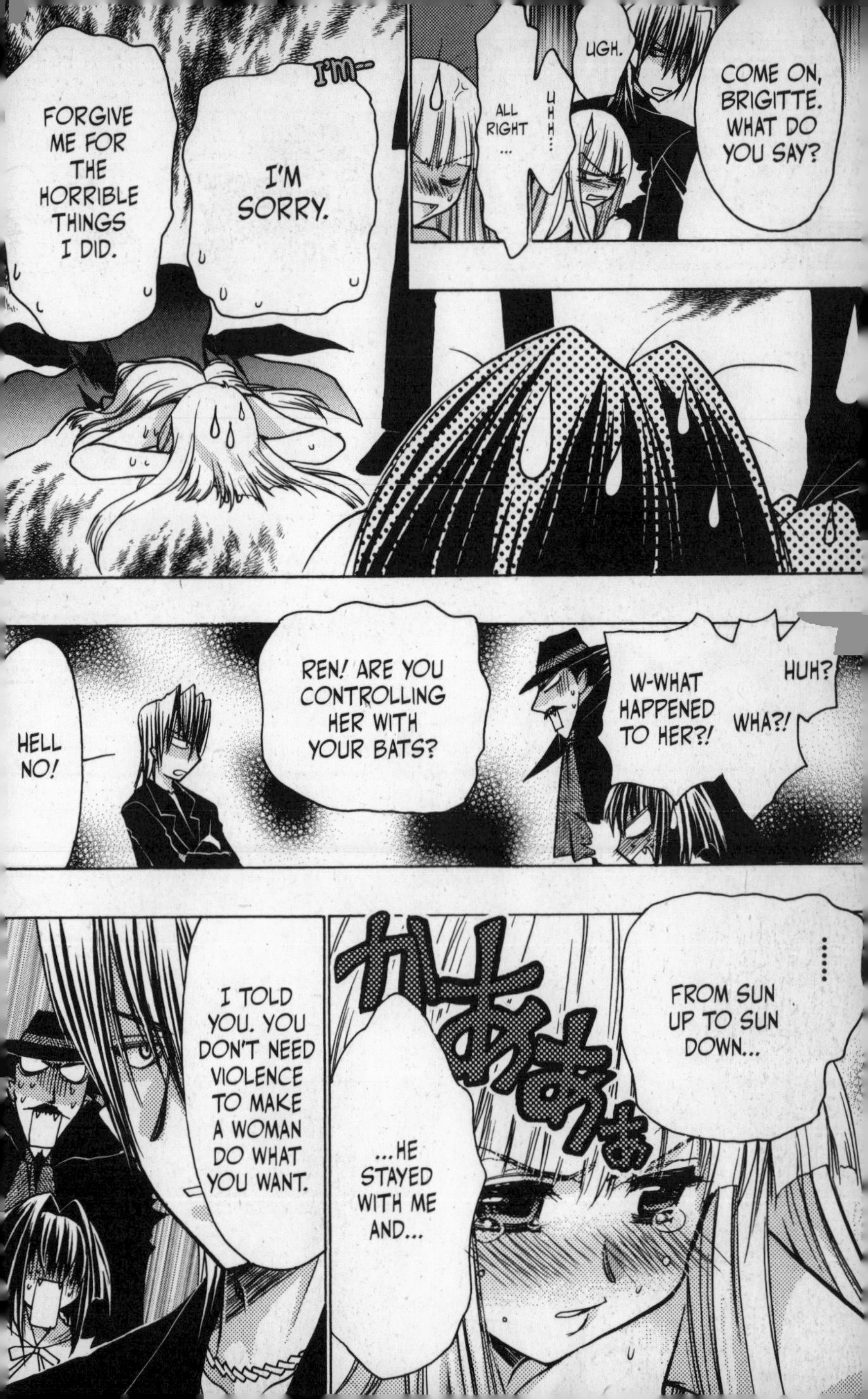
COME ON, BRIGITTE. WHAT DO YOU SAY?
UGH.
UHH...
ALL RIGHT...
I'M—
I'M SORRY.
FORGIVE ME FOR THE HORRIBLE THINGS I DID.
HUH?
WHA?!
W-WHAT HAPPENED TO HER?!
REN! ARE YOU CONTROLLING HER WITH YOUR BATS?
HELL NO!
......
FROM SUN UP TO SUN DOWN...
かあああ
...HE STAYED WITH ME AND...
I TOLD YOU. YOU DON'T NEED VIOLENCE TO MAKE A WOMAN DO WHAT YOU WANT.

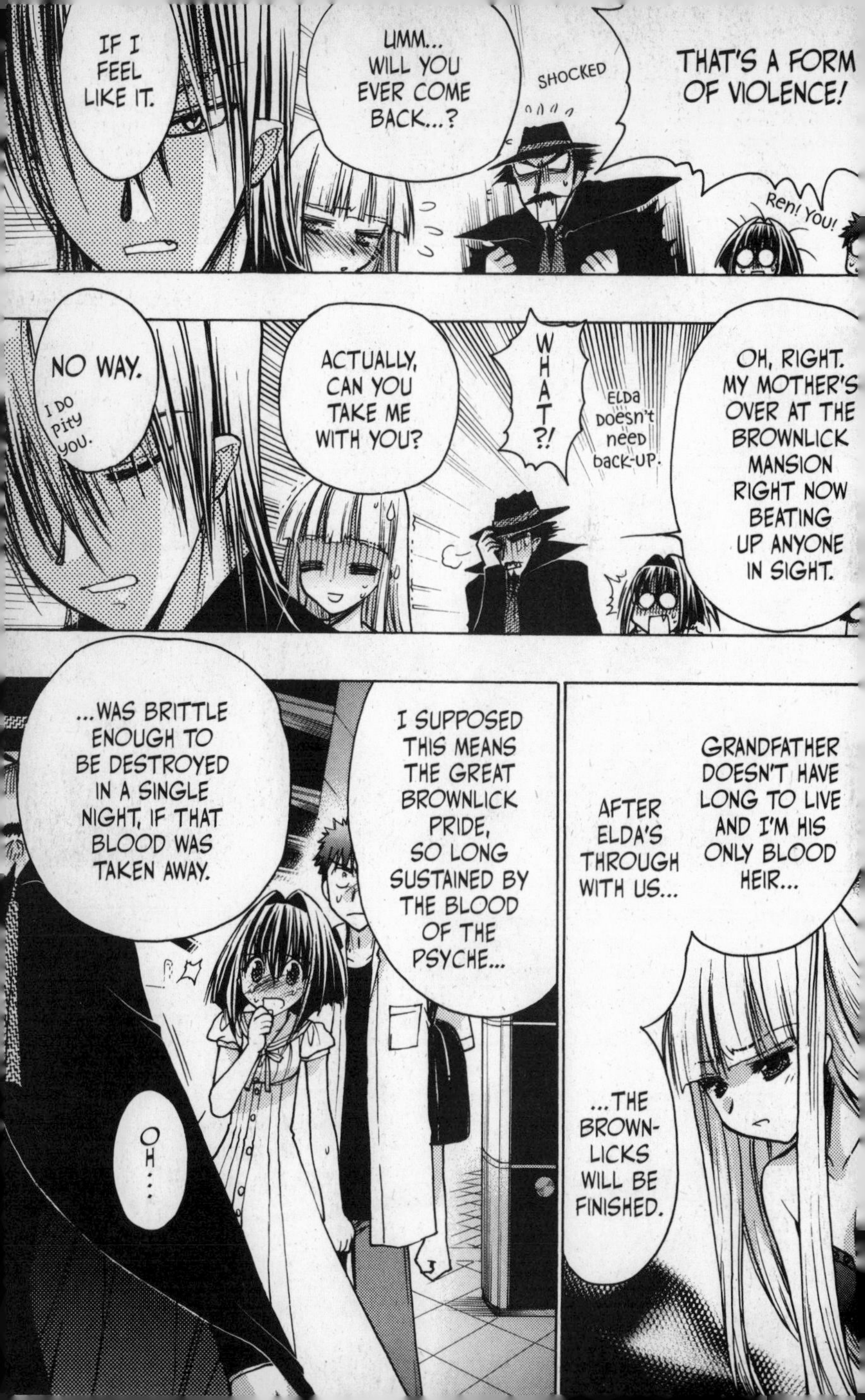
THAT'S A FORM OF VIOLENCE!
Ren! You!
SHOCKED
UMM... WILL YOU EVER COME BACK...?
IF I FEEL LIKE IT.
OH, RIGHT. MY MOTHER'S OVER AT THE BROWNLICK MANSION RIGHT NOW BEATING UP ANYONE IN SIGHT.
Elda doesn't need back-up.
WHAT?!
ACTUALLY, CAN YOU TAKE ME WITH YOU?
NO WAY.
I do pity you.
GRANDFATHER DOESN'T HAVE LONG TO LIVE AND I'M HIS ONLY BLOOD HEIR...
AFTER ELDA'S THROUGH WITH US...
...THE BROWN-LICKS WILL BE FINISHED.
I SUPPOSED THIS MEANS THE GREAT BROWNLICK PRIDE, SO LONG SUSTAINED BY THE BLOOD OF THE PSYCHE...
...WAS BRITTLE ENOUGH TO BE DESTROYED IN A SINGLE NIGHT, IF THAT BLOOD WAS TAKEN AWAY.
OH...

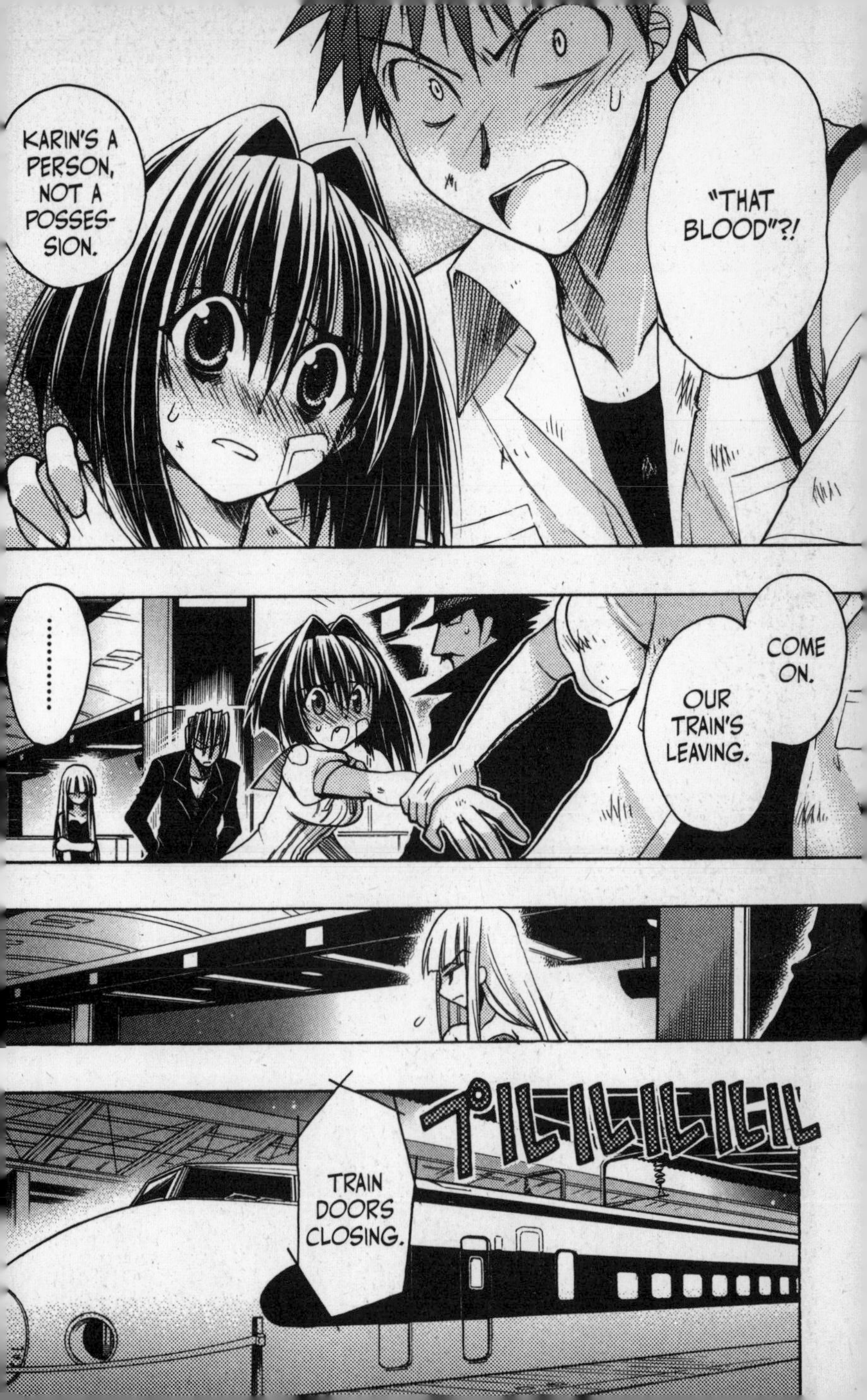
"THAT BLOOD"?!
KARIN'S A PERSON, NOT A POSSES-SION.
COME ON.
OUR TRAIN'S LEAVING.
....
TRAIN DOORS CLOSING.

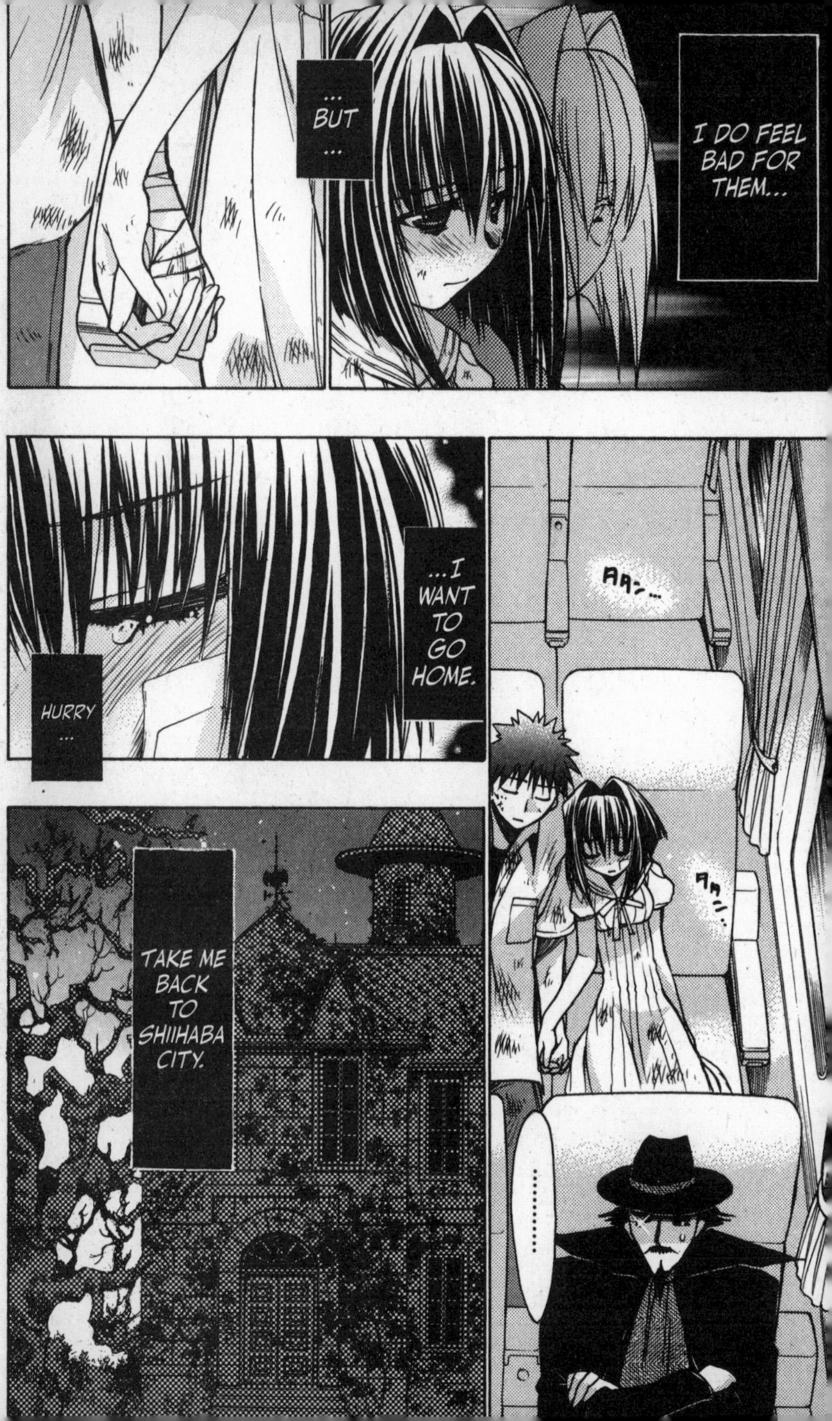

I DO FEEL BAD FOR THEM...
...BUT...
タタン…
タタン…
……
...I WANT TO GO HOME.
HURRY...
TAKE ME BACK TO SHIIHABA CITY.

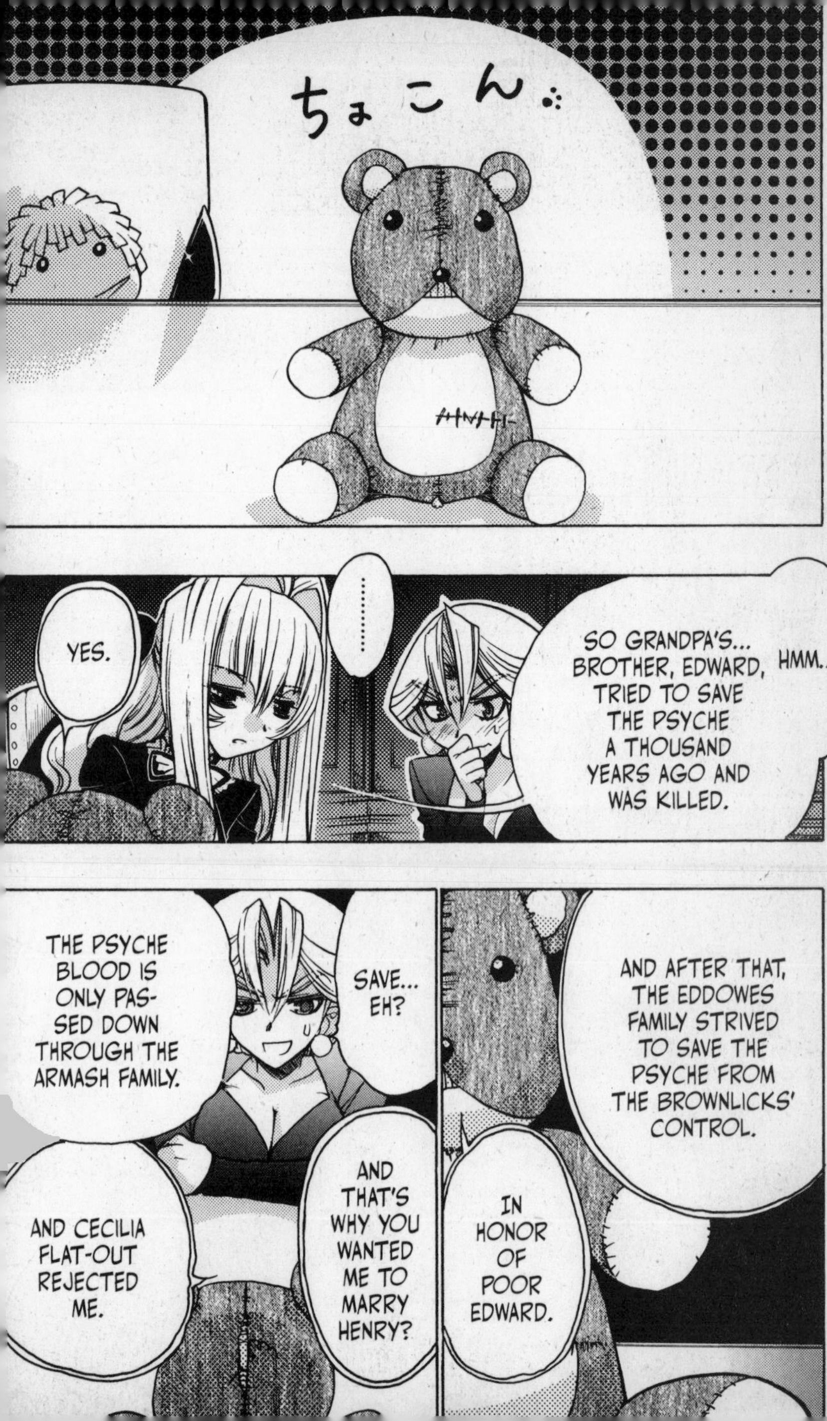
ちょこん
HMM...
SO GRANDPA'S... BROTHER, EDWARD, TRIED TO SAVE THE PSYCHE A THOUSAND YEARS AGO AND WAS KILLED.
......
YES.
AND AFTER THAT, THE EDDOWES FAMILY STRIVED TO SAVE THE PSYCHE FROM THE BROWNLICKS' CONTROL.
IN HONOR OF POOR EDWARD.
SAVE... EH?
THE PSYCHE BLOOD IS ONLY PAS-SED DOWN THROUGH THE ARMASH FAMILY.
AND THAT'S WHY YOU WANTED ME TO MARRY HENRY?
AND CECILIA FLAT-OUT REJECTED ME.

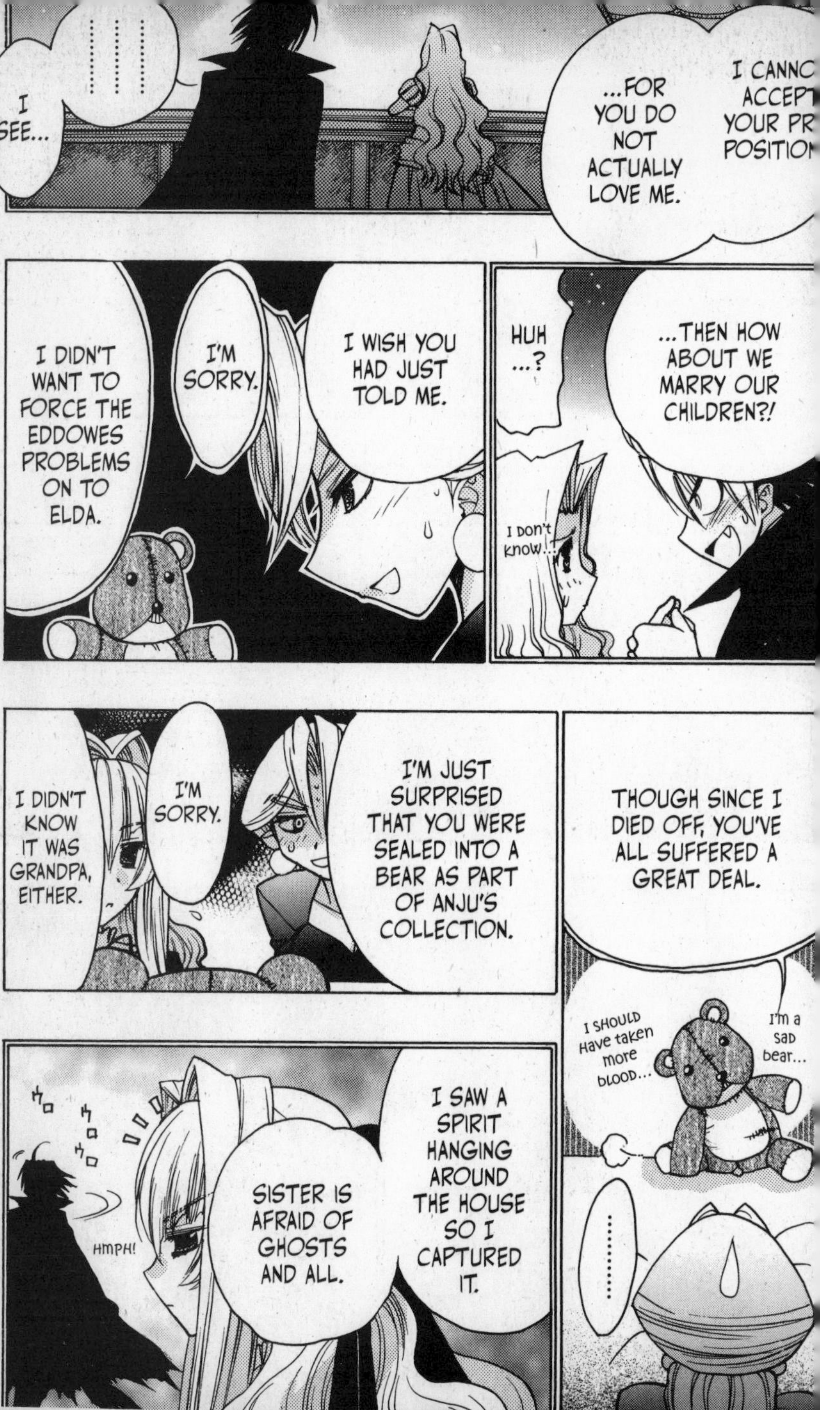
I CANN ACCEP YOUR P POSITIO
...FOR YOU DO NOT ACTUALLY LOVE ME.
......
I SEE...
...THEN HOW ABOUT WE MARRY OUR CHILDREN?!
HUH ...?
I Don't know...
I WISH YOU HAD JUST TOLD ME.
I'M SORRY.
I DIDN'T WANT TO FORCE THE EDDOWES PROBLEMS ON TO ELDA.
THOUGH SINCE I DIED OFF, YOU'VE ALL SUFFERED A GREAT DEAL.
I'm a sad bear...
I SHOULD Have taken more blood...
......
I'M JUST SURPRISED THAT YOU WERE SEALED INTO A BEAR AS PART OF ANJU'S COLLECTION.
I'M SORRY.
I DIDN'T KNOW IT WAS GRANDPA, EITHER.
I SAW A SPIRIT HANGING AROUND THE HOUSE SO I CAPTURED IT.
SISTER IS AFRAID OF GHOSTS AND ALL.
HMPH!

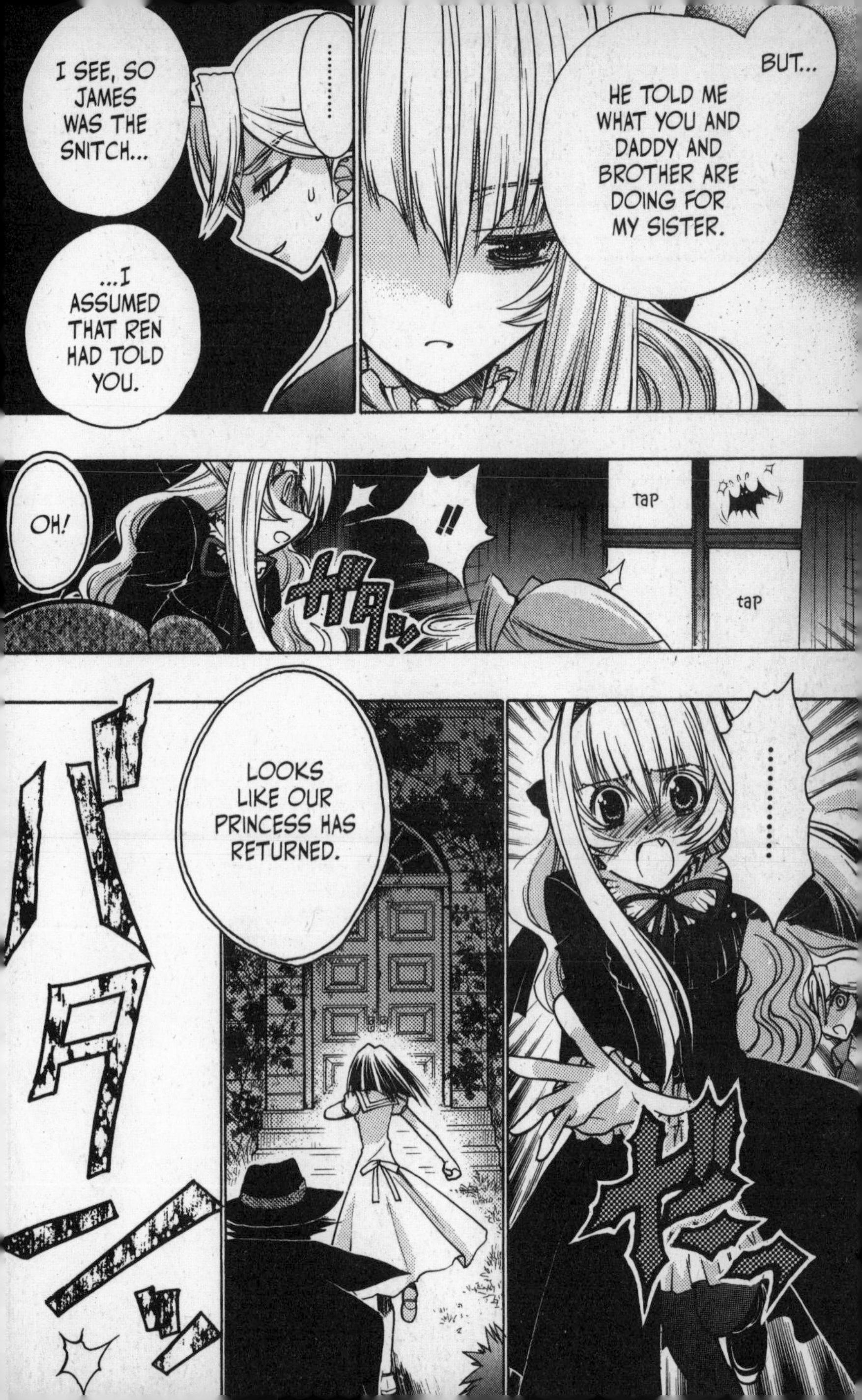
BUT...
HE TOLD ME WHAT YOU AND DADDY AND BROTHER ARE DOING FOR MY SISTER.
......
I SEE, SO JAMES WAS THE SNITCH...
...I ASSUMED THAT REN HAD TOLD YOU.
tap
tap
!!
OH!
......
LOOKS LIKE OUR PRINCESS HAS RETURNED.

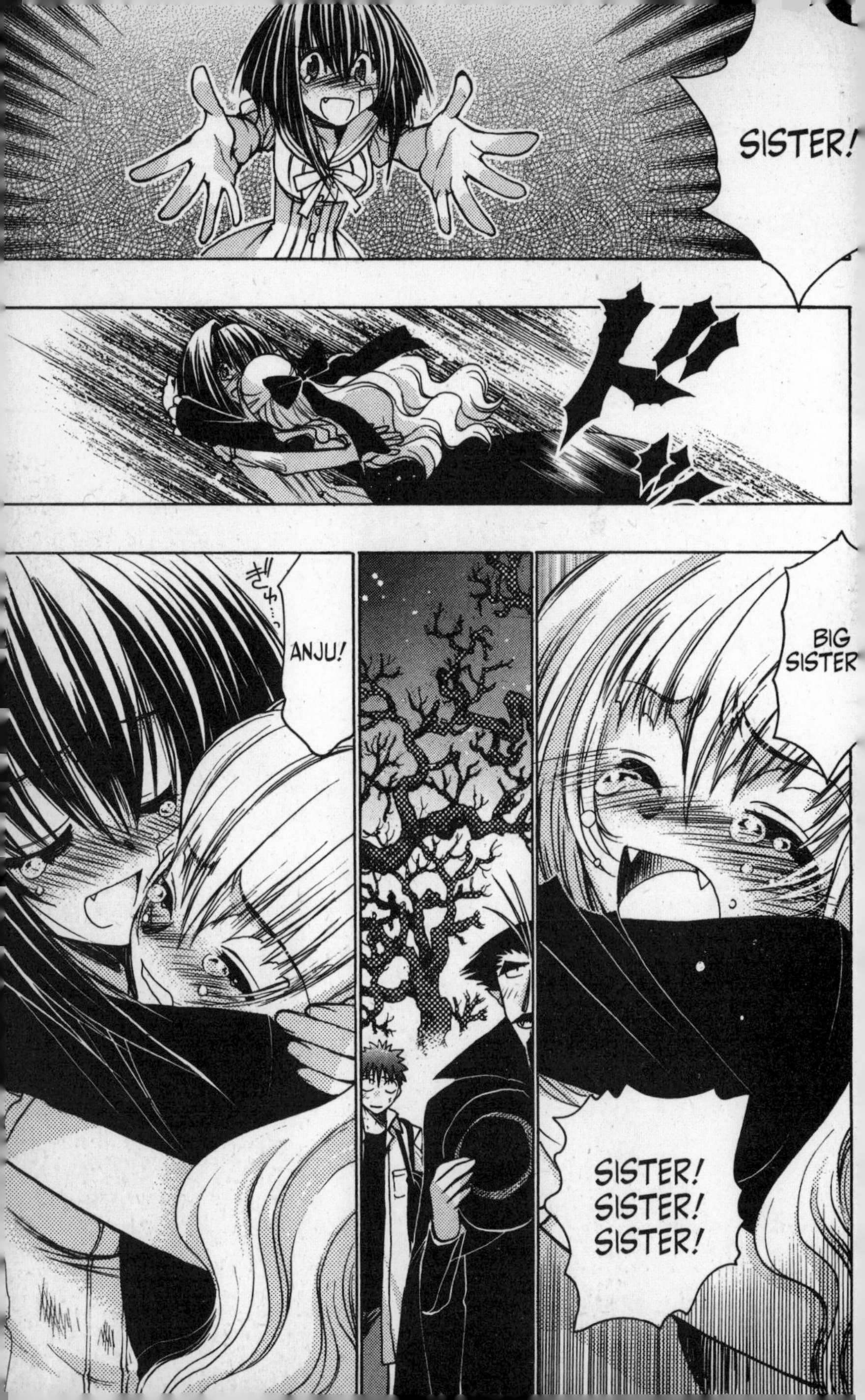
SISTER!
BIG SISTER
SISTER! SISTER! SISTER!
ANJU!
ぎゅ…っ

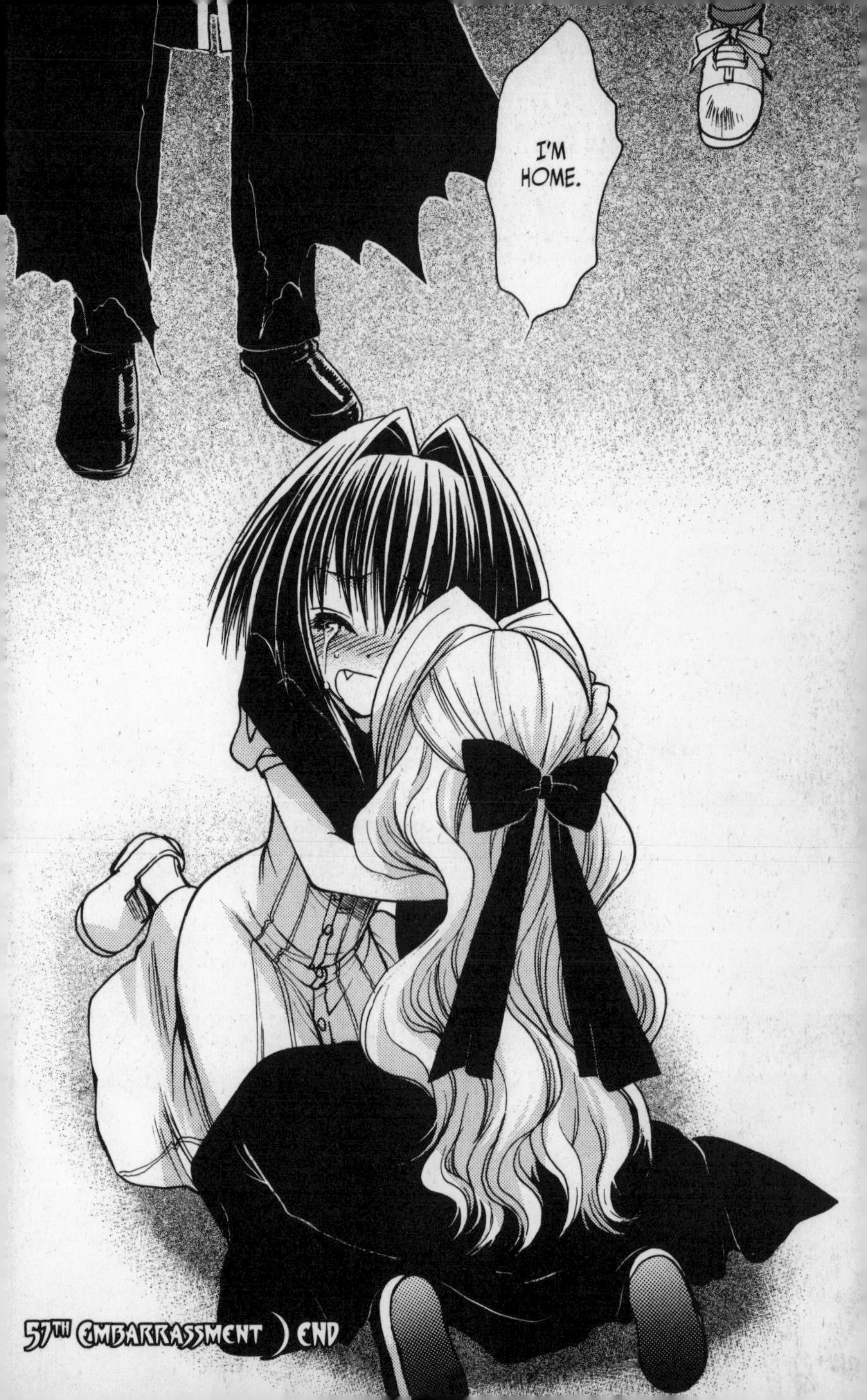
I'M HOME.
57TH EMBARRASSMENT) END

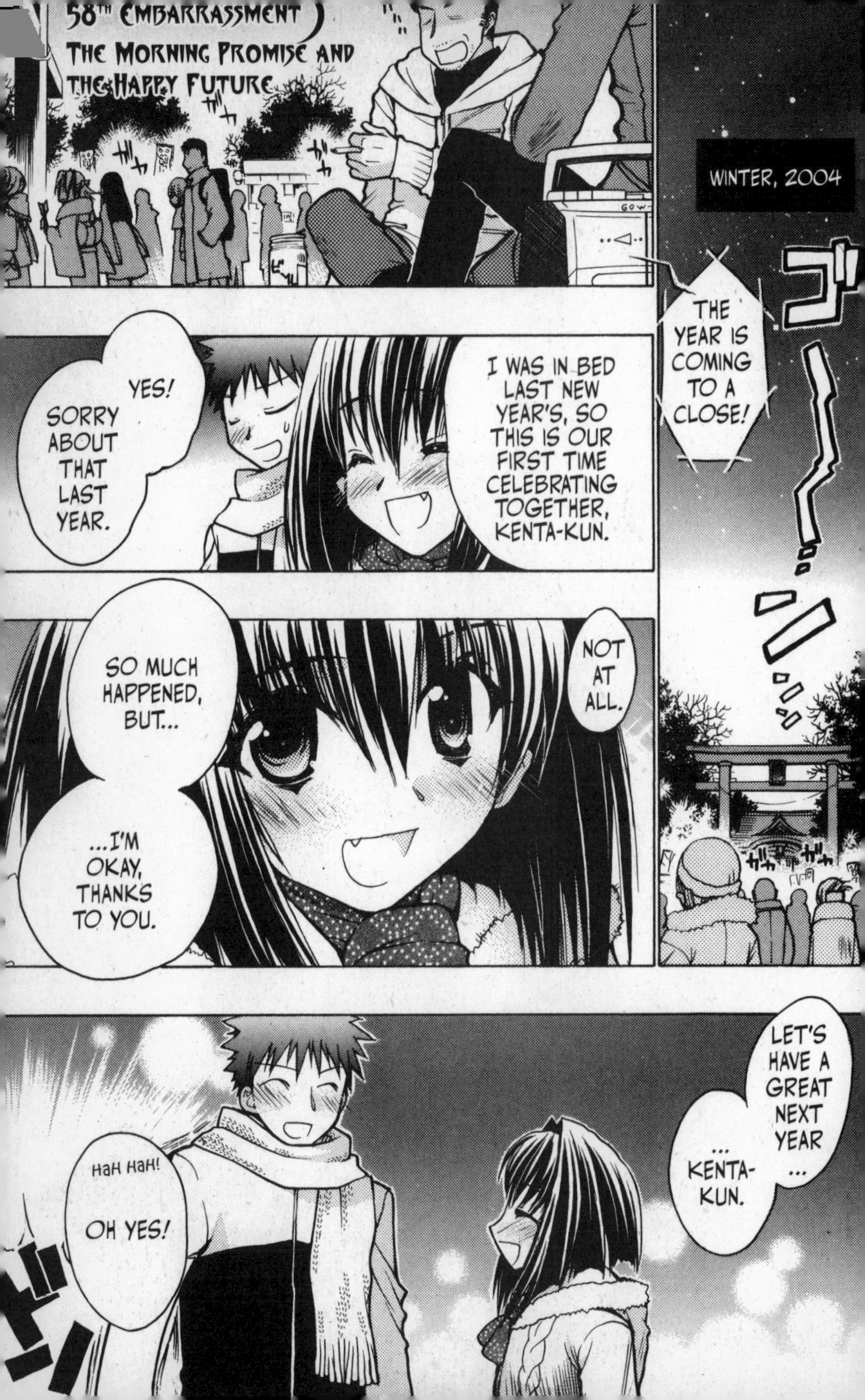
WINTER, 2004
THE YEAR IS COMING TO A CLOSE!
58TH EMBARRASSMENT
THE MORNING PROMISE AND THE HAPPY FUTURE
I WAS IN BED LAST NEW YEAR'S, SO THIS IS OUR FIRST TIME CELEBRATING TOGETHER, KENTA-KUN.
YES! SORRY ABOUT THAT LAST YEAR.
NOT AT ALL.
SO MUCH HAPPENED, BUT...
...I'M OKAY, THANKS TO YOU.
LET'S HAVE A GREAT NEXT YEAR... ...KENTA-KUN.
HAH HAH!
OH YES!

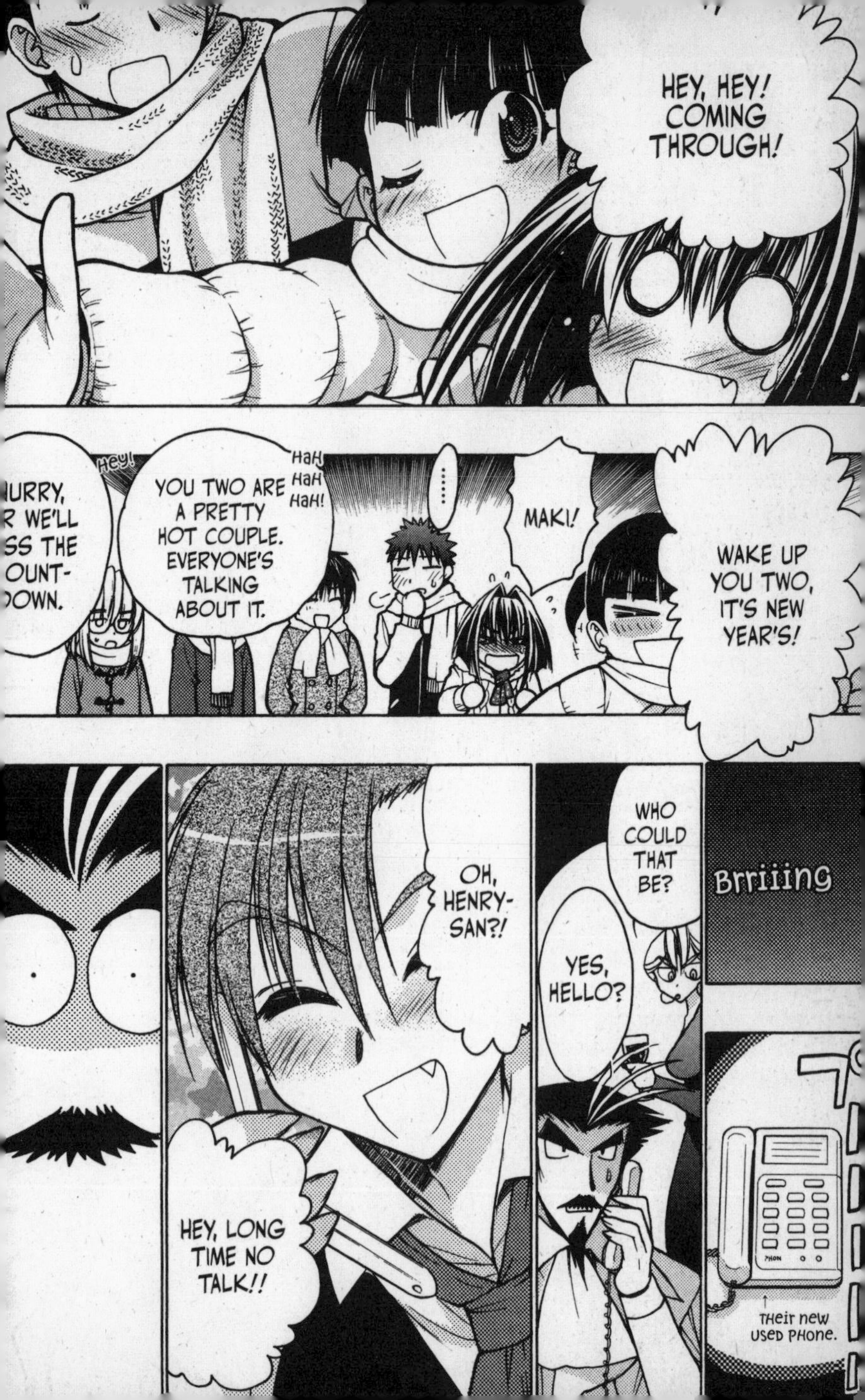
HEY, HEY! COMING THROUGH!
WAKE UP YOU TWO, IT'S NEW YEAR'S!
MAKI!
......
HaH HaH HaH!
YOU TWO ARE A PRETTY HOT COUPLE. EVERYONE'S TALKING ABOUT IT.
HEY!
URRY, R WE'LL SS THE OUNT- OWN.
Brriiing
Their new used phone.
WHO COULD THAT BE?
YES, HELLO?
OH, HENRY-SAN?!
HEY, LONG TIME NO TALK!!

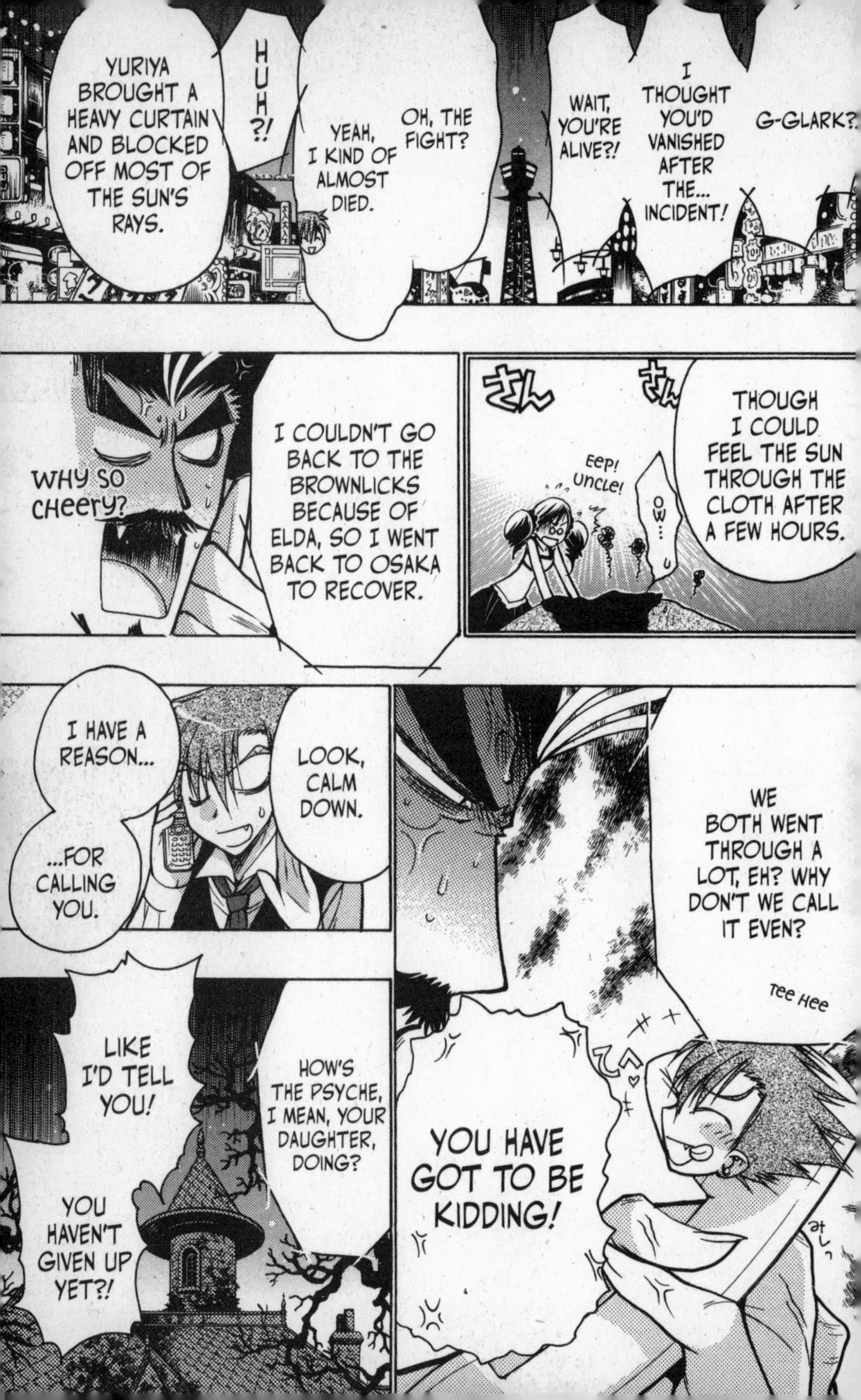
G-GLARK?!
I THOUGHT YOU'D VANISHED AFTER THE... INCIDENT!
WAIT, YOU'RE ALIVE?!
OH, THE FIGHT?
YEAH, I KIND OF ALMOST DIED.
HUH?!
YURIYA BROUGHT A HEAVY CURTAIN AND BLOCKED OFF MOST OF THE SUN'S RAYS.
さん
さん
THOUGH I COULD FEEL THE SUN THROUGH THE CLOTH AFTER A FEW HOURS.
OW...
Eep! Uncle!
I COULDN'T GO BACK TO THE BROWNLICKS BECAUSE OF ELDA, SO I WENT BACK TO OSAKA TO RECOVER.
WHY SO CHEERY?
WE BOTH WENT THROUGH A LOT, EH? WHY DON'T WE CALL IT EVEN?
Tee Hee
YOU HAVE GOT TO BE KIDDING!
LOOK, CALM DOWN.
I HAVE A REASON...
...FOR CALLING YOU.
HOW'S THE PSYCHE, I MEAN, YOUR DAUGHTER, DOING?
LIKE I'D TELL YOU!
YOU HAVEN'T GIVEN UP YET?!

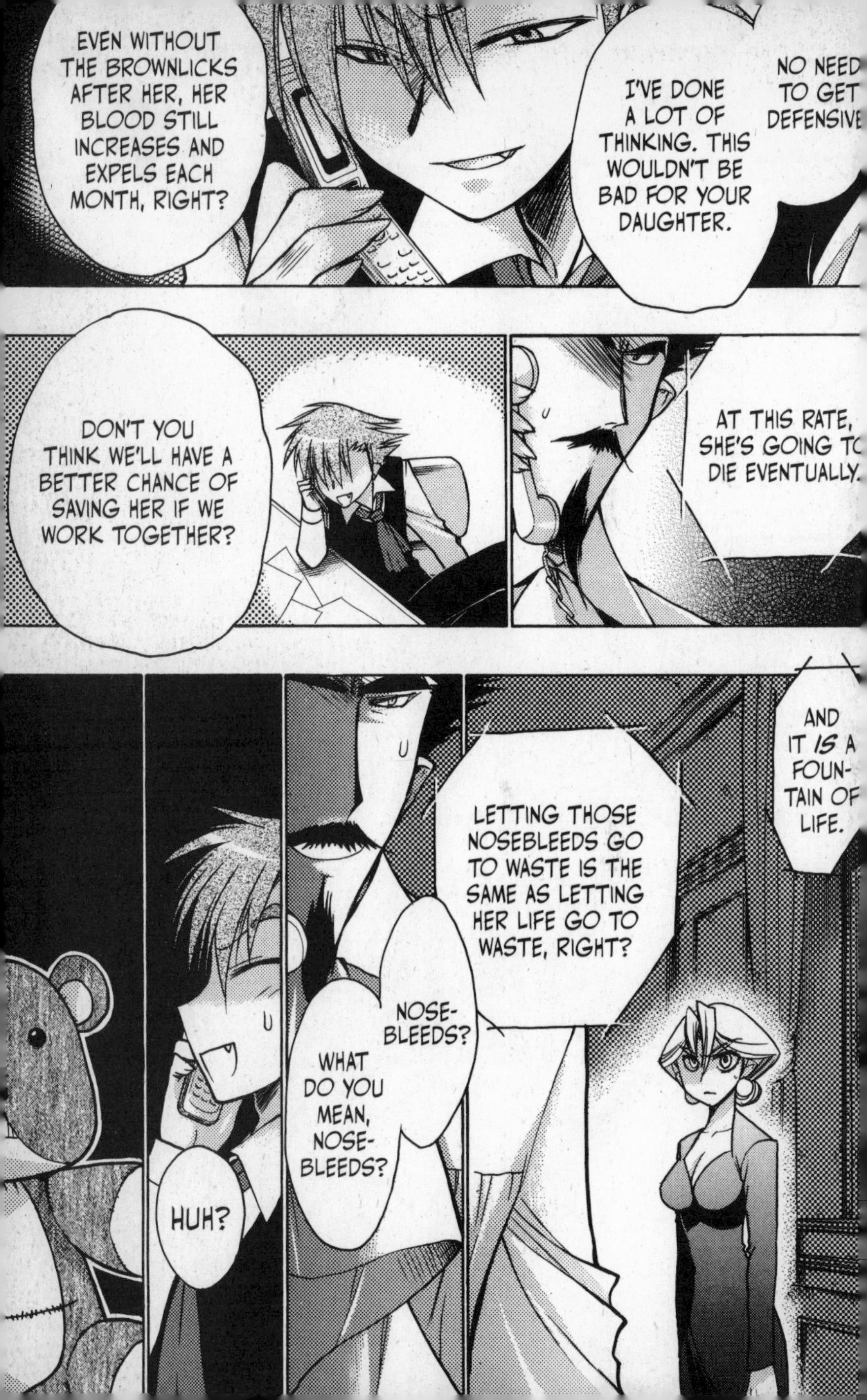
NO NEED TO GET DEFENSIVE
I'VE DONE A LOT OF THINKING. THIS WOULDN'T BE BAD FOR YOUR DAUGHTER.
EVEN WITHOUT THE BROWNLICKS AFTER HER, HER BLOOD STILL INCREASES AND EXPELS EACH MONTH, RIGHT?
AT THIS RATE, SHE'S GOING TO DIE EVENTUALLY.
DON'T YOU THINK WE'LL HAVE A BETTER CHANCE OF SAVING HER IF WE WORK TOGETHER?
AND IT *IS* A FOUN-TAIN OF LIFE.
LETTING THOSE NOSEBLEEDS GO TO WASTE IS THE SAME AS LETTING HER LIFE GO TO WASTE, RIGHT?
NOSE-BLEEDS?
WHAT DO YOU MEAN, NOSE-BLEEDS?
HUH?

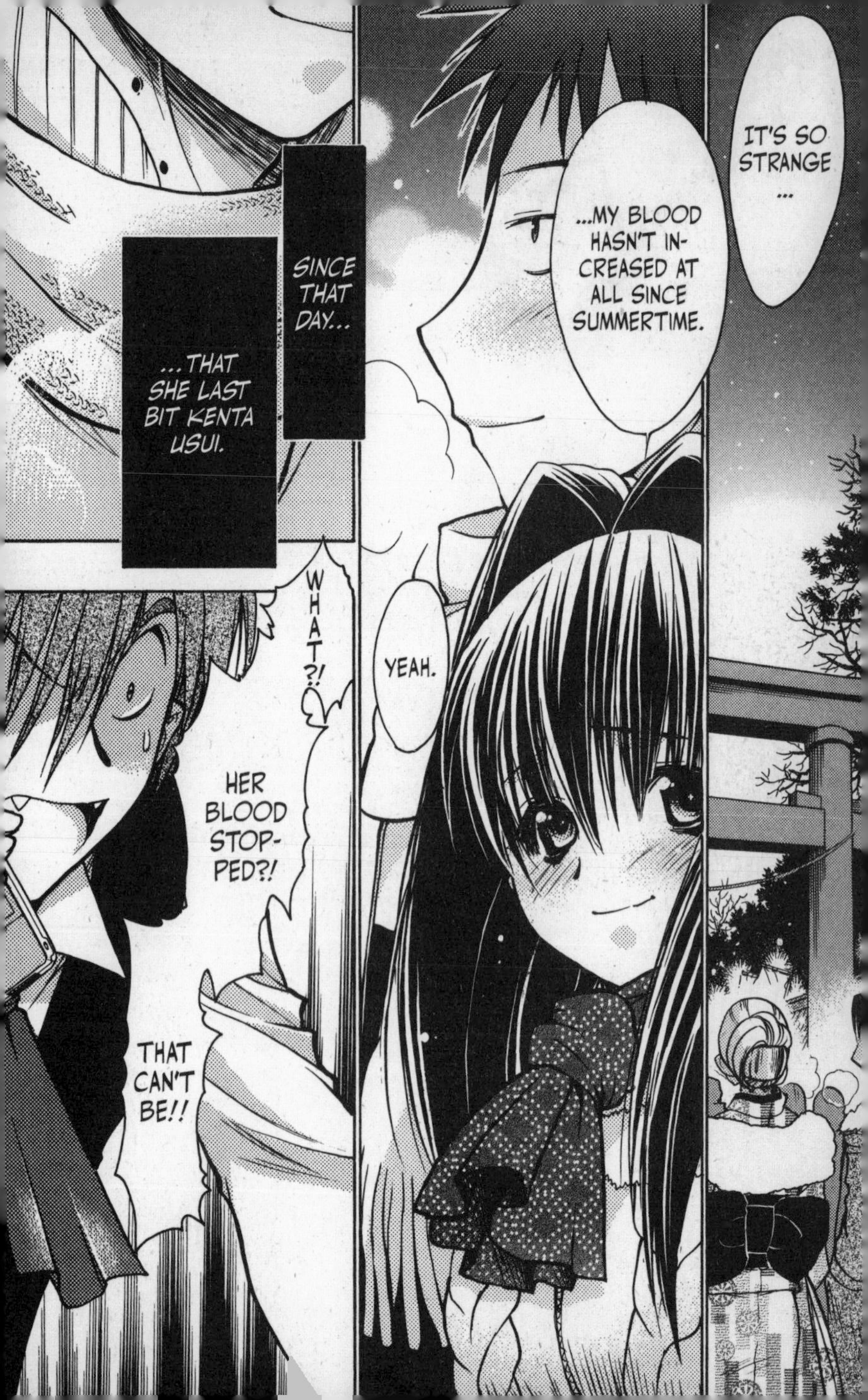
IT'S SO STRANGE ...
...MY BLOOD HASN'T IN-CREASED AT ALL SINCE SUMMERTIME.
YEAH.
SINCE THAT DAY...
...THAT SHE LAST BIT KENTA USUI.
WHAT?!
HER BLOOD STOP-PED?!
THAT CAN'T BE!!

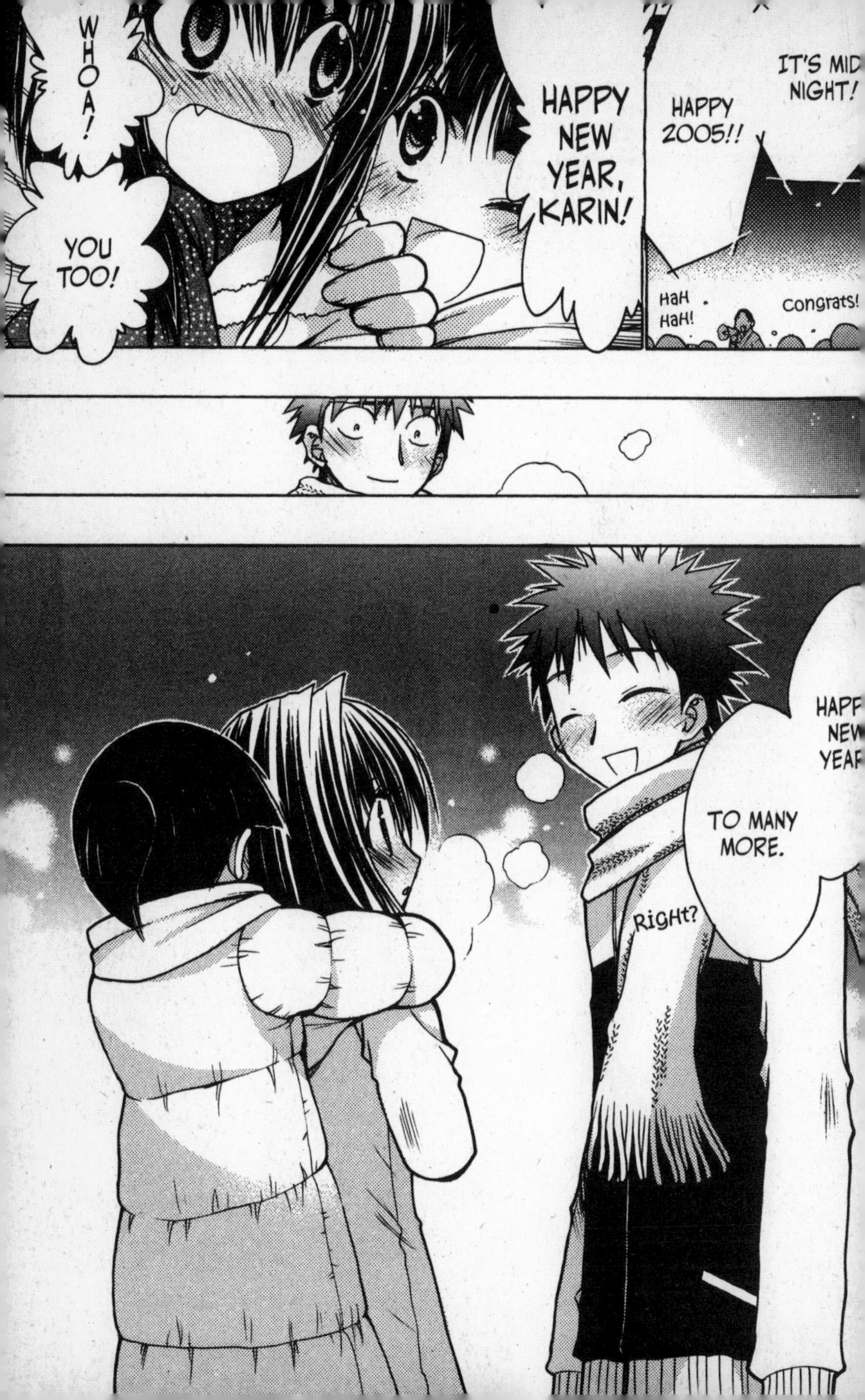
IT'S MID NIGHT!
HAPPY 2005!!
HaH HaH!
Congrats!
HAPPY NEW YEAR, KARIN!
WHOA!
YOU TOO!
HAPP NEW YEA
TO MANY MORE.
RiGHt?

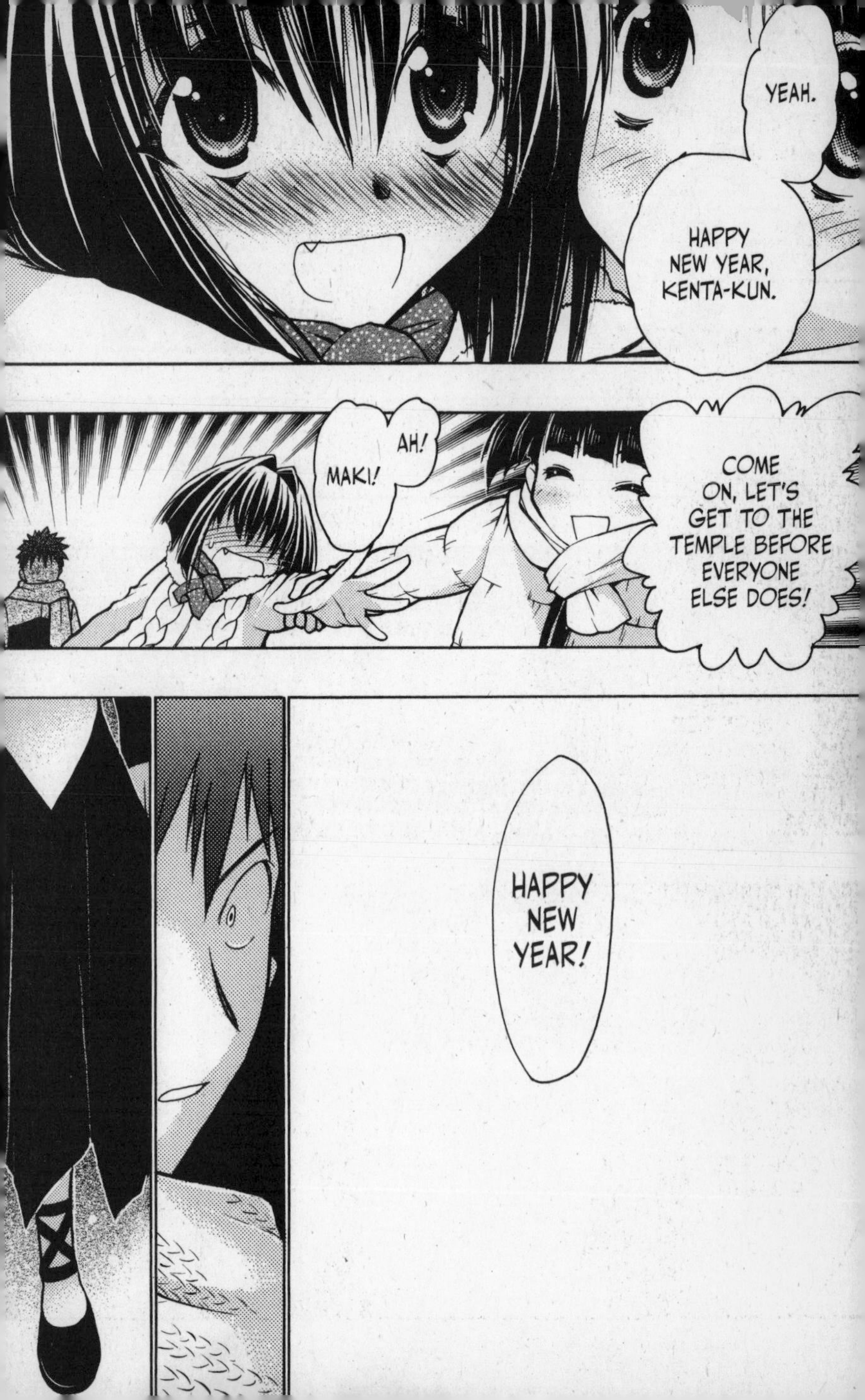
YEAH.
HAPPY NEW YEAR, KENTA-KUN.
COME ON, LET'S GET TO THE TEMPLE BEFORE EVERYONE ELSE DOES!
AH! MAKI!
HAPPY NEW YEAR!

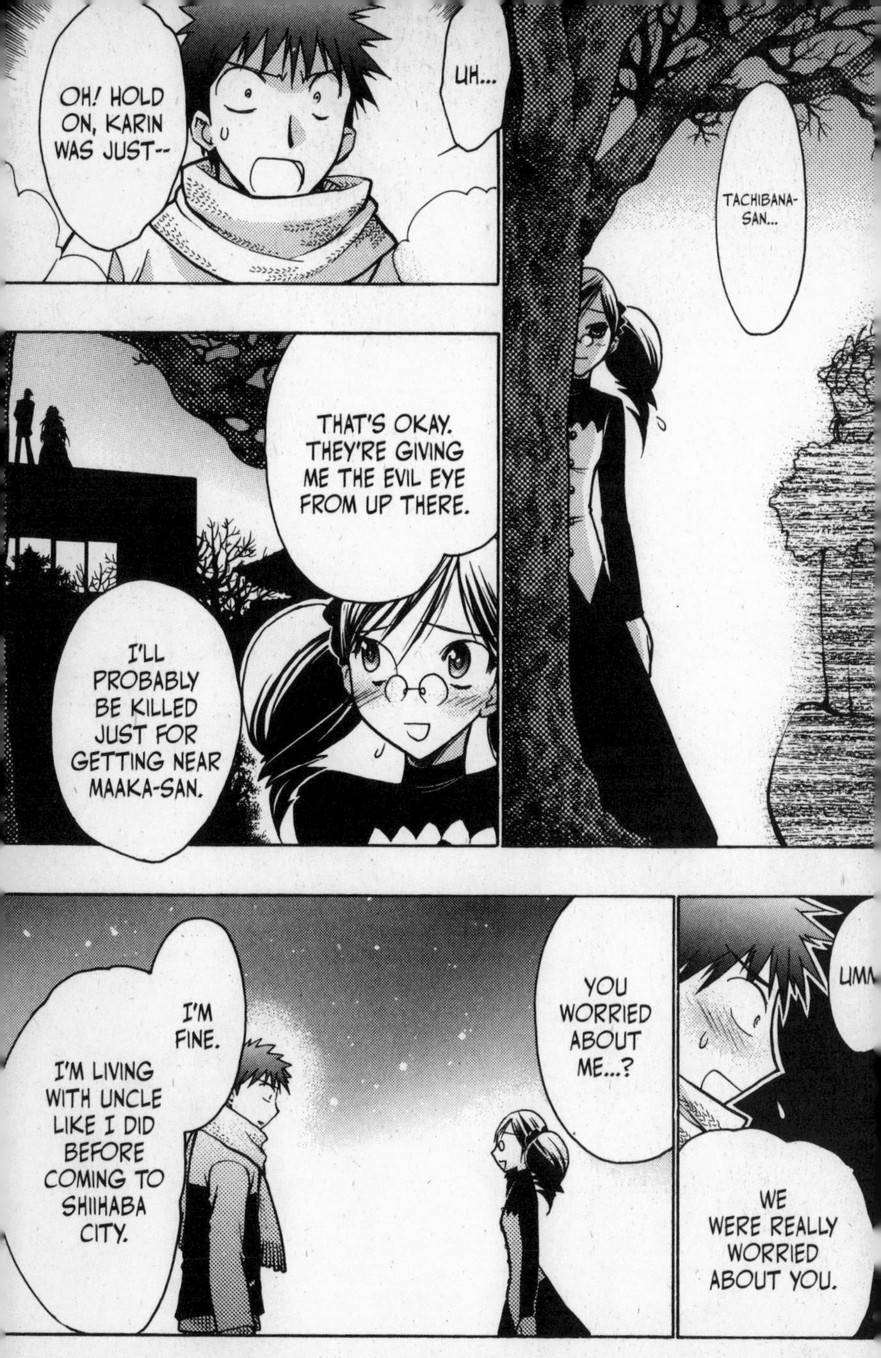
TACHIBANA-SAN...
UH...
OH! HOLD ON, KARIN WAS JUST--
THAT'S OKAY. THEY'RE GIVING ME THE EVIL EYE FROM UP THERE.
I'LL PROBABLY BE KILLED JUST FOR GETTING NEAR MAAKA-SAN.
UMM
WE WERE REALLY WORRIED ABOUT YOU.
YOU WORRIED ABOUT ME...?
I'M FINE.
I'M LIVING WITH UNCLE LIKE I DID BEFORE COMING TO SHIIHABA CITY.

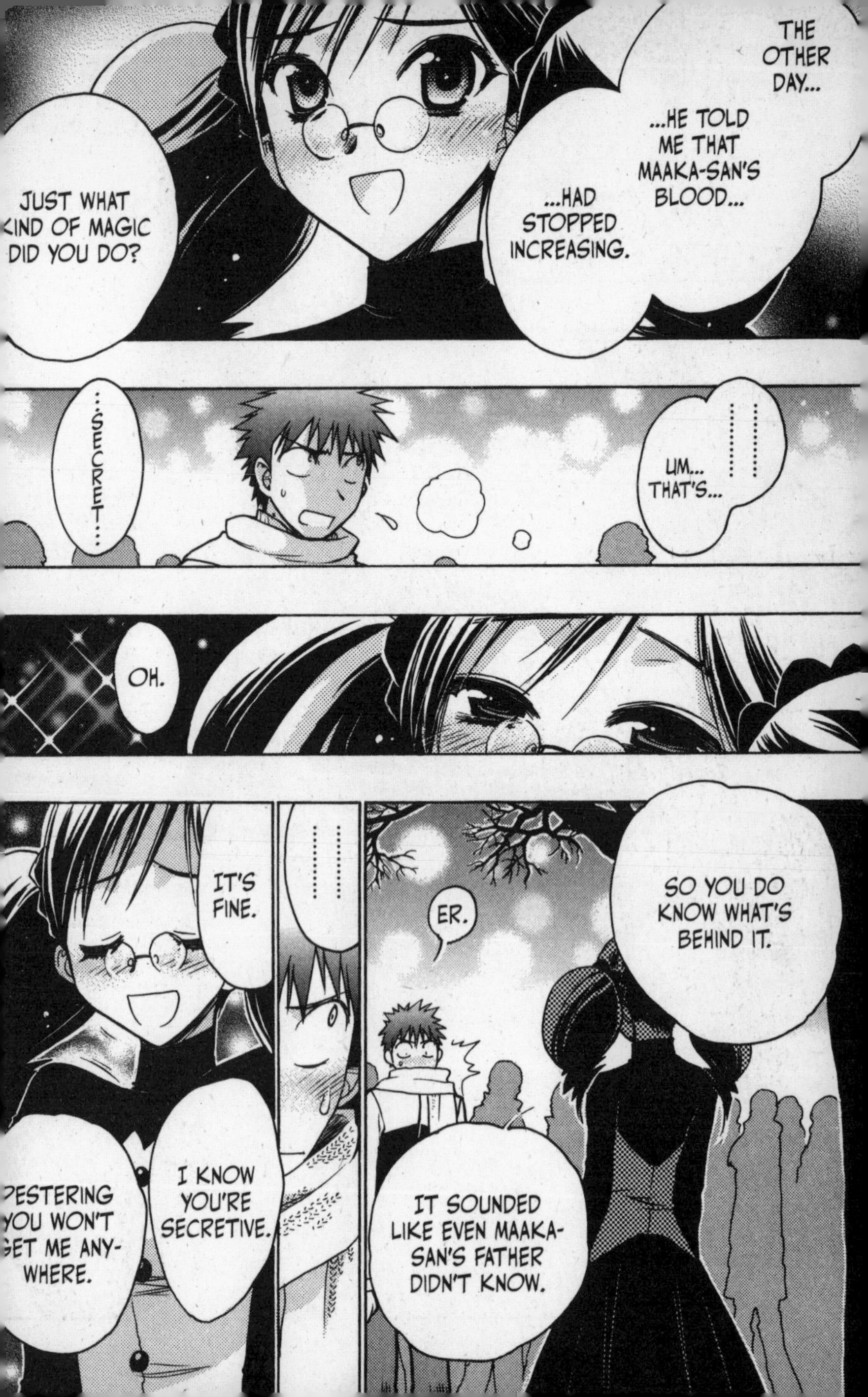
THE OTHER DAY...
...HE TOLD ME THAT MAAKA-SAN'S BLOOD...
...HAD STOPPED INCREASING.
JUST WHAT KIND OF MAGIC DID YOU DO?
......
UM... THAT'S...
...SECRET...
OH.
SO YOU DO KNOW WHAT'S BEHIND IT.
ER.
IT SOUNDED LIKE EVEN MAAKA-SAN'S FATHER DIDN'T KNOW.
......
IT'S FINE.
I KNOW YOU'RE SECRETIVE.
PESTERING YOU WON'T GET ME ANY-WHERE.

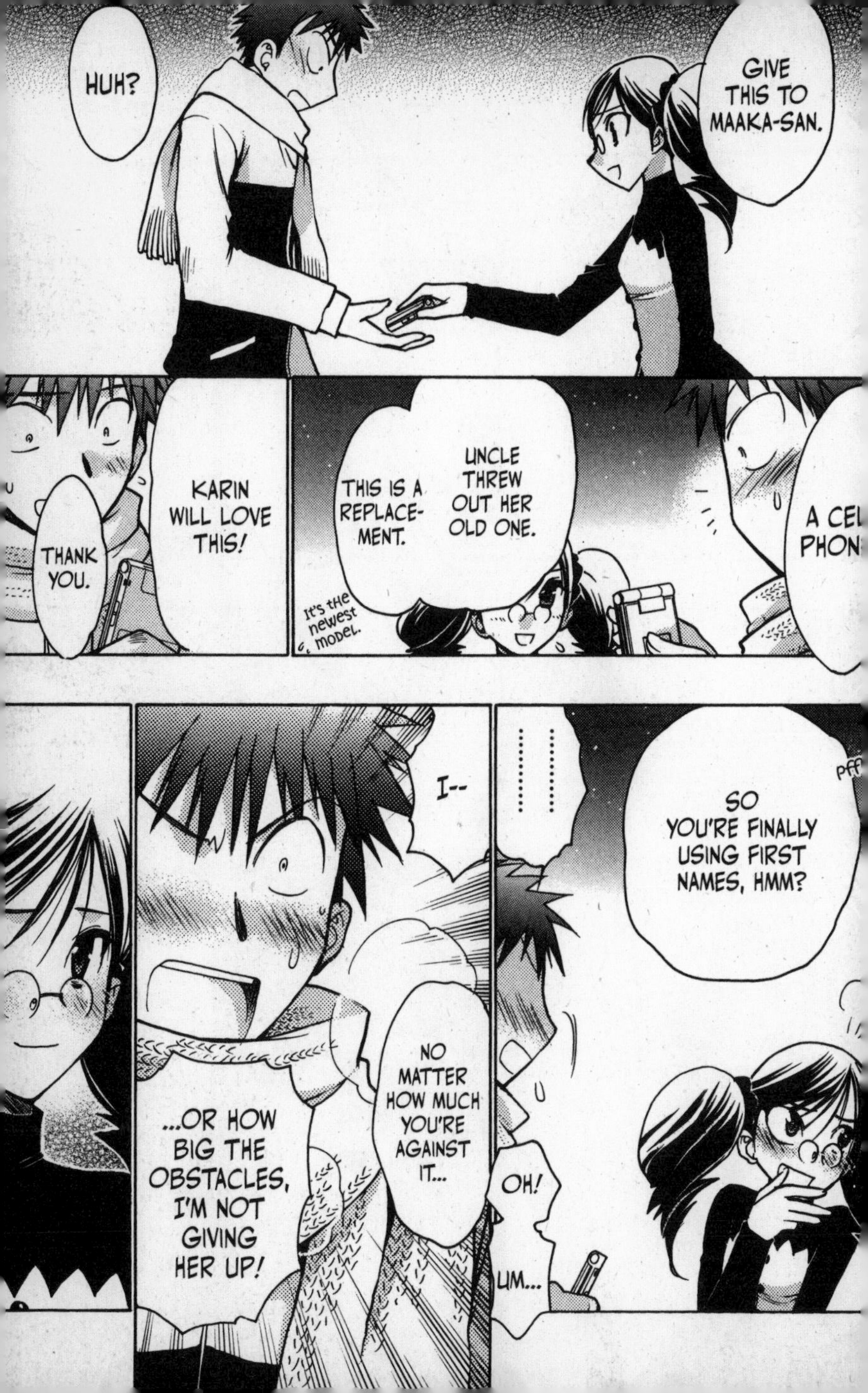
GIVE THIS TO MAAKA-SAN.
HUH?
A CEL PHON
UNCLE THREW OUT HER OLD ONE.
THIS IS A REPLACE-MENT.
It's the newest model.
KARIN WILL LOVE THIS!
THANK YOU.
pff
SO YOU'RE FINALLY USING FIRST NAMES, HMM?
......
OH!
UM...
I--
NO MATTER HOW MUCH YOU'RE AGAINST IT...
...OR HOW BIG THE OBSTACLES, I'M NOT GIVING HER UP!

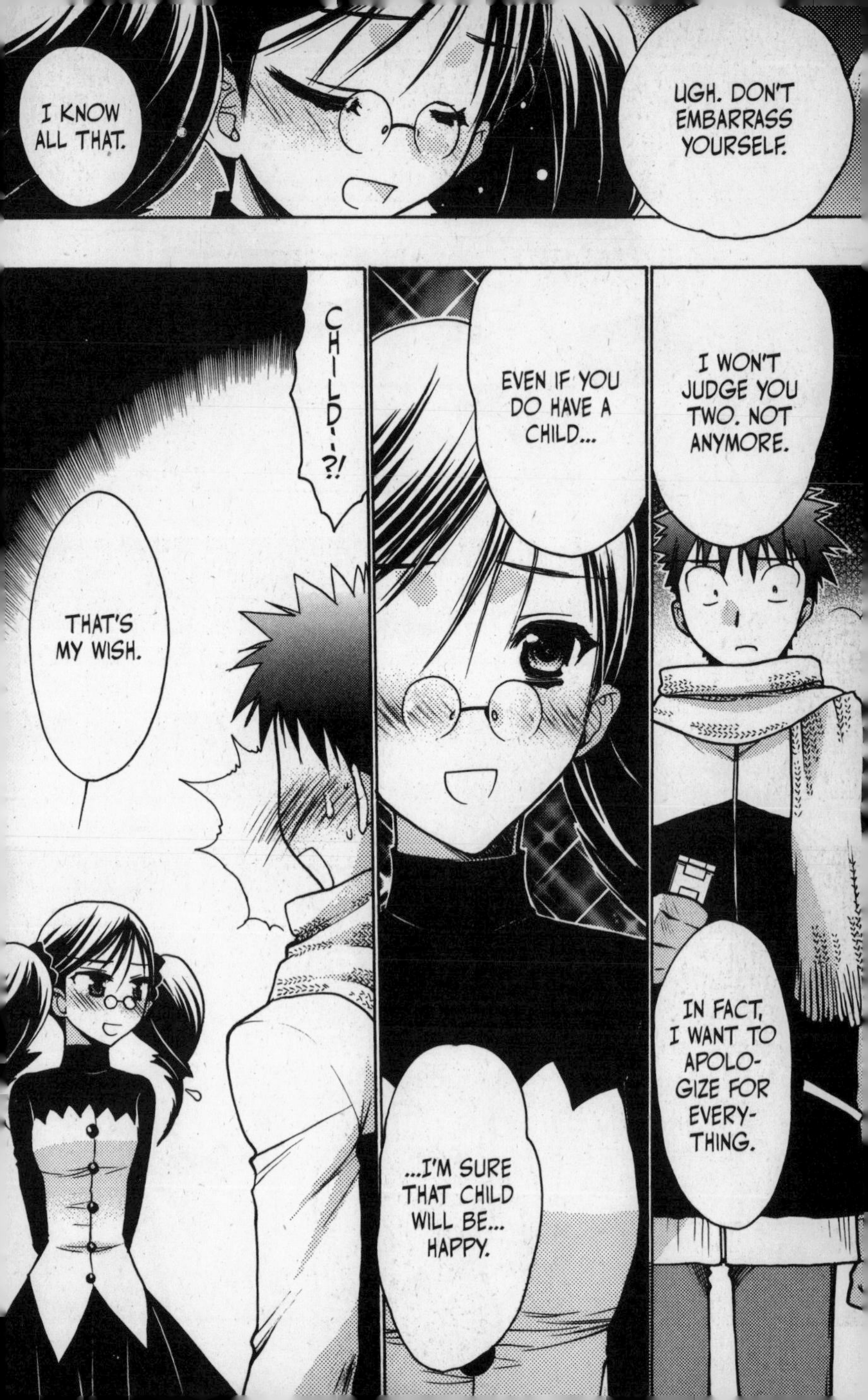
UGH. DON'T EMBARRASS YOURSELF.
I KNOW ALL THAT.
I WON'T JUDGE YOU TWO. NOT ANYMORE.
IN FACT, I WANT TO APOLO-GIZE FOR EVERY-THING.
EVEN IF YOU DO HAVE A CHILD...
...I'M SURE THAT CHILD WILL BE... HAPPY.
CHILD...?!
THAT'S MY WISH.

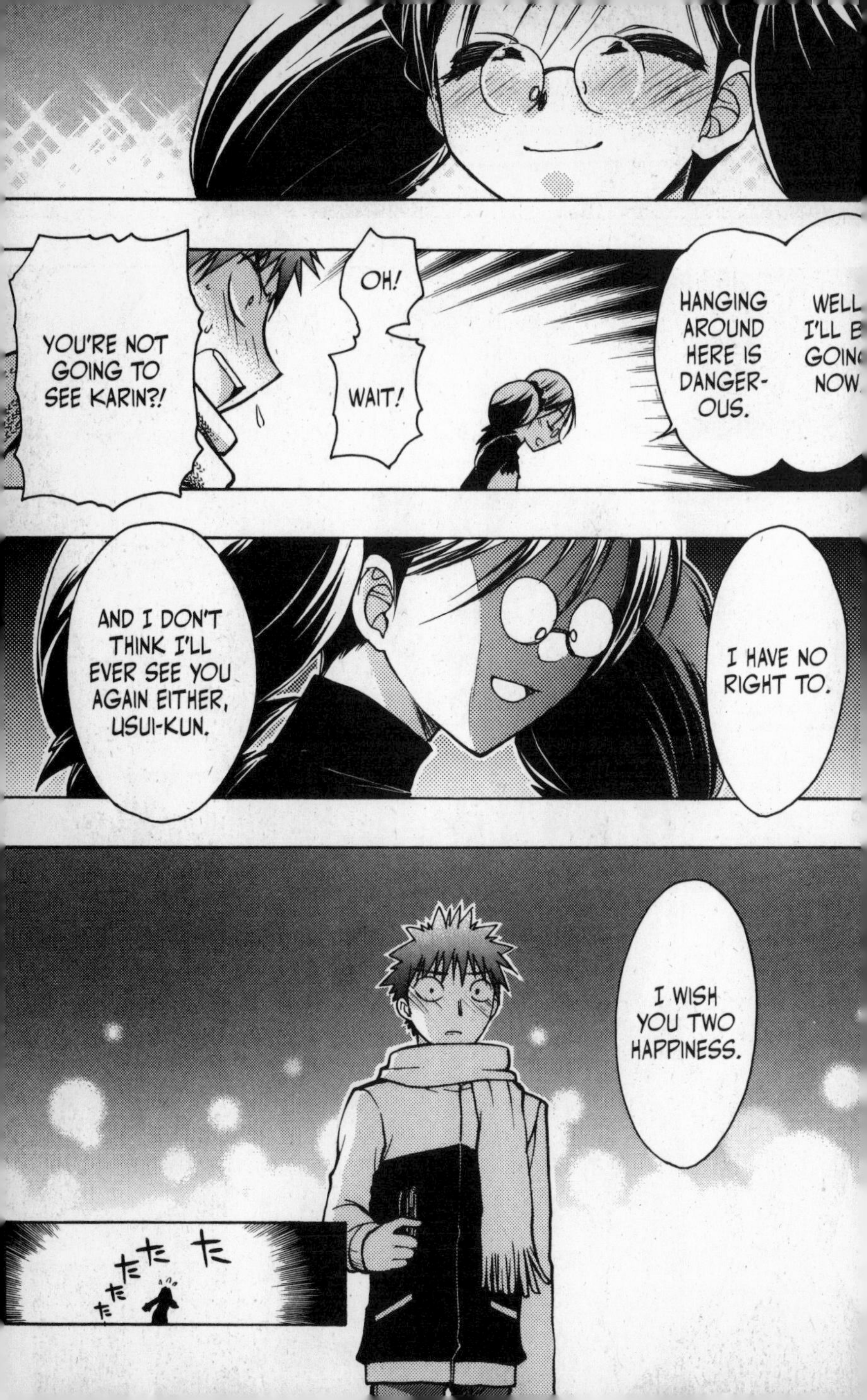
WELL I'LL B GOIN NOW.
HANGING AROUND HERE IS DANGER-OUS.
OH! WAIT!
YOU'RE NOT GOING TO SEE KARIN?!
I HAVE NO RIGHT TO.
AND I DON'T THINK I'LL EVER SEE YOU AGAIN EITHER, USUI-KUN.
I WISH YOU TWO HAPPINESS.
たたたたた

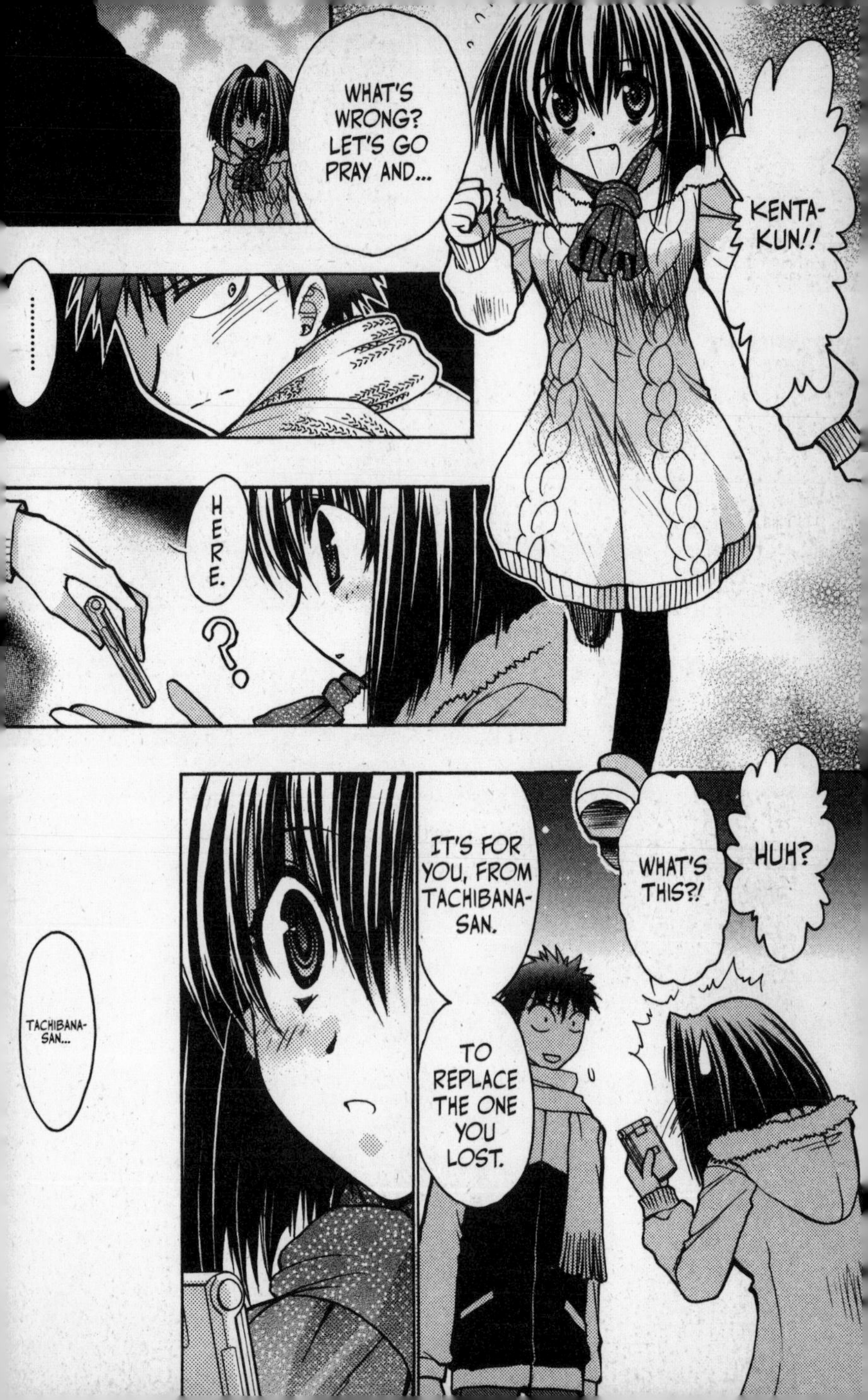
KENTA-KUN!!
WHAT'S WRONG? LET'S GO PRAY AND...
......
HERE.
?
HUH?
WHAT'S THIS?!
IT'S FOR YOU, FROM TACHIBANA-SAN.
TO REPLACE THE ONE YOU LOST.
TACHIBANA-SAN...

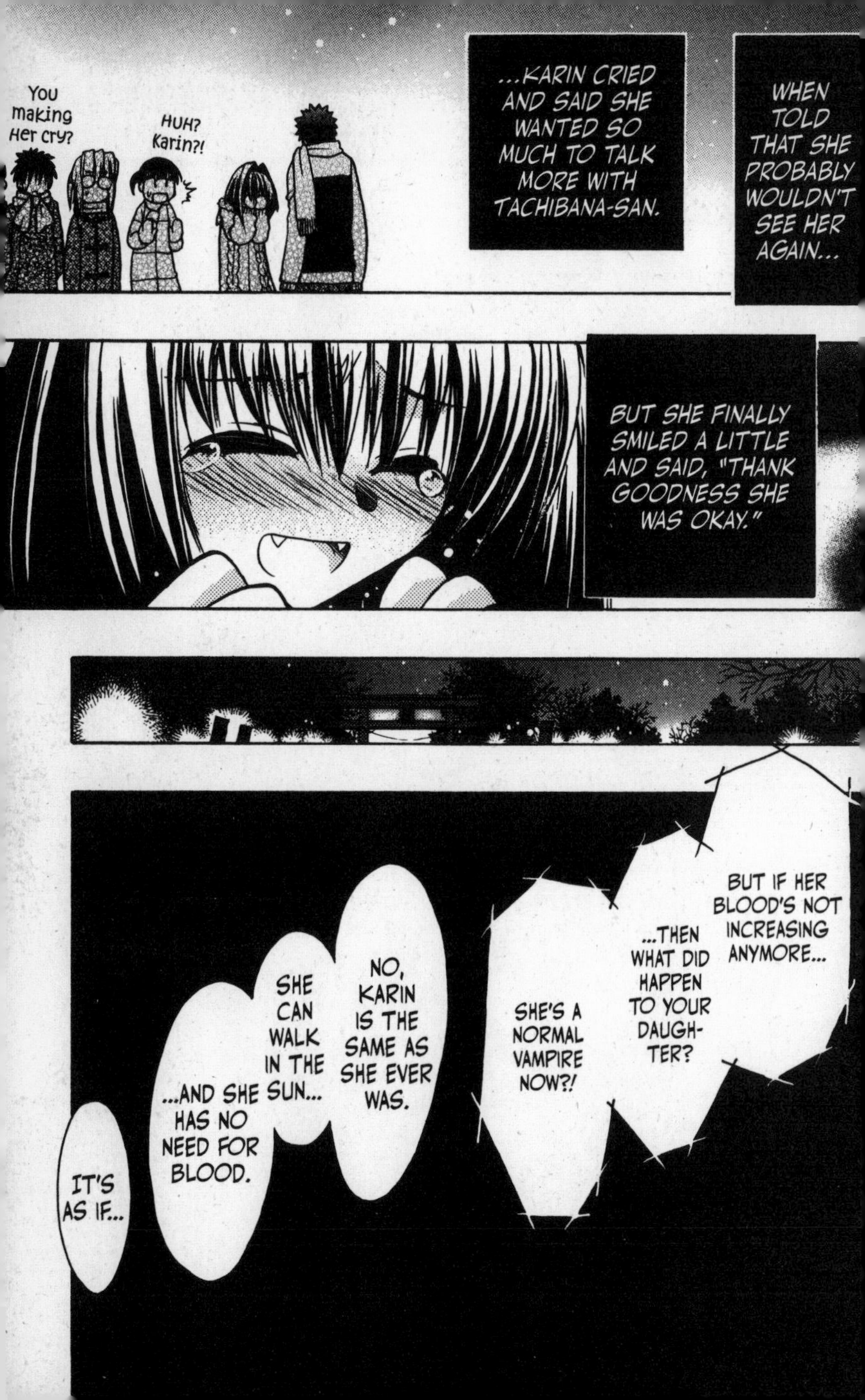
WHEN TOLD THAT SHE PROBABLY WOULDN'T SEE HER AGAIN...
...KARIN CRIED AND SAID SHE WANTED SO MUCH TO TALK MORE WITH TACHIBANA-SAN.
HUH? Karin?!
You making Her cry?
BUT SHE FINALLY SMILED A LITTLE AND SAID, "THANK GOODNESS SHE WAS OKAY."
BUT IF HER BLOOD'S NOT INCREASING ANYMORE...
...THEN WHAT DID HAPPEN TO YOUR DAUGHTER?
SHE'S A NORMAL VAMPIRE NOW?!
NO, KARIN IS THE SAME AS SHE EVER WAS.
SHE CAN WALK IN THE SUN...
...AND SHE HAS NO NEED FOR BLOOD.
IT'S AS IF...

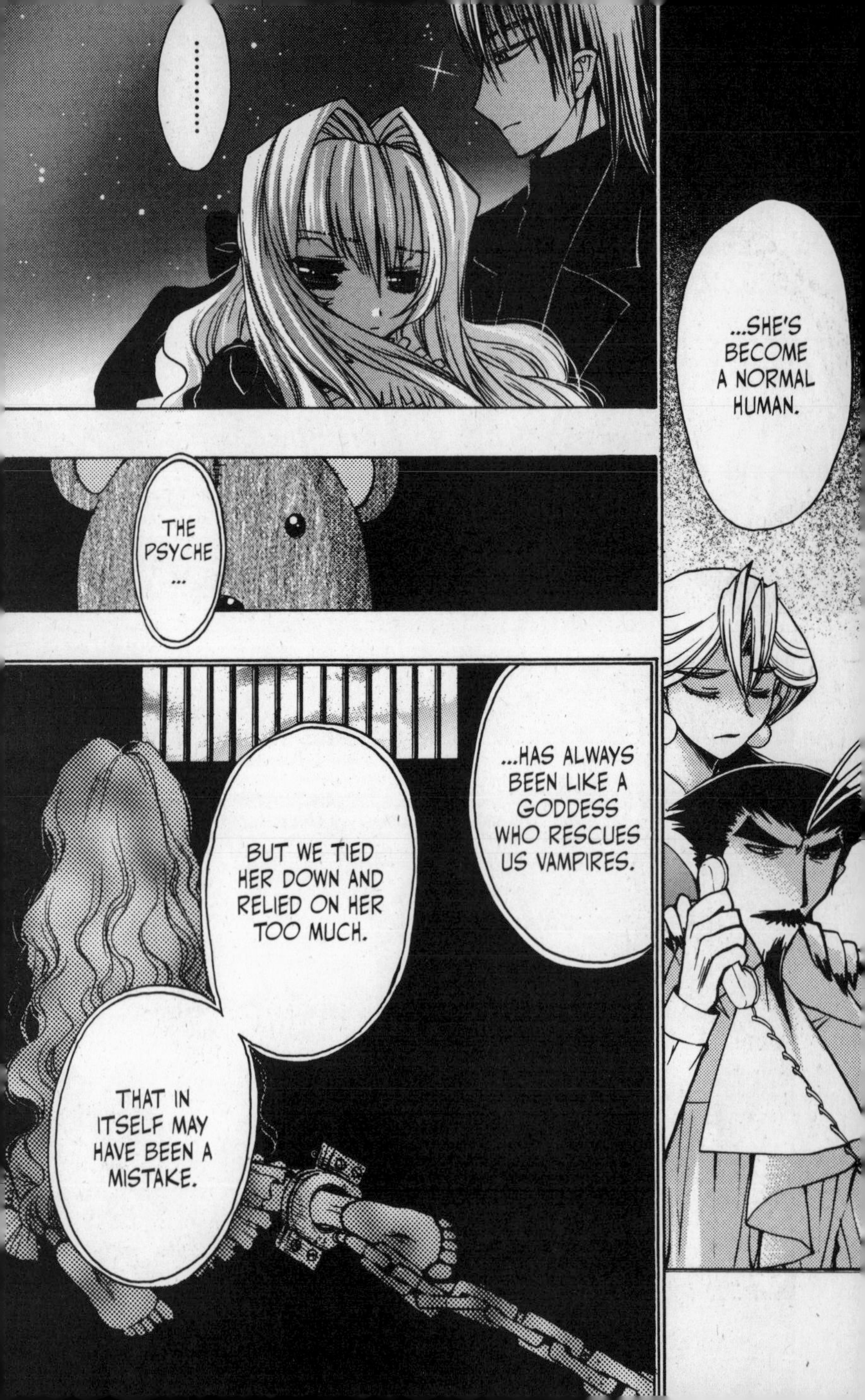

...SHE'S BECOME A NORMAL HUMAN.
......
THE PSYCHE ...
...HAS ALWAYS BEEN LIKE A GODDESS WHO RESCUES US VAMPIRES.
BUT WE TIED HER DOWN AND RELIED ON HER TOO MUCH.
THAT IN ITSELF MAY HAVE BEEN A MISTAKE.

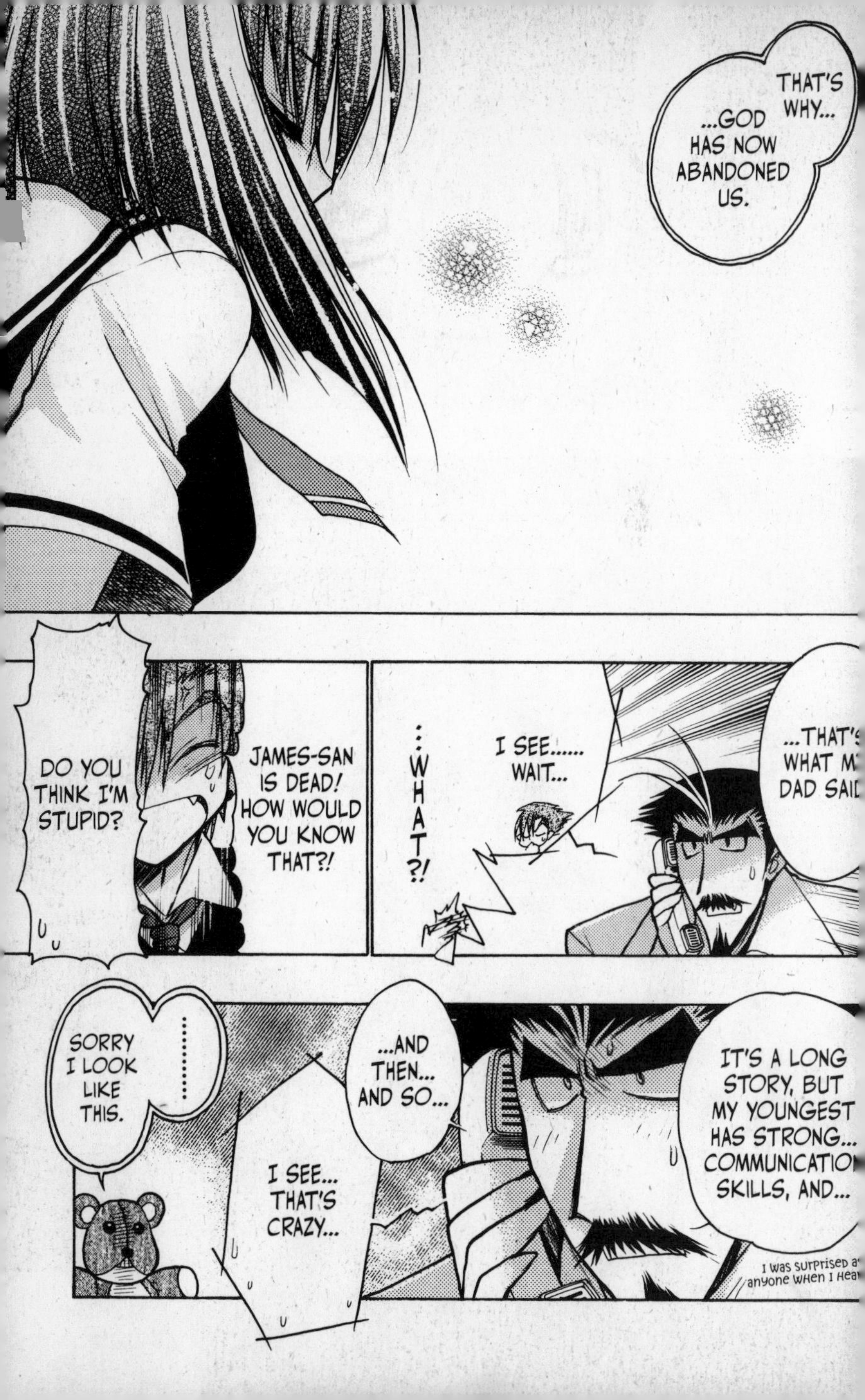
THAT'S WHY... ...GOD HAS NOW ABANDONED US.
...THAT'S WHAT M DAD SAI
I SEE...... WAIT...
...WHAT?!
JAMES-SAN IS DEAD! HOW WOULD YOU KNOW THAT?!
DO YOU THINK I'M STUPID?
IT'S A LONG STORY, BUT MY YOUNGEST HAS STRONG... COMMUNICATIO SKILLS, AND...
I was surprised a anyone when I Hea
...AND THEN... AND SO...
I SEE... THAT'S CRAZY...
....
SORRY I LOOK LIKE THIS.

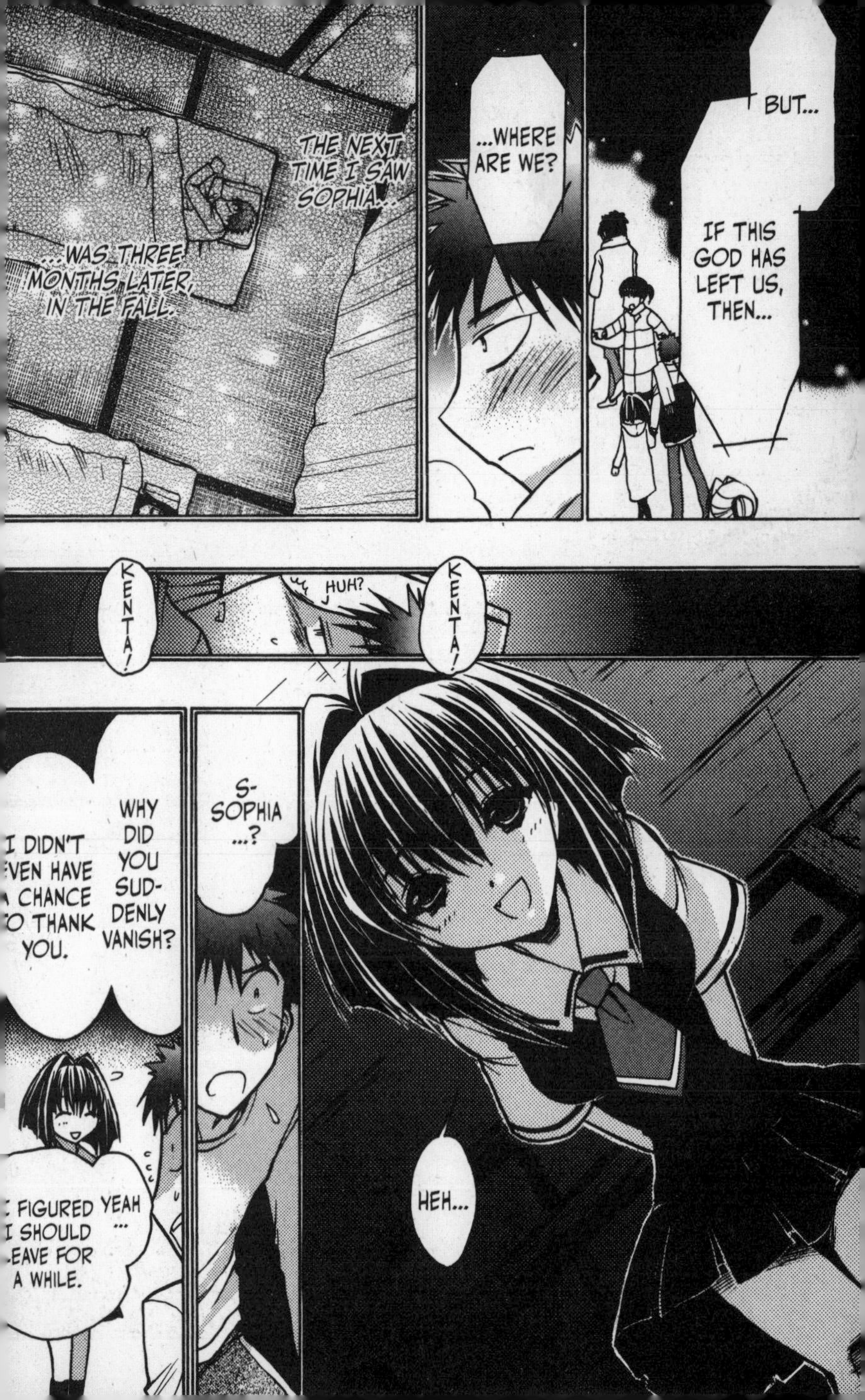
BUT...
IF THIS GOD HAS LEFT US, THEN...
...WHERE ARE WE?
THE NEXT TIME I SAW SOPHIA...
...WAS THREE MONTHS LATER, IN THE FALL.
KENTA!
HUH?
KENTA!
HEH...
S-SOPHIA...?
WHY DID YOU SUD-DENLY VANISH?
I DIDN'T EVEN HAVE A CHANCE TO THANK YOU.
YEAH...
I FIGURED I SHOULD LEAVE FOR A WHILE.

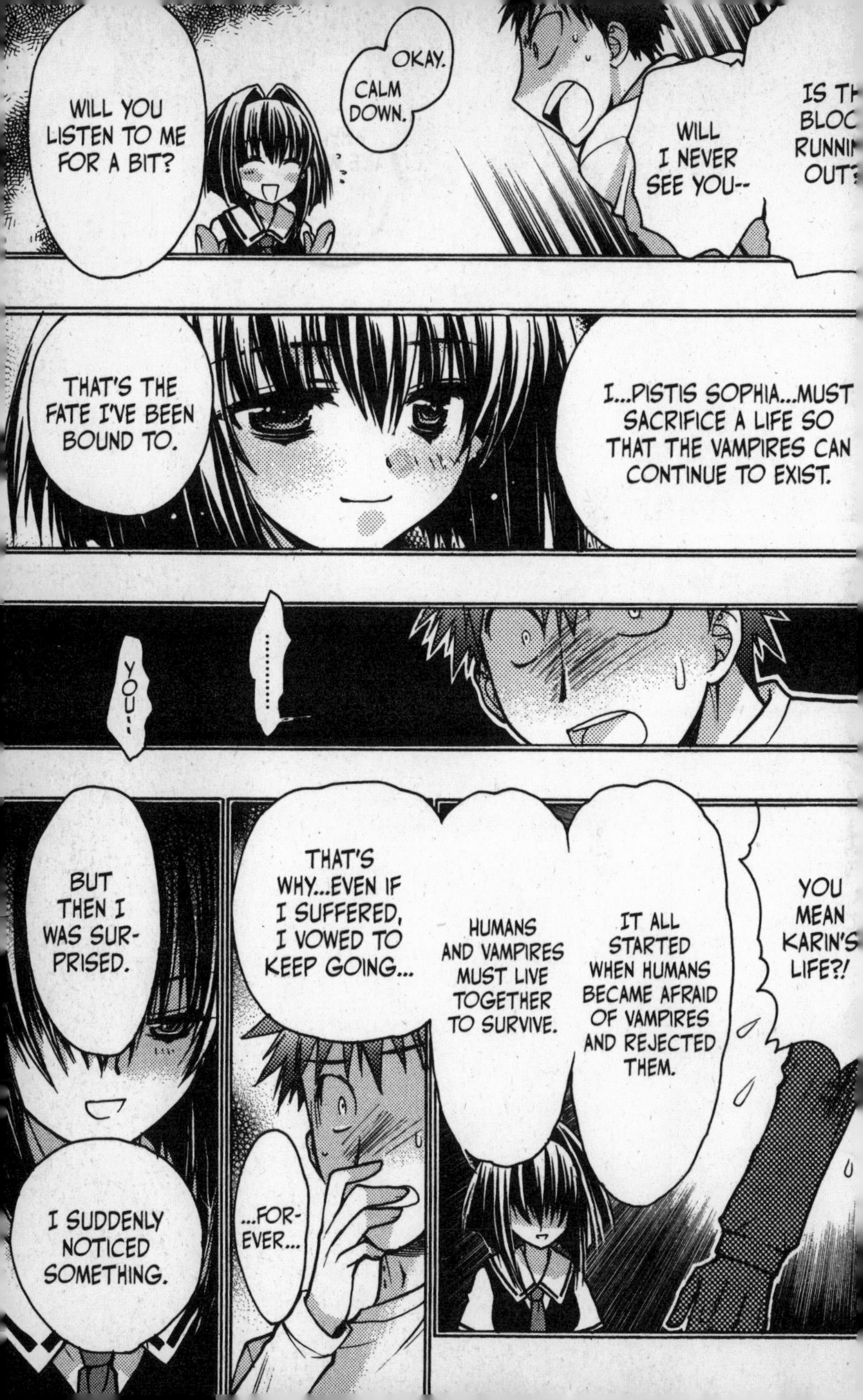
IS TH BLOC RUNNI OUT?
WILL I NEVER SEE YOU--
OKAY. CALM DOWN.
WILL YOU LISTEN TO ME FOR A BIT?
I...PISTIS SOPHIA...MUST SACRIFICE A LIFE SO THAT THE VAMPIRES CAN CONTINUE TO EXIST.
THAT'S THE FATE I'VE BEEN BOUND TO.
......
YOU...
YOU MEAN KARIN'S LIFE?!
IT ALL STARTED WHEN HUMANS BECAME AFRAID OF VAMPIRES AND REJECTED THEM.
HUMANS AND VAMPIRES MUST LIVE TOGETHER TO SURVIVE.
THAT'S WHY...EVEN IF I SUFFERED, I VOWED TO KEEP GOING...
...FOR-EVER...
BUT THEN I WAS SUR-PRISED.
I SUDDENLY NOTICED SOMETHING.

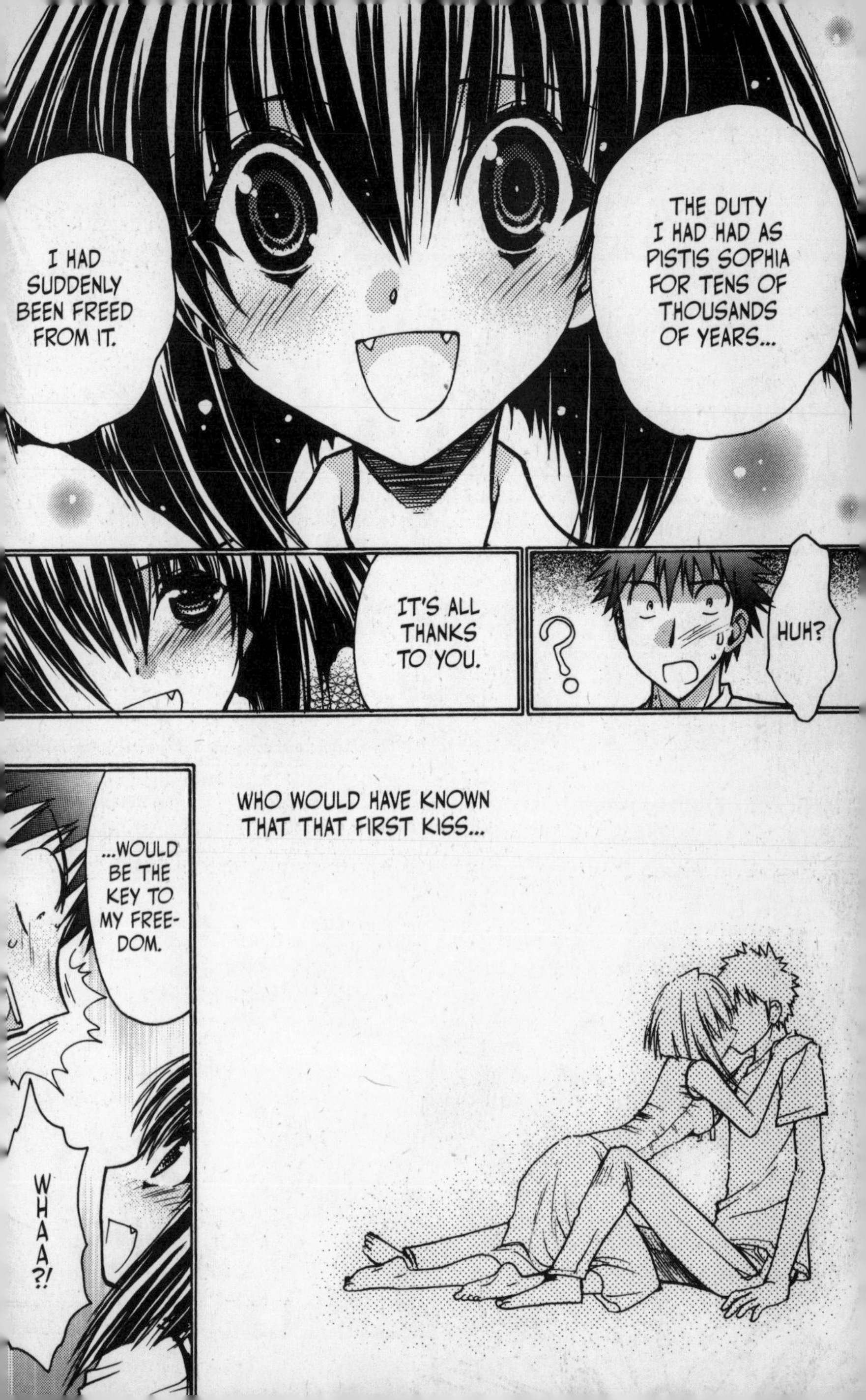
THE DUTY I HAD HAD AS PISTIS SOPHIA FOR TENS OF THOUSANDS OF YEARS...
I HAD SUDDENLY BEEN FREED FROM IT.
HUH?
IT'S ALL THANKS TO YOU.
WHO WOULD HAVE KNOWN THAT THAT FIRST KISS...
...WOULD BE THE KEY TO MY FREE-DOM.
WHAAA?!

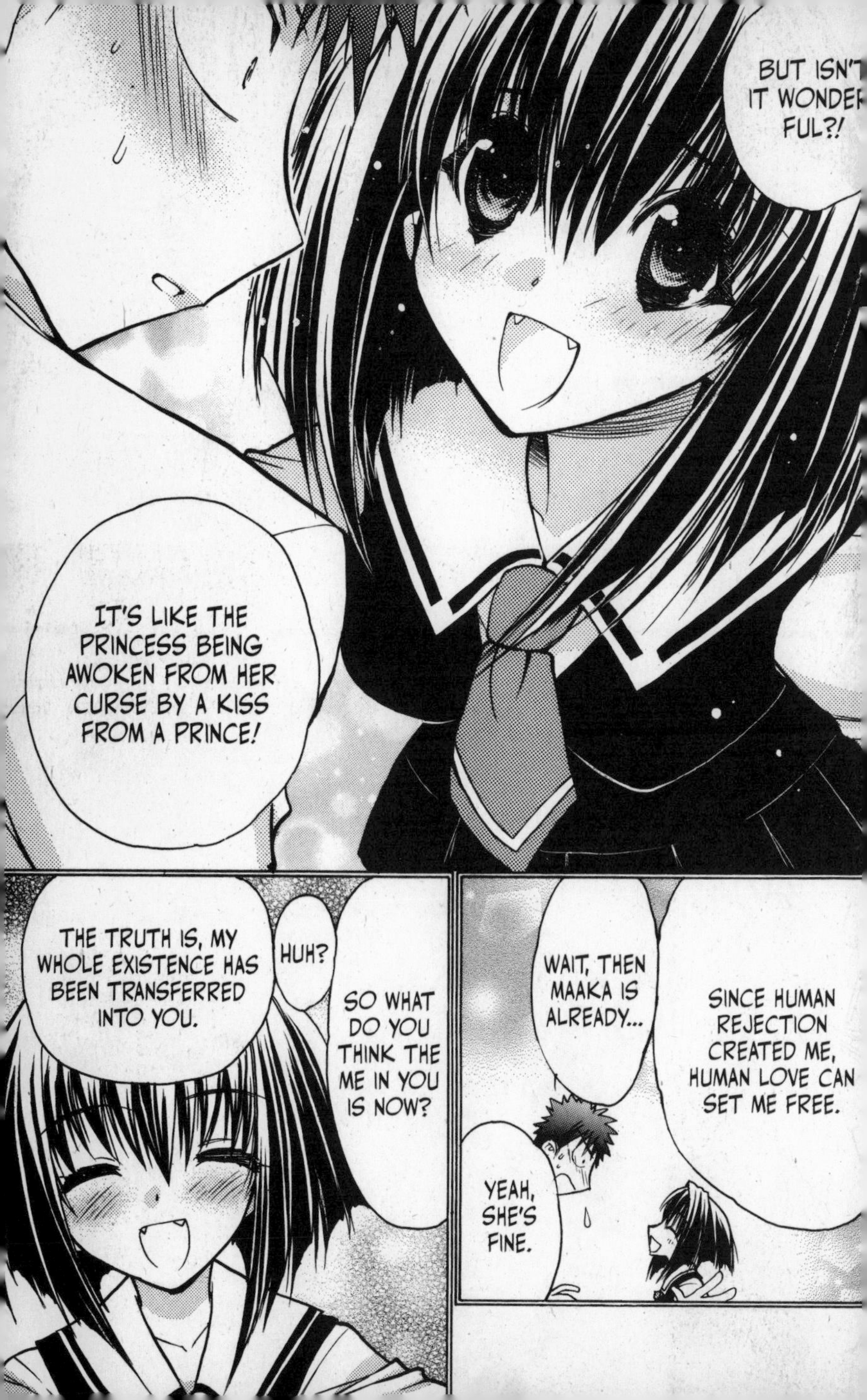
BUT ISN'T IT WONDERFUL?!
IT'S LIKE THE PRINCESS BEING AWOKEN FROM HER CURSE BY A KISS FROM A PRINCE!
SINCE HUMAN REJECTION CREATED ME, HUMAN LOVE CAN SET ME FREE.
WAIT, THEN MAAKA IS ALREADY...
YEAH, SHE'S FINE.
SO WHAT DO YOU THINK THE ME IN YOU IS NOW?
HUH?
THE TRUTH IS, MY WHOLE EXISTENCE HAS BEEN TRANSFERRED INTO YOU.

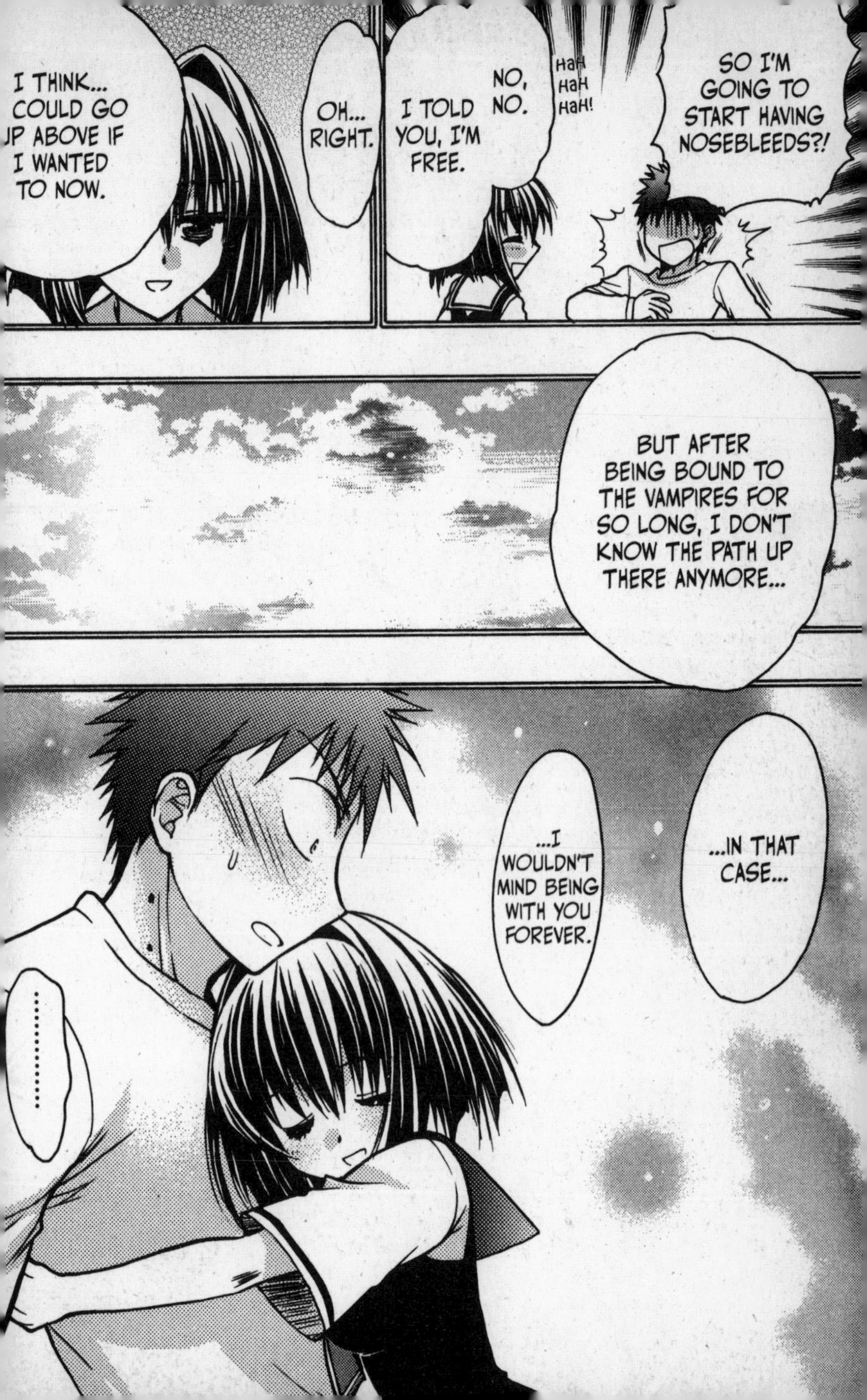
SO I'M GOING TO START HAVING NOSEBLEEDS?!
HaH HaH HaH!
NO, NO.
I TOLD YOU, I'M FREE.
OH... RIGHT.
I THINK... COULD GO P ABOVE IF I WANTED TO NOW.
BUT AFTER BEING BOUND TO THE VAMPIRES FOR SO LONG, I DON'T KNOW THE PATH UP THERE ANYMORE...
...IN THAT CASE...
...I WOULDN'T MIND BEING WITH YOU FOREVER.
....

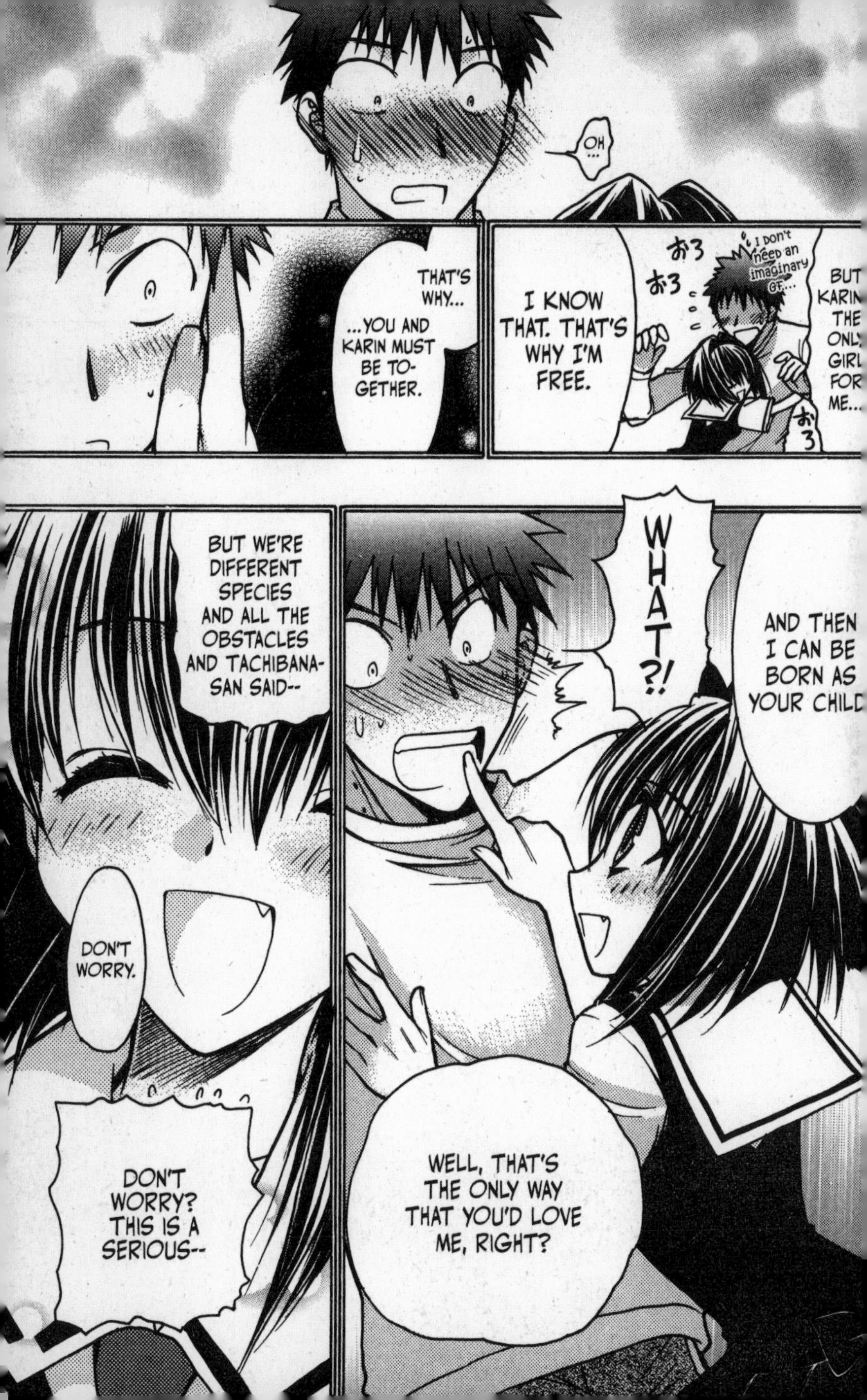
OH...
BUT KARIN THE ONLY GIRL FOR ME...
I don't need an imaginary GF...
おろ
おろ
おろ
I KNOW THAT. THAT'S WHY I'M FREE.
THAT'S WHY...
...YOU AND KARIN MUST BE TO-GETHER.
AND THEN I CAN BE BORN AS YOUR CHILD
WHAT?!
WELL, THAT'S THE ONLY WAY THAT YOU'D LOVE ME, RIGHT?
BUT WE'RE DIFFERENT SPECIES AND ALL THE OBSTACLES AND TACHIBANA-SAN SAID--
DON'T WORRY.
DON'T WORRY? THIS IS A SERIOUS--

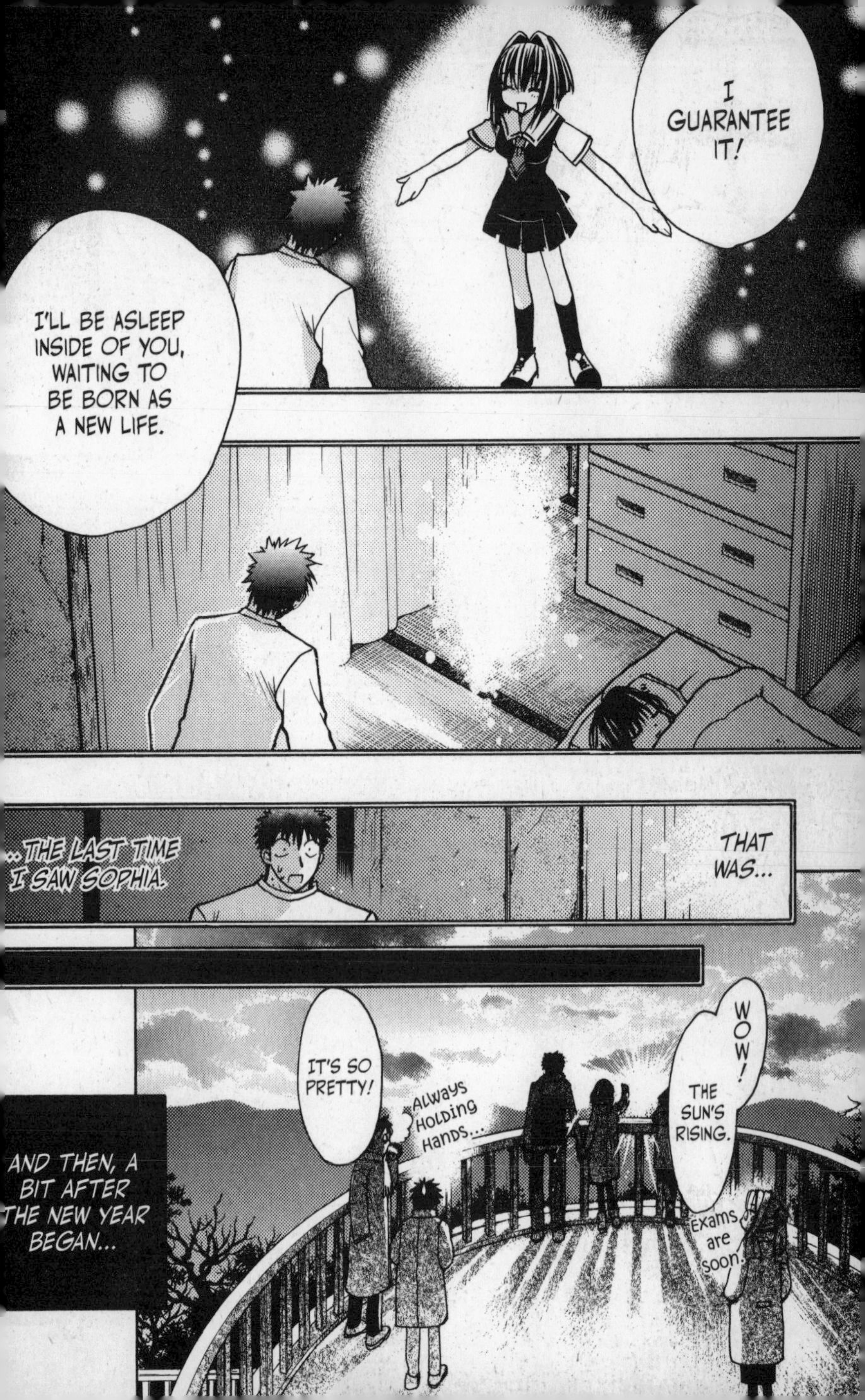
I GUARANTEE IT!
I'LL BE ASLEEP INSIDE OF YOU, WAITING TO BE BORN AS A NEW LIFE.
THAT WAS...
...THE LAST TIME I SAW SOPHIA.
WOW! THE SUN'S RISING.
IT'S SO PRETTY!
Always Holding Hands...
Exams are soon.
AND THEN, A BIT AFTER THE NEW YEAR BEGAN...

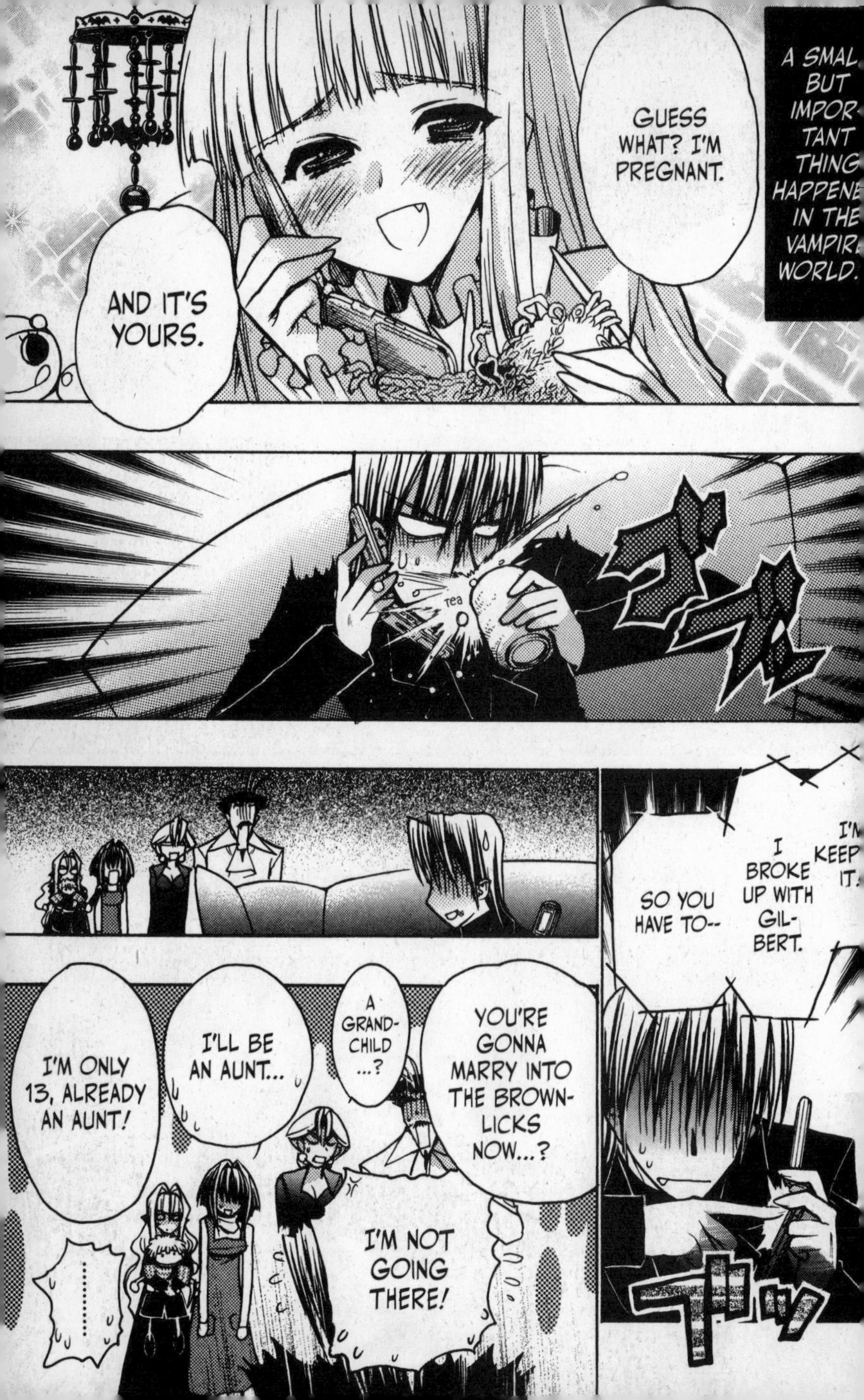
A SMAL BUT IMPORTANT THING HAPPENE IN THE VAMPIR WORLD.
GUESS WHAT? I'M PREGNANT.
AND IT'S YOURS.
tea
I'M KEEP IT.
I BROKE UP WITH GILBERT.
SO YOU HAVE TO--
YOU'RE GONNA MARRY INTO THE BROWNLICKS NOW...?
A GRANDCHILD ...?
I'LL BE AN AUNT...
I'M ONLY 13, ALREADY AN AUNT!
I'M NOT GOING THERE!
......

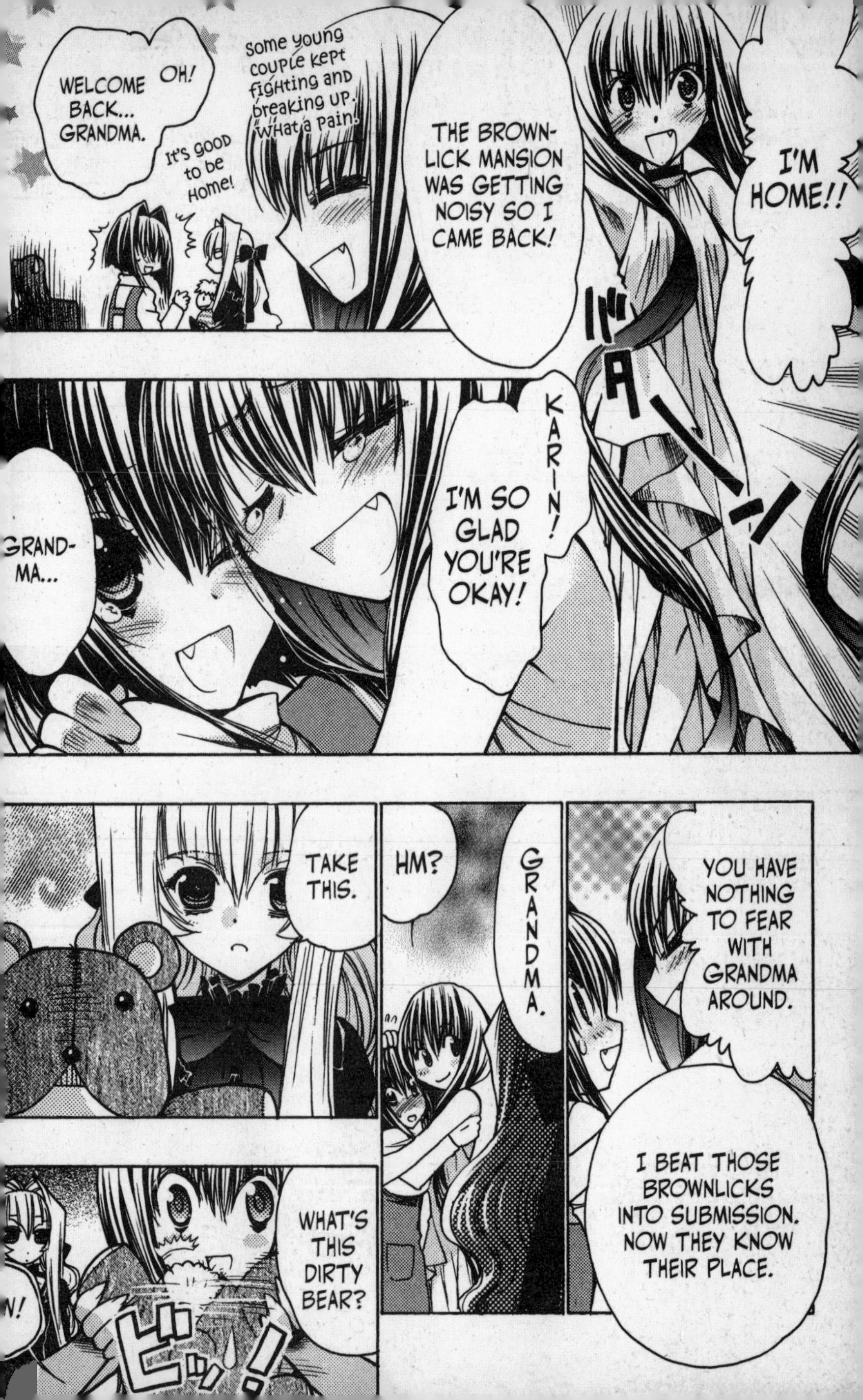
I'M HOME!!
THE BROWN-LICK MANSION WAS GETTING NOISY SO I CAME BACK!
Some young couple kept fighting and breaking up. What a pain.
OH!
WELCOME BACK... GRANDMA.
It's good to be home!
KARIN!
I'M SO GLAD YOU'RE OKAY!
GRAND-MA...
YOU HAVE NOTHING TO FEAR WITH GRANDMA AROUND.
I BEAT THOSE BROWNLICKS INTO SUBMISSION. NOW THEY KNOW THEIR PLACE.
GRANDMA.
HM?
TAKE THIS.
WHAT'S THIS DIRTY BEAR?

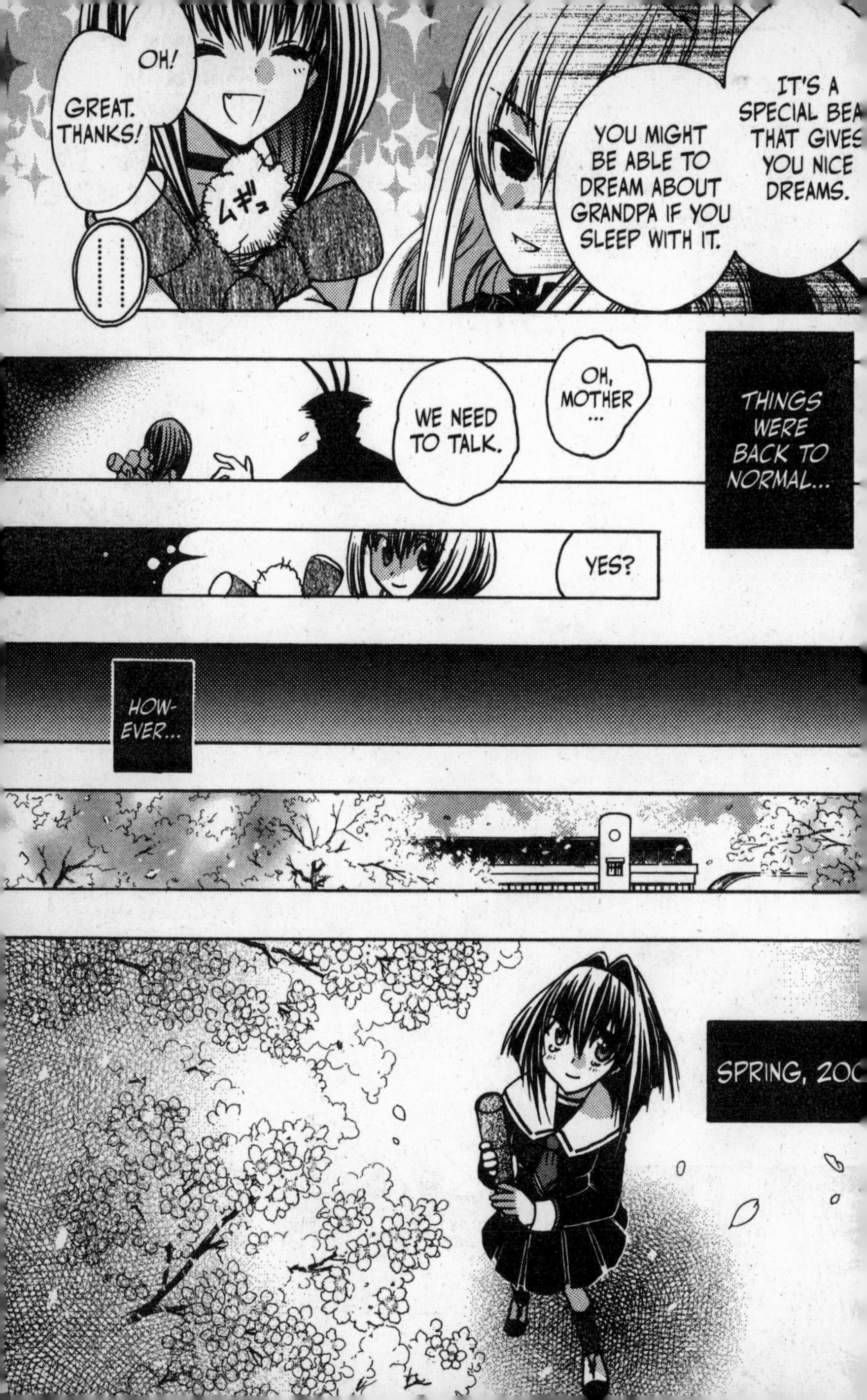
IT'S A SPECIAL BEA THAT GIVES YOU NICE DREAMS.
YOU MIGHT BE ABLE TO DREAM ABOUT GRANDPA IF YOU SLEEP WITH IT.
OH!
GREAT. THANKS!
ムギュ
......
THINGS WERE BACK TO NORMAL...
OH, MOTHER ...
WE NEED TO TALK.
YES?
HOW-EVER...
SPRING, 200

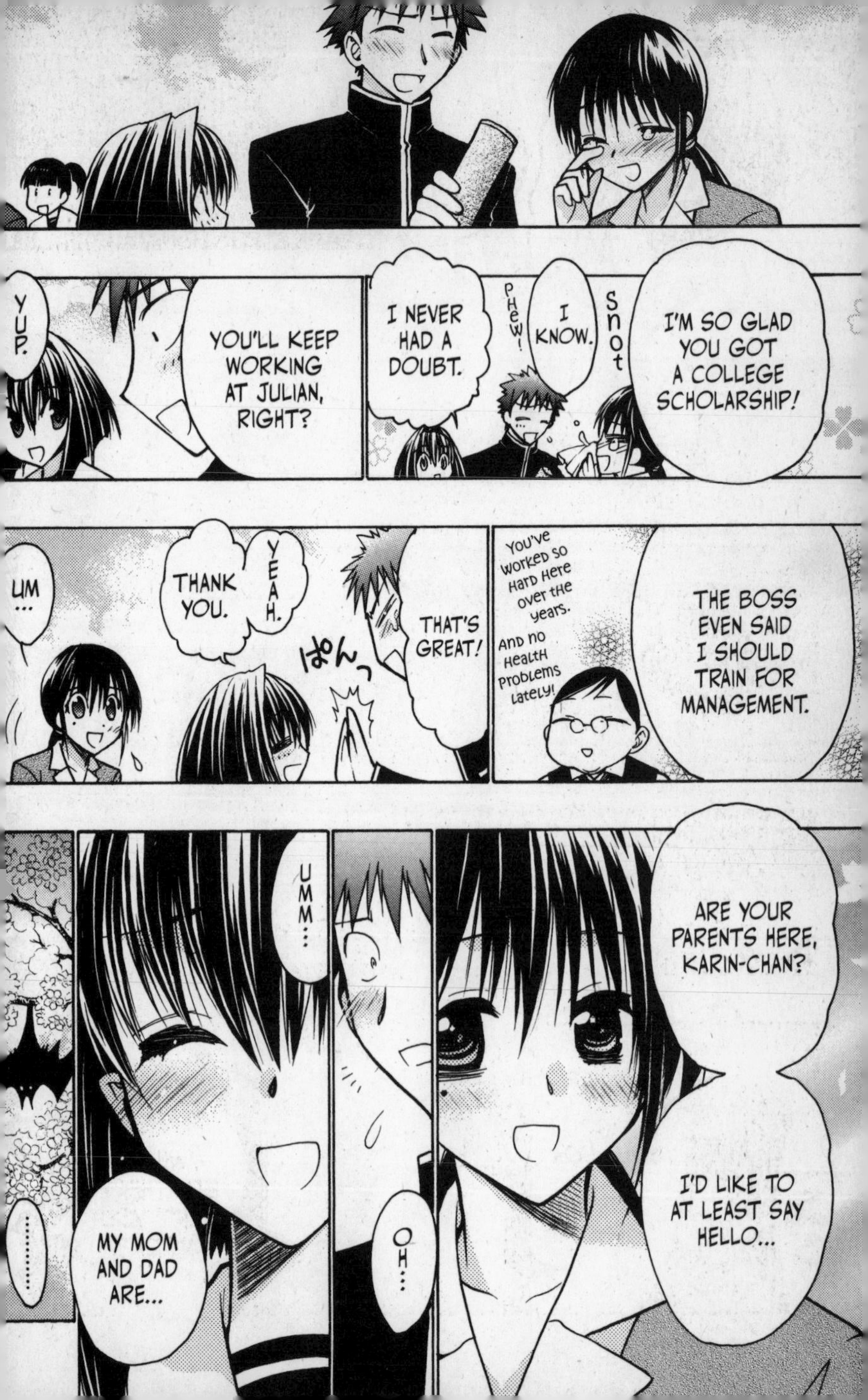
I'M SO GLAD YOU GOT A COLLEGE SCHOLARSHIP!
Snot
I KNOW.
Phew!
I NEVER HAD A DOUBT.
YOU'LL KEEP WORKING AT JULIAN, RIGHT?
YUP.
THE BOSS EVEN SAID I SHOULD TRAIN FOR MANAGEMENT.
You've worked so hard here over the years.
And no health problems lately!
THAT'S GREAT!
ぱんっ
YEAH.
THANK YOU.
UM...
ARE YOUR PARENTS HERE, KARIN-CHAN?
I'D LIKE TO AT LEAST SAY HELLO...
UMM...
OH...
MY MOM AND DAD ARE...
....

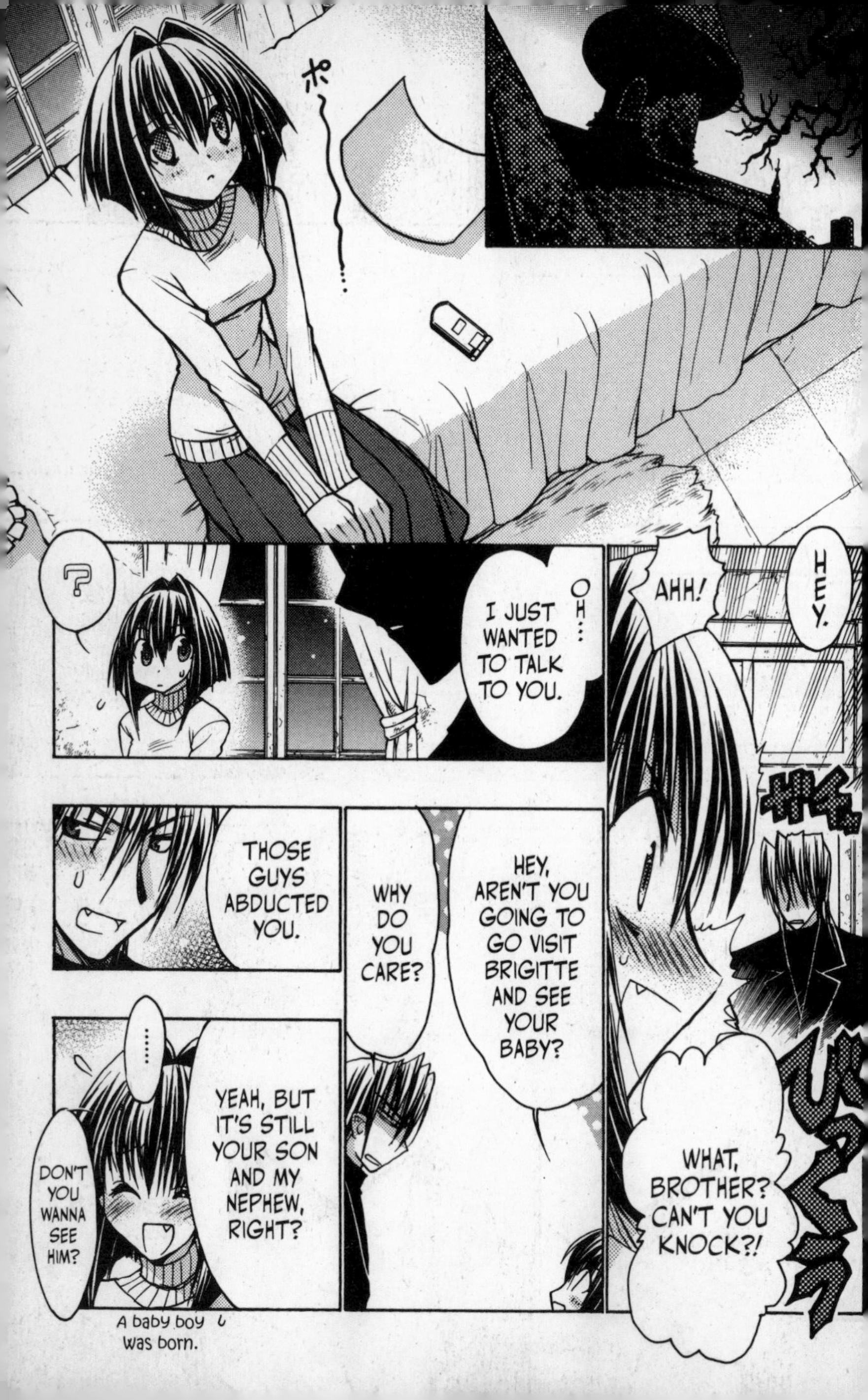
ポ〜…
HEY.
AHH!
WHAT, BROTHER? CAN'T YOU KNOCK?!
OH... I JUST WANTED TO TALK TO YOU.
?
HEY, AREN'T YOU GOING TO GO VISIT BRIGITTE AND SEE YOUR BABY?
WHY DO YOU CARE?
THOSE GUYS ABDUCTED YOU.
YEAH, BUT IT'S STILL YOUR SON AND MY NEPHEW, RIGHT?
......
DON'T YOU WANNA SEE HIM?
A baby boy was born.

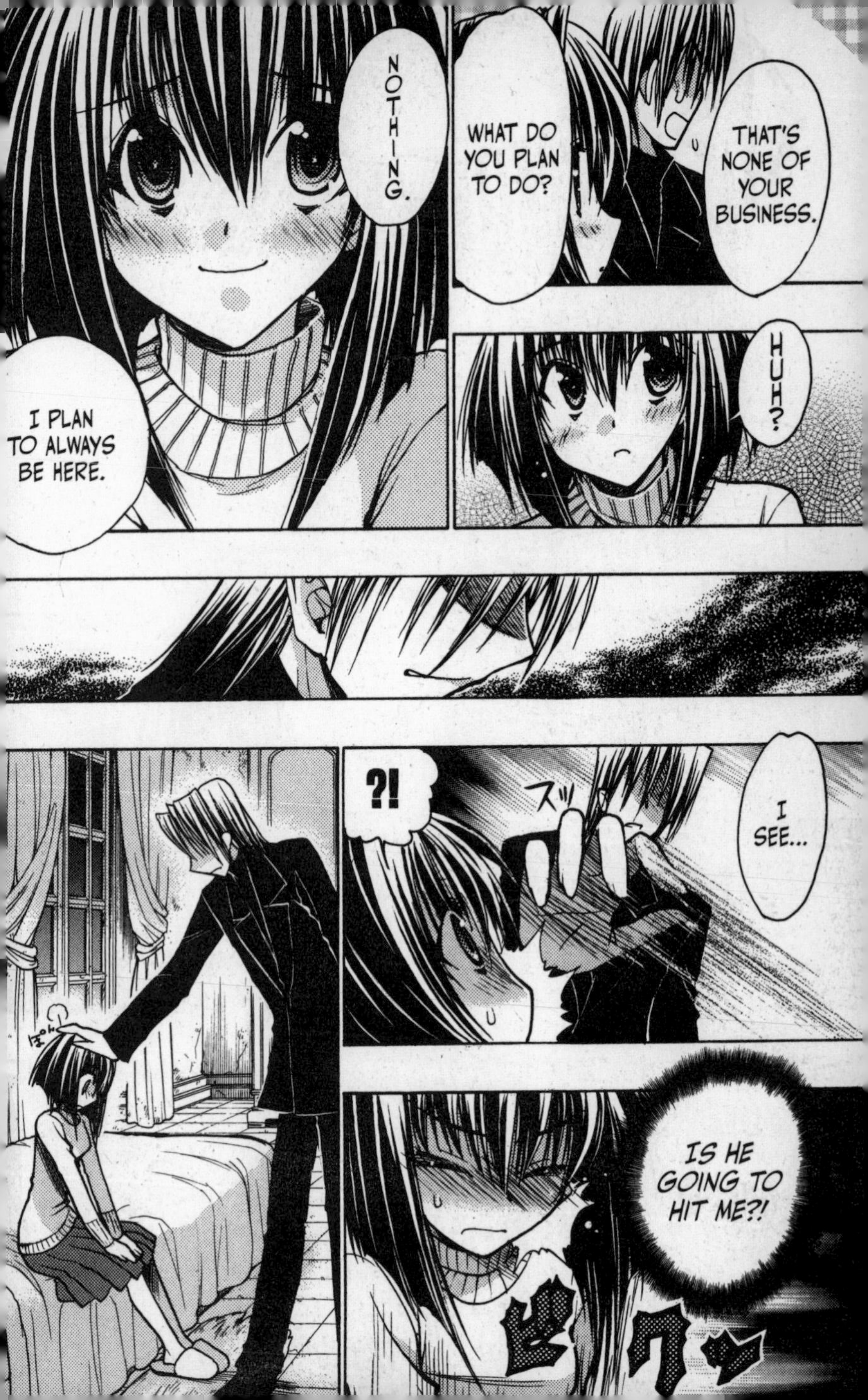
THAT'S NONE OF YOUR BUSINESS.
WHAT DO YOU PLAN TO DO?
HUH?
NOTHING.
I PLAN TO ALWAYS BE HERE.
I SEE...
ズッ
?!
IS HE GOING TO HIT ME?!
ビクッ

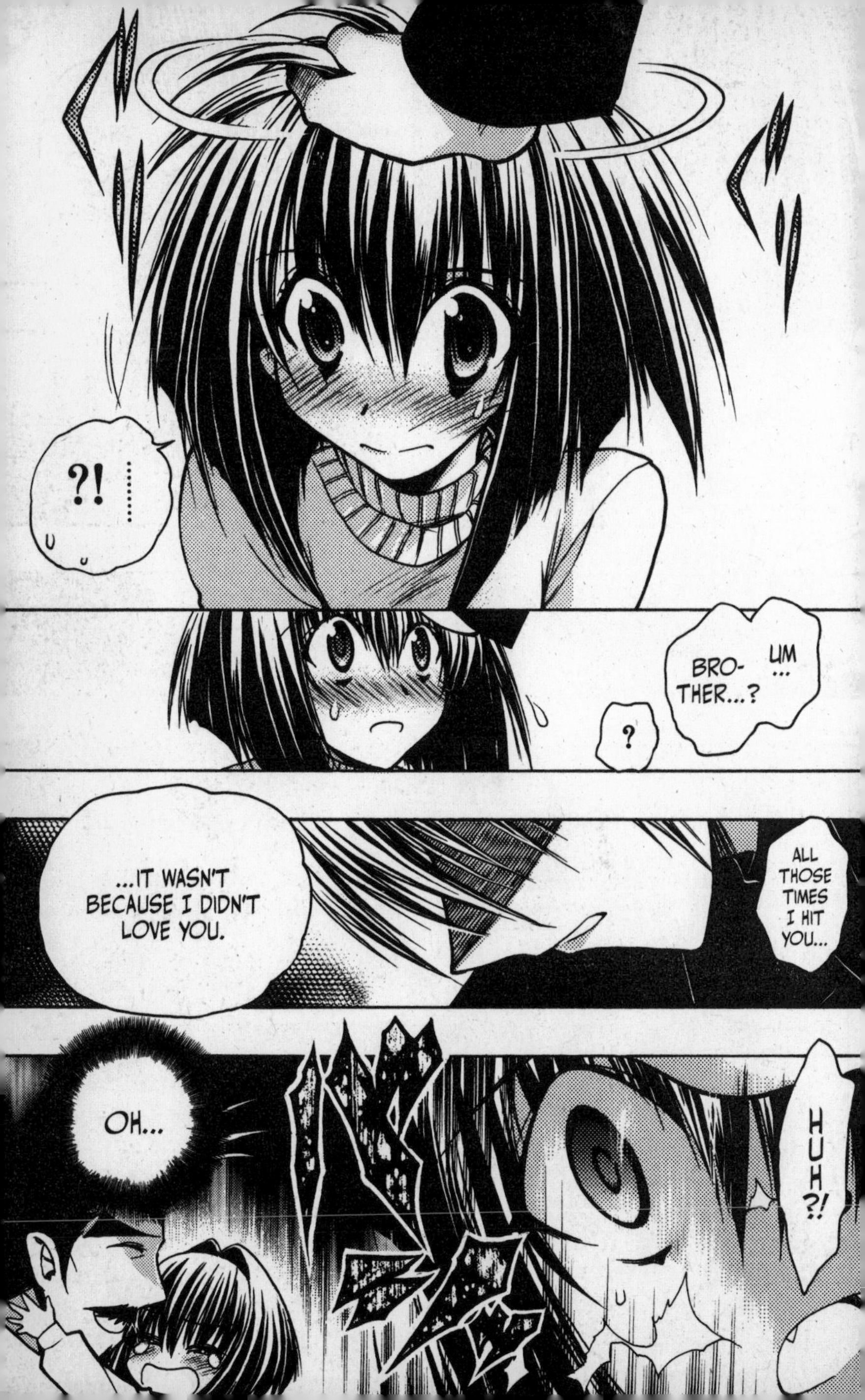
?!......
UM... BRO-THER...?
?
ALL THOSE TIMES I HIT YOU...
...IT WASN'T BECAUSE I DIDN'T LOVE YOU.
HUH?!
OH...

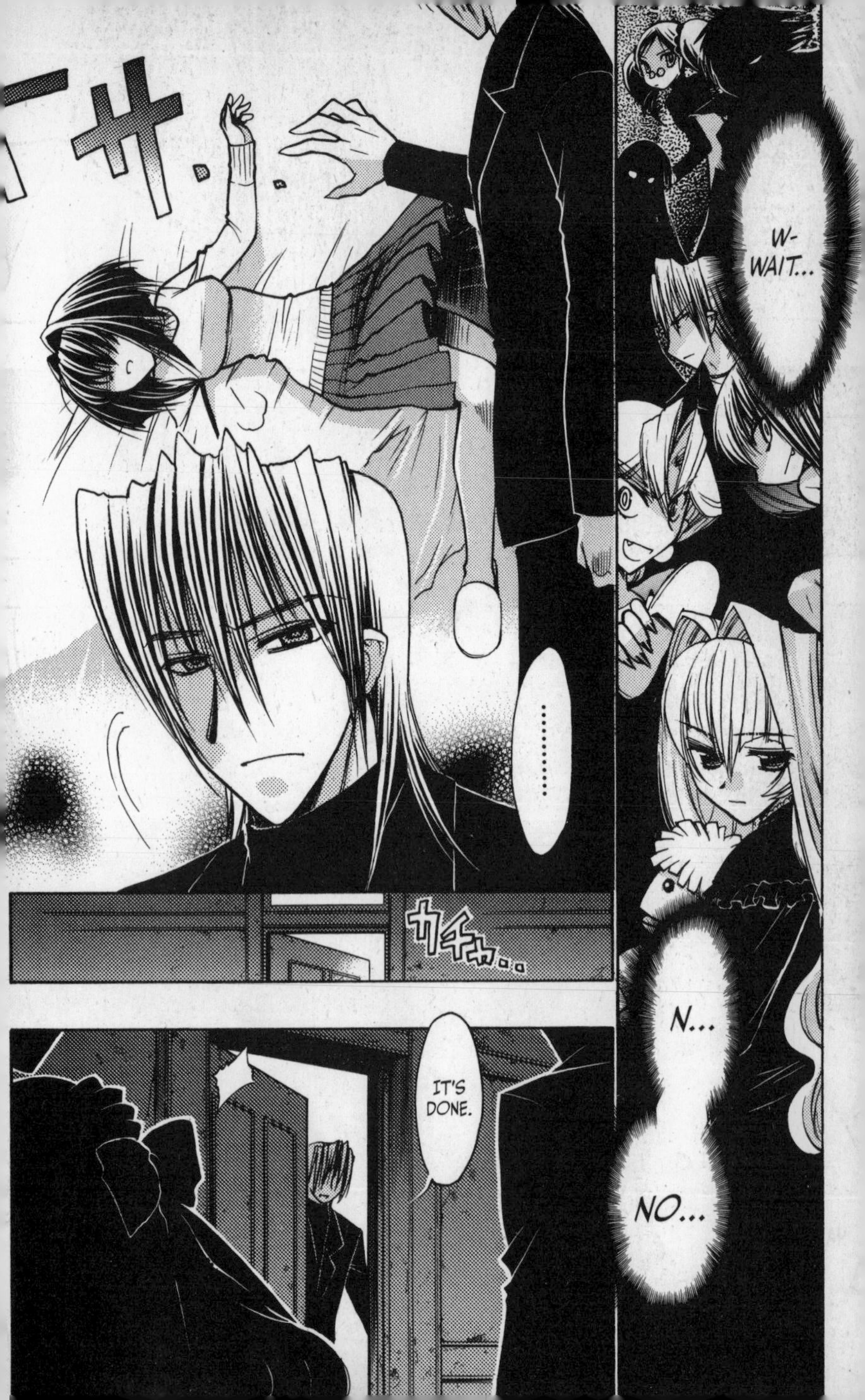
W-WAIT...
N...
NO...
......
カチャ..
IT'S DONE.

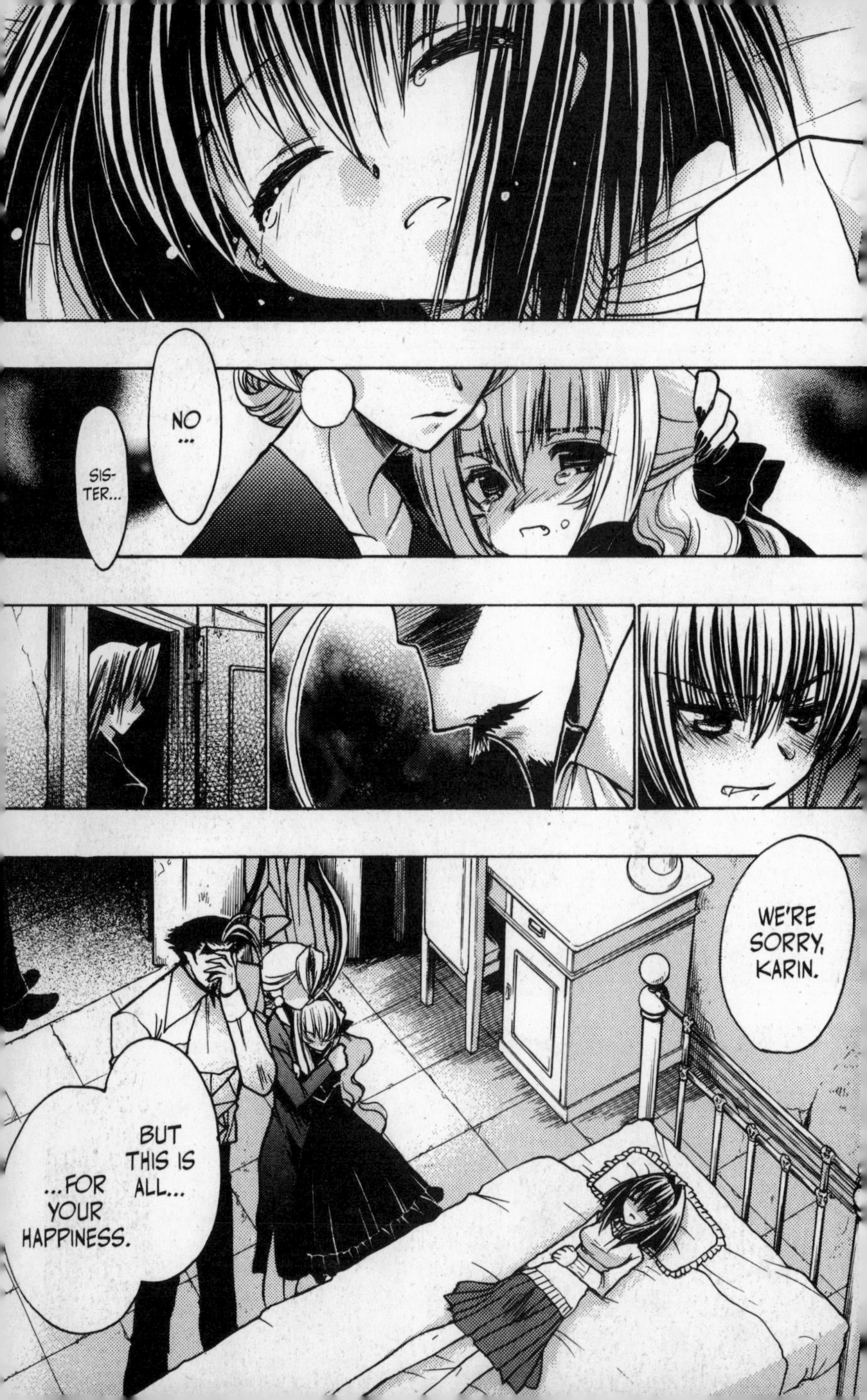
NO...
SISTER...
WE'RE SORRY, KARIN.
BUT THIS IS ALL...
...FOR YOUR HAPPINESS.

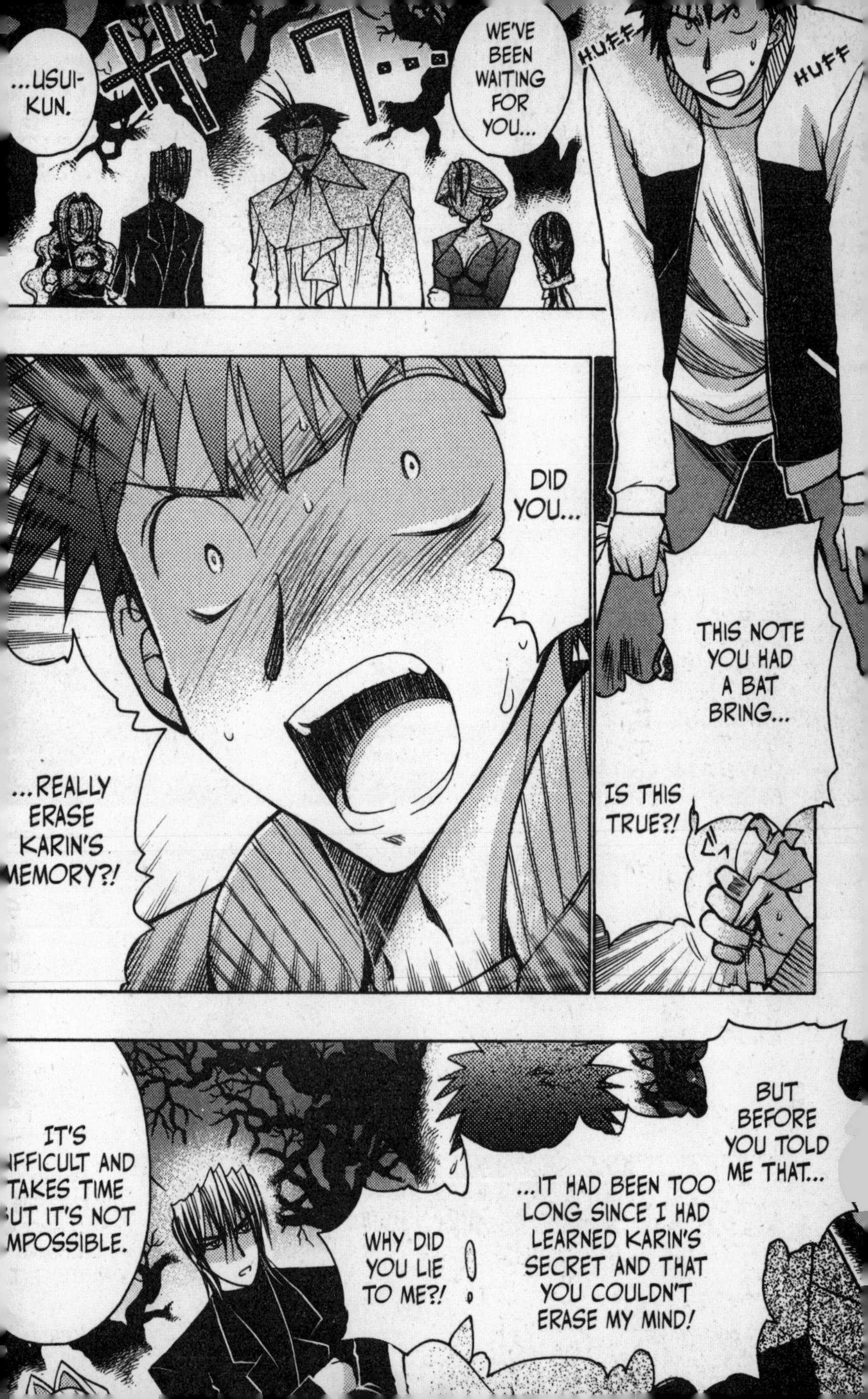
HUFF
HUFF
THIS NOTE YOU HAD A BAT BRING...
IS THIS TRUE?!
WE'VE BEEN WAITING FOR YOU...
...USUI-KUN.
DID YOU...
...REALLY ERASE KARIN'S MEMORY?!
BUT BEFORE YOU TOLD ME THAT...
...IT HAD BEEN TOO LONG SINCE I HAD LEARNED KARIN'S SECRET AND THAT YOU COULDN'T ERASE MY MIND!
WHY DID YOU LIE TO ME?!
!
IT'S IFFICULT AND TAKES TIME UT IT'S NOT MPOSSIBLE.

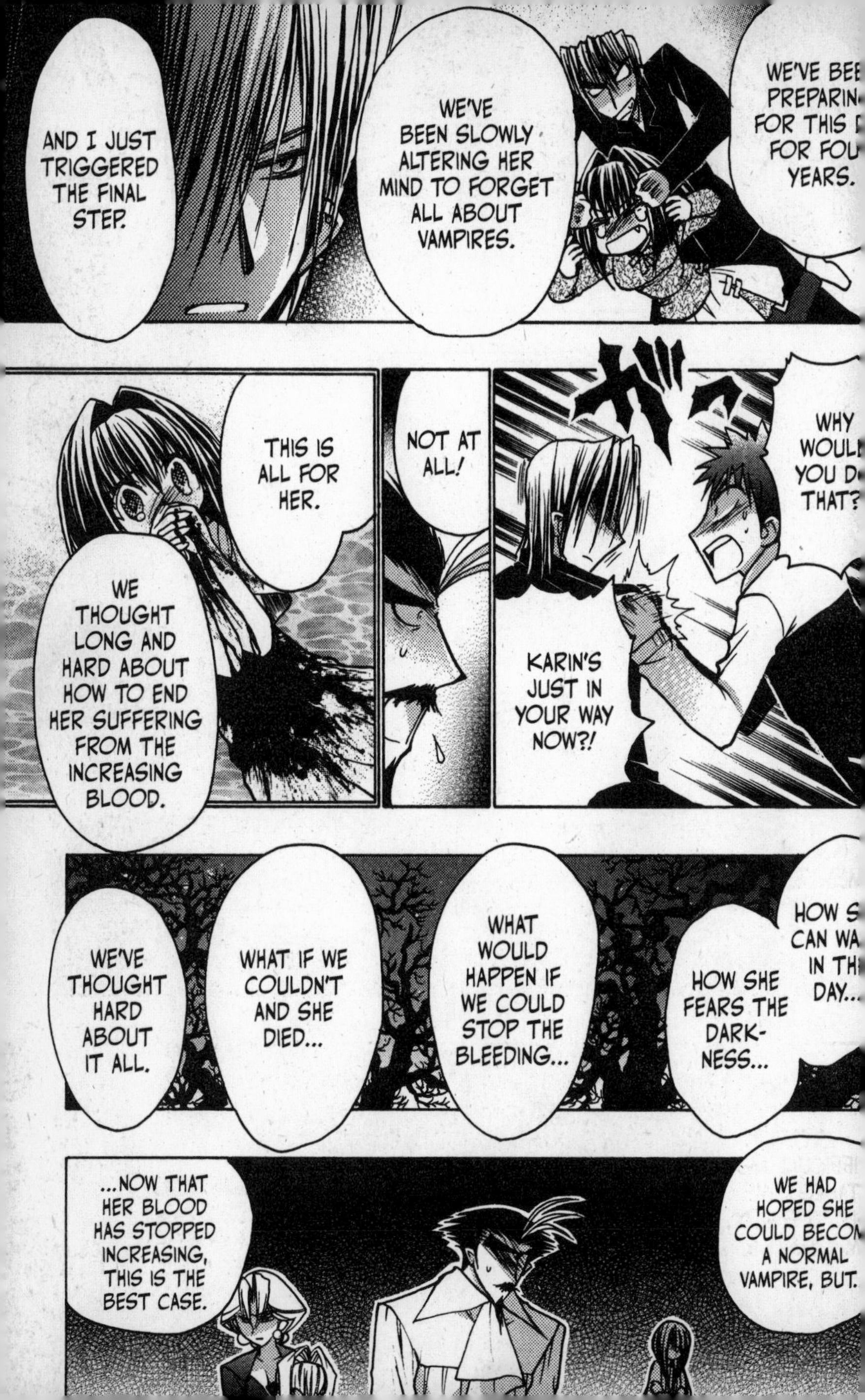
WE'VE BEE PREPARIN FOR THIS FOR FOU YEARS.
WE'VE BEEN SLOWLY ALTERING HER MIND TO FORGET ALL ABOUT VAMPIRES.
AND I JUST TRIGGERED THE FINAL STEP.
WHY WOUL YOU D THAT?
KARIN'S JUST IN YOUR WAY NOW?!
NOT AT ALL!
THIS IS ALL FOR HER.
WE THOUGHT LONG AND HARD ABOUT HOW TO END HER SUFFERING FROM THE INCREASING BLOOD.
HOW S CAN WA IN TH DAY...
HOW SHE FEARS THE DARK-NESS...
WHAT WOULD HAPPEN IF WE COULD STOP THE BLEEDING...
WHAT IF WE COULDN'T AND SHE DIED...
WE'VE THOUGHT HARD ABOUT IT ALL.
WE HAD HOPED SHE COULD BECOM A NORMAL VAMPIRE, BUT...
...NOW THAT HER BLOOD HAS STOPPED INCREASING, THIS IS THE BEST CASE.

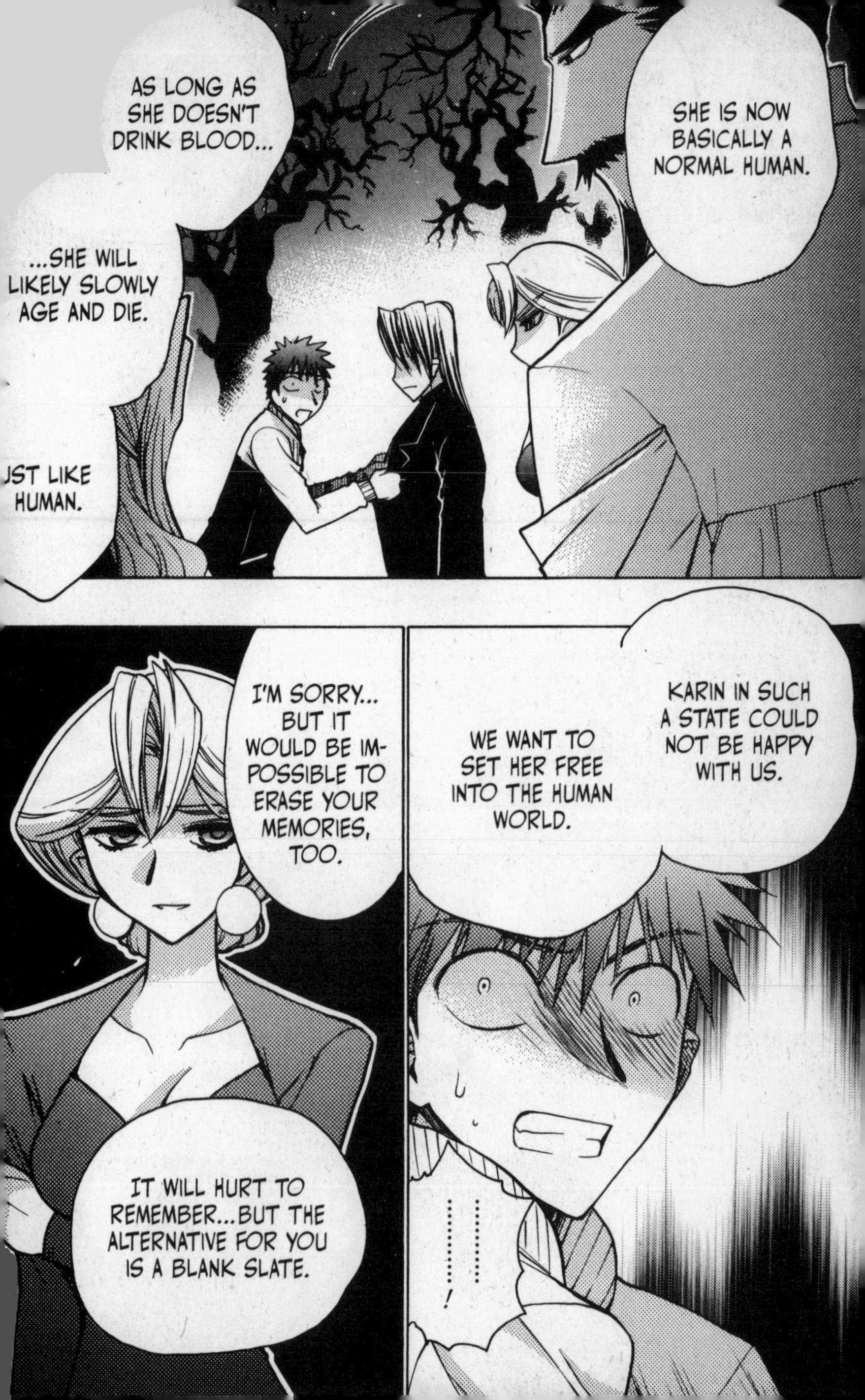
SHE IS NOW BASICALLY A NORMAL HUMAN.
AS LONG AS SHE DOESN'T DRINK BLOOD...
...SHE WILL LIKELY SLOWLY AGE AND DIE.
JST LIKE HUMAN.
KARIN IN SUCH A STATE COULD NOT BE HAPPY WITH US.
WE WANT TO SET HER FREE INTO THE HUMAN WORLD.
......!
I'M SORRY... BUT IT WOULD BE IM-POSSIBLE TO ERASE YOUR MEMORIES, TOO.
IT WILL HURT TO REMEMBER...BUT THE ALTERNATIVE FOR YOU IS A BLANK SLATE.

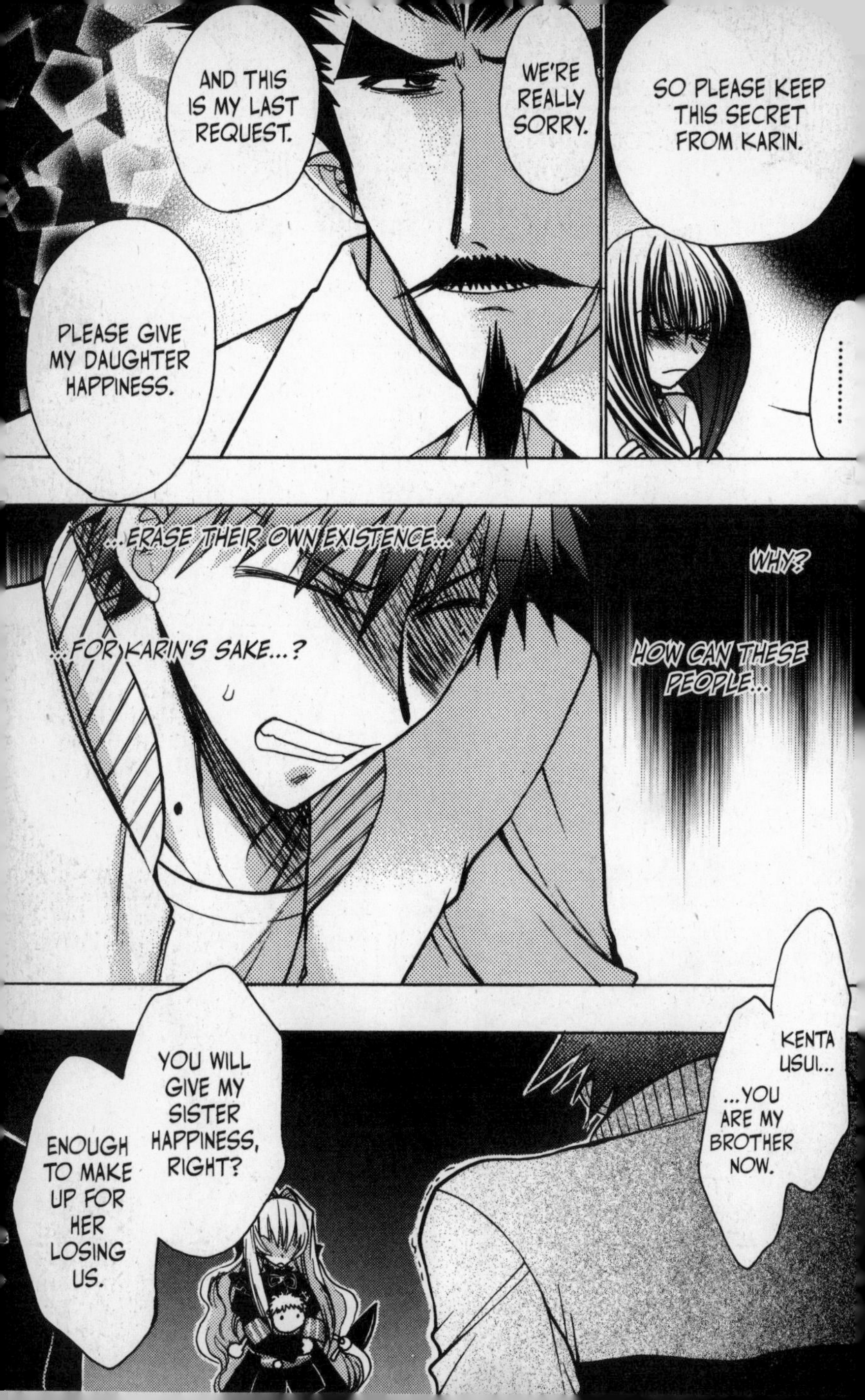
SO PLEASE KEEP THIS SECRET FROM KARIN.
......
WE'RE REALLY SORRY.
AND THIS IS MY LAST REQUEST.
PLEASE GIVE MY DAUGHTER HAPPINESS.
WHY?
HOW CAN THESE PEOPLE...
...ERASE THEIR OWN EXISTENCE...
...FOR KARIN'S SAKE...?
KENTA USUI...
...YOU ARE MY BROTHER NOW.
YOU WILL GIVE MY SISTER HAPPINESS, RIGHT?
ENOUGH TO MAKE UP FOR HER LOSING US.

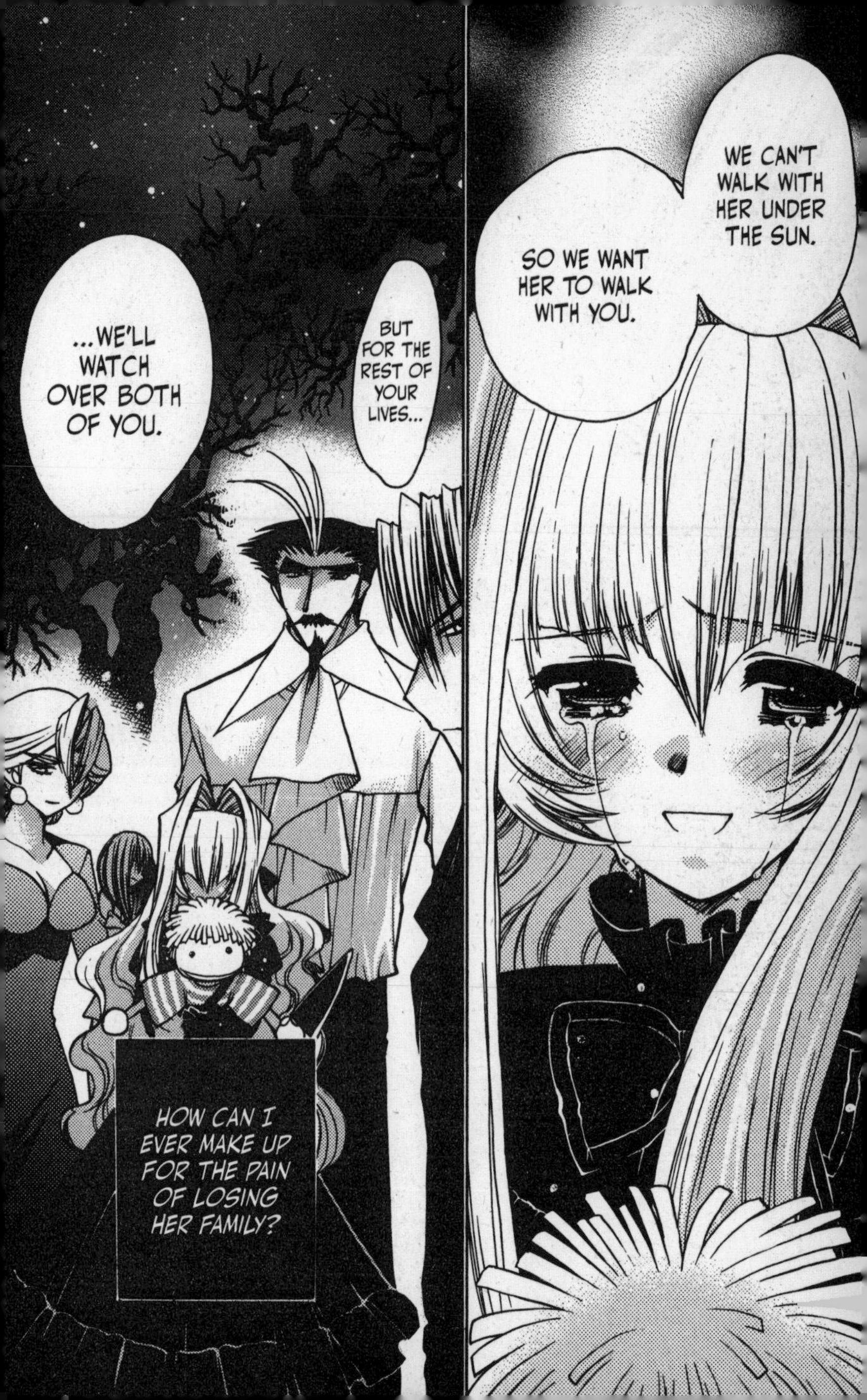
WE CAN'T WALK WITH HER UNDER THE SUN.
SO WE WANT HER TO WALK WITH YOU.
BUT FOR THE REST OF YOUR LIVES...
...WE'LL WATCH OVER BOTH OF YOU.
HOW CAN I EVER MAKE UP FOR THE PAIN OF LOSING HER FAMILY?

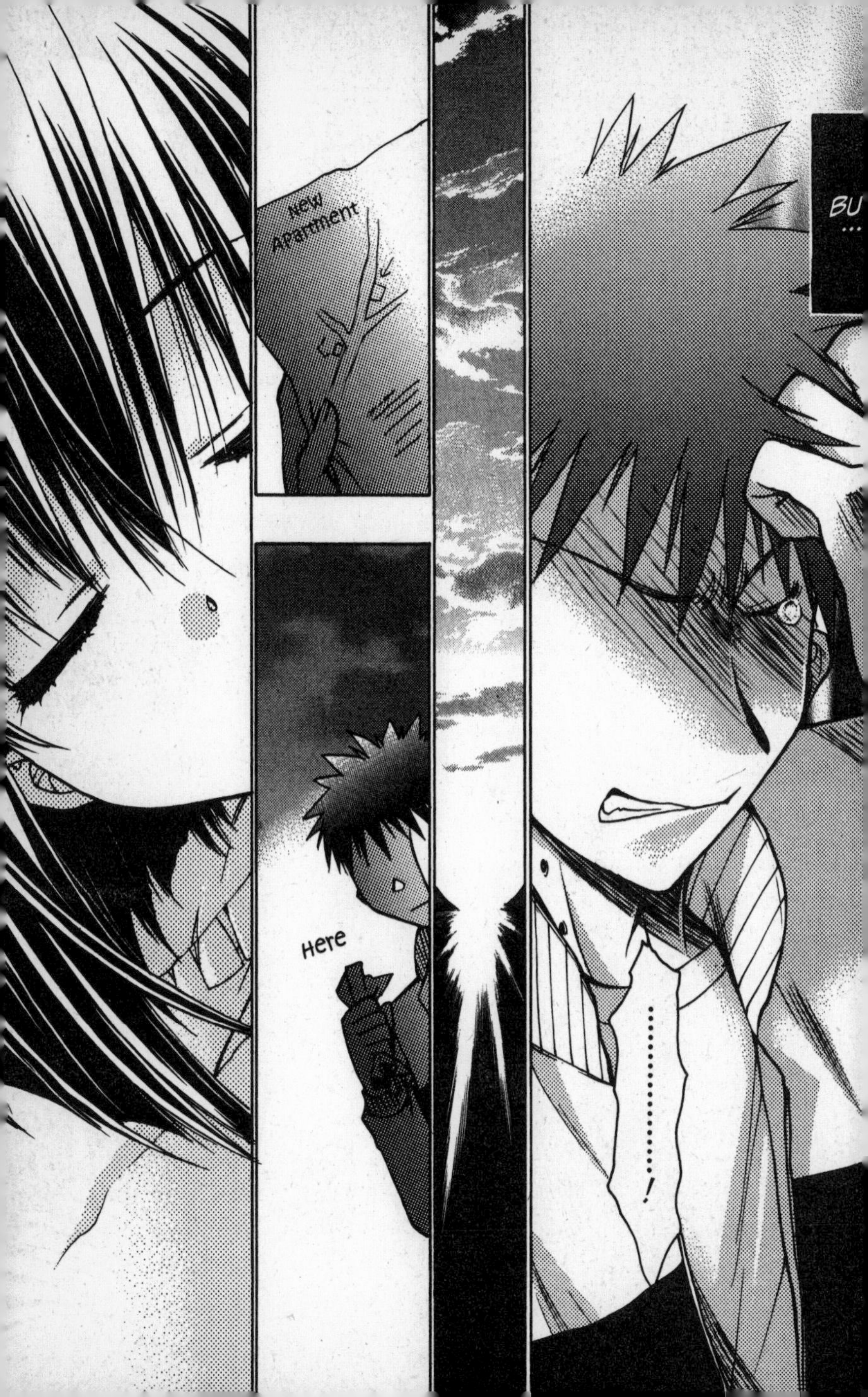
BU...
......!
New Apartment
Here

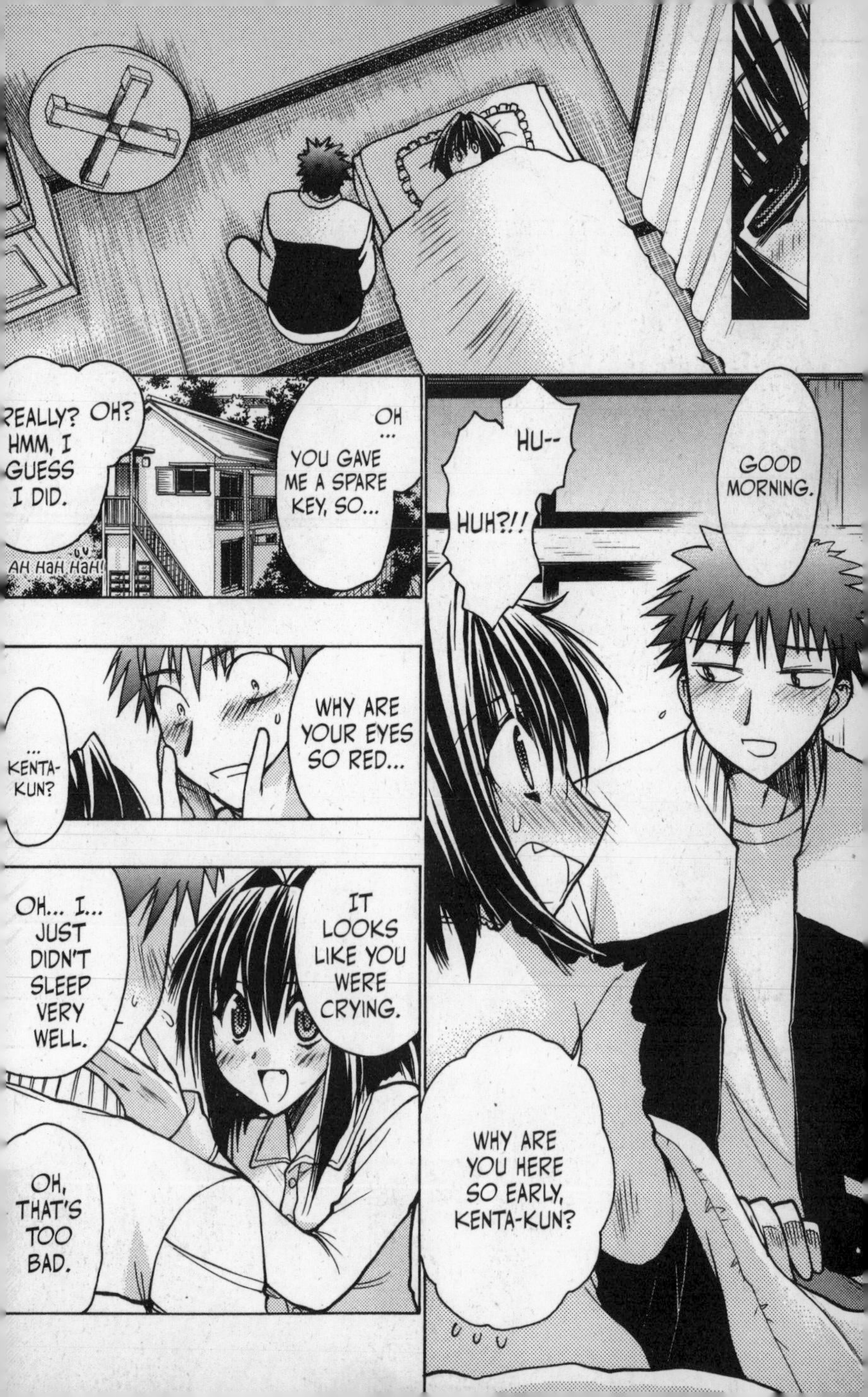
GOOD MORNING.
HU--
HUH?!!
WHY ARE YOU HERE SO EARLY, KENTA-KUN?
OH... YOU GAVE ME A SPARE KEY, SO...
OH? REALLY? HMM, I GUESS I DID.
AH HAH HAH!
WHY ARE YOUR EYES SO RED...
... KENTA-KUN?
IT LOOKS LIKE YOU WERE CRYING.
OH... I... JUST DIDN'T SLEEP VERY WELL.
OH, THAT'S TOO BAD.

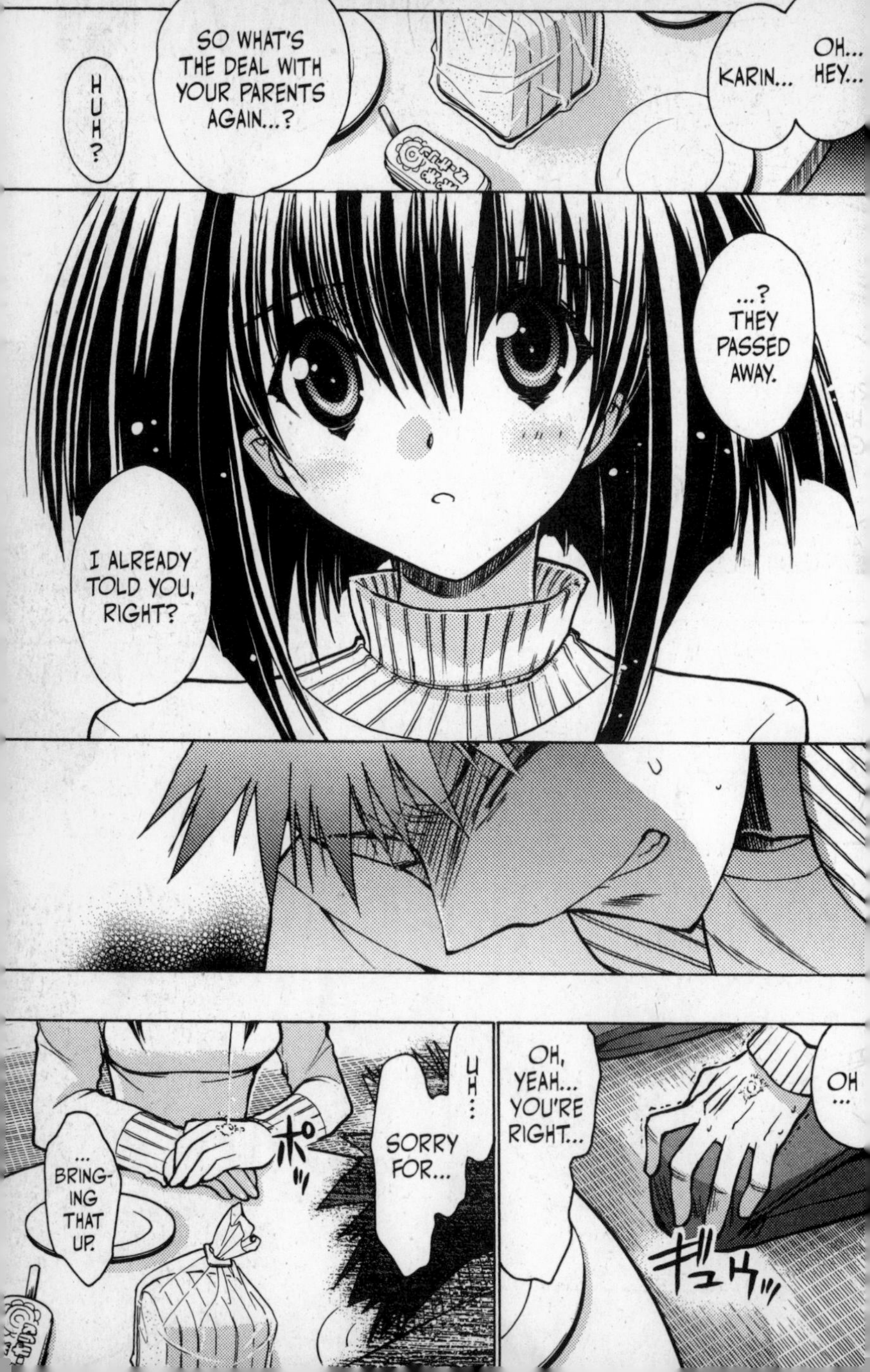
OH... HEY... KARIN...
SO WHAT'S THE DEAL WITH YOUR PARENTS AGAIN...?
HUH?
...? THEY PASSED AWAY.
I ALREADY TOLD YOU, RIGHT?
OH ...
OH, YEAH... YOU'RE RIGHT...
ギュウッ
UH...
SORRY FOR...
...BRINGING THAT UP.
ポッ

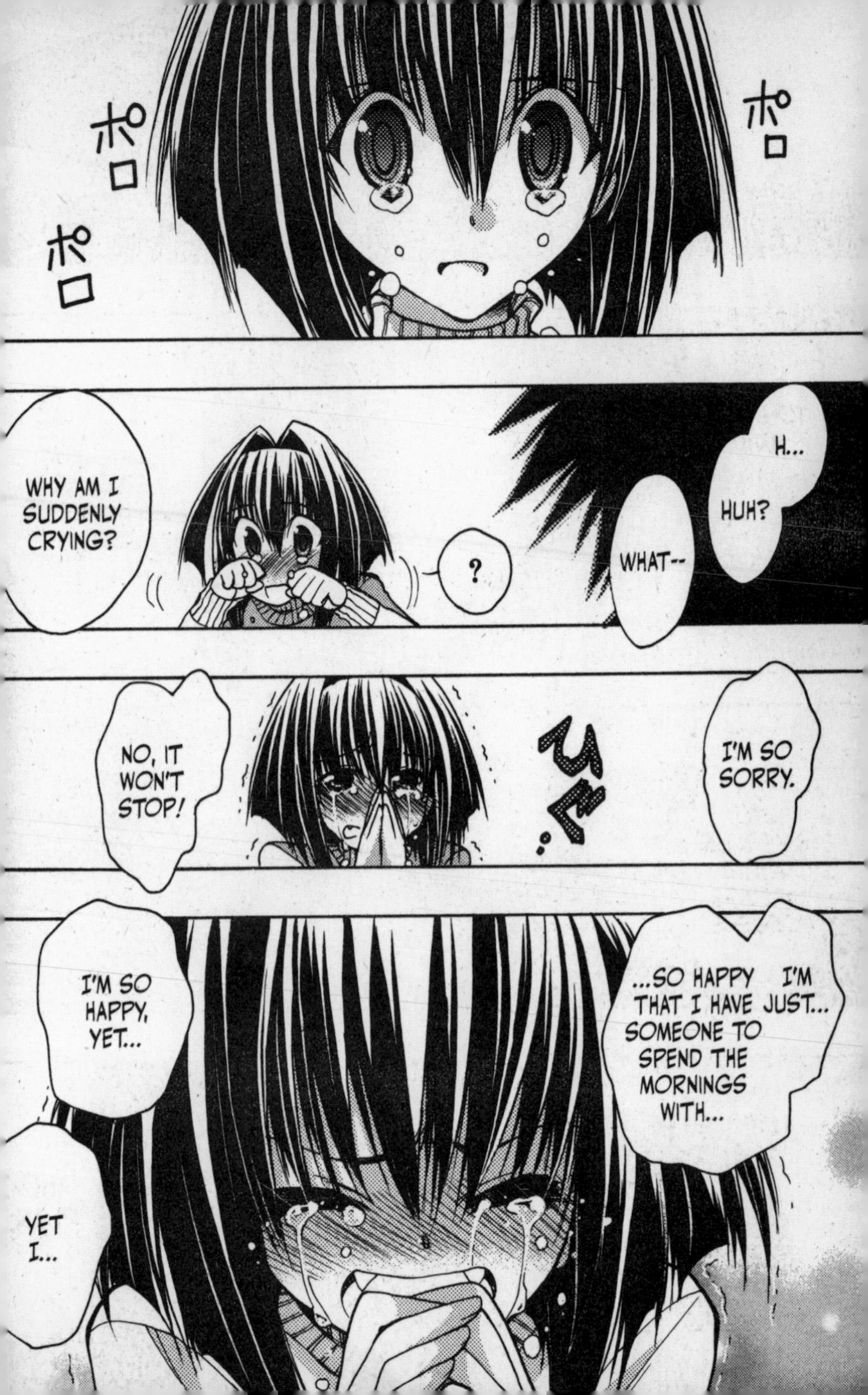
ポロ
ポロ
ポロ
H...
HUH?
WHAT--
?
WHY AM I SUDDENLY CRYING?
I'M SO SORRY.
ひぐ‥
NO, IT WON'T STOP!
I'M JUST...
...SO HAPPY THAT I HAVE SOMEONE TO SPEND THE MORNINGS WITH...
I'M SO HAPPY, YET...
YET I...

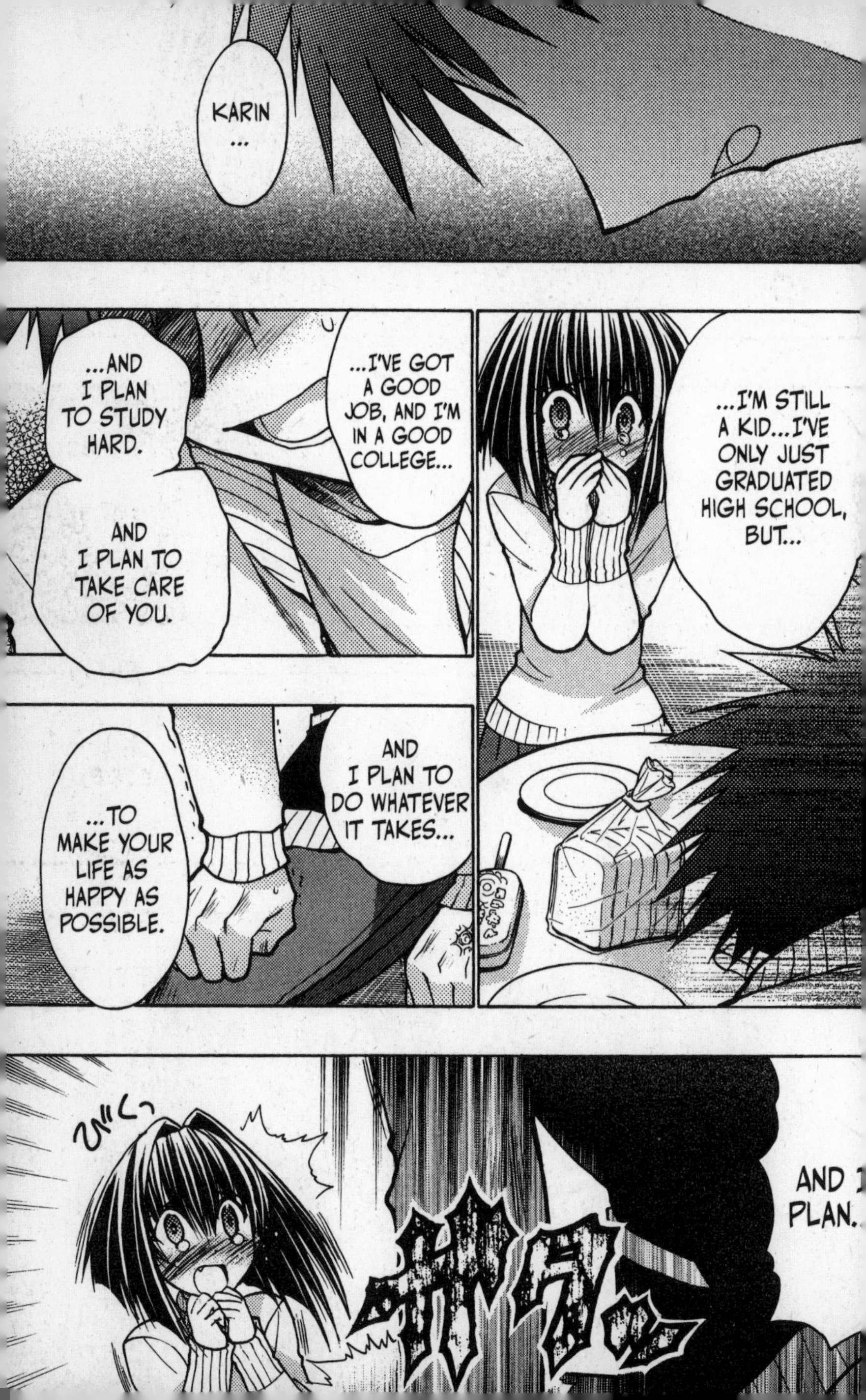
KARIN ...
...I'M STILL A KID...I'VE ONLY JUST GRADUATED HIGH SCHOOL, BUT...
...I'VE GOT A GOOD JOB, AND I'M IN A GOOD COLLEGE...
...AND I PLAN TO STUDY HARD.
AND I PLAN TO TAKE CARE OF YOU.
AND I PLAN TO DO WHATEVER IT TAKES...
...TO MAKE YOUR LIFE AS HAPPY AS POSSIBLE.
AND I PLAN...
びくっ

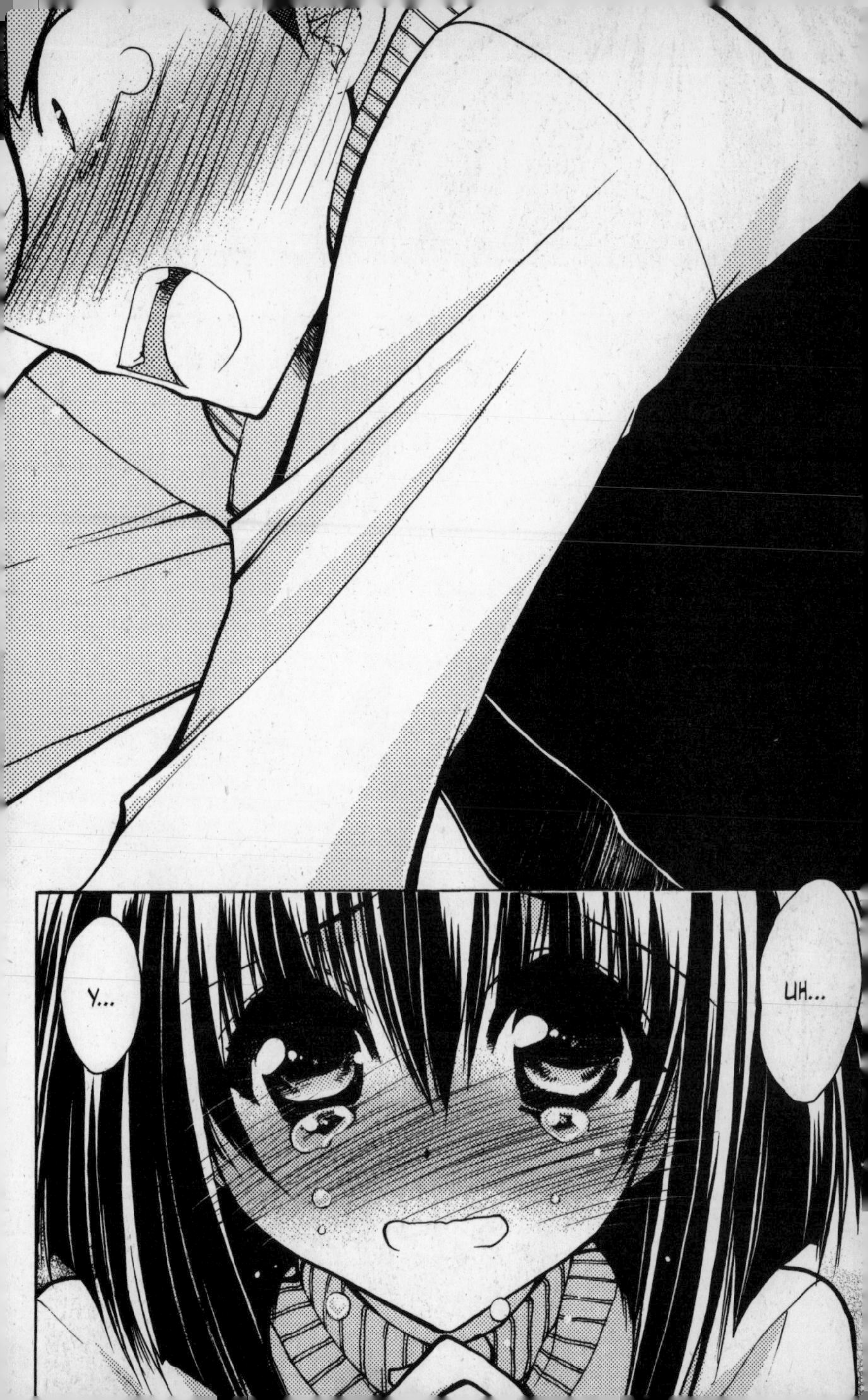
UH...
Y...

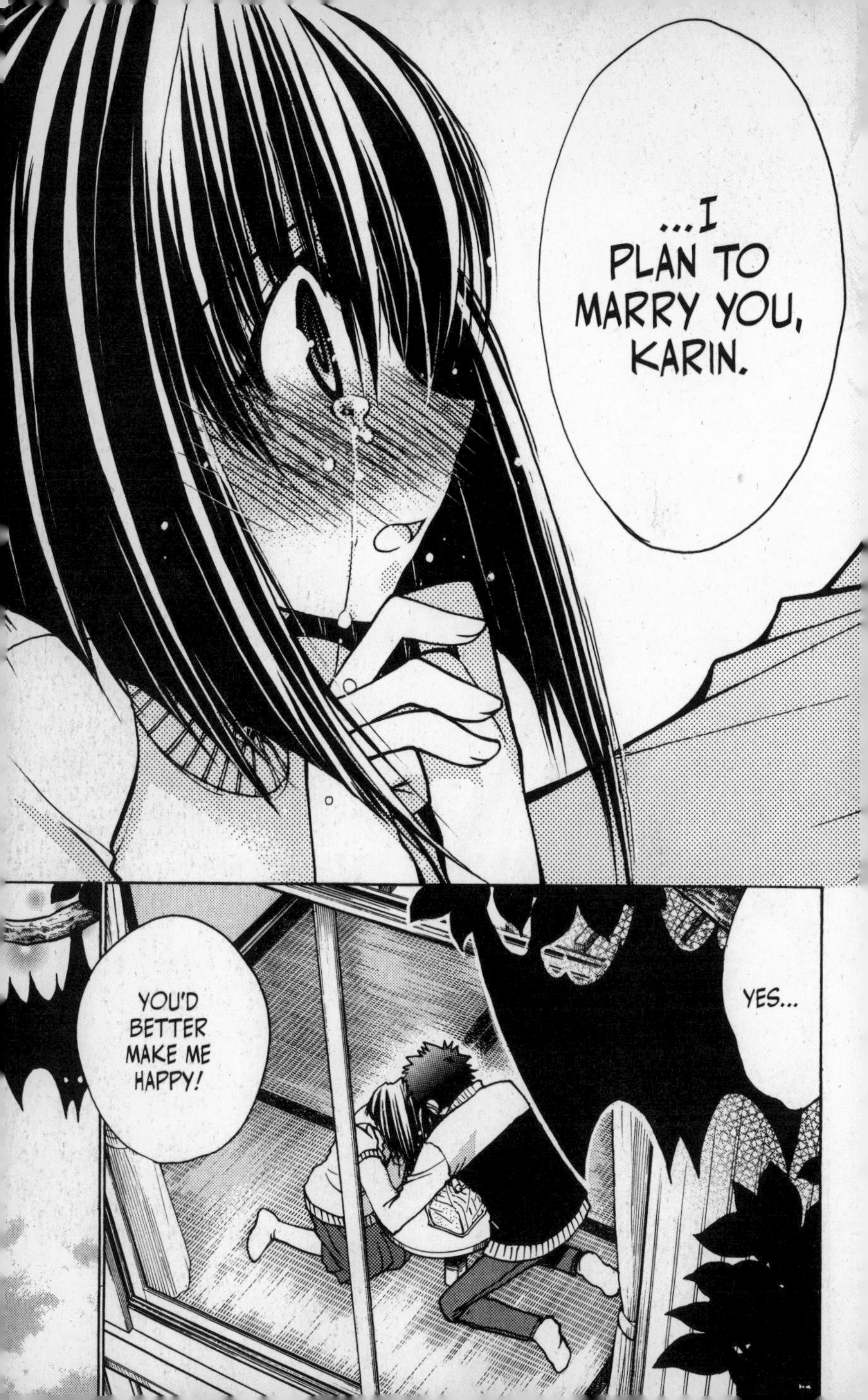
...I PLAN TO MARRY YOU, KARIN.
YES...
YOU'D BETTER MAKE ME HAPPY!

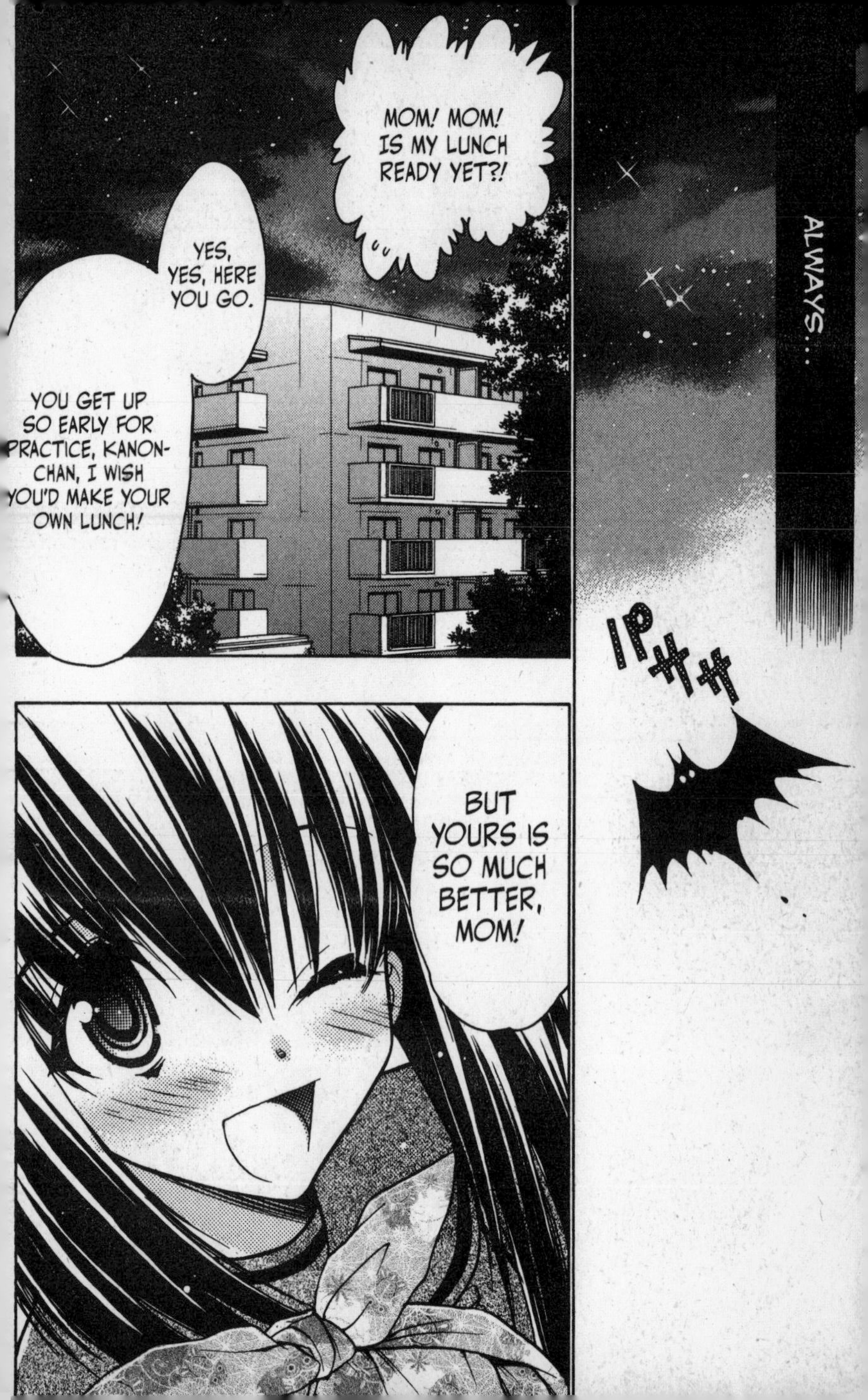
ALWAYS...
MOM! MOM! IS MY LUNCH READY YET?!
YES, YES, HERE YOU GO.
YOU GET UP SO EARLY FOR PRACTICE, KANON-CHAN, I WISH YOU'D MAKE YOUR OWN LUNCH!
BUT YOURS IS SO MUCH BETTER, MOM!

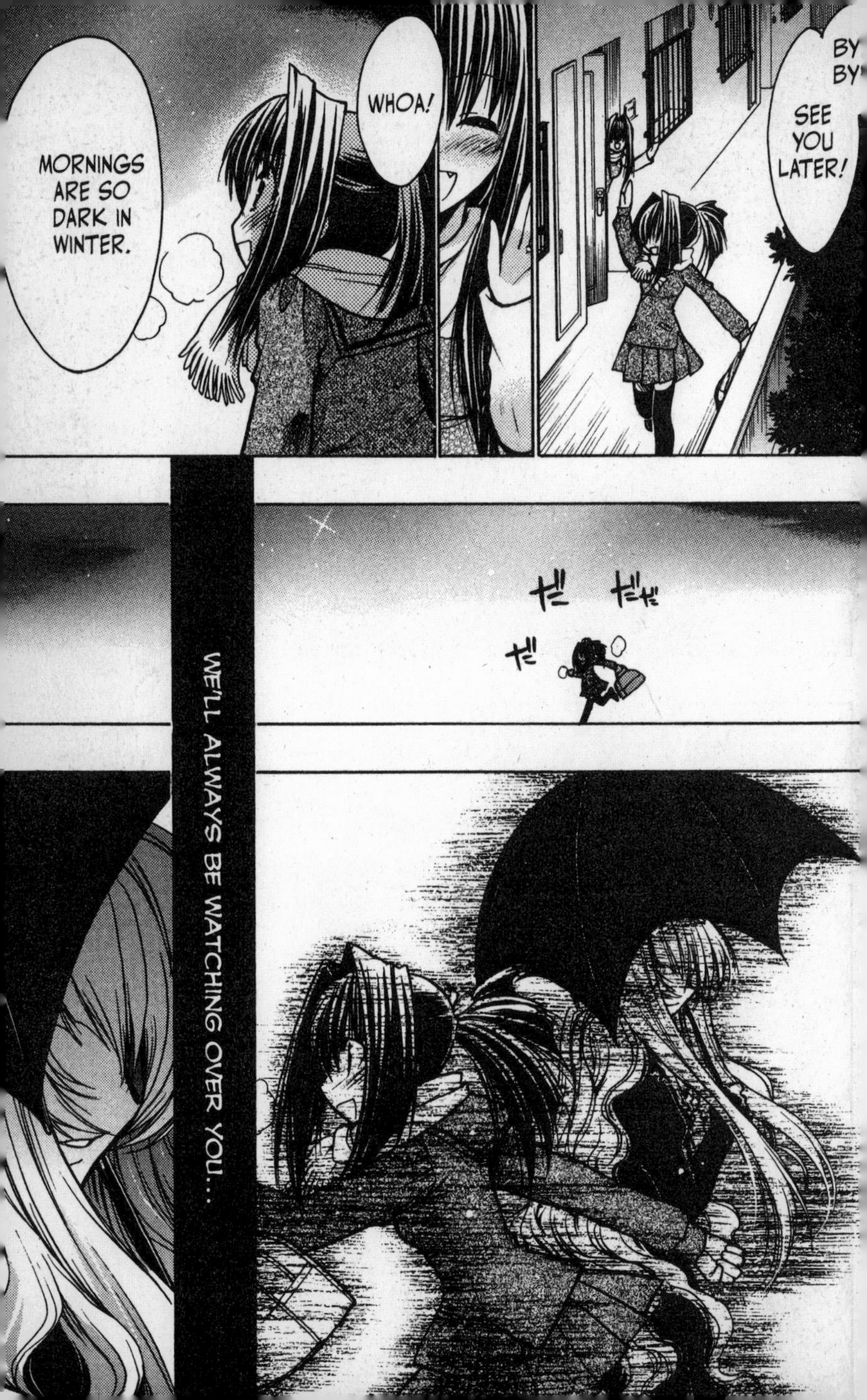
BY BY
SEE YOU LATER!
WHOA!
MORNINGS ARE SO DARK IN WINTER.
だ
だだ
だ
WE'LL ALWAYS BE WATCHING OVER YOU...

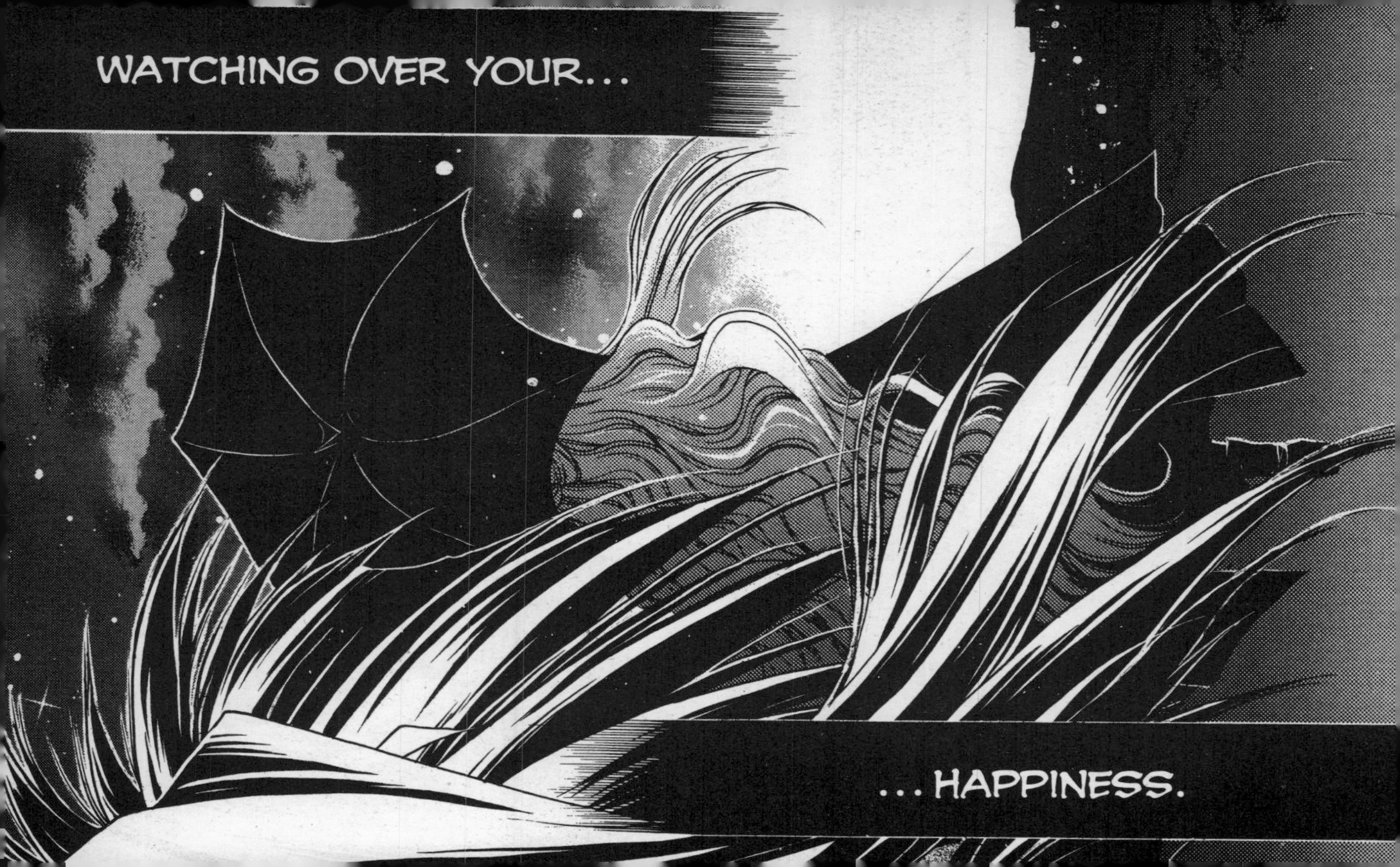
WATCHING OVER YOUR...
...HAPPINESS.

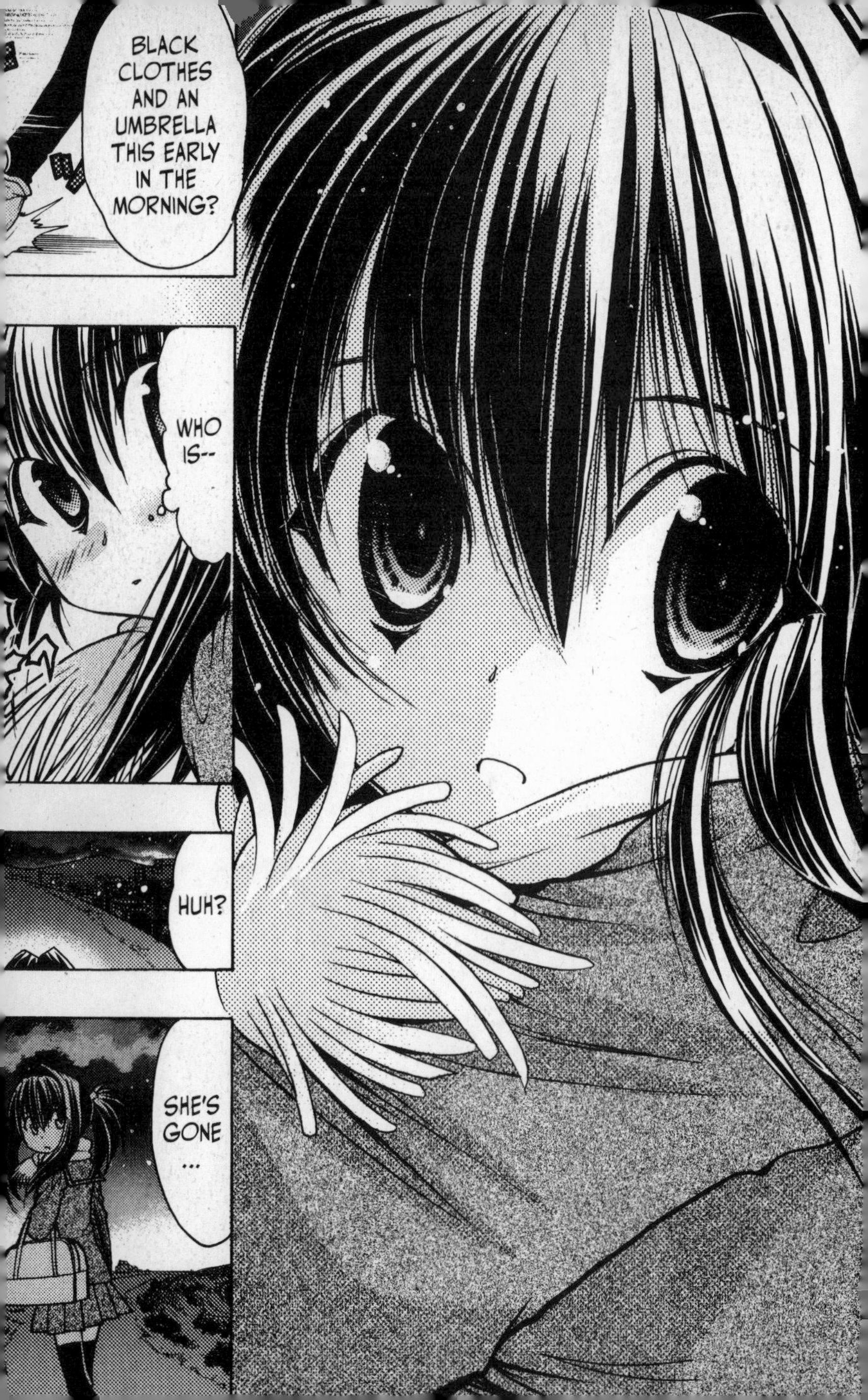
BLACK CLOTHES AND AN UMBRELLA THIS EARLY IN THE MORNING?
WHO IS--
HUH?
SHE'S GONE ...

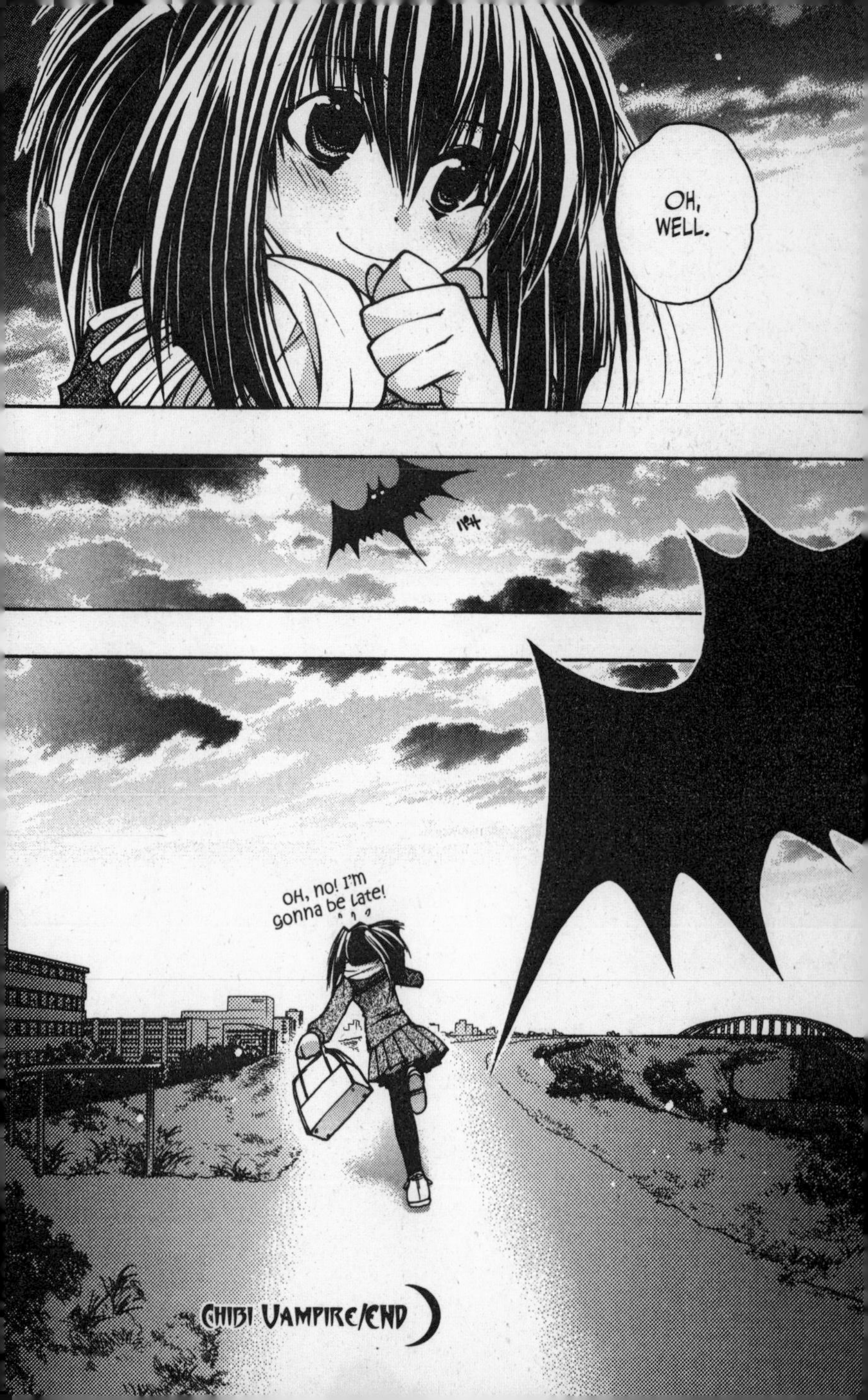
OH, WELL.
OH, no! I'm gonna be late!
CHIBI VAMPIRE/END

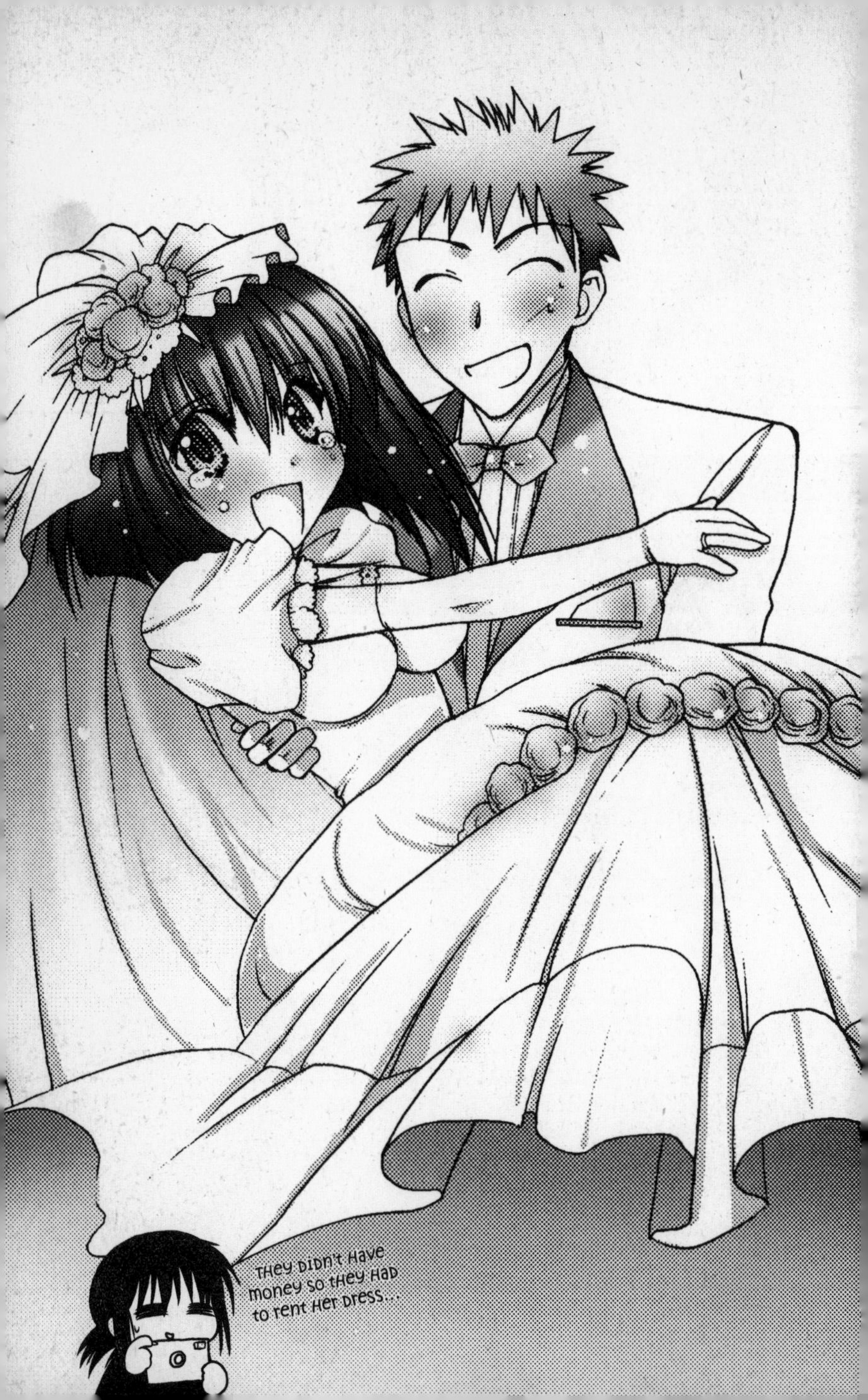
THEY DIDN'T HAVE MONEY SO THEY HAD TO RENT HER DRESS...

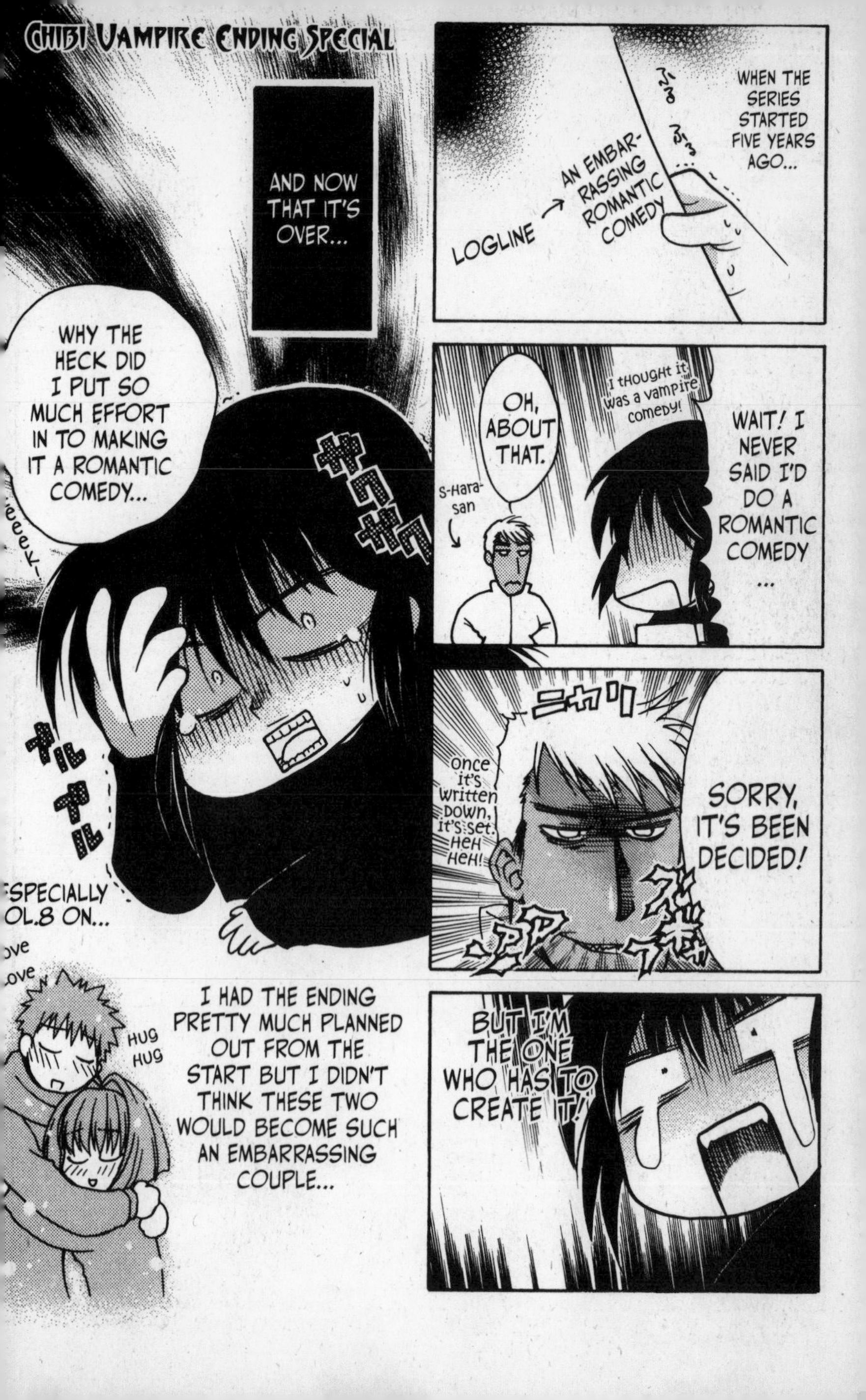

CHIBI VAMPIRE ENDING SPECIAL
WHEN THE SERIES STARTED FIVE YEARS AGO...
LOGLINE
AN EMBARRASSING ROMANTIC COMEDY
WAIT! I NEVER SAID I'D DO A ROMANTIC COMEDY...
I thought it was a vampire comedy!
OH, ABOUT THAT.
S-Hara-san
ニヤリ
SORRY, IT'S BEEN DECIDED!
once it's written down, it's set. HEH HEH!
BUT I'M THE ONE WHO HAS TO CREATE IT!
AND NOW THAT IT'S OVER...
WHY THE HECK DID I PUT SO MUCH EFFORT IN TO MAKING IT A ROMANTIC COMEDY...
eeek-
SPECIALLY
OL.8 ON...
HUG HUG
I HAD THE ENDING PRETTY MUCH PLANNED OUT FROM THE START BUT I DIDN'T THINK THESE TWO WOULD BECOME SUCH AN EMBARRASSING COUPLE...

ENGAGEMENT ♡

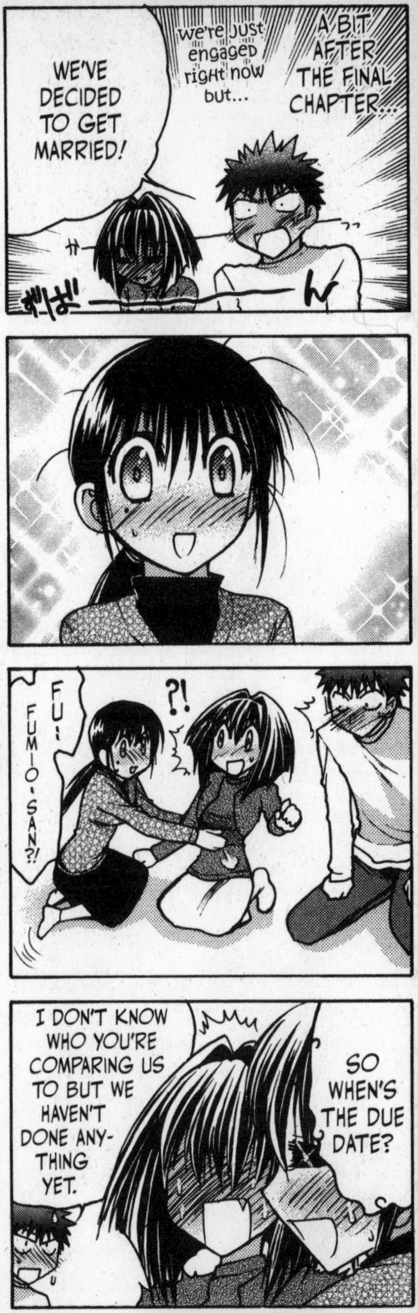
A BIT AFTER THE FINAL CHAPTER...
We're just engaged right now but...
WE'VE DECIDED TO GET MARRIED!
ずばーん
?!
FU!
FUMIO-SAN?!
SO WHEN'S THE DUE DATE?
I DON'T KNOW WHO YOU'RE COMPARING US TO BUT WE HAVEN'T DONE ANYTHING YET.

OH, Kenta. So much like your father...(LOL)

THE CURSE CONTINUES?

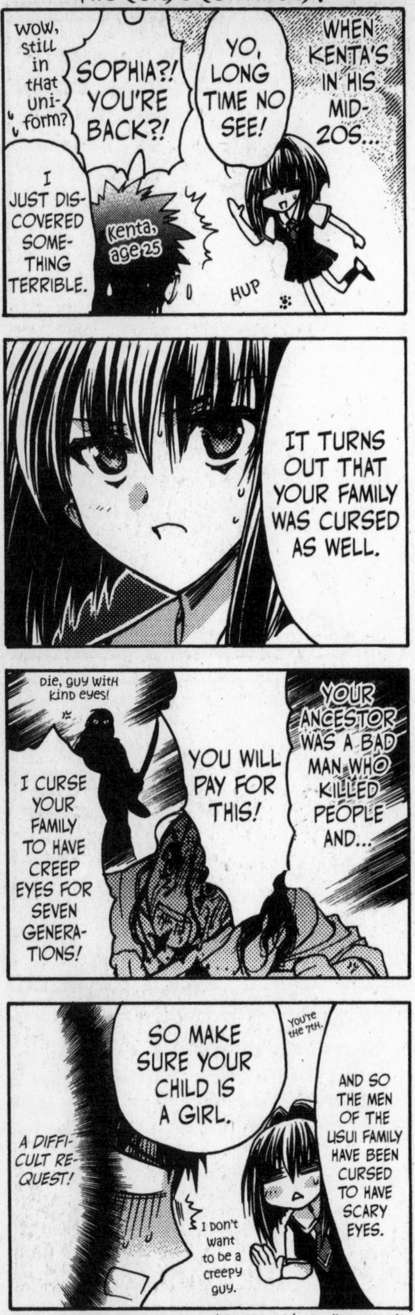
WHEN KENTA'S IN HIS MID-20S...
YO, LONG TIME NO SEE!
SOPHIA?! YOU'RE BACK?!
Wow, still in that uniform?
I JUST DISCOVERED SOMETHING TERRIBLE.
Kenta, age 25
HUP
IT TURNS OUT THAT YOUR FAMILY WAS CURSED AS WELL.
YOUR ANCESTOR WAS A BAD MAN WHO KILLED PEOPLE AND...
YOU WILL PAY FOR THIS!
Die, guy with kind eyes!
I CURSE YOUR FAMILY TO HAVE CREEP EYES FOR SEVEN GENERATIONS!
AND SO THE MEN OF THE USUI FAMILY HAVE BEEN CURSED TO HAVE SCARY EYES.
You're the 7th.
SO MAKE SURE YOUR CHILD IS A GIRL.
A DIFFICULT REQUEST!
I don't want to be a creepy guy.

The reason why the ancestor became a killer: "I couldn't make any friends because of these creepy eyes!"

Using your Brain is Tough

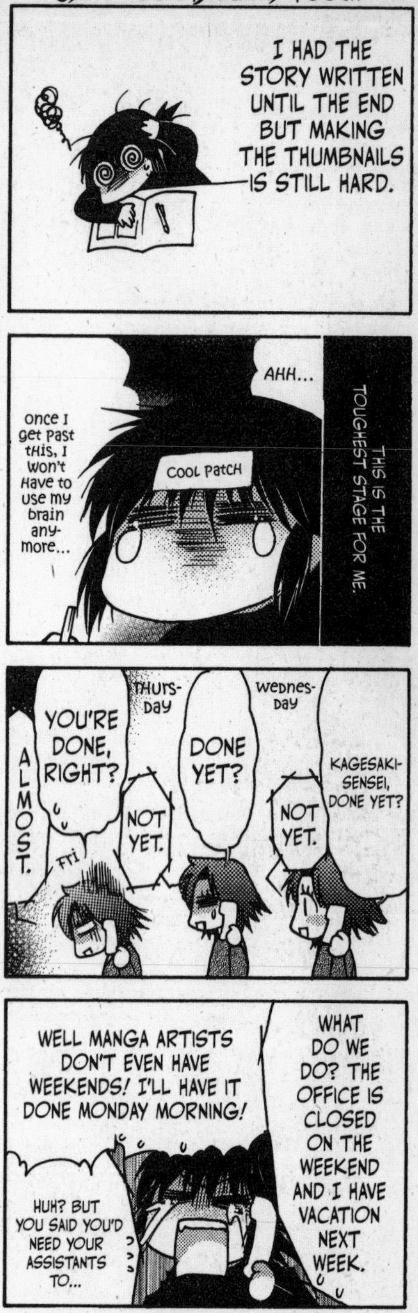
I HAD THE STORY WRITTEN UNTIL THE END BUT MAKING THE THUMBNAILS IS STILL HARD.
THIS IS THE TOUGHEST STAGE FOR ME.
AHH...
COOL PATCH
Once I get past this, I won't have to use my brain anymore...
Wednesday
KAGESAKI-SENSEI, DONE YET?
NOT YET.
Thursday
DONE YET?
NOT YET.
YOU'RE DONE, RIGHT?
ALMOST.
Fri
WHAT DO WE DO? THE OFFICE IS CLOSED ON THE WEEKEND AND I HAVE VACATION NEXT WEEK.
WELL MANGA ARTISTS DON'T EVEN HAVE WEEKENDS! I'LL HAVE IT DONE MONDAY MORNING!
HUH? BUT YOU SAID YOU'D NEED YOUR ASSISTANTS TO...

And this is repeated every month...

Getting Ahead

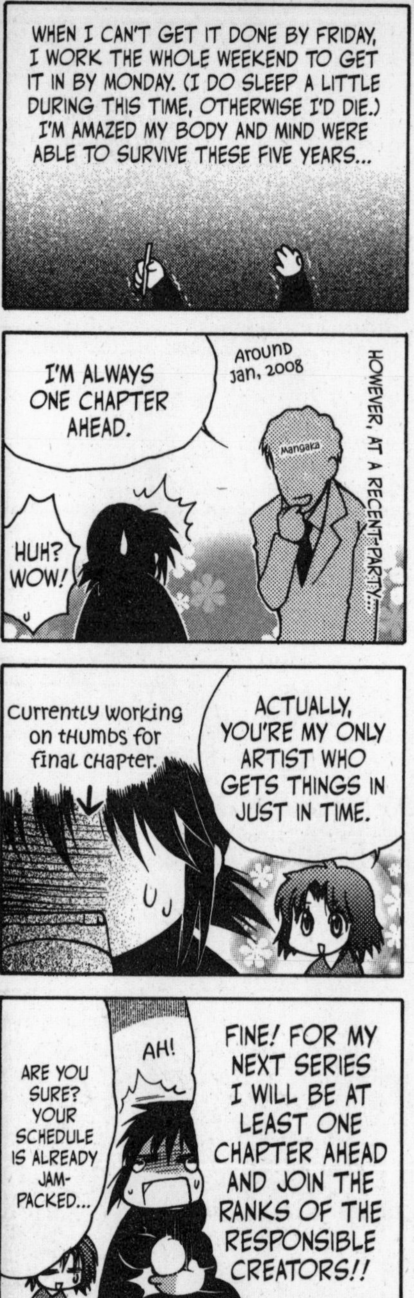
WHEN I CAN'T GET IT DONE BY FRIDAY, I WORK THE WHOLE WEEKEND TO GET IT IN BY MONDAY. (I DO SLEEP A LITTLE DURING THIS TIME, OTHERWISE I'D DIE.) I'M AMAZED MY BODY AND MIND WERE ABLE TO SURVIVE THESE FIVE YEARS...
HOWEVER, AT A RECENT PARTY...
Around Jan, 2008
Mangaka
I'M ALWAYS ONE CHAPTER AHEAD.
HUH? WOW!
ACTUALLY, YOU'RE MY ONLY ARTIST WHO GETS THINGS IN JUST IN TIME.
Currently working on thumbs for final chapter.
FINE! FOR MY NEXT SERIES I WILL BE AT LEAST ONE CHAPTER AHEAD AND JOIN THE RANKS OF THE RESPONSIBLE CREATORS!!
AH!
ARE YOU SURE? YOUR SCHEDULE IS ALREADY JAM-PACKED...

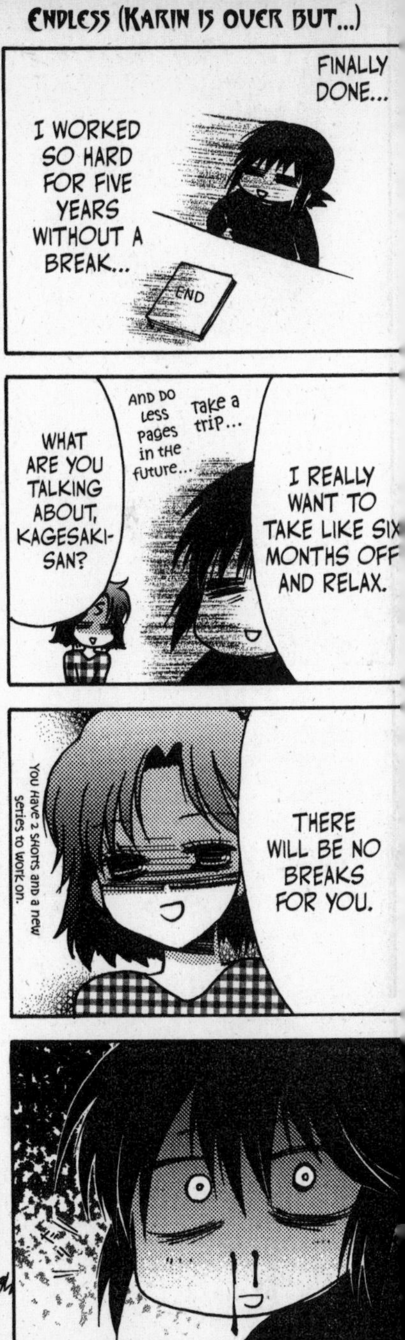
ENDLESS (KARIN IS OVER BUT...)
FINALLY DONE...
I WORKED SO HARD FOR FIVE YEARS WITHOUT A BREAK...
END
I REALLY WANT TO TAKE LIKE SIX MONTHS OFF AND RELAX.
Take a trip...
And do less pages in the future...
WHAT ARE YOU TALKING ABOUT, KAGESAKI-SAN?
THERE WILL BE NO BREAKS FOR YOU.
You have 2 shorts and a new series to work on.

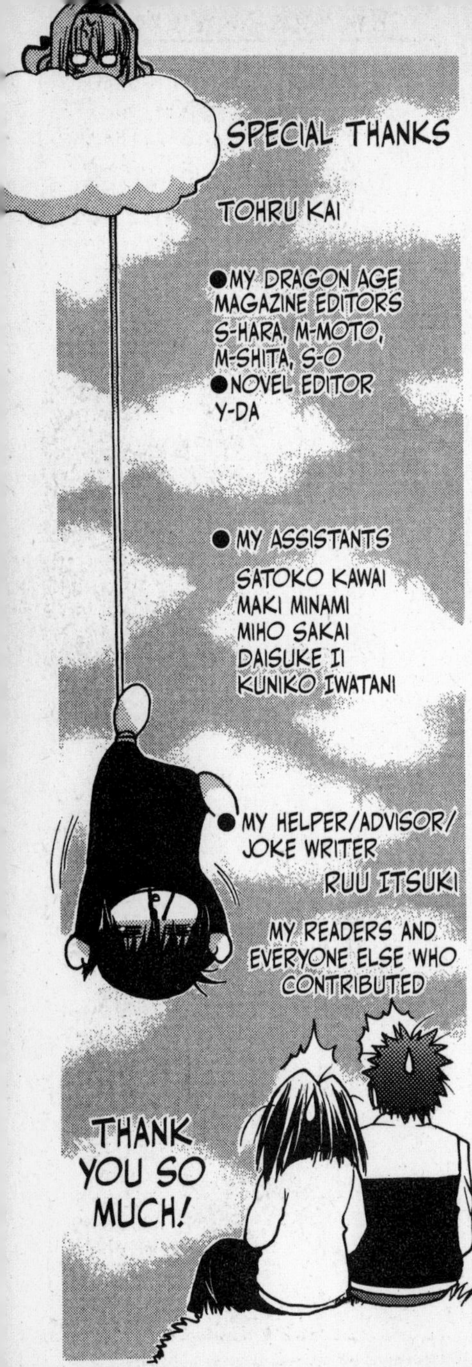
SPECIAL THANKS
TOHRU KAI
●MY DRAGON AGE MAGAZINE EDITORS S-HARA, M-MOTO, M-SHITA, S-O
●NOVEL EDITOR Y-DA
●MY ASSISTANTS
SATOKO KAWAI
MAKI MINAMI
MIHO SAKAI
DAISUKE II
KUNIKO IWATANI
●MY HELPER/ADVISOR/JOKE WRITER
RUU ITSUKI
MY READERS AND EVERYONE ELSE WHO CONTRIBUTED
THANK YOU SO MUCH!

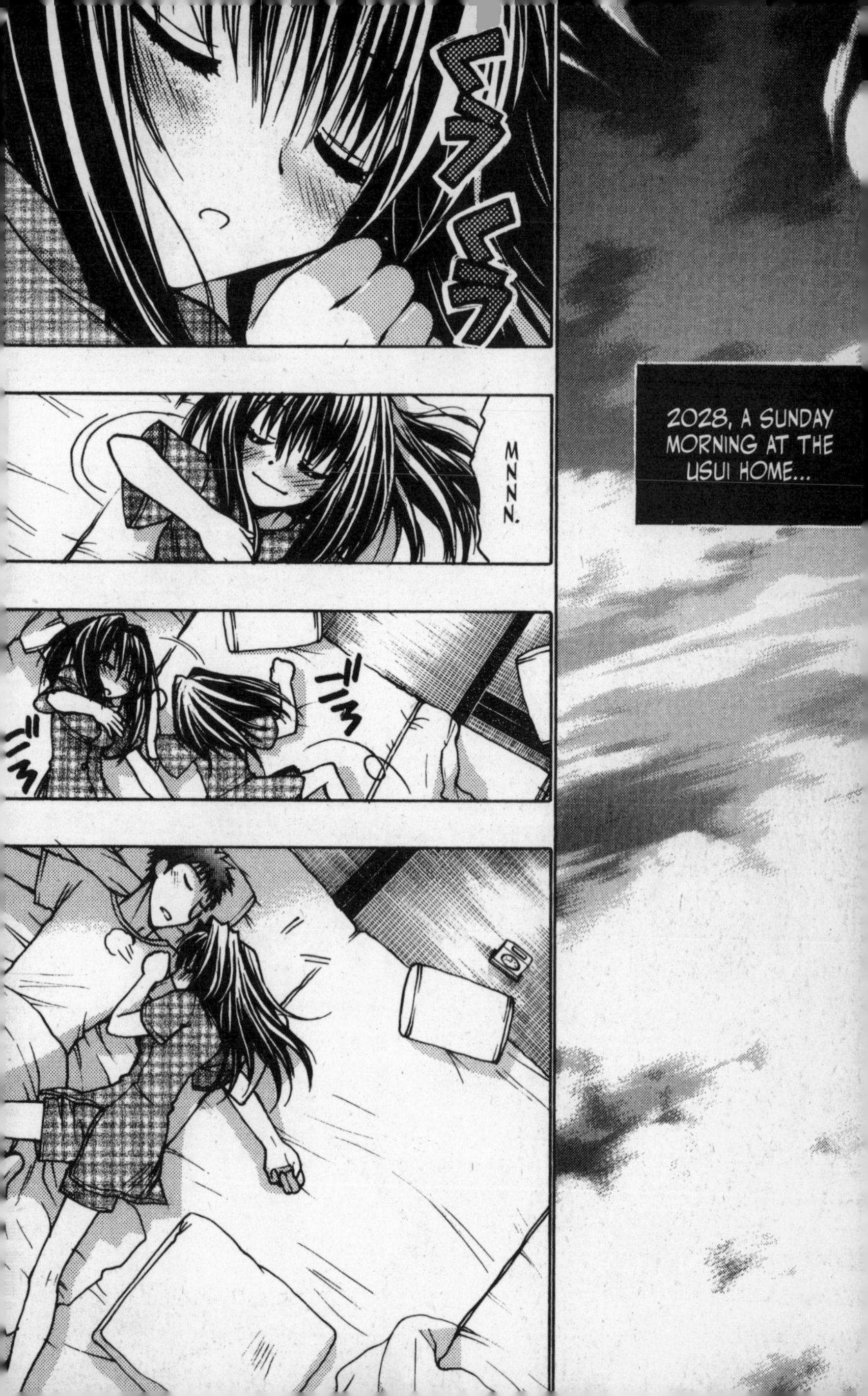
2028, A SUNDAY MORNING AT THE USUI HOME...
MNNN.

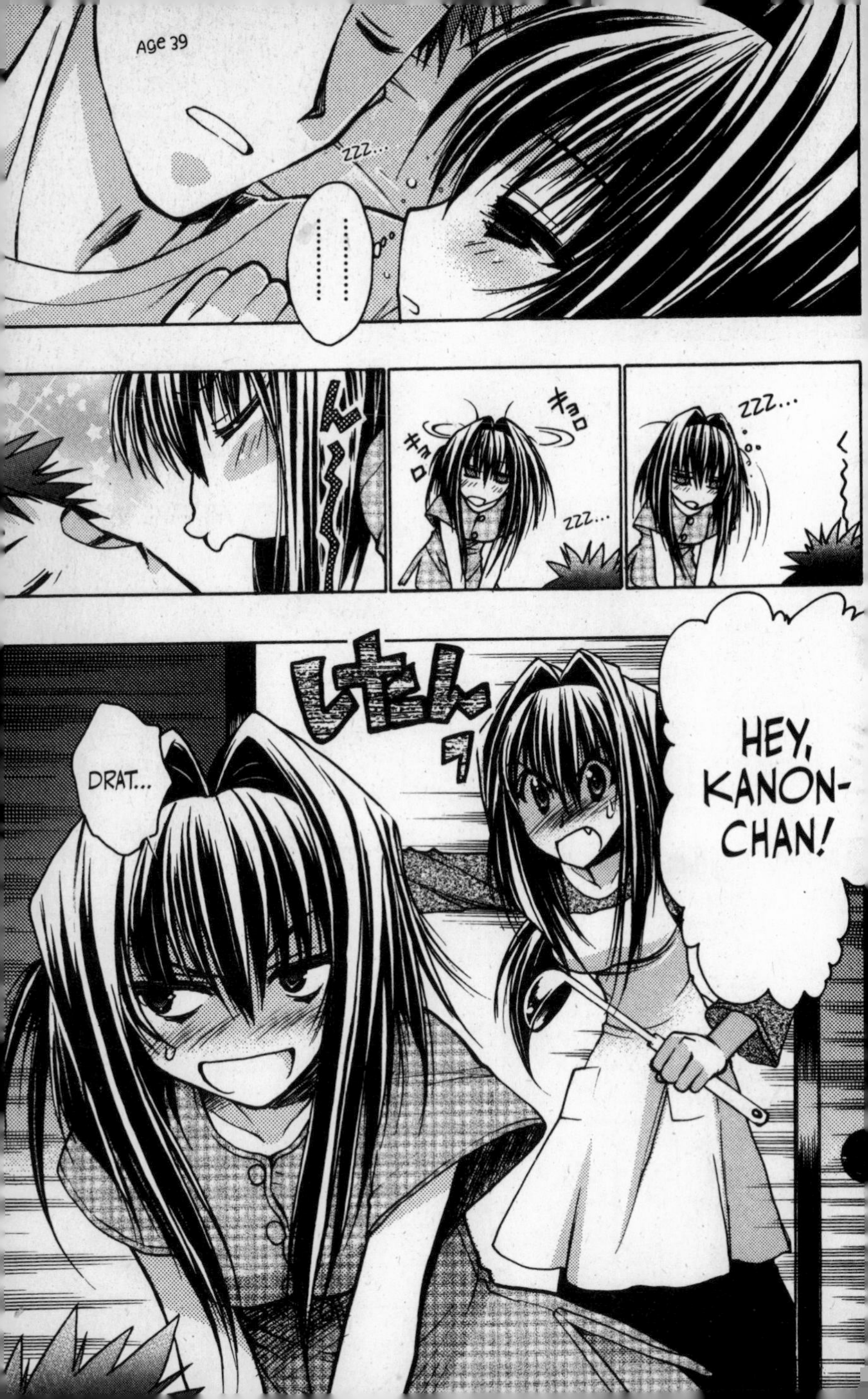
Age 39
ZZZ...
......
ZZZ...
キョロ
キョロ
ZZZ...
HEY, KANON-CHAN!
DRAT...

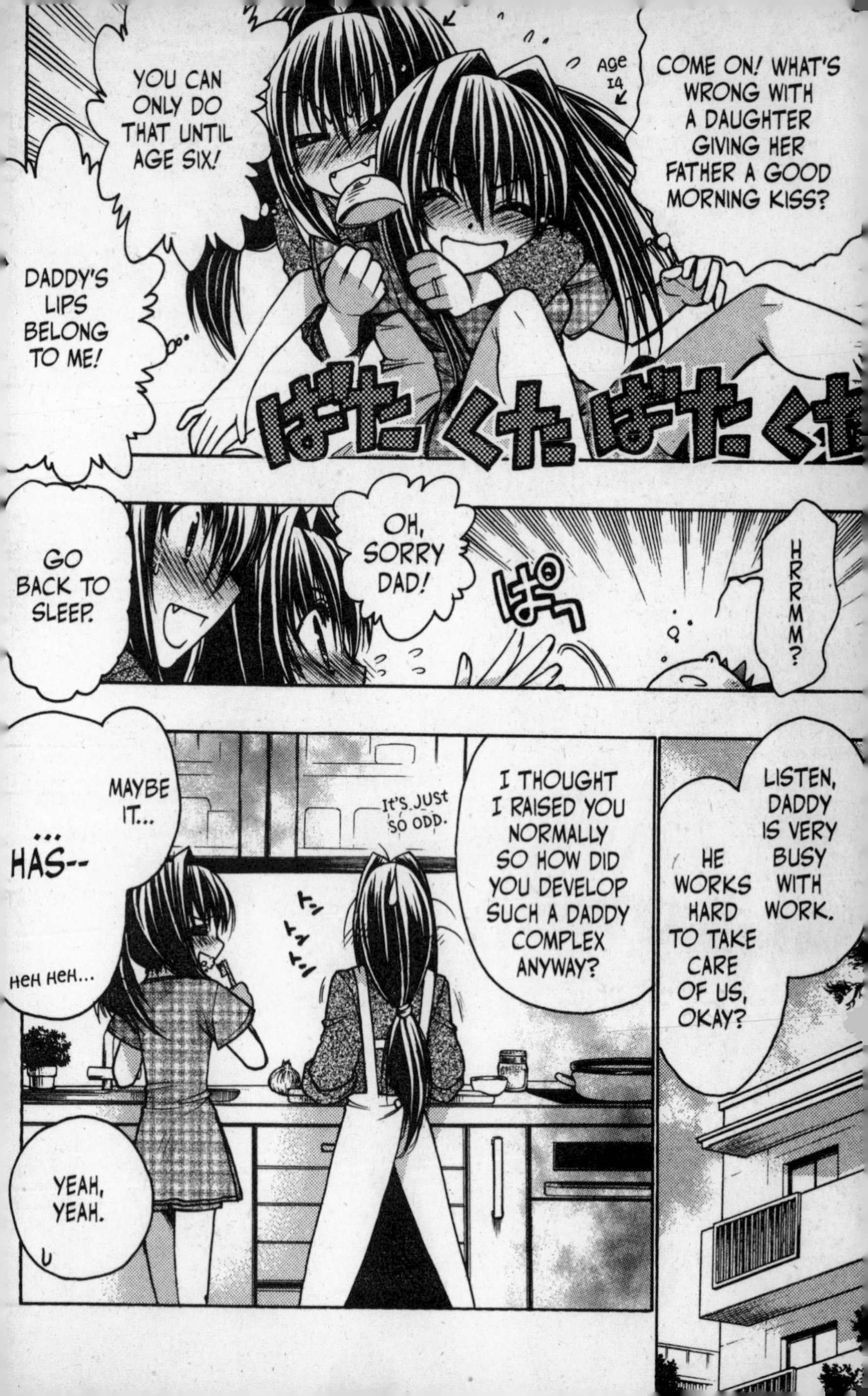
COME ON! WHAT'S WRONG WITH A DAUGHTER GIVING HER FATHER A GOOD MORNING KISS?
AGE 14
YOU CAN ONLY DO THAT UNTIL AGE SIX!
DADDY'S LIPS BELONG TO ME!
ばたくたばたくた
HRRMMM?
ぱっ
OH, SORRY DAD!
GO BACK TO SLEEP.
LISTEN, DADDY IS VERY BUSY WITH WORK.
HE WORKS HARD TO TAKE CARE OF US, OKAY?
I THOUGHT I RAISED YOU NORMALLY SO HOW DID YOU DEVELOP SUCH A DADDY COMPLEX ANYWAY?
IT'S JUST SO ODD.
MAYBE IT...
...HAS--
HEH HEH...
YEAH, YEAH.

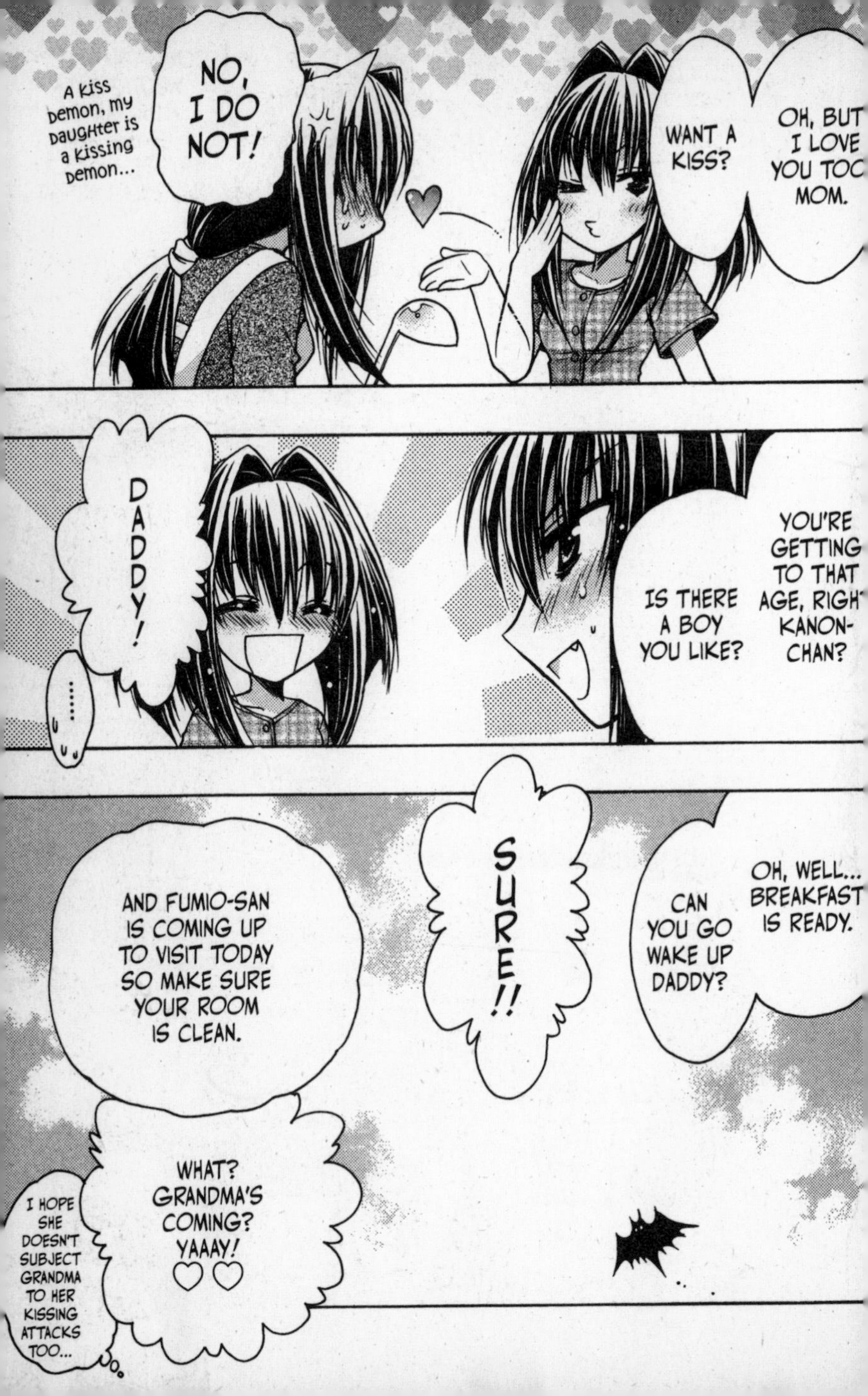

OH, BUT I LOVE YOU TOO MOM.
WANT A KISS?
NO, I DO NOT!
A kiss demon, my daughter is a kissing demon...
YOU'RE GETTING TO THAT AGE, RIGH KANON-CHAN?
IS THERE A BOY YOU LIKE?
DADDY!
......
OH, WELL... BREAKFAST IS READY.
CAN YOU GO WAKE UP DADDY?
SURE!!
AND FUMIO-SAN IS COMING UP TO VISIT TODAY SO MAKE SURE YOUR ROOM IS CLEAN.
WHAT? GRANDMA'S COMING? YAAAY! ♡ ♡
I HOPE SHE DOESN'T SUBJECT GRANDMA TO HER KISSING ATTACKS TOO...

MAKI-CHAN GIVES USUI-KUN A LESSON IN GOOD TASTE!

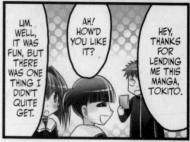

HEY, THANKS FOR LENDING ME THIS MANGA, TOKITO.
AH! HOW'D YOU LIKE IT?
UM. WELL, IT WAS FUN, BUT THERE WAS ONE THING I DIDN'T QUITE GET.
AROUND HERE, IN THE CLIMACTIC SCENE...
YAMADA-KUN...
ぱら...
AND THEN ON THE NEXT PAGE WE'RE HERE ALL OF A SUDDEN.
CHIRP CHIRP
パラ...
サラ....ッ
WHAT WITH THE SCENE CHANGE, I'M NOT SURE WHAT HAPPENED.
I specifically gave it to him because it wasn't explicit!
THIS'S BAD! HE DOESN'T GET WHY IT'S MORNING AND THE BIRDS ARE SINGING?!
Ke... Kenta-kun...
うぅ

KARIN'S FUTURE PROSPECTS SUDDENLY DIM...

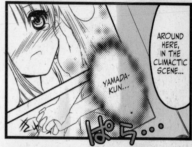

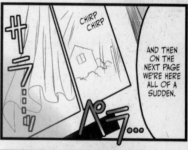

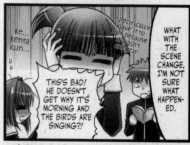

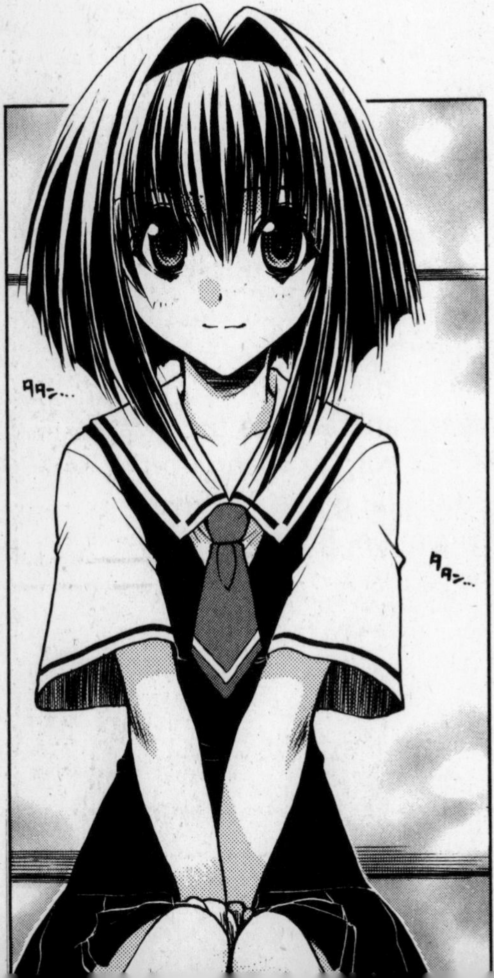
タタン…
タタン…

DEADMAN WONDERLAND

Ten years have passed since the Great Tokyo Earthquake, and the people's memories of the disaster have faded. Ganta Igarashi, a middle school evacuee, has finally begun to live a normal life...That is, until the day "Red Man" appears at his school and Ganta's fate is changed forever. Convicted of a horrendous crime he didn't commit, Ganta is sentenced to death and sent to the bizarre prison known as "Deadman Wonderland." An insane and brutal game of prison survival begins!

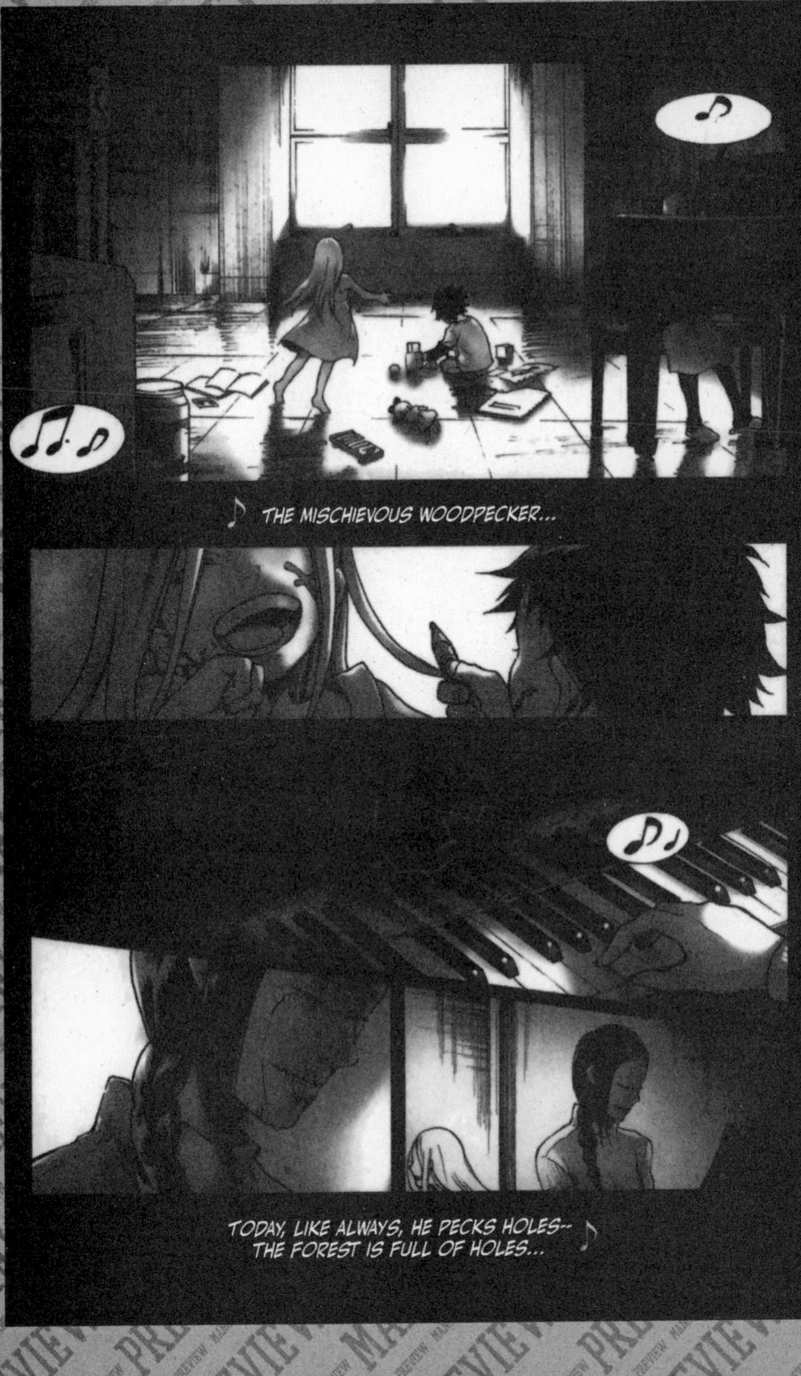
THE MISCHIEVOUS WOODPECKER...
TODAY, LIKE ALWAYS, HE PECKS HOLES--
THE FOREST IS FULL OF HOLES...

THE WOOD GOD WAS ANGERED, SO HE MADE HIS BEAK POISONOUS... ♪

THE WOODPECKER WAS TROUBLED, HIS NEST BECAME POISONED,
AND HIS FOOD BECAME POISONED...

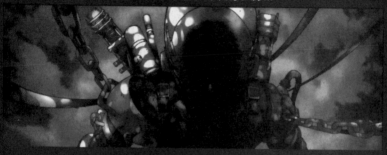

♪ IF HE TOUCHED HIS FRIENDS THEY WOULD ALL DIE...

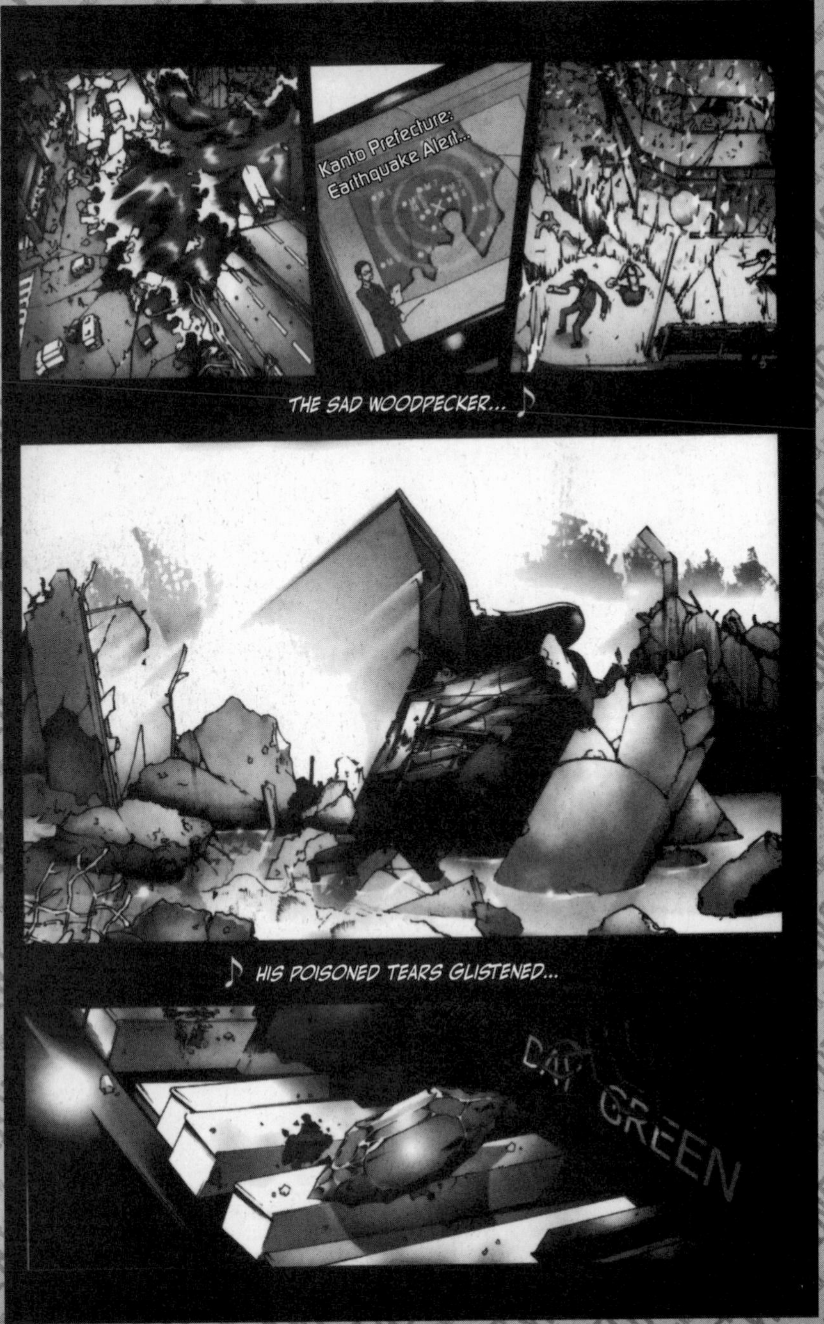
Kanto Prefecture:
Earthquake Alert...
THE SAD WOODPECKER... ♪
♪ HIS POISONED TEARS GLISTENED...
GREEN

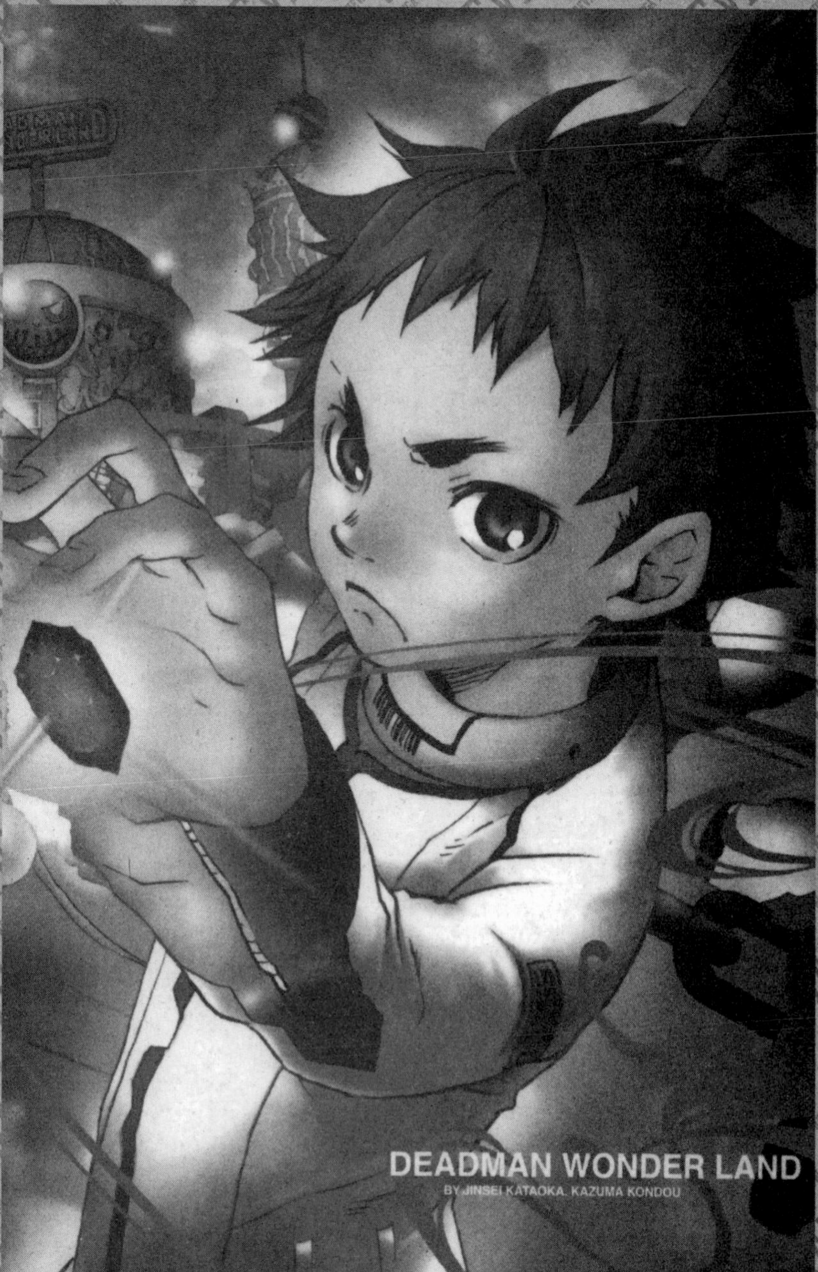
DEADMAN WONDER LAND
BY JINSEI KATAOKA. KAZUMA KONDOU

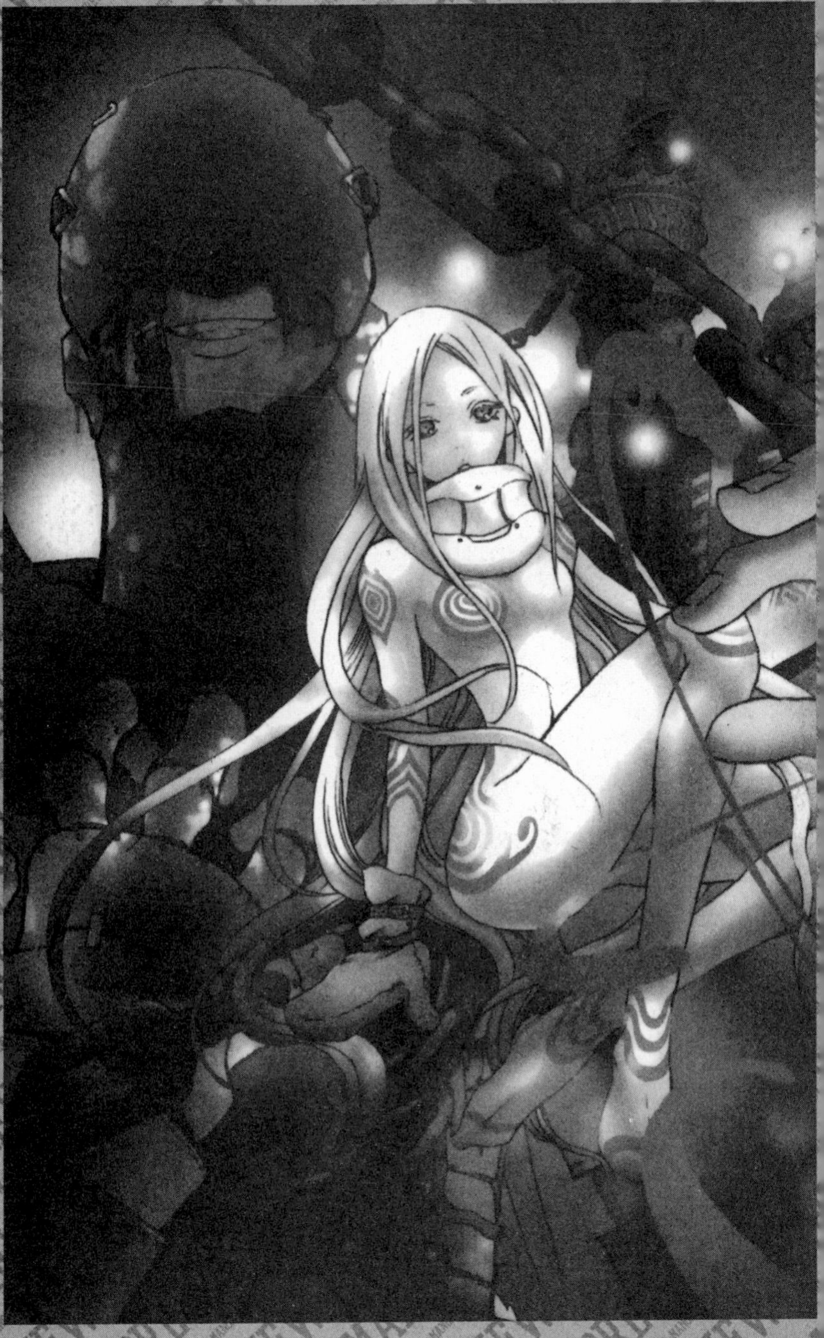

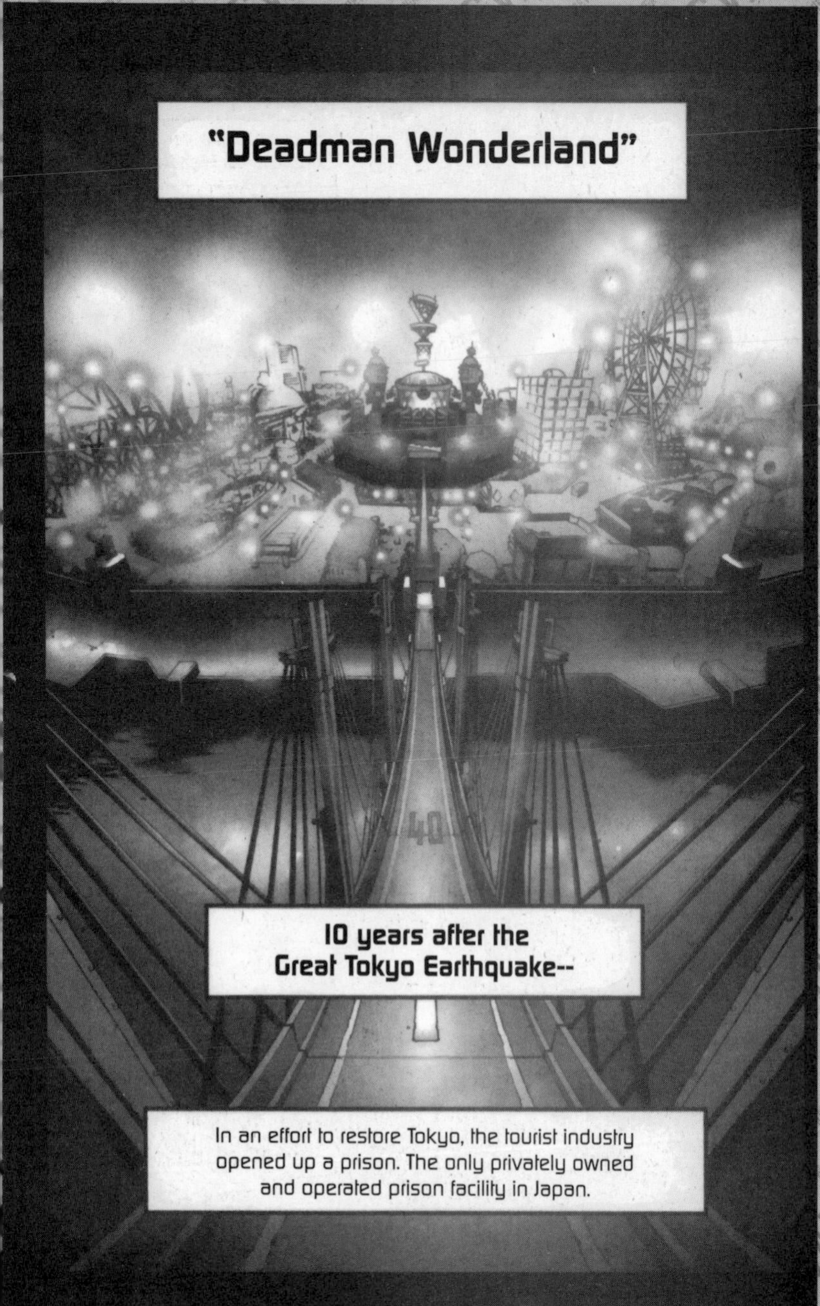
"Deadman Wonderland"
40
10 years after the Great Tokyo Earthquake--
In an effort to restore Tokyo, the tourist industry opened up a prison. The only privately owned and operated prison facility in Japan.

01 Who killed Cock Robin?

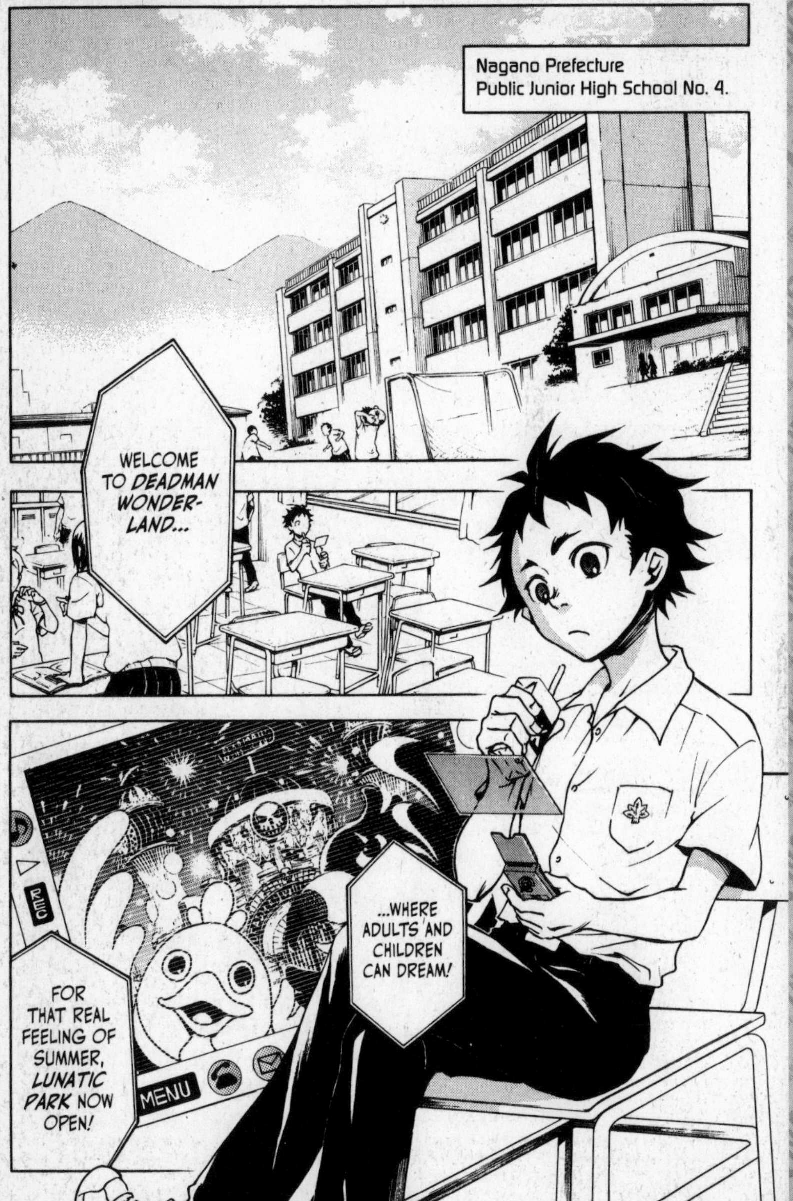
Nagano Prefecture
Public Junior High School No. 4.
WELCOME TO *DEADMAN WONDER-LAND...*
...WHERE ADULTS AND CHILDREN CAN DREAM!
REC
MENU
FOR THAT REAL FEELING OF SUMMER, *LUNATIC PARK* NOW OPEN!

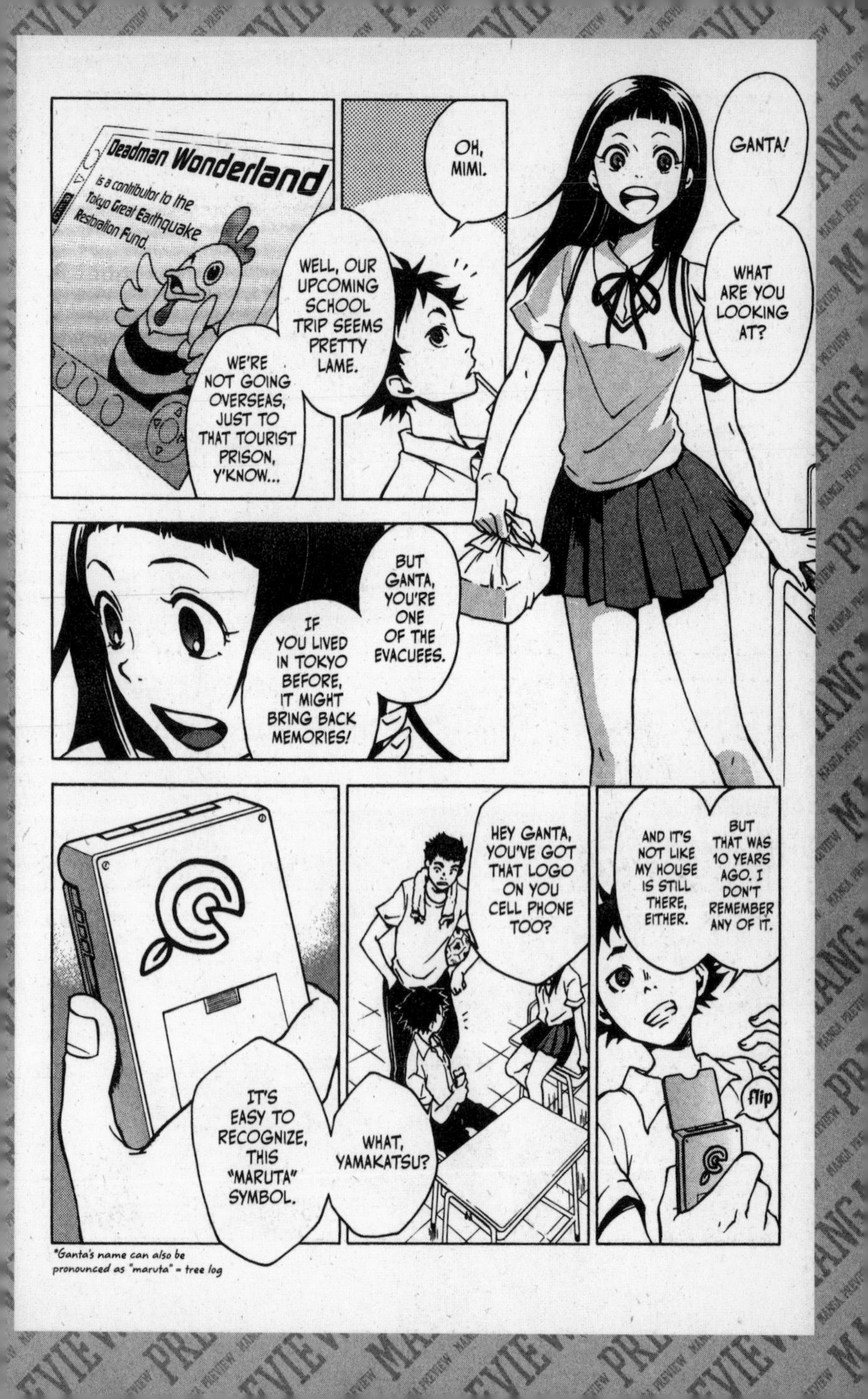
GANTA!
WHAT ARE YOU LOOKING AT?
OH, MIMI.
WELL, OUR UPCOMING SCHOOL TRIP SEEMS PRETTY LAME.
WE'RE NOT GOING OVERSEAS, JUST TO THAT TOURIST PRISON, Y'KNOW...
Deadman Wonderland
is a contributor to the Tokyo Great Earthquake Restoration Fund.
BUT GANTA, YOU'RE ONE OF THE EVACUEES.
IF YOU LIVED IN TOKYO BEFORE, IT MIGHT BRING BACK MEMORIES!
BUT THAT WAS 10 YEARS AGO. I DON'T REMEMBER ANY OF IT.
AND IT'S NOT LIKE MY HOUSE IS STILL THERE, EITHER.
flip
HEY GANTA, YOU'VE GOT THAT LOGO ON YOU CELL PHONE TOO?
WHAT, YAMAKATSU?
IT'S EASY TO RECOGNIZE, THIS "MARUTA" SYMBOL.

*Ganta's name can also be pronounced as "maruta" = tree log

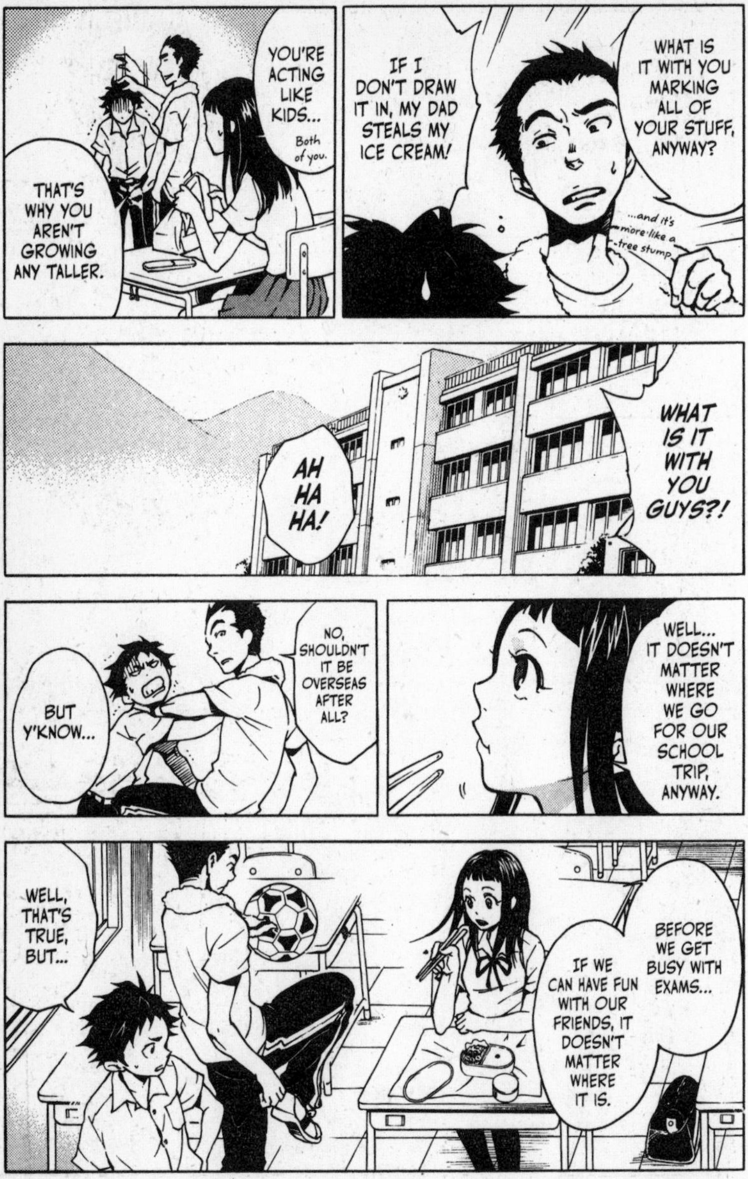
WHAT IS IT WITH YOU MARKING ALL OF YOUR STUFF, ANYWAY?
...and it's more like a tree stump
IF I DON'T DRAW IT IN, MY DAD STEALS MY ICE CREAM!
YOU'RE ACTING LIKE KIDS...
Both of you.
THAT'S WHY YOU AREN'T GROWING ANY TALLER.
WHAT IS IT WITH YOU GUYS?!
AH HA HA!
WELL... IT DOESN'T MATTER WHERE WE GO FOR OUR SCHOOL TRIP, ANYWAY.
NO, SHOULDN'T IT BE OVERSEAS AFTER ALL?
BUT Y'KNOW...
BEFORE WE GET BUSY WITH EXAMS...
IF WE CAN HAVE FUN WITH OUR FRIENDS, IT DOESN'T MATTER WHERE IT IS.
WELL, THAT'S TRUE, BUT...

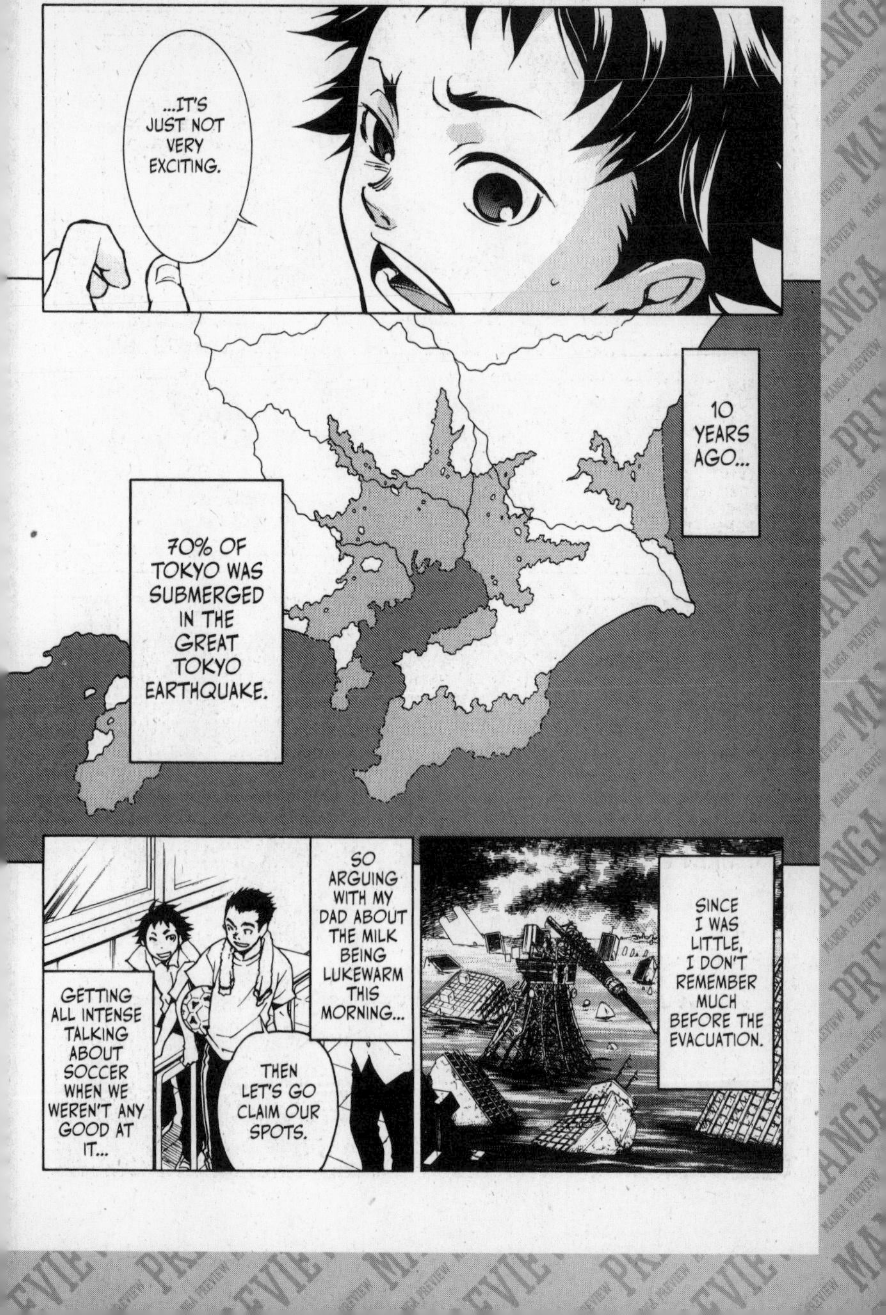
...IT'S JUST NOT VERY EXCITING.
10 YEARS AGO...
70% OF TOKYO WAS SUBMERGED IN THE GREAT TOKYO EARTHQUAKE.
SINCE I WAS LITTLE, I DON'T REMEMBER MUCH BEFORE THE EVACUATION.
SO ARGUING WITH MY DAD ABOUT THE MILK BEING LUKEWARM THIS MORNING...
GETTING ALL INTENSE TALKING ABOUT SOCCER WHEN WE WEREN'T ANY GOOD AT IT...
THEN LET'S GO CLAIM OUR SPOTS.

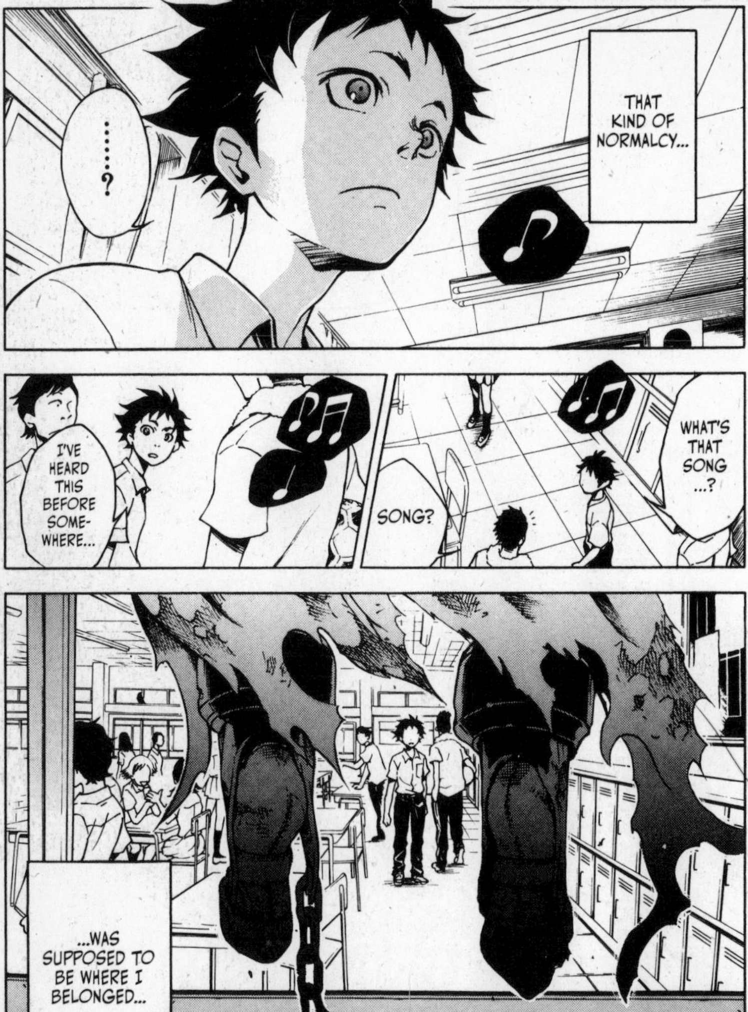
THAT KIND OF NORMALCY...
......?
WHAT'S THAT SONG ...?
SONG?
I'VE HEARD THIS BEFORE SOME-WHERE...
...WAS SUPPOSED TO BE WHERE I BELONGED...

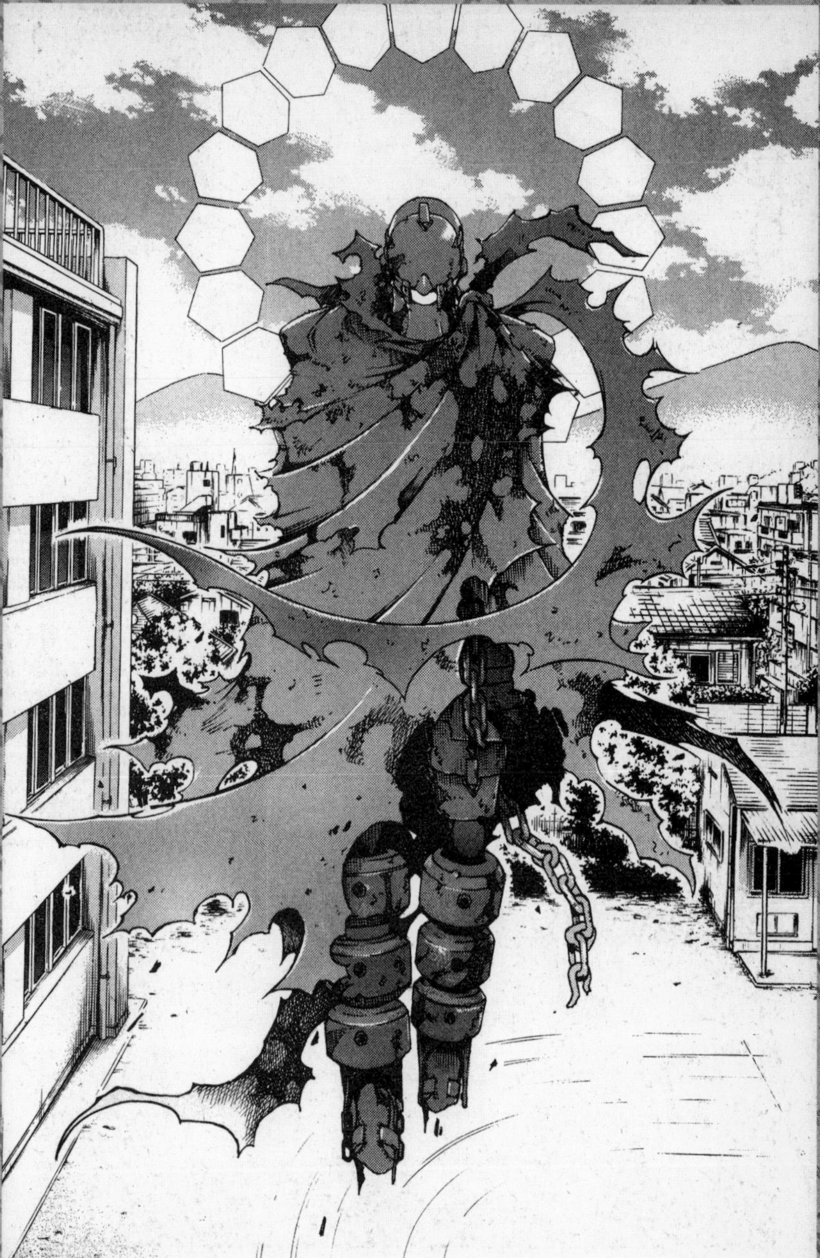

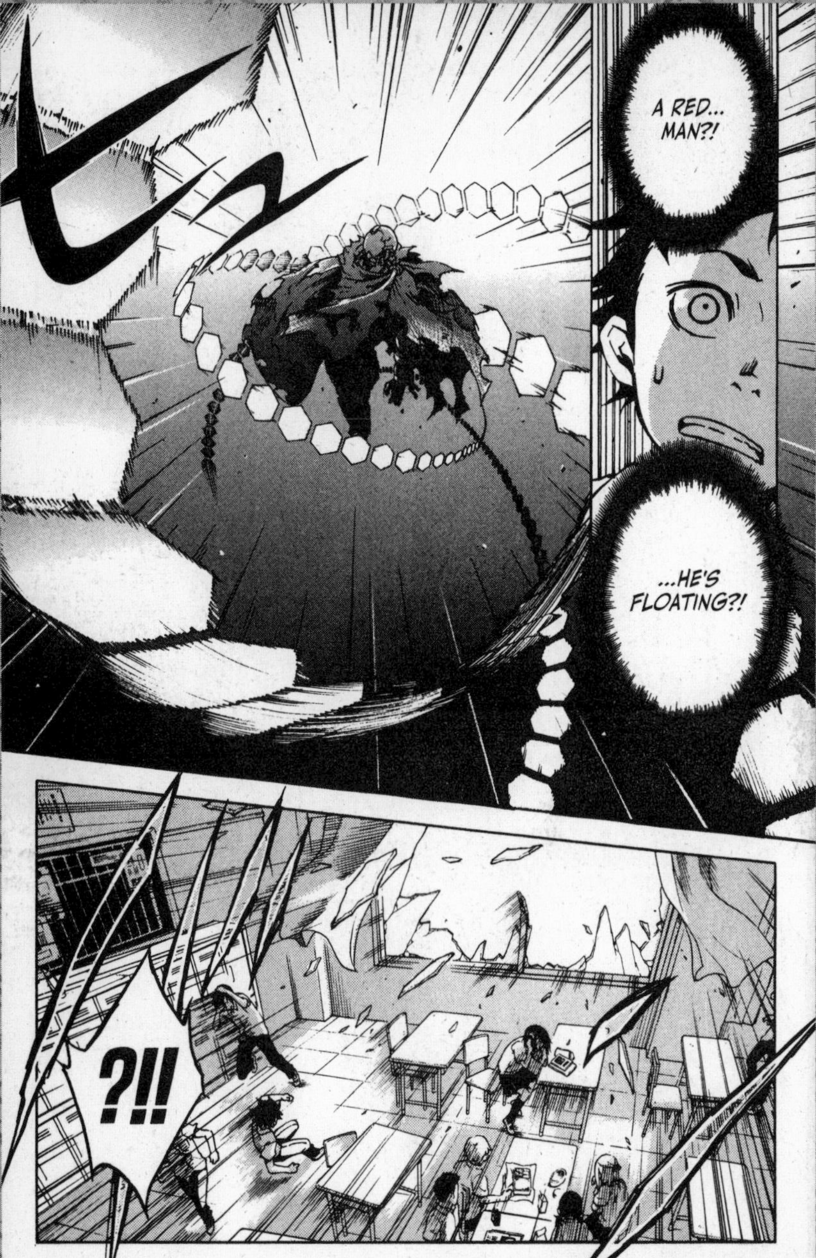
A RED... MAN?!
...HE'S FLOATING?!
?!!

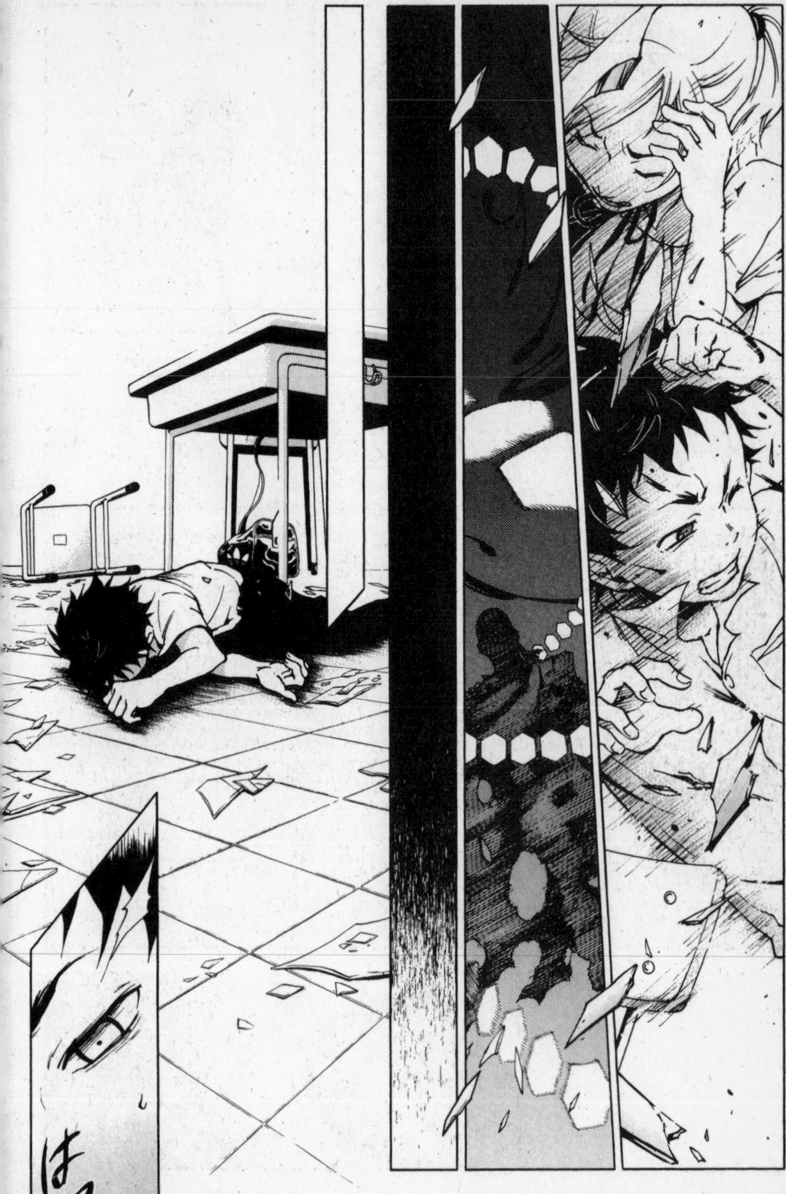
はっ

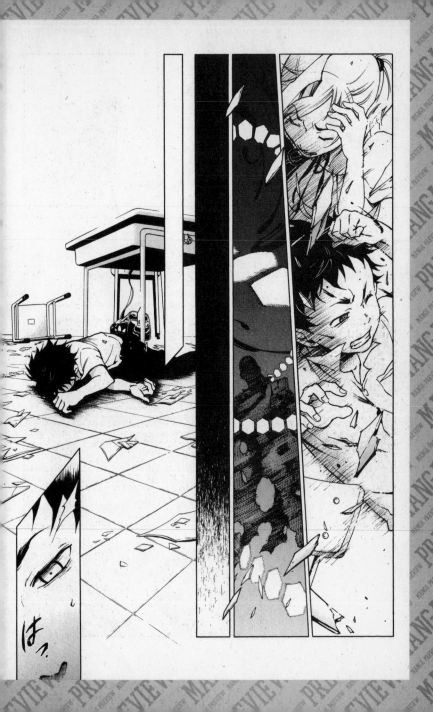

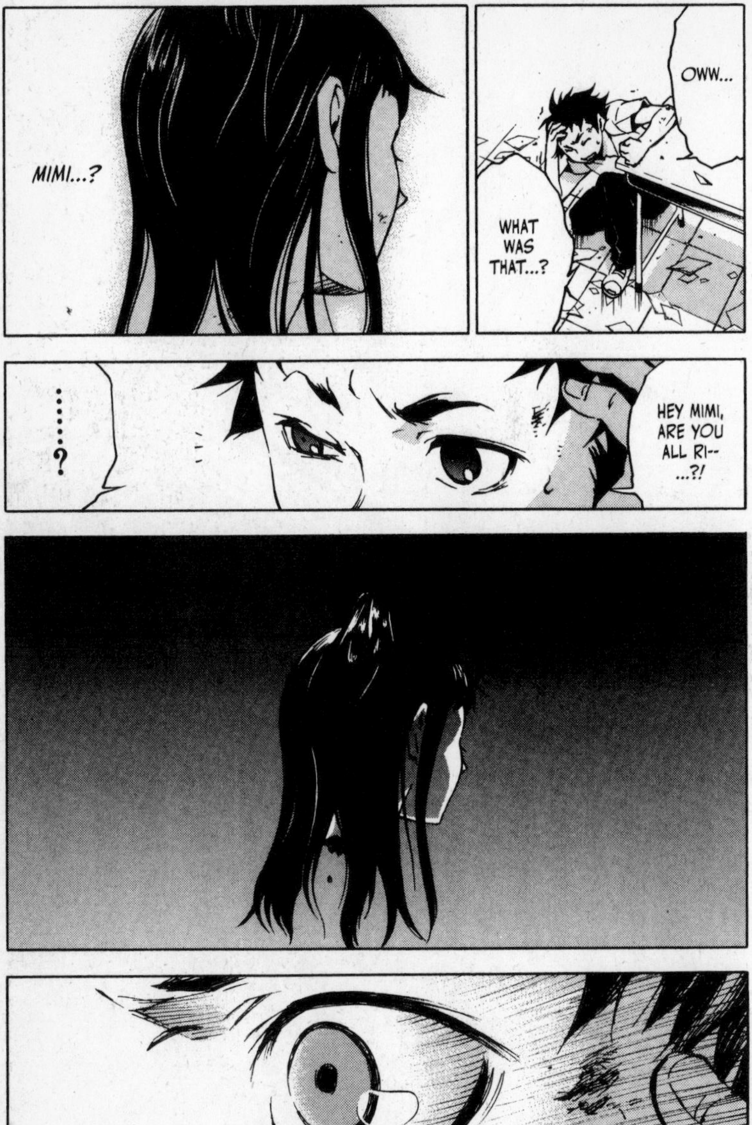
OWW...
WHAT WAS THAT...?
MIMI...?
HEY MIMI, ARE YOU ALL RI-- ...?!
......?

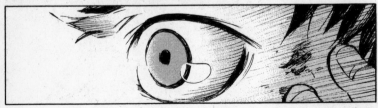

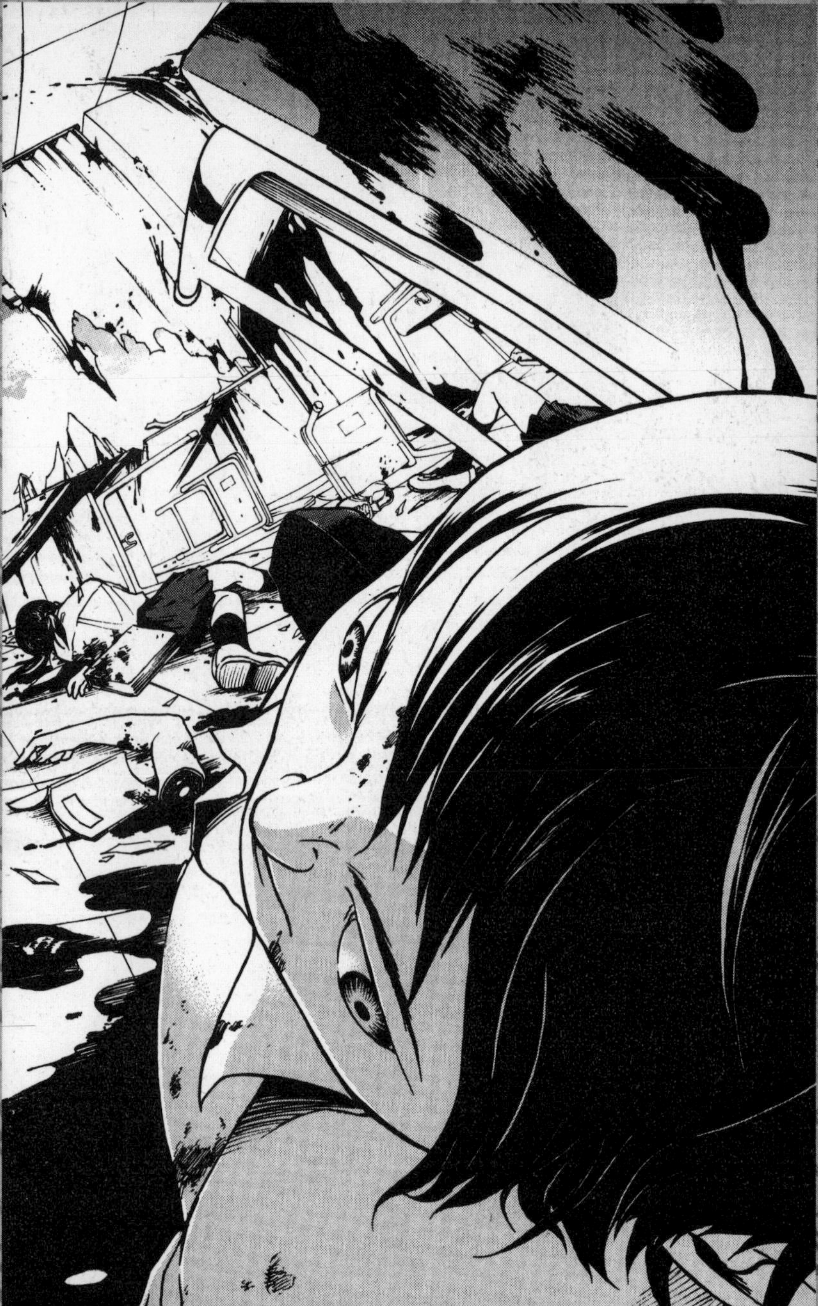

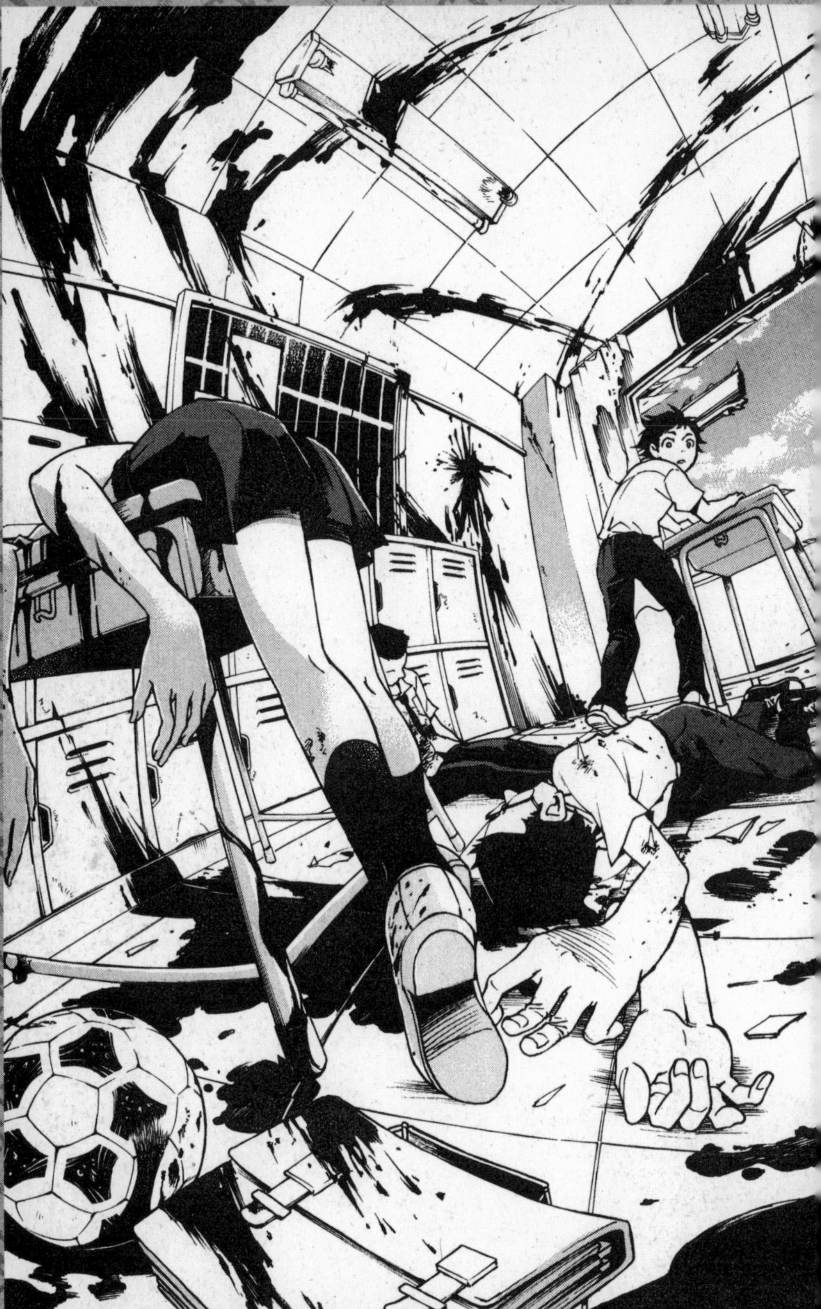

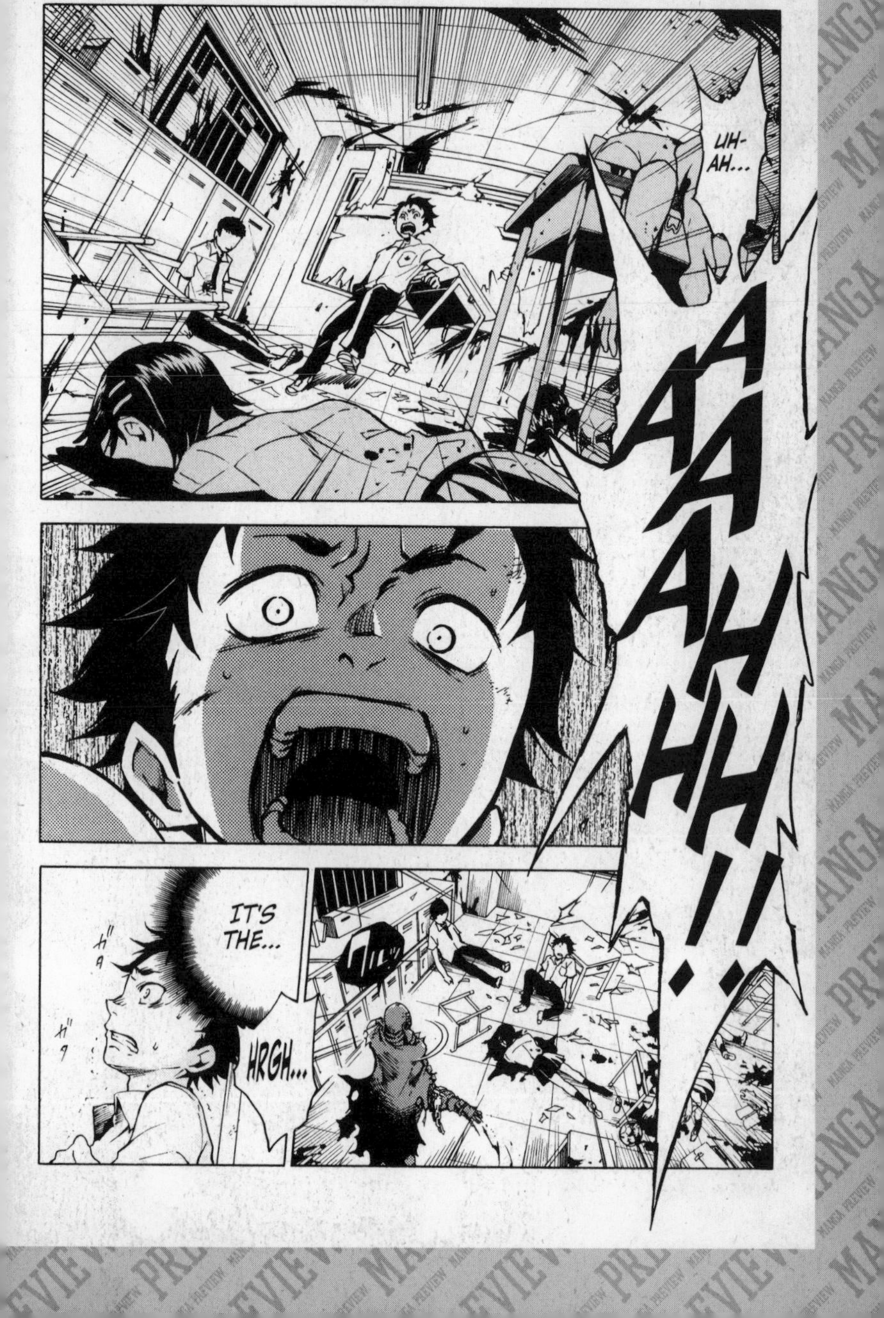
UH-AH...
AAAHHHH!!!
IT'S THE...
ガタ
ガタ
HRGH...

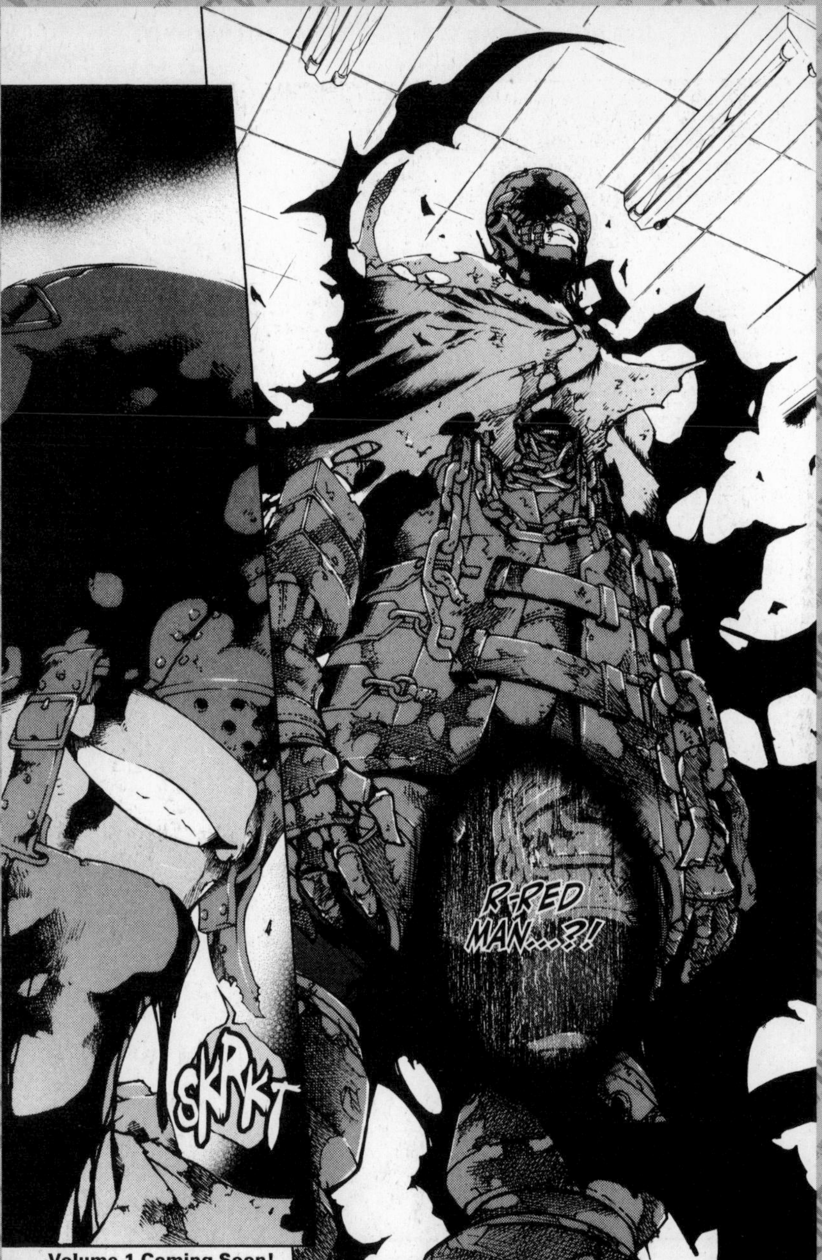
R-RED MAN...?!
SKRKT
Volume 1 Coming Soon!

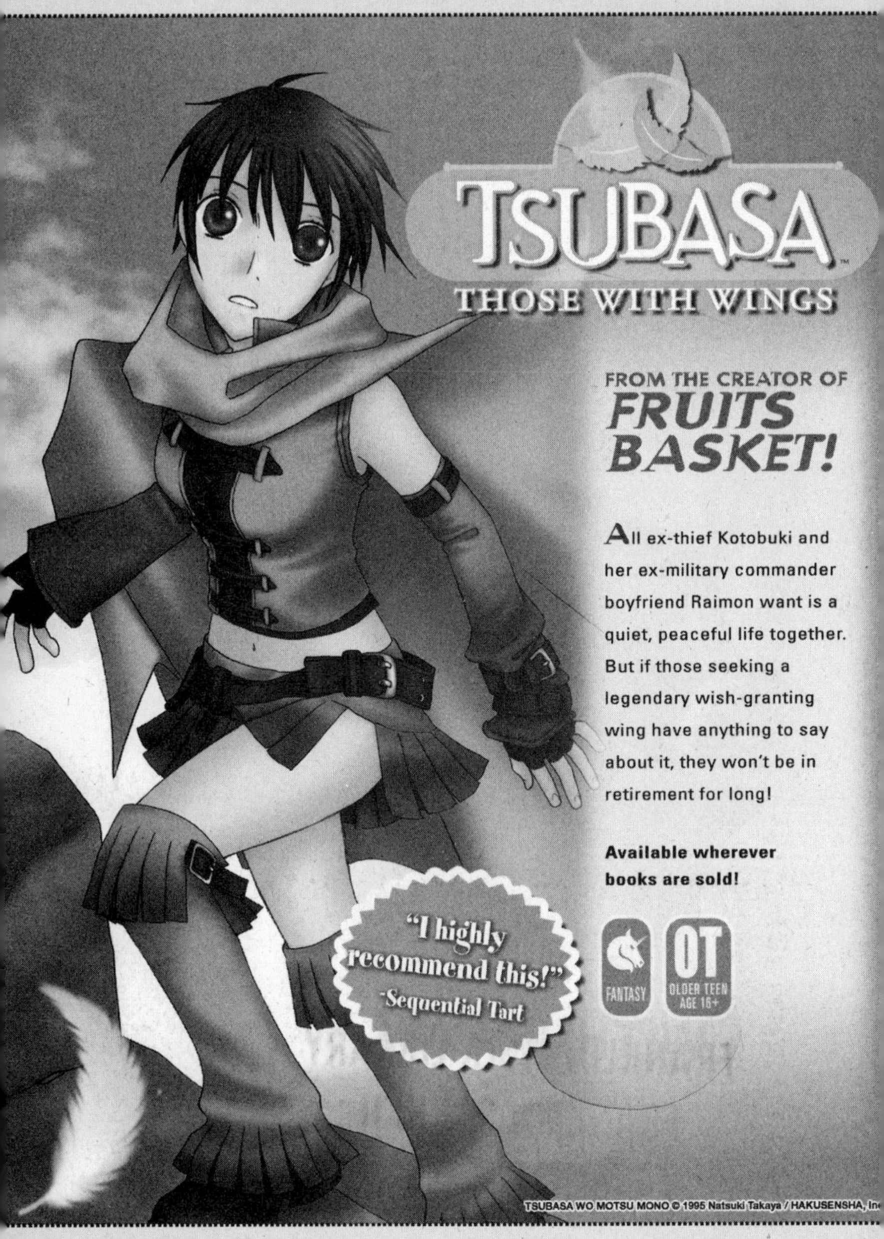
TSUBASA
THOSE WITH WINGS
FROM THE CREATOR OF FRUITS BASKET!
All ex-thief Kotobuki and her ex-military commander boyfriend Raimon want is a quiet, peaceful life together. But if those seeking a legendary wish-granting wing have anything to say about it, they won't be in retirement for long!
Available wherever books are sold!
"I highly recommend this!" -Sequential Tart
FANTASY
OT OLDER TEEN AGE 16+
TSUBASA WO MOTSU MONO © 1995 Natsuki Takaya / HAKUSENSHA, Inc

Maid Sama!™

The class president has a little secret she's keeping from the sexy bad boy in school...

CHIBI VAMPIRE
392-7079

It's love at first fight in this shojo romantic comedy—with a hilarious spin on geek culture and... student government?!

As President of the Student Council, the overachieving feminist Misaki really socks it to the boys in an attempt to make the former all-boys' school attract a more female student body. But what will she do when the hottest boy in class finds out Misaki's after-school gig is in a maid café?!

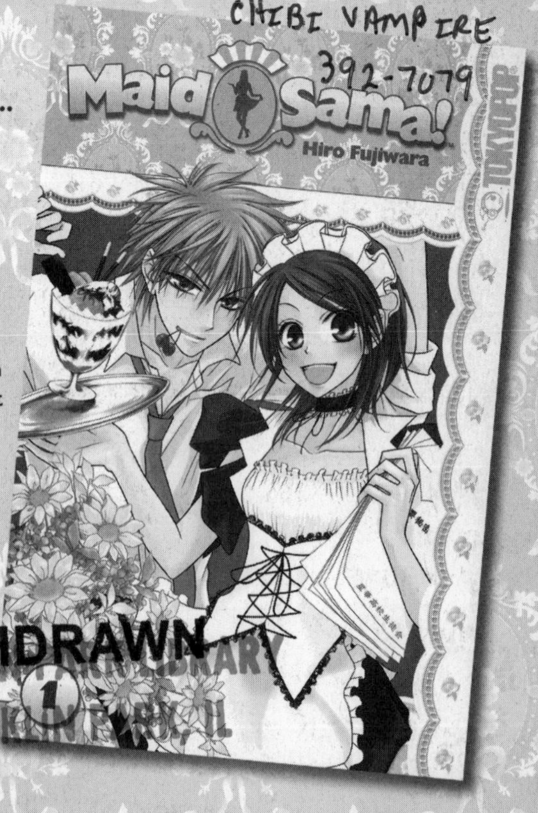
Maid Sama!
Hiro Fujiwara
TOKYOPOP
1

ROMANCE

T
TEEN AGE 13+

BE SURE TO VISIT WWW.TOKYOPOP.COM/SHOP FOR EVERYTHING YOU COULD EVER WANT!

STOP!

6/11

This is the back of the book. You wouldn't want to spoil a great ending!

This book is printed "manga-style," in the authentic Japanese right-to-left format. Since none of the artwork has been flipped or altered, readers get to experience the story just as teh creater intended. You've been asking for it, so TOKYOPOP® delivered: authentic, hot-off-the-press, and far more fun!

1
2
3
4
5
6
7
8
9
10

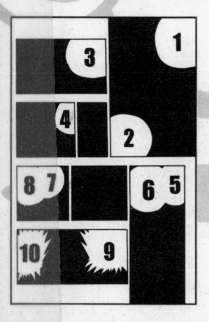

DIRECTIONS

If this is your first time reading manga-style, here's a quick guide to help you understand how it works.

It's easy... just start in the top right panel and follow the numbers. Have fun, and look for more 100% authentic manga from TOKYOPOP®!

THE MANGA REVOLUTION • LEADING THE MANGA REVOLUTION • LEADING
漫画革命